DEATH AT THE DOWER HOUSE

PIPPA DARLING MYSTERIES
BOOK 2

JENNA BENNETT

Copyright © 2023 by Jenna Bennett/Magpie Ink

All rights reserved.

No part of this book may be reproduced in any form or by any electronic or mechanical means, including information storage and retrieval systems, without written permission from the author, except for the use of brief quotations in a book review.

Cover design by Dar Albert/Wicked Smart Designs

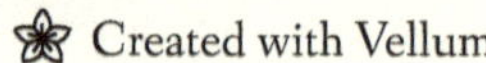 Created with Vellum

England, May, 1926

After the funerals of the late Duke of Sutherland and his daughter-in-law, Charlotte, (and of course Grimsby, the blackmailing valet), the younger members of the family—Philippa Darling, her cousins Christopher and Francis, and Crispin, Viscount St George—are invited to a weekend party at the Dower House in Dorset by Dowager Lady Peckham's children, Constance and Gilbert.

Once in Dorset, things go sideways very quickly. Lady Peckham's ward, the lovely Dutch emigree Johanna de Vos, has been making a dead set at Crispin, and has had him all to herself for the past few days. Constance's time has been monopolized by Francis, while Pippa wouldn't throw Crispin a rope if he were going under for the third time. However, the house party also includes the beautiful Lady Laetitia Marsden, a former dalliance of Crispin's, and she doesn't take the competition for his affections—or his title and fortune—lying down.

As a result, when the lovely Johanna is found murdered, the suspects are plentiful. Did Lady Laetitia decide to remove her rival? Did Lord Geoffrey, her brother, the handsy one, lose control and strangle the woman he was trying to seduce? Or perhaps Crispin was tired of the relentless pursuit, and took matters into his own hands?

When Lady Peckham also dies, miles away in Wiltshire, the case develops yet one more wrinkle. Now Pippa, with some help from Christopher, must figure out who wanted the two women dead, hopefully before the murderer can consign her to the same fate.

"She could not have gazed at him with a more rapturous intensity if she had been a small child and he a saucer of ice cream."

P.G. WODEHOUSE

ONE

"I CAN'T BELIEVE we're doing this again," Christopher grumbled, as he heaved my weekender bag down from the train's luggage rack and onto the seat below.

"I know." I picked it up, while I watched him reach above his head again for his own.

Tuesday a week ago, we'd done this in reverse. It had been the afternoon of the morning Her Grace, Aunt Charlotte, Duchess of Sutherland, was found dead in bed, and all we had really wanted to do at that time, was put as much distance between ourselves and the events of the previous weekend as we could. Three deaths plus an attempted murder is enough to discomfit even the most intrepid of Bright Young Things, and that's true even for those of us who imagine ourselves far too modern for finer feelings.

Neither Christopher nor I realized, or at least it wasn't discussed between us, that we would have to return to Wiltshire and Sutherland Hall for the funerals just over a week later.

In addition to Her Grace, Lady Charlotte, the dead

included Christopher's grandfather Henry, the Duke of Sutherland (the one before Aunt Charlotte's husband, Uncle Harold, ascended to the title; poor Aunt Charlotte only got to enjoy being a duchess for a couple of days before she was dead, too), as well as Grimsby, the late duke's valet.

We wouldn't be attending that funeral, of course. That was for the below-stairs, and any family or personal friends Grimsby might have had. Given that he was a sneak and a blackmailer, I imagined there might not be many attendees.

But we would definitely be required to be there both for the late duke's ceremonials, and for the late duchess's. They would both be buried in the family plot in the small graveyard outside the village of Little Sutherland in Wiltshire, so we'd had to make the trip from London via train to Salisbury, and by car from there to Sutherland Hall, yet again.

"I hope Wilkins is here with the motorcar," Christopher groused. "I'm starved."

"I'm sure he will be. I phoned from the box in the station and told Tidwell when to expect us. And if you hadn't over-slept, you would have had more time for breakfast."

"I wanted luncheon," Christopher said petulantly.

"Well, I'm sorry, but we were on the train at lunch time. Assuming Wilkins doesn't make us wait, we'll reach the hall about halfway between luncheon and tea, but perhaps Mrs. Sloane can find you a biscuit to tide you over."

Christopher opened his mouth again, surely to say something else thoroughly unhelpful, and I added, "You know, I can see why some people have such a hard time telling you and your cousin Crispin apart. You both act like spoiled brats when you don't get what you want."

"I do *not* act like a spoiled brat!" Christopher said, offended, and then he seemed to hear himself, because he flushed. "I do, don't I? Sorry, Pippa."

"It's all right," I told him as we carried our bags towards the train station exit. "I didn't really mean it, you know. I've never had a problem telling you and your cousin apart. And I know neither one of us is looking forward to the next two days. Last weekend was horrific, and this week will be even worse."

Christopher made a face. "Bad enough if they'd all died of natural causes. But when one of them killed the other two and then herself..."

I nodded. "I'm amazed your uncle and St George have managed to keep it out of the newspapers. Could you imagine what kind of money your mother would have got for the inside scoop that the Duchess of Sutherland killed her father-in-law, his valet, and then herself?"

"Let's not talk about my mother and her little sideline right now."

He pushed the door open for me and then followed me out. It was early May in Southern England, and the sun shone warmly on the red brick of the train station. Everything was perfectly lovely until Christopher said, "Brace yourself, Pippa."

"For—" *What?* was left unsaid, because I saw immediately the reason I needed bracing.

Heard it, as well.

"Afternoon, Darling. Kit."

There, just beyond the red-brick pavement, in a slot clearly designated for 'drop off' and not 'pick up,' sat the bright blue Hispano-Suiza H6 racing car that was the pride and joy of Christopher's cousin. The formerly Honorable Crispin Astley, now the Right Honorable Viscount St George since his grandfather's death a week and a half hence, was lounging in the driver's seat, a soft cap pulled low over his face—to keep the afternoon sun out of his eyes, I assumed, or perhaps to allow him to size up young women without their noticing—and the usual smug smirk on his lips. He made absolutely no move to get out of the car and help with the luggage. Instead, he reached back and pulled open the back door without ever stirring from behind the wheel. "Make yourselves at home."

"I'll take the back seat," I told Christopher, since I didn't fancy spending the next hour sitting next to St George, who is by way of being my least favorite person. For being so physically like Christopher that a lot of people have a problem deciding which is which, Crispin is nothing like Christopher in personality. As a result, I do my utmost to avoid spending any time with him whatsoever.

In this case, I couldn't avoid the motorcar, but I could make Christopher bear the brunt of his cousin's company while I hid myself away in the back. Christopher was brought up to be a gentleman, and he minds Crispin less than I do, anyway.

He bowed me into the back seat and then dumped his bag on the seat next to me. That done, he circled the car and got into the passenger seat next to his cousin.

"Ready?" the latter asked, even before Christopher had properly latched the door behind him. "Let's blouse."

The H6 took off down Western Road, roared up Mill Street, and scattered traffic to cross the bridge over the River Avon. (This is not the same Avon that Shakespeare waxed poetic about, in case you wondered. There are five Rivers Avon in England, three more in Scotland, and one in Wales. The Salisbury Avon is the third longest, and it runs from Pewsey in Wiltshire through Hampshire and Dorset before it empties out into the English Channel at Mudeford.)

From the bridge, we barreled down the old High Street past the Salisbury Cathedral and the Magna Carta Charter House —"Might as well do the scenic tour," Crispin yelled from the front seat—before we proceeded out of town on our way in a south-easterly direction towards Sutherland Hall.

I made myself comfortable in the back and watched the

scenery fly by. The one good thing about the Hispano-Suiza and Crispin's love of speed is that he drives so fast that there was no way I could partake in any conversation taking place in the front seat. Any words either of them spoke were literally ripped from their mouths as soon as they were uttered, and dissipated in the wind long before they reached me. I had no idea what they were discussing, so I spent the time watching the landscape outside go from Salisbury proper to scattered households on the outskirts of town to rural fields and pastures as we drove further into the countryside. And occasionally, when he turned sideways to say something to Christopher, I looked at Crispin, and wondered what the last week had been like for him.

When Christopher and I had scurried away from Sutherland Hall last Tuesday, like rats leaving a sinking ship, Crispin had just been taken off by a chief inspector in Scotland Yard for an interview. Aunt Charlotte had been found dead in bed that morning, with what amounted to a suicide note—or at least a letter addressed to her only son—left on the writing table. That was after an attempted murder of me—or possibly Christopher —the previous day, the discovery of the dead valet the morning before that, and the death of the old duke the afternoon prior to that again. It had been quite an eventful weekend, and while none of the deaths had really affected me personally—the old duke hadn't been my grandfather, and Christopher's aunt hadn't liked me much at all, a feeling which was decidedly mutual—they were obviously much closer to Crispin's heart (assuming he had one). The duke had been his grandfather, he'd lived in the same house as the valet, and Christopher's aunt was his mother, who had adored him. I imagined the last week couldn't have been easy.

And if I looked closely, I could see it. There were dark circles under his eyes, as if he hadn't been resting well, and his skin wasn't just pale, it was pasty. The eyes themselves were bloodshot, and if I had to guess, I would have said he'd lost half a stone in the week since I'd last seen him. All in all, he made a perfect picture of a young man who didn't sleep, didn't eat, and didn't exercise, but spent much too much time in a bottle.

"You look awful, St George," I told him when we had finally arrived at our destination, Sutherland Hall outside the village of Little Sutherland in southern Wiltshire, and he was standing in the courtyard holding the car door open for me.

He sneered. "Thanks ever so, Darling."

"I mean it. Haven't you bothered to eat since we left last week?"

He shrugged, and moved past me to close the car door, before lifting the weekender bags out of the back seat and handing them over to Alfred, the second footman, who had appeared out of thin air to receive them.

"Same rooms as last time," Crispin instructed him.

I made a face, since I knew that that would put me in the west wing, as far away from Christopher's room in the east wing as it was possible for me to get.

Alfred headed into the foyer with the bags and Crispin arched a brow. "Problem, Darling? Did you want to be closer to the action?"

"I thought it was your mother who was obsessed with keeping me away from the men's wing," I told him, without really thinking about what I was saying.

And then, of course, I realized what I had said when he grimaced. "Oh, no. I'm sorry, St George. I didn't mean..."

"I'm sure," Crispin said dryly. "No reason why you would take any special care with my feelings."

He paused expectantly, probably for me to express doubts as to his possessing any. Under the circumstances I refrained, since I could tell quite well that he was still reeling from his mother's death.

So instead I steeled myself before I put a hand on the arm of his tweed coat and said, as sincerely as I could, "I'm sorry, St George. Truly. I forgot for a moment."

He looked down at my hand, appalled or perhaps just astonished that I was actually touching him, before he nodded. "I do that, too. Go along as normal, until suddenly I remember that my mother is dead. And then the world ends all over again."

His eyes met mine for a moment, storm-cloud gray, before he twitched his arm out from under my hand and took a step back. "At any rate, it made sense to put Christopher and Francis into the rooms they had last time. The only other empty room in the east wing is my mother's, and I'm sure you wouldn't want to sleep there."

No, I definitely wouldn't. If I had a choice between the room where Aunt Charlotte had died, and the west wing, I'd take the west wing every time.

"You won't be alone in the west wing this time," Crispin added. "Aunt Roslyn and Uncle Herbert will be here by supper. And my mother's old friend Lady Peckham is staying for a few nights. She's bringing her daughter and her ward, along with her son. They'll be in the west wing, too."

"Constance Peckham?" I asked. "Her mother and brother?"

He nodded. "How do you know Constance?"

There was a faint sneer to his expression, as if he didn't think much of Constance Peckham. I wanted to chastise him for it, but the truth was that I had never thought much of Constance Peckham myself.

That may have made it sound as if I had something against Constance, which wouldn't be true at all. It wasn't that I thought she was stuck up or unpleasant or anything like that. She was merely very quiet and unassuming, and as such, very easy to dismiss. It galled me that I couldn't take Crispin to task for his cavalier attitude towards someone who was, by all accounts, a very sweet-natured young lady, and certainly a much better person than he was. But it was hard to do so when I had mostly dismissed her as mealy-mouthed myself, for as long as I had known her.

I decided on the spot to be especially nice to Constance when she turned up.

"We went to Godolphin together," I told him, "while you and Christopher were away at Eton."

This might have been the longest, most civil conversation I'd had with St George in eons. It made me feel strange, and I looked around for Christopher, for something else to focus on. He was standing on the other side of the Hispano-Suiza looking from one to the other of us with a strange expression on his face. Couldn't believe the lack of hostilities either, probably. Or perhaps he was preparing to interfere when the lack of hostilities invariably came to an end. "Did you hear, Christopher? Constance Peckham is expected."

Christopher nodded warily. "Do I know Constance?"

"I doubt it," I told him. "She and I weren't close. She was a very meek sort of girl. Kind and well-meaning and all that, just very unassuming. Not St George's type at all."

Crispin sneered. "And what would you know about my type, Darling?"

Whatever truce we'd temporarily enjoyed was obviously over, and we were back to snide remarks and verbal slaps.

I can give as good as I get when it comes to that, so I waded into the fray.

"Everyone in London knows your type, St George. And it isn't quiet and unassuming. Those of your conquests I'm familiar with all have flashy looks and fast reputations and not much of substance between the ears."

The corner of his mouth quirked. "Are you suggesting I like my women stupid, Darling?"

His women, were they? How deplorably chauvinistic.

I looked at him down the length of my nose. He's a few inches taller than I am, but I tilted my head back and gave it my best. "You said it, not me. Although they'd have to be, wouldn't they? They fall for *you*, after all."

He nodded pleasantly. "So they do. Although I don't know why *you* would take offense, Darling. No one would call you mousey. You're more of a shrew, aren't you?"

"Oh, lovely." I put my hands together for a couple of slow claps. "You're so clever, St George. Not a mouse, but a shrew. Imagine coming up with that. You're brilliant, you are."

He flushed. "Get stuffed, Darling."

"You know," I told him, "I think I will. Christopher?"

Christopher offered me his arm, the way any well-trained young gentleman would do when addressed in this manner, and we swept into the foyer of Sutherland Hall leaving Crispin to no doubt grit his teeth in our wake in the courtyard.

"MR. ASTLEY." Tidwell the butler was waiting just inside the front door. "Miss Darling."

"Tidwell," I said warmly. "How lovely to see you."

Tidwell blinked, since it's not usual for the above-stairs to address the staff quite so exuberantly. But this was the effect Crispin had on me: after talking to him, I felt so much more fondly towards the entire rest of the world, which had, after all, the benefit of not being Crispin St George.

"You're in your usual room in the west wing, Miss Darling," Tidwell informed me once he'd got his countenance back, "and

Mr. Astley, you're in your usual room in the east wing. Tea will be served in the parlor at five o'clock."

"Lovely, Tidwell."

I must have verged on sounding maniacally friendly again, because Christopher gave me a quelling sort of look before addressing Tidwell himself.

"We missed luncheon, Tidwell. Do you suppose there's any chance Cook could rustle up some victuals early?"

"I can ask Cook for a tray, Mr. Astley." Tidwell bowed politely. "Do you wish a tray too, Miss Darling?"

"I'll share Christopher's," I said. "Just have her send two of everything. Cups, saucers, plates..."

Tidwell nodded. "Very well, Miss Darling. To Mr. Astley's room?"

"That'll be fine," I said. "Unless..."

I lowered my voice and leaned a little closer. "When was the last time Lord St George ate a solid meal, Tidwell? He looks like a ghost."

"The last week has been hard on the young master," Tidwell said blandly, which was surely an understatement if I'd ever heard one.

"He left before luncheon, too, didn't he? To pick us up?"

"Yes, Miss Darling."

"Then have Cook send enough for three," I said, "and put it in the breakfast room or somewhere like that. Scotland Yard has finished with the breakfast room, I assume?"

The breakfast room was where Chief Inspector Pendennis and his two underlings, Detective Sergeants Finchley and Gardiner, had set up their incident room last week, after Grimsby's murder.

Tidwell nodded. "Yes, Miss Darling. The breakfast room is currently used for breakfast."

"Then we'll eat there. Where we won't disturb any preparations for tea that might be going on in the salon."

Tidwell nodded. "Very well, Miss Darling."

He withdrew. I turned to Christopher. "Go get your cousin before he decides to get back in the motorcar and take off again."

I was honestly surprised we hadn't heard the roar of the Hispano-Suiza's engine already.

"He's probably waiting for it to be time to go pick up the Peckhams," Christopher said.

"All the more reason to force some food into him before he leaves again. He looks ill."

"You'd look—" Christopher began, and then shook his head. "Sorry, Pippa."

"Think nothing of it. You're right. If I had lost my mother under the circumstances he lost his—" instead of to the influenza epidemic that had ravaged the Continent seven years ago, "I'm sure I'd look terrible, too."

I hadn't seen my mother in five years by that point. I'm sure that made the loss easier to bear. So did the fact that I had a new family around me, to hold me and pet me and make sure I was all right. It didn't seem as if Crispin had anyone. No siblings, and a father who had never seemed to be very affectionate even when his son was small.

And that didn't make him my problem, especially as he was someone I didn't particularly like, who didn't particularly like me back. But even so—

I turned toward the staircase. "I'm going to wash my hands before we eat. Get him inside, Christopher. I don't care how you do it. Hit him over the head and drag him into the breakfast room if you have to. If he doesn't take better care of himself, he's going to die, too, and that won't help anyone in the slightest."

Except perhaps Uncle Herbert, who would be second in line for the title with Crispin out of the way. But that was a horrible thing to think, and would be a worse one to express, especially to Uncle Herbert's son, so I didn't mention it.

Christopher nodded. "I'll get him."

"I'll be down by the time the tray arrives," I said, and headed up the staircase to the lavatory while Christopher went in the other direction, toward the door to the outside and the courtyard.

TWO

THE PECKHAM FAMILY arrived in time for tea, and they did not need Crispin's help in doing so. Instead, they had their own enclosed Crossley saloon car, similar to the touring car the old duke kept for outings, but with a burgundy body instead of shiny black. It was driven by a chauffeur, while Mr. Peckham, Constance's brother, sat enthroned in the passenger seat in solitary splendor.

I had never met the man, but I had a vague picture of Constance in my head, from the last time I had seen her five years ago, and he looked like an older, male version of the girl I remembered. Soft, brown hair and brown eyes in a pleasantly round, somewhat placid face. He was dressed in the same style of casual newsboy cap Crispin had on earlier, with a similar, belted, sport-back tweed coat. But while Crispin is tallish and trim, young Mr. Peckham was shorter and stout. The emphasis the belt put on his waistline was not as flattering as it had been for St George.

Naturally, I would never say so. Not to St George, and

certainly not to Mr. Peckham. Nor did I have the chance. Peckham bounded out of the car and directly to the back seat, where he made a very big deal out of handing a young lady out of the motorcar and onto the gravel of the courtyard with exquisite care.

She wasn't his sister. And it was difficult to blame him for his enthusiasm, as the lady was stunning.

I have no particular doubts about my own attractiveness, to be fair. Nor do I think I estimate my looks in any way too highly, either. I'm a reasonably attractive young woman of twenty-three, with bobbed, brown hair, a trim figure, and even features. Although St George has been known to call my nose pointy—as in, "Keep your pointy nose out of my affairs, Darling!"—I have it on good authority—Christopher's—that it is actually more upturned than pointy.

I don't generally scare any eligible gentlemen off with my looks, in other words. But I know when I'm beaten, and this was someone on a different level of attractiveness than I could ever aspire to be.

Tall and slim, she must have been close to Christopher's height, and taller than Mr. Peckham, at least in her elegant triple-strap shoes. I would call her build willowy, which means it was perfect for the drop-waist dresses that were popular this decade. (My own figure is also well-suited to the current fashions. I'm not willowy, however, but rather what they call boyish.) The frock she had on was a gorgeous creation of pink and blue crepe de chine that simultaneously managed to play up the blue of her eyes, the pink in her cheeks, and the sunny gold of her hair. I heard simultaneous indrawn breaths on either side of me, and deduced that even Christopher wasn't immune to such splendor. And it appeared that she had managed to put roses into Crispin's cheeks, for which I supposed she ought to be commended. Not that I planned to do any commending anytime soon.

"Philippa?"

Unnoticed by any of us, during the time it had taken Mr. Peckham to withdraw the vision of beauty from our side of the motorcar, the chauffeur had extricated his employer as well as Miss Constance Peckham from the other side, and now Constance was standing in front of me, looking nervous.

I smoothed out the cynical expression I was certain was on my face, and dredged up a pleasant, welcoming smile instead. "Constance! It's lovely to see you, after such a long time!"

I leaned down—she's quite a bit shorter than me, and decidedly not boyish—and air-kissed both her cheeks. She made smooching noises in return, and we leaned back and assessed one another.

"You look good," I said, and hoped I managed to keep the surprise out of my voice. It might just have been getting out of the Godolphin uniform that made her look so much better than I remembered. In the younger forms, it was pinafores, but towards the end, the uniform had consisted of shirts and ties, heavy dark stockings, lace-up shoes and boaters, and nobody looks good like that.

Well, let me rephrase the sentiment: the only people who look good like that are the golden goddesses, like the one who was being swept towards the front entrance right now by a combination of Mr. Peckham, who held jealously onto her arm, and Crispin, who was doing his best imitation of the young lord of the manor, welcoming the new guests into his domain.

Christopher, showing more sense than his cousin, had offered Lady Peckham his arm, while Tidwell conversed with the Peckhams' chauffeur, probably about where to stow the motorcar. Alfred and the first footman, Hugh—the Astleys isn't the sort of family to rename their footmen James and John—were pulling bags from the boot of the Crossley and dragging them into the house. For a group of people who were only planning to stay two nights, the Peckhams had brought a lot of luggage.

"Who's the beauty queen?" I asked Constance, since we were perfectly alone by then, and nobody could hear me.

She made a face. "My mother's ward. A friend's daughter from the Continent, come to live with us."

"Really?" I was from the Continent myself, and had lived with the Astleys since 1914, when my mother, Aunt Roz's sister, sent me away to England for my safety.

Constance nodded. "Her name is Johanna de Vos, from Holland. Her parents were killed in the shelling."

Perhaps best not to mention, to Johanna or Lady Peckham, that my father had been German. He was killed in the war, too, but it would be better to be careful, I thought. Some things were still delicate, even eight years after the fighting stopped.

"I'm sorry to hear it," I said politely.

Constance snorted, and I glanced at her, surprised. The girl I'd known at Godolphin wouldn't have been that direct. "I saw the way you looked at her," she told me. "You didn't like her any better than I do."

Likely not. "She's just so very..." I hesitated, "obvious about it."

Constance nodded. "You should try to live with her."

I shuddered. "No, thank you."

"I suppose I can't convince you to come home with us after the funerals tomorrow, then?"

She tucked her arm through mine as we turned towards the house.

"Come home with you?" I echoed.

She nodded. "Mother wants to have a weekend party. I

think she's hoping that one of your cousins will meet me and fall in love, but I don't see any signs of that happening."

She gestured to where Crispin and Christopher had vanished into the house without giving her a second look before adding, "Although I suppose she'd probably be happy enough to have Johanna snag a duke's grandson. Better if it were the viscount, of course."

"That's Crispin," I said, "and she's welcome to him. But she can't have Christopher. I like him too much."

Constance giggled. "I don't know either of them well enough to say. I think I might have met Christopher once while you and I were at Godolphin together. I mostly know the viscount by reputation."

"You and everyone else," I said. "He's not the kind of man I would wish on someone I cared about."

And especially not someone as seemingly sweet and innocent as Constance. Crispin would have her in tears in five minutes flat, and with nothing worse than cold sarcasm.

Not that cold sarcasm isn't bad enough, but he wouldn't have to touch her, wouldn't have to berate her, wouldn't have to raise his voice, wouldn't have to do anything but be his cold, distant self. For a sensitive, romantic soul, the undiluted effect of Crispin Astley, Viscount St George, would be more than enough.

And then there was the chance that he'd pour on the charm —which I knew he could do, having watched other girls succumb to it—only to withdraw after Constance was well and truly hooked. That would be even worse.

"Stay away from Crispin," I told her. "If you want a husband, we'll find you a nice, kind one."

She brightened. "Christopher?"

"Perhaps not Christopher. He's..."

I hesitated. The plain, unvarnished truth was that Christopher prefers men, but that's not something one can just come out and say. Not even in the thoroughly modern year of 1926. And not to someone one doesn't know well.

Besides, it wasn't something I necessarily wanted to get out. It's no one else's concern, for one thing, and for another, the buggery laws are still in effect. In the end, I came up with a polite, old-fashioned euphemism I thought solved the problem nicely. "Christopher's affections are engaged elsewhere."

So were Crispin's, if he were to be believed. (Although of course I didn't. His supposed infatuation with some unsuitable girl his father wouldn't let him marry didn't slow him down enough for it to be remotely likely that he was telling the truth.)

Constance nodded thoughtfully. "I hadn't heard that. But people don't say much about Mr. Astley. They mostly talk about Lord St George."

I'm sure they did. "Out of curiosity," I said, "who do you know who travels in the same circles as Crispin?"

Because she really didn't strike me as someone who had friends in the Bright Young Set that Crispin ran with when he was in Town. It was a very fast crowd, and Constance, although she was more spirited than I remembered from Godolphin, struck me as anything but fast.

"Oh." She flushed. "The Marsdens live nearby. Do you know Lady Laetitia?"

I didn't. Or not well, at any rate.

"By name mostly." More specifically, her name had been on a list of women that Grimsby the valet-cum-blackmailer had assembled to give to the late duke two weeks ago. A list of women who knew Crispin, in the Biblical or some other way.

"She'll probably be there this weekend," Constance offered, "if you'd like to meet her."

Oh, would she?

I wondered whether that would make Crispin more or less

likely to agree to go. If he was trying to pursue the golden Johanna, the presence of Laetitia might put a crimp in that plan.

On the other hand, he might simply switch his attentions from Johanna to Laetitia instead. Or, I supposed, he might try to juggle them both. He seemed to have juggled so many women for so long that it was quite possible he could handle two in the same weekend.

Or, if we were all very lucky, he might decide to stay home to avoid the whole situation, and we wouldn't be burdened with him for the weekend.

"I'll ask Christopher," I said. "Are you expecting anyone else I might know?"

"Laetitia has a brother," Constance answered. "And isn't there an older Mr. Astley, as well? I'm sure my mother would like him to come."

"I assume you mean Francis and not my Uncle Herbert?" I nodded to Tidwell, who was standing sentry in the foyer. "Where is Miss Peckham's room, Tidwell? Is she next to me, or across the hall?"

"Miss Peckham's room is next to your room, Miss Darling," Tidwell intoned. "Her ladyship and Miss de Vos are across the hall. Miss Peckham's bag should be empty and her clothes put in the wardrobe by now."

"Thank you, Tidwell. Did the others go upstairs, or...?"

Tidwell's impassive face became, somehow, even more impassive. "The young gentlemen are in the billiards room, Miss Darling. Lady Peckham and her ward retired upstairs."

"Thank you, Tidwell." I turned to Constance. "Do you want to go upstairs to your mother and Johanna, or would you rather see what's going on in the billiard room?"

I could see the struggle on her face. I'm sure she felt she was supposed to join her mother. But let's be honest, who would want to spend any more time than necessary in the company of the Golden One?

Well, I'm sure all the men would. But among the rest of us? Not many, I fancied.

"Billiard room it is," I said briskly. "Do let us know when it's time for tea, Tidwell."

"I'll ring the gong as usual, Miss Darling."

"Thank you, Tidwell." I ushed Constance down the hallway in the west wing, towards the billiards room.

It should really, more properly, be called the game room. There was a billiards table at pride of place in the middle of the room, yes. There were also several smaller tables intended for games of canasta and bridge and whist and the like. But the walls were covered with the stuffed heads of game—deer and elk and the occasional zebra or antelope—all looking down on the proceedings with accusing black eyes.

I avoided looking at them as I pulled Constance behind me into the room. "Gentlemen."

They were gathered around the billiards table. Or rather, Crispin was lining up a shot while Christopher and Mr. Peckham eyed him, Christopher somewhat complacently and Mr. Peckham with a bit of consternation. I guess he didn't know Crispin well enough to realize just how competitive he is. He's the youngest of all of us, even if it's only by a couple of months in Christopher's case, and I suppose he feels at a bit of a disadvantage. It was clear that Mr. Peckham had managed to stir him up, and equally obvious that the latter had no idea how to deal with it.

"Careful, Mr. Peckham," I told him lazily, "St George is not above bouncing balls off the table when he's in a mood."

Crispin straightened and showed teeth. "Mind your own, Darling."

His cheeks were nicely flushed, and he was looking a lot

less ghostly. Under different circumstances, I would have congratulated Peckham on the accomplishment.

Instead, I said mildly, "I'm just warning Mr. Peckham that he might be in danger, St George. He doesn't know you like we do."

"You don't know me at all, Darling."

He dismissed me with a flick of a glance and went back to the table.

"I know you well enough to be able to ruin your concentration," I told him. "It's polite to let the guests win, you know."

"I'm not running a charity," Crispin retorted, between clenched teeth, and took his shot. The ball bounced off the edge, hit something else, and then it was Peckham's turn.

He sniggered. "She has your number, St George."

Crispin gave me a fulminating stare. "That's not all she has."

I smirked back. "In this case you're right. I also have news. You missed making her acquaintance outside, dangling after Miss de Vos the way you did, but this is Miss Constance Peckham, who has kindly invited us all to a house party at the Dower House this weekend."

I let this announcement sit for a moment before I added, sweetly, "Laetitia Marsden will be there, St George. I thought you'd be particularly interested."

Peckham gave Crispin a narrow look, while I kept a pleasant expression on my face.

I had hoped he'd give some indication that he either wanted, or didn't want, to spend time with Lady Laetitia. He didn't. Instead, he did what I had worried he would do, which was turn to Constance and boost the charm.

"Miss Peckham." The smile was boyish and just rueful enough to look like genuine regret. "Please forgive my inattention. I'm delighted to meet you. Darling has already told us so much about you."

He snatched up her hand and brought it to his lips. And kept it there slightly longer than necessary. Constance blushed beet red, while her brother's eyes sharpened.

"Take your mouth off her hand, St George," I told him. "Nobody wants your cooties."

Crispin's eyes narrowed, but he kept his temper for long enough to give Constance her hand back in a polite manner—and with a brush of his thumb across her knuckles—before he turned to me. "I beg to differ, Darling. Plenty of people want my cooties. Laetitia Marsden, for one."

"Ewww." My face twisted. "I didn't need that image in my head, St George."

"Then you should have known better than to bring it up, shouldn't you?" Crispin turned back to the billiards table. "My turn, is it?"

I rolled my eyes. "Come on, Constance. Let's go to the salon, and leave the boys to their amusements. Tea should be ready in a moment."

Constance nodded, but not without a glance at her brother, who looked back at her stonily, and Crispin, who didn't look at her at all, but kept his attention on the table and the balls, and finally Christopher, who gave her a slightly apologetic smile and a small bow. "Christopher Astley," he told her. "At your service."

Constance gave him a quick curtsey, but she didn't blush the way she'd done over Crispin. When she turned towards the door, however, Christopher shifted his attention to me and winked.

"Coming?" I asked him.

He nodded. "This won't take much longer. We'll be there in a few minutes."

"We'll see you in the salon, then." I followed Constance out the door. "Eyes on the ball, St George."

As I crossed the threshold, I heard the smack of wood against ivory behind me, and so quickly that it was almost simultaneous, a growl from Crispin.

"Bad luck, old chum," Peckham said insincerely. I sniggered, loudly enough that I thought he'd certainly be able to hear me, as I headed down the hallway after Constance.

I WON'T BORE you by recounting the ways all the men stumbled over their feet and their words over tea, dribbling on themselves and the table while the lovely Johanna sipped the genial beverage and pretended she didn't notice. It was quite clearly pretense, because they were so obvious about it that there was simply no way she could have been unaware. I would frankly be delighted to assign an imbecilic level of stupidity to her, but no one is that oblivious.

But we made it through tea, and then the boys vied for Johanna's attention while Constance and I took a walk through the grounds. The weather was nice, and the formal gardens were lovely, bursting with spring flowers now at the beginning of May.

As we progressed from the gravel paths on the east side of the house towards the rear, Constance dropped her voice. "Is that where...?"

That was indeed where Grimsby the valet had met his demise.

"The garden maze," I nodded. "I followed St George into it last Sunday week—Christopher told me I had to apologize for having been unkind over breakfast—and there he was."

Or there they were, more accurately. Crispin on his knees

beside Grimsby's dead body. It hadn't been until I got closer that I'd seen the blood.

Constance gave a half-frightened, half-delighted little shudder. "Can we...?"

"You want to go inside the maze?"

That I hadn't expected. I hadn't been back inside since, and I had no real desire to go now. But perhaps she had been reading the works of Agatha Christie, as I had. Before I saw several freshly dead bodies in the flesh, so to speak, last weekend, I'd been curious, too.

Constance nodded, her eyes bright and her hands wound together in front of her.

"Of course," I murmured politely. She was a guest, after all, and as a representative of the family, even a distant one, it was my duty to give her what she wanted.

So in we went, Right, then left, then left again. I had plotted the hedge maze at twelve, after Crispin had left me crying inside it one too many times. He, of course, had grown up here, and had had it memorized by the time he was five.

And speaking of St George... there he was, in the heart of the maze as we rounded the final corner into the central section, where the sundial and the wrought iron benches were.

Grimsby had been lying beside the sundial, so that's where my eye went first. It took me a few seconds more to spy Crispin, sitting on a bench side by side with the lovely Johanna.

Or more accurately, I noticed him when he shot to his feet at the sight of us. The movement out of the corner of my eye was what caused me to turn in that direction, in time to take in the flush on his cheeks and the way his collar was just a centimeter or so out of alignment.

I looked at it for a second too long, quite deliberately, before I arched my brows. "Petting party, St George?"

The flush deepened, while Constance gave a sort of horrified titter behind me. Johanna didn't say anything, but her lips curved in a very self-satisfied way.

"Don't be crude, Darling," Crispin managed, but it was without most of his usual insouciance, and completely without vitriol.

I waved him off, pseudo-magnanimously. "No, no. Don't let me stop you. We're just here to view the scene of the crime. Although I have to say, St George, you could have found a more romantic setting for your tryst. There was a dead body here just over a week ago. I know you remember. We both stood here and looked at it, didn't we? And hadn't you told me, just a few minutes before that, that you weren't the type to bed anyone on the grass in the garden maze?"

Constance choked on another horrified laugh, and by this point, Crispin's cheeks were so red they must have been hurting him. "Good God, Darling," he choked, "don't you ever shut up?"

I smiled sweetly, the equivalent of a condescending pat on the head. "Of course, St George. We'll be out of your way in a jiffy. Come on, Constance. The body was over there, by the sundial, although we should probably come back another time. We don't want to get in the way of St George bagging yet another conquest. He must be up to an even dozen for the year by now, and it's hardly even May yet."

I ushered Constance back into the maze, while behind me, Crispin's voice rose in a cry. "Damn you, Darling! When I get my hands on you—"

"In your dreams, St George," I told him over my shoulder, while beside me, Constance was practically convulsing with silent laughter. "The only way you'll get your hands on me, is in your dreams."

We disappeared out of sight between the yew hedges. I smiled grimly while Constance battled little hiccoughing bouts of horrified laughter as we made our way through the maze and out, at a much faster clip than we'd gone in. It wasn't that I really expected Crispin to abandon Johanna in the middle of the maze to come running after me to strangle me, but on the other hand, it didn't seem entirely out of the realm of possibility that I'd pushed him far enough that he'd try, either.

THREE

"I'M SORRY," Constance told me when we were back in the open again. She was still battling occasional bursts of mirth, but she did her best to sound sober and serious. "I don't know what came over me. He just looked so alarmed being caught that way, practically with his hand in the biscuit jar..."

My mind supplied a picture of Johanna as the biscuit jar and Crispin's hands going somewhere they had no business to go, and I fought back a combination snort-wince of mingled amusement and revulsion. Once I had myself under control again, I told her, "When your family arrived, I got the impression that your brother was staking his claim on Johanna."

"Oh, no." Constance tucked her hand through my arm as we made our way back toward the front of the house. "Mother would never allow that. Johanna is a foreigner with no title and no money. Gilbert is supposed to find himself an heiress with a title and fortune of her own."

"So between you, Gilbert, and Johanna, she's expecting three advantageous marriages where you all come out better than you went in?"

Constance nodded. "I'm expected to find an heir, preferably with a title but certainly with a fortune. Your cousin St George would be ideal—"

"He's not my cousin," I said. "He's Christopher's cousin, and there's nothing about him that's ideal."

"—although your cousin Christopher would be acceptable."

"You can't have Christopher, and I would recommend that you stay away from Crispin, as well."

While he had both title and fortune, he was not a good risk for marriage, if you asked me.

"Yes, Pippa," Constance said demurely. "You made that abundantly clear back there."

"Back...?"

"In the maze," Constance said. "Perhaps I ought to have picked up on it sooner, but you could have just explained that you and Lord St George have some sort of understanding, Pippa."

My jaw dropped. "Me and... we... you think Crispin and I...?"

"It certainly sounded that way," Constance said brightly.

I began shaking my head, and ended up shaking it faster and faster. It was imperative that I convey the impossibility of this suggestion. "Oh, no. No, no, no. No, definitely not. Not in a thousand years. Not possibly. No."

Constance smirked. "Those are a lot of Nos."

"I can't possibly object to Crispin strongly enough," I explained. "It takes a lot of Nos to do it justice."

"He's handsome. Wealthy. Titled."

He was all those things. I couldn't argue with any of them. "He's also a brat," I said. "A childish, self-indulgent little horror. He's a philanderer. A cad, if that isn't too old-fashioned a word. He beds women indiscriminately. A girl with a baby showed up at Sutherland House in London a couple of months ago. A baby, Constance!"

"Dear me," Constance said.

I nodded. "I don't think he'd stop doing it if he were married, either."

Not unless he was allowed to marry the girl he claimed to be in love with, at any rate. The foreign one his late grandfather and mother had objected to, along with his still-very-much-alive father. If he got her, maybe he'd be happy enough that he wouldn't feel the need to stray.

And speaking of foreign girls with no title or money...

"I don't suppose there's any chance St George might have made Johanna's acquaintance before now, is there?"

From the scene we'd stumbled on in the maze, things had moved rather quickly for two people who had never laid eyes on each other before today. And she was clearly both foreign and penniless. Just as he was, clearly, quite smitten with her.

"I have no idea," Constance said, as we came around the corner of the conservatory. There was the sound of a motorcar off in the distance, and as we made our way toward the front of the Hall and the courtyard, it came closer. "She's never mentioned him before. Then again, we don't talk much, Johanna and I..."

No, I wouldn't want to talk to Johanna, either. The thought of living with her, even just for the next few days, was unpleasant. I couldn't imagine how Constance put up with it.

"Who else is coming?" Constance wanted to know, as a shiny black motorcar made its way up the drive from the road into the courtyard. The evening sun shone on a fair head behind the wheel, while a dignified brown Derby along with a green-on-green appliqued cloche took up the back seat.

"Hullo, Pipsqueak!" a voice called out.

I raised a hand in response. "That's the rest of the Astleys.

My Aunt Roslyn and Uncle Herbert and Cousin Francis. Christopher's parents and his eldest—well, only now —brother."

"You lost a cousin in the war," Constance interpreted, with her eyes still on the motorcar as it zoomed around the curve of the driveway and into the courtyard.

I nodded. "Francis was the eldest, Christopher the youngest. Too young to serve. You know that; he's the same age as we are."

"Eleven when the war started," Constance said.

"Precisely. Francis was eighteen and Robert sixteen. By the time conscription started, they were both called up. Francis made it through. Robert didn't."

"And that's Francis." Constance watched as my eldest cousin pulled the motorcar to a stop beside the fountain in the courtyard and jumped out. Tidwell, meanwhile, had opened the front door from the Hall and now proceeded majestically towards the automobile to open the door for Uncle Herbert while Francis did the honors for Aunt Roz. Alfie and Hugh descended on the car to carry the bags upstairs, and Francis came our way.

"Pipsqueak!"

I grimaced. "I wish so much you wouldn't call me that, Francis."

"I know, Pippa. That's why I do it." He put an arm around my shoulders and gave me a squeeze before smiling down at Constance. "Who do we have here?"

"Constance," I said formally, "this is my cousin, Mr. Francis Astley. Francis, my friend from Godolphin, Miss Constance Peckham. The Peckhams are here for the funeral. Lady Peckham was a friend of Aunt Charlotte's."

Francis nodded. "Delighted to meet you, Miss Peckham." He appropriated her hand and did the Crispin-bow over it, complete with kiss. Constance tittered and blushed again, and Francis winked at her.

"Behave yourself," I admonished. He was red-cheeked and bright-eyed and looked flushed and healthy, and like all the Astley men, he's quite good-looking. But while the high color and high spirits may have been the result of the invigorating drive here from Beckwith Place, he might equally well have indulged in some sort of stimulant before setting out. Francis has a problem with self-medication, and I'm sure he wasn't looking forward to tomorrow and the funerals.

"I always do, Pippa." He turned the wink on me before offering his arm "May I escort you two lovely ladies inside?"

"Of course." I tucked my hand through his elbow. "You missed tea, I'm sorry to say."

On the other side of Francis, Constance did the same, delicately but gamely.

"And be warned," I added, as we headed for the front door, "there's a gold-digger on the premises."

"You don't say?" Francis peered down at Constance. "Not this one, surely?"

"No, no." I shook my head, and so did she. "Constance is expected to snag a husband, too, but the It Girl has St George cornered in the maze."

Francis smothered a laugh. "Such a curse, being young, handsome, and titled."

"Isn't it just? At any rate, she's Lady Peckham's ward, or companion, or special project, from the Continent."

"Like you are *our* special project from the Continent," Francis said and squeezed my hand.

"Exactly like that. Except your mother doesn't seem to care whether I snag a husband with a title or not."

"No." He shook his head. "Mum has her own thoughts on that score."

"Must be nice," Constance muttered.

It *was* nice, actually. However— "Surely Aunt Roz doesn't think I'm going to marry Christopher, does she?"

"Of course not," Francis said. "Our mother knows both of you better than that."

Good to know. "So back to the girl. Her name is Johanna, and she's Flemish or Belgian or something like that. Dutch, maybe. Tall, blond, and exceptionally beautiful. Crispin seems altogether smitten. And while she seems focused on him right now, if something goes wrong there, she could come after you. We both know Christopher isn't in the market for a wife..."

Francis shook his head.

"And that means you're the fallback. Eldest grandson of a duke—"

"Not anymore," Francis reminded me. "Since a week ago, I'm just the eldest nephew of a duke. One with a son of his own. Crispin's the one with the title and fortune."

"Still. You're the grandson of a duke—all right, the grandson of a *dead* duke—and if she strikes out with Crispin and Christopher isn't interested..."

"I'll guard my virtue carefully," Francis promised, and guided us both through the front door into the foyer, "I guess I may assume you don't want this chippy in the family?"

"Not if I can help it." I extricated my hand from his arm. "She's welcome to St George. If I never have to deal with him again, it won't be too soon. But she can't have any of the rest of you. Aunt Roz would absolutely hate every inch of her."

"Then I'll be careful," Francis said, and removed Constance's hand from his arm with a lot more care than he'd shown mine. "I should go get situated in my room. I assume we're changing for dinner?"

"I think you can safely assume that. I'm sure Lady Peckham

and the Continental Project have a gown waiting that's designed to take everyone's breath away."

Constance nodded confirmation.

"Then we'll just have to uphold the family honor the best we can," Francis said, and smacked his heels together in a way I didn't think I'd seen him do since he was in uniform. "Miss Peckham. A pleasure."

Constance dropped a sort of abbreviated curtsey.

"Pipsqueak." He nodded to me.

"We'll see you downstairs at eight o'clock," I said, and then we watched as he headed up the stairs and into the east wing. When he had vanished, I turned to Constance, who was still looking at the spot where he had turned the corner. "So that's Francis."

She nodded, without looking at me.

"He was on his best behavior, I admit, but you can see why he's preferable to St George in practically every particular."

Constance hummed agreement.

"What do you want to do now?" I asked, and she finally took her attention off the stairs to attend to our conversation.

"I suppose I should go upstairs and see if Mother needs any help getting ready for dinner. She didn't bring her lady's maid with us..."

"If Hughes is still around," I said, "Aunt Charlotte's maid, you know, I'm sure she'd be happy to help your mother."

Of course, with Aunt Charlotte gone, Hughes might have left the Hall already, too. Unless she was staying until after the funeral. Or unless Uncle Harold had offered to keep her on. I had no idea what sort of job he'd be able to find for her, though. He had no need of a lady's maid, nor did Crispin, and I doubted Hughes would be enthused about being demoted to chambermaid.

Constance looked doubtful, and I added, forcefully. "You

absolutely do not owe Johanna any help. If you want to do something useful, go make yourself as beautiful as you can. She could use some competition, instead of having it all her own way."

"I'd rather just be myself," Constance demurred, which was a lovely sentiment as far as it went. However—

"Is there a reason you can't be yourself as well as look beautiful?"

She looked at me with all the self-confidence of a wilted wallflower. I sighed. "Come on. Show me what you brought to wear."

"You don't have to..." Constance demurred, but by then I was dragging her towards the staircase and she was coming willingly.

Upstairs, we went in the opposite direction of Francis, who had headed for his usual room in the east wing. Someone must have told him where to go, or perhaps he had simply assumed he'd be in the same room as last time.

Constance and I went left, past the door to the duchess's chamber—which would have been Aunt Charlotte's now, if she had only lived long enough to take possession of it—and the room Aunt Roz and Uncle Herbert use when they're visiting, and then around the corner and down the hall in the west wing toward my room and Constance's.

Mine's in the far corner, as far from the east wing and Christopher's room as it's possible to get, and Tidwell had said Constance's room was next to mine. Last week, Inspector Pendennis of Scotland Yard had slept there for a couple of nights.

There was no need to mention that, of course, so I didn't.

The door to the room stood open, and we pushed inside. Constance looked around while I busied myself with lighting the electric lamps. Sutherland Hall had been converted from gas to the electric grid in the years since the war, and it was lovely to flip a switch and have bright light burst out immediately.

"Gown?" I asked Constance when she made no move toward the wardrobe. "Tidwell said your things had been unpacked."

"I'm only staying for two nights, and tomorrow we're all expected to wear black, so I only brought one option for dinner tonight."

"That's fine," I said. "I'm not much better off. Although after we got stuck here much longer than expected last weekend, I packed a few extra things this time, just in case."

She gave me a look over her shoulder as she opened the wardrobe and reached in. "Surely you're not expecting another murder?"

"Of course not. That would be silly."

I eyed the gown that appeared from the wardrobe. It was a dull tobacco brown crepe with bronze beads and mahogany embroidery and little cap sleeves made from chiffon. It was a really poor color choice for Constance, who already had the look of a plump sparrow with her shiny brown hair and dark eyes.

"That's..." I stopped myself before I could say 'unfortunate,' because really and truly, the frock wasn't bad. It was well made, the embroidery exquisite; it was just not right for Constance, who was already fading into the paneling and needed no further help in making herself invisible.

"I know." She eyed it with displeasure. "Johanna said I looked beautiful, and of course Mother insisted I had to have it."

"The cow," I said.

Constance looked at me with a giggle. "Did you just call my mother a cow, Pippa?"

"Not your mother. Johanna." Although Lady Peckham might well be a cow, too, if she allowed her ward to diminish her daughter in this way. "Wait here a second. I have something that might work better."

I had brought two evening gowns with me this time, just in case we got stuck here another day and I needed an extra. Last week I hadn't had a spare, and I was determined not to be put in that position again. So my weekender bag—or more accurately, the wardrobe in the next room—also held clothes I didn't plan to wear, that I had only brought in the event we were taken by surprise again.

As indeed we had been, with the impromptu invitation to the house party at the Dower House that Constance had issued. I wouldn't have time to go back to London to pack, so it was a good thing I had brought extras.

Among them was the butter-yellow evening dress with silver spangles I had worn to dinner last week. I had brought it again, as a spare, along with an apple green silk dress with diamante embroidery I had been planning to wear tonight. It was brand new, and I wasn't about to loan it to anyone before I'd had a chance to wear it myself, but the yellow was fair game. Everyone in the family had already seen that. It would be a bit long on Constance, who was several inches shorter than me, but the uneven hem would help, and the yellow would at least be brighter with her complexion than the tobacco brown.

I fished it out of my wardrobe and stepped back into the hallway with it. Just in time to come face to face with Johanna, who was going into her own room on the opposite side of the hall.

She was humming.

Her cheeks were flushed, her golden curls were rumpled, as if someone had had his hands in them, and her lipstick was mostly just a memory. She looked like a girl who had been thoroughly used, and despite not liking her much at all, I felt as if I ought—woman to woman—give her fair warning. "He's not a good bet for marriage."

She turned slowly, eyes moving over me from top to bottom and back. I think she would have liked very much to sneer, but it so happens that I don't look bad enough to sneer at, and I also don't look like someone who would take being sneered at very well. So instead she merely asked, "Excuse me?" in a very snotty voice.

"Lord St George," I explained, as if she didn't already know quite well who we were talking about. "He's not someone you should pin your hopes on for a marriage proposal."

Her eyes narrowed. "Do you imagine you can stop me?"

Her voice had a lilting sort of accent, very melodic, and I could quite imagine that if she murmured sweet nothings into someone's ear in that voice, he'd be putty in her hands.

I laughed. "Oh, Lord, no. He doesn't care what I think. Nor do I care who he marries. In fact, if he were mine to give away, and it would get him out of my hair, I would have him giftwrapped and handed over to you right now. But I happen to know that he won't be a good husband to anyone at the moment. You're familiar with his reputation, I'm sure."

It wasn't a question, since I was absolutely certain she was. Word had got around, and almost anyone our age, or a bit younger or a bit older, was familiar with Crispin's escapades.

As she must have been, because she gave a nonchalant little shrug. "Boyish exuberance."

"He's twenty-two," I said. "Almost twenty-three. Hardly a boy anymore." While she was surely at least a few years older, and clearly ready to settle down. "Although he did just lose his mother. Perhaps he's looking for a substitute."

That hit home, anyway. Her lips flattened.

I held up a hand in a gesture of peace. It would have been

both hands, but I was carrying the yellow gown with the other. "Listen, Miss de Vos. I'm trying to do you a favor. He's in love. He wants a woman he can't have, and because he can't have the woman he wants, he uses every other woman he comes across who'll let him. You can certainly let him use you if you want—you won't be the first or the last; if you're familiar with his reputation, you already know that—but he won't marry you. If he can't get his father's permission to marry the girl he's in love with, he won't get his father's permission to marry you."

She was just as foreign, after all, and presumably just as penniless and without prospects as Crispin's ladylove.

"But feel free to waste your time on him anyway," I told her, magnanimously. "Just don't say I didn't warn you."

I left her standing there, and flounced down the hall to Constance's room. By the time I let myself in, Johanna was still standing where I'd left her, staring after me with an expression that ought to have left me as nothing more than a wet smear on the floor of the hall.

FOUR

CONSTANCE LOOKED RATHER FETCHING in my yellow gown, and I didn't look too bad in her brown one. There's nothing particularly sparrow-like about me, so I could carry it off much better than she could, and with a whole lot more attitude, too, especially when I remembered my suspicion that Johanna had talked Lady Peckham into buying it for the sole purpose of making Constance look drab so Johanna could shine more brightly.

Additionally, because I had a few inches on Constance, I got to flash a little more leg, too, which is never a bad thing. I have it on good authority—Christopher's—that my legs are excellent, so I don't mind a chance to show them off.

Of course, there was absolutely no way for either of us to outshine Johanna. Certainly not in borrowed gowns. The Golden Goddess wore flame-colored crepe de chine with flounce upon flounce of beads, clearly straight from Paris. She had paired the gown with a golden headband and gold strap shoes, and I knew I was beaten as soon as she walked into the room.

Aunt Roz's eyebrows disappeared up her forehead. "Well, well."

I nodded. "I know. That's Lady Peckham's ward, Johanna de Vos. Here to snag a husband, clearly."

"Couldn't be much clearer," Aunt Roz agreed. "I suppose I ought to make sure she knows Herbert is taken."

"I don't think she's interested in Uncle Herbert. She has her eye on Crispin, I think."

"Good Lord," Aunt Roz said, and turned her attention to her nephew, who was standing behind his chair on the other side of the table, elegant in black tie evening kit. For some reason, it made him look younger rather than older. "She'd eat him for breakfast."

"I think he's more than capable of holding his own," I told her dryly. "He's not without experience, you know."

Aunt Roz had to acquiesce to that. Nonetheless, she shook her head. "He's not equal to that, surely. She'll have him hogtied and halfway to the altar if we're not careful."

"They've invited us to a weekend party at the Dower House," I told her. "We're to go directly there the day after tomorrow."

Aunt Roz looked serious. "You'll have to make sure she doesn't compromise him, Pippa."

"Compromise him?" I stared at her. What were we, Victorians? "I hardly think he can be compromised, Aunt Roz. Not considering the kinds of things he gets up to every time he goes up to London. Which reminds me, Laetitia Marsden is going to be there, too. And you know he's already dallied with her before."

"So it'll be a pitched battle between the two of them," Aunt Roz said brightly. "Now I'm rather sorry I wasn't invited."

I rolled my eyes. "Just what we'd all like to see, I'm sure.

Two women squabbling over St George like he is the last, dried-up cucumber sandwich on the tray."

"Just keep an eye on things," Aunt Roz told me. "We can't let someone like that get her hooks in him."

She tilted her head sideways to take in the golden glow of Johanna. "Just look at the way she's smiling at Harold now. Indecent is what it is."

It was, actually. Aunt Roz clicked her tongue. "I'd better go rescue him. Lady Peckham clearly isn't going to do it."

No, she wasn't. She simply stood there, beaming, as Johanna turned all her youth and beauty on the grieving widower, whose wife wasn't even in the ground yet.

"Looks like your new ladylove is looking to trade up already," I told Crispin across the table as Aunt Roz set off. He had been watching Johanna, too, so there was no need to explain what I was talking about. I did it anyway, of course. "Why bother with the viscount when she can go directly to the duke?"

It was intended as a rhetorical question, not something that required a response, but I wasn't surprised when he couldn't resist the bait. There was even a hint of offended color in his cheeks. "Perhaps she's just getting to know her future father-in-law, Darling."

"Oh, God," I said. "St George, please. Don't tell me you're actually thinking of proposing marriage? Have you lost whatever's left of your tiny mind?"

"Why would I have to have lost my mind?" He gestured to where Johanna was fluttering her eyelashes at Uncle Harold. They were exceptionally long and curly, of course. Just like everything else about her. "Look at her, Darling. She's stunning."

Of course she was. However— "Is that really all you're looking for? Someone pretty?"

"She's quite a lot more than pretty, Darling."

Pretty enough that he had a problem taking his eyes off her, it seemed. I don't appreciate people not looking at me when I'm talking to them, and my voice surely made it clear.

"What about the girl you swore up and down you were in love with last weekend? The one who was so important to you that you wanted me to forget all about her? She's just out the window now, is she?"

He sent me a scowl. "It's not like I can have her, is it? At least this," another glance at Johanna, but this one didn't stick, "is someone I can have."

"I wouldn't be too sure," I told him. "She's just as foreign as your other girl, isn't she? And just as poor, too, probably. Surely your father won't approve that? And from the way she's looking at him, she might just decide that she'd rather have him than you, anyway. You could end up with a stepmother who's a year or two older than you."

And not just that, but a stepmother he'd kissed in the garden maze earlier.

My face twisted at the reminder, and so did his. "You're vile, Darling."

"Oh, am I? Would you like to know what I think is vile? For a woman to kiss a man in the garden maze, and then, less than an hour later, look at his father like she'd like to do the same to him."

He opened his mouth, presumably to object to something I had said—what, I can't imagine—and I barreled right over him. "That woman is a piranha, St George, and for your own sake, if you know what's good for you, you'll stay far, far away from her."

Since no one seemed to be making any effort to sit down at the supper table, I flounced off, too, in the opposite direction of the one Aunt Roz had taken. Over to where Francis had engaged Constance in conversation, with a little help from Christopher.

They both seemed immune to Johanna's glory, I was happy to see. Of course, with Christopher, that was hardly a surprise. She's not even remotely his type. But it seemed my warning to Francis had done the trick, or perhaps he simply preferred Constance to her flashier counterpart.

It appeared mutual, too, as she was quite visibly blushing and dimpling under his gaze.

I hid a sigh. Now I'd have to caution Constance about Francis, I supposed, and unlike my warnings to both Francis and Crispin about Johanna, this one I wasn't looking forward to having to give. I love Francis, and want all the best for him, but he's perhaps not a great marital risk right now either, especially for someone so much younger and as innocent as Constance. She hadn't experienced the war up close the way we had.

But that was a warning for another day. This wasn't the right occasion for it. So I smiled pleasantly as I approached, and was reeled in by Christopher.

"Pippa." He put out a hand, and I stepped into the group. He looked me up and down. "That's a pretty frock. New?"

We live together, so he's fairly familiar with the contents of my wardrobe.

"Constance's," I said. "We traded."

He looked at Constance, and then back at me. "It looks better on you. And that—" The yellow dress, "looks better on *you*." This was Constance, who flushed.

"I have a feeling Johanna talked Lady Peckham into buying it so Constance wouldn't outshine her," I said, and ran my hand over the embroidery. "It's a beautiful dress, but not something that stands out in a crowd."

"Constance doesn't need help standing out in a crowd,"

Francis declared gallantly, and Constance looked half gratified, half appalled.

"Of course." I certainly couldn't disagree; that would be rude. "But the perfect dress never hurts."

I caught Christopher's eye. He looked amused, as well he should. My closet at home is full of gorgeous evening dresses in Christopher's size. If anyone knows the impact of a beautiful dress, it's my cousin.

Unfortunately, they're all the wrong colors for me—pinks and pale blues and such, things that make me look washed out. Otherwise, I could have doubled my wardrobe in one blink.

"I saw you talking to Crispin," Christopher said, and I rolled my eyes.

"We found him in the garden maze earlier, snuggled up to Johanna. I caught her sneaking into her room later, all disheveled, with her hair mussed up and her lipstick mostly gone. And now she's over there, looking at your uncle like she'd like to have him for supper. I merely pointed out the futility of pinning his hopes on that."

"I imagine that went over well," Francis said, eyes lit with amusement. He looked fairly healthy tonight, not like he was under the influence of anything stronger than Constance's company.

I made a face. "As well as my conversations with St George ever go. It ended with him calling me vile and me suggesting that he might brace himself for a new stepmother, before I walked over here."

Constance looked concerned, and Francis hastened to reassure her. "They're like that. Always have been. Pippa's been with us since 1914, and she and Crispin got off on the wrong foot almost immediately."

"Apparently I poached his best friend," I said, with a glance at Christopher, "something I wasn't even aware of doing until last week."

Francis nodded thoughtfully. "I suppose there's something to that."

"If I had realized it sooner, there might have been something I could have done about it. Made sure I included him more, perhaps. But by now I'm afraid it's too late."

"Definitely," Francis said. "I don't think friendship—"

He stopped with a wince, as if someone had kicked him in the ankle.

"What?" I looked down. If he'd been kicked, it was not immediately apparent. No one's foot was hanging about temptingly close to Francis's ankle.

He cleared his throat. "I was going to say, I don't think his friendship with Christopher is what's motivating him anymore. I'm sure he's over that by now."

"Oh, clearly. They get along simply fine, anyway. But he still doesn't like me."

I sent a disgruntled look across the room, to where Crispin was still standing alone, hand on the back of his chair, still watching the byplay over by the door, between his father, his uncle, Lady Peckham, Mr. Peckham, the lovely Johanna, and now Aunt Roz as well.

"He looks lonely," Constance said, and I glanced at her and back at Crispin.

To me he looked sulky, like he had been excluded from the group of popular children and it bothered him, but perhaps that was the same thing she was seeing, and she just interpreted it differently. He was standing alone, anyway, while all the rest of us were bunched into groups. That alone might have been enough to put the idea into her head.

"We'll go and find our seats," Francis told her, with the air of one trying to remedy the situation, "and that way he won't be standing alone anymore."

Constance nodded, and he offered his arm gallantly, for the few steps from where we were standing over to the table. Constance blushed when she rested her hand on it. I wanted to roll my eyes, but I refrained.

WE WERE ELEVEN FOR DINNER. An uneven number, which made the seating arrangements a bit peculiar. No doubt Tidwell had been tearing his hair out quietly while getting everything ready, and it wasn't made any easier by the fact that I'm fairly certain Mr. Peckham didn't sit where he was supposed to, between Aunt Roz and his sister to the left of Uncle Harold, when it came time to be seated. Instead, he pounced on the seat between his mother and Johanna on Uncle Harold's right. That left Uncle Herbert to sit next to his wife, which is never supposed to happen. But of course one couldn't tell the honored male guest that he'd made a mistake, whether on purpose or not, so Peckham stayed where he was, and Uncle Herbert obligingly sat between Aunt Roz and Constance on the left side of the table.

On the other side of Constance was Francis, which was nice for them both, and perfectly appropriate, except Constance ought really to be on the other side of the table between what should have been Uncle Herbert and Crispin, and it was Johanna who should have been on the off-side with the non-titled Astleys. Constance was Lady Peckham's real daughter, and as such more prominent than Johanna; she should have been the one seated next to the son of the house.

Of course Constance had absolutely no desire to converse with Crispin, who surely felt the same way about her, so they were both fine with the snub, and so, naturally, was Francis. But it was all very irregular.

I should have been sitting between Francis and Christopher, I suppose. Or at least I would have sat there, if I'd truly been their sister.

Or perhaps not. Perhaps I should have been sitting between Francis and Christopher if I were *not* their sister. Either way, and for whatever reason, Tidwell had decided to put me on the other side of the table next to Crispin. Perhaps it was so that we'd at least match from side to side. With eleven at table, and Uncle Harold at the head, that left five chairs on either side. Which I suppose made more sense to Tidwell than six on one side and four on the other, even if Christopher and Francis ended up sitting next to each other.

Crispin realized it at the same time I did. He curled his lip. "It appears you're over here next to me, Darling."

I rolled my eyes. "Should make for a quiet meal, then."

Francis smothered a laugh. "How can you possibly say that, Pipsqueak? The two of you bicker relentlessly."

"I'm sure St George will be busy amusing the dining companion on his other side," I said, as I prepared to make my way around the table.

His eyes narrowed. "Are you suggesting I haven't been taught the proper etiquette, Darling? You're to my right, so I'll be conversing with you during the first course."

"And then leave me to myself for the rest of the meal, I suppose."

He didn't say anything to that, or perhaps I was just too far away to hear his response at that point. Perhaps it was muttered under his breath and didn't carry far. He did pull out the chair for me when I arrived next to him, however, and seated me properly before sitting down himself. I shook the napkin out and draped it over my lap while I waited for Tidwell to bring the soup.

"So tell me how you've been, St George."

"Good God," Crispin said, and looked like he was thinking about putting his head down on the table, "you're going to make me do it, aren't you?"

I held back a smirk. "Do what?"

"Converse politely with you."

On the other side of the table, Francis stifled a burst of laughter, but when I glanced at him, his attention was on Constance, so maybe she was the one who had made him laugh.

"It's not going to kill you, St George," I told him. "Besides, I'm serious. It must have been a difficult week, and you're not looking particularly well."

"Thanks ever so, Darling." He slanted me a scowl. "If you know that, I'm sure you can guess how I've been."

I could, as a matter of fact, but a stubborn part of me wanted to hear him say it. "Just talk to me, St George. You don't have anyone else to talk to right now, and for the next few minutes, you're required to talk to me. Just do it. Tell me how you've been."

"Fine. You want to know?" His eyes flicked up to mine for a second and then away again. "I'll tell you. My mother died. My mother killed two people, and then herself. My father is... hell, I don't even know, Darling. He mostly hasn't said a word to me all week, except to tell me that no, I can't go to London where there *are* people I can actually talk to. My throat hurts from not talking."

"He was probably afraid you'd go to London and make a spectacle of yourself and end up on the cover of The Daily Yell again," I told him, "which wouldn't look good when your mother hasn't been buried yet."

"Don't you think I know that, Darling? I know exactly what he's afraid of. But I've been going crazy here by myself."

I nodded. "I'm sorry, St George. You could have contacted us, you know. We would have taken you in."

The look he gave me this time was sardonic. "You, take me in? No, you wouldn't have, Darling. You hate me. Besides, your flat is in London. Father wouldn't have let me go there."

That was a valid point. Everything he'd said was valid, actually. Except for the bit about me hating him. I didn't. Disliked him, certainly. Abhorred him, sometimes. Wanted to argue him into submission, always. Although at the moment I couldn't dredge up much of any of that, except pity, and anger that he'd had to go through this all alone.

"Aunt Roz, then," I said. "You could have taken the Hispano-Suiza and driven to Beckwith Place in less than an hour. Aunt Roz would have taken you in, and taken care of you."

He glanced across the table, and his eyes stayed on Aunt Roz for a moment. She was seated next to Uncle Herbert, and was smiling at him, tapping his nose with a finger. She looked happy, and loving, and kind, everything a mother ought to be, and for a second, the expression on Crispin's face was one of pure longing.

Until he wiped it away, or had it wiped for him, when Johanna turned to him with a dazzling smile. "Lord St George."

"Miss de Vos." I couldn't see the expression on his face any longer, as he'd had to turn away from me to respond to her. That was probably the point. She didn't want him talking to another woman while she was sitting next to him, even if etiquette dictated that he was supposed to.

I rolled my eyes. On the other side of the table, Christopher smirked, Francis grinned, and Constance looked uncomfortable.

"Johanna," she said softly, carefully, as if she thought there was any chance at all that Johanna didn't know exactly what she was doing, "Gilbert is your conversational partner for this course. Not Lord St George."

She accompanied the admonition with a glance at her mother, as if afraid Lady Peckham would notice Johanna's *faux pas* and take her to task over it. As if she were trying to save Johanna from being chastised by Lady P, in other words. And then she completed the performance by looking apologetically at Crispin, seemingly embarrassed at the breach of etiquette by her mother's ward.

I smothered the urge to laugh out loud. It was beautifully done. With one carefully worded statement, Constance had made Johanna look like she either didn't know proper etiquette or simply chose to flout it, which you really don't want to do in front of a duke and a viscount, especially not when you hope to entice one or the other into marriage. She had managed to make Johanna look bad, in other words, and I wanted to applaud.

It wasn't quite so funny when Johanna leveled a look across the table at Constance that could have blown her hair back. But by then Crispin had turned back to me, and Francis was looking at her with admiration, and it seemed as if Constance was able to ignore Johanna's murderous expression just fine.

FIVE

THE FUNERALS TOOK place the next day, and the less said about them, the better. Johanna looked divine in black, of course. Constance looked frumpy, and I decided to lay that at Johanna's door, too. Uncle Harold looked dignified, pale but composed, while Crispin fidgeted through the entirety of his grandfather's funeral, like a little boy who'd rather be anywhere else. By the time Aunt Charlotte's coffin was lowered into the ground, however, he was practically catatonic, so he had most likely indulged in something calming at some point, to make it through the ordeal. I couldn't even blame him. It's difficult to lose your mother under any circumstances, and these were particularly heinous.

Johanna didn't seem to notice his condition, so she was either stupid or, more likely, simply oblivious to the fact that he was both high as a kite and grieving.

Or perhaps she simply didn't care. I had the very distinct impression, which I had also communicated to St George (and to anyone else who would listen), that she was much more interested in his title and fortune than in his person.

Francis seemed mostly sober, calm but not unnaturally so, and he stayed close to Constance the entire day. Uncle Herbert remained with Uncle Harold, as did Lady Peckham, and Christopher and Aunt Roz never strayed too far from Crispin. I didn't think my help in propping up St George would be welcomed, by him or by Johanna, so I kept to myself, and occasionally to Francis and Constance. And so we made it through the day and into bed for the second night.

The next morning after breakfast we all packed our bags and prepared to decamp for Dorset and the Dower House. By then it was Friday, just the right time for the beginning of a weekend party, and Lady Peckham announced that she was staying at Sutherland Hall through Sunday, to "support poor Harold in his time of grief."

I wasn't the only one arching my brows at that. Aunt Roz was doing the same thing on the other side of the table in the breakfast room, and Christopher looked like he was having a difficult time keeping a straight face.

"Here I thought she was siccing Johanna on Uncle Harold," I whispered to him, "and all along she was planning to catch him for herself?"

Christopher nodded, the corners of his mouth twitching with amusement. "Looks like she's planning a double score. She gets Uncle Harold and Johanna gets Crispin."

Or even a triple. Constance got Francis, except he wasn't as much of a prize, without any title of his own.

Before I could say anything about it, however, Christopher had gone on. "I'm surprised she didn't throw Gilbert Peckham at you, honestly."

"I'm not worth enough," I said. "Nor am I a Sutherland. I'm sure she's planning to have Gilbert woo Lady Laetitia Marsden this weekend."

"That should be interesting. Isn't she an old flame of Crispin's?"

He glanced over at his cousin, who was contemplating his own plate with a conspicuous lack of enthusiasm. He was seated on the other side of the table and down a bit; far enough away, and distracted enough, that I didn't think we had to worry about him overhearing what we were saying.

"She was on the list of women Grimsby compiled," I nodded. "And he mention her to me once."

"She might be reluctant to let him go."

"I suspect he's already let her go," I told him, "not that I think it was serious to begin with. He doesn't appear to hang on to any of them for long. Given the number of women he's amused himself with in the past few years, I doubt she was under any illusions about keeping him."

"Still." Christopher contemplated his cousin silently for a moment. "If she sees someone else go after him, she might decide to keep her own hand in."

I suppose she might. "Your mother used the words 'pitched battle.' I suppose it could turn out to be amusing."

"As long as they attack each other and not him," Christopher said.

"I wouldn't mind if they attacked him. If anyone needs to have some sense smacked into him, it's St George."

He heard that, at any rate, because his eyes lifted from the plate and turned our way. They were bloodshot, like he hadn't got much sleep last night, but the sneer was as beautifully executed as always. "Plotting, Darling?"

"Not me," I said. "I'm just looking forward to seeing which of your many girlfriends goes for your throat first."

Christopher smothered a chuckle. Crispin looked at him for a moment before he turned back to me. "You really should endeavor to curb these violent tendencies, Darling."

"And you should eat some of your food. You'll need your strength if you plan to keep juggling several women this weekend."

He glanced down at the plate. And back up at me. And then he picked up a halved, cooked mushroom—with his fingers—and popped it in his mouth. And chewed it, slowly and thoroughly, while very deliberately keeping his eyes on mine.

"St George!" Uncle Harold barked, shocked, and Crispin swallowed, a pink flush on his cheekbones.

"Sorry, Father."

It was my turn to smother a laugh, which netted me a fuming look. "Just wait, Darling. One of these days..."

"I'll look forward to it, St George," I told him, and went back to moving the remains of my own breakfast around my plate, but not before I had shared an amused look with Christopher.

AFTER THE MEAL, we all gathered in the courtyard for the drive to the Dower House. Crispin had the Hispano-Suiza pulled out, of course, and was planning to make the drive himself, while Gilbert Peckham was negotiating with his mother how they'd handle their own motorcar, and the chauffeur who had come with it.

"If St George takes the two Astleys and Miss Darling with him, I can drive the Crossley back with Johanna and Constance."

He clearly planned to put Johanna next to himself in the front seat, while Constance would be languishing in the back by herself. And the chauffeur, I assumed, would be twiddling his thumbs in Wiltshire until Gilbert saw fit to come back and fetch him and his mother.

"Don't be ridiculous, Gilbert," Lady Peckham said. "You can't drive all that way by yourself."

Which was a ridiculous statement, when she'd had no qualms whatsoever about having the chauffeur do it. It wasn't like he was made of different material than Gilbert Peckham. Besides, it wasn't much of a drive at all. Crispin regularly drove from Wiltshire to London by himself, and that was much farther. The Dower House were just an hour or so southwest of us, into Dorset.

"I don't know that I feel good about leaving the children alone by themselves for the weekend," Aunt Roz said, which of course resulted in us all telling her that we weren't children anymore, we were all adults, and we certainly didn't need chaperones. "One of us should be there. What if something goes wrong?"

"The servants—" Lady Peckham began, but she stopped without finishing the sentence when Aunt Roz looked at her. I've been on the receiving end of Aunt Roz's looks, so I knew exactly why Lady P had stopped talking. Most people do, when Aunt Roz looks at them like that.

"Francis can chaperone," I said, tilting my head onto his shoulder for a moment. "He's practically Father Time. Aren't you, Francis?"

"Be careful with the epithets, Pipsqueak," Francis told me, but without heat. "I'm still on the right side of thirty, I'll have you know."

He stole a glance at Constance, perhaps to see how she'd react to this evidence of his advanced age. If it bothered her at all, she showed no signs of it.

"For two whole months," I jeered. "And I did say practically!"

"Not Francis," Aunt Roz said firmly, which put paid to that

idea. "No offense, Francis, but for purposes of this discussion, you're a child, too."

Francis didn't look like he minded. And I have to say I understood where Aunt Roz was coming from. Between the drug habit and his newfound interest in Constance, he was hardly chaperone material.

"Why don't you come with us, Harold?" Lady Peckham suggested next. "Charlotte used to love to visit me at the Dower House. And it would do you good to get away from the Hall. All that sadness."

Uncle Harold looked like he didn't quite know what to say, and Crispin had the appearance of someone who had accidentally bitten into a lemon. With his father around, I guess all his plans for Johanna, or Laetitia, or both of them, would go up in smoke.

"There's not enough room at the Dower House for anyone else," Gilbert piped up. I guess the prospect of having to watch Crispin make eyes at Johanna, and Francis do the same with Constance, all weekend long, was already enough for him. He didn't want to watch his mother, or perhaps Johanna, playing up to Uncle Harold, too. "We're going to have to double up as it is. And I'm sure His Grace wouldn't want to share."

No, indeed. The idea of the Duke of Sutherland going to a country house and having to share a room with anyone was laughable. Uncle Harold paled at the thought.

"We're all adults, Aunt Roz," I told her. "I know we still look like your children to you—"

Or at least Christopher and Francis did, and perhaps I did, and by a stretch perhaps Crispin did, now that he was motherless.

"But we're all of age, and more than. Francis is almost thirty. Christopher and I are twenty-three. St George is still infantile, admittedly—"

"Speak for yourself, Darling."

"—but we'll make sure he doesn't do anything too irresponsible."

Aunt Roz looked at me. I did my best to look responsible.

Then she looked at Christopher, who would certainly be responsible in this situation, since a house party at a noble country estate, full of ladies looking for husbands, isn't the sort of place where he lets down his hair.

Then she looked at Francis, who had in fact behaved quite responsibly for the past two days. I hadn't seen any evidence of illicit drug use at all since he'd come to Sutherland Hall.

Finally she looked at Crispin, who made no attempt to look responsible, but I guess she decided he simply wasn't her burden to bear. Nor were the Peckhams and their hangers-on.

She sighed. "On your own heads be it, then."

A subdued cheer went up, or at least Gilbert tried to get one going. The rest of us stared at him, and he stopped.

"Back to the motorcars, then," Crispin said. "I can take four aside from myself."

"And I have an idea," Francis added. "Why don't we leave the Peckhams' Crossley here, with the chauffeur, that way Lady Peckham will have a way to get home at the end of the weekend."

He gave Constance's mother a modified bow. She looked at him with approval, which had probably been the point of the exercise. "I'll drive our car to the Dower House—"

He glanced at his father, and got Uncle Herbert's nod, "—and Mother and Father can either get a ride home with Lady Peckham, or have Wilkins take them home in Uncle Harold's Crossley when it's convenient. Or they can stay here until we come back."

"That will leave us with two motorcars to bring back to Sutherland Hall at the end of the weekend," I pointed out.

"Or one for Sutherland and one for Beckwith Place, at any rate."

"But some of us may choose to stay longer," Crispin said, and smirked wickedly.

I assumed he was insinuating that he might choose to spend more time with Johanna, or perhaps with Lady Laetitia Marsden, and if he did, it was certainly no business of mine.

"It's a good thing the rest of us can fit in Francis's motorcar, then, if you're planning to stay behind. Constance—" I snagged her arm, "why don't you ride with us."

It wasn't a question, and I didn't make it sound like one, just towed her toward Francis, who gave her a polite bow.

"You can sit up front with Francis," I told her, "while Christopher and I huddle in the back. Meanwhile, Crispin can take Miss de Vos and Mr. Peckham."

Johanna looked delighted, Gilbert Peckham did not. Crispin looked like he wasn't sure what to think, which was surprising. I'd have thought he'd be pleased to have Johanna. Gilbert's presence would derail anything too untoward from taking place, of course, but then Crispin's need to actually drive the motorcar ought to have taken care of that in the first place.

I added, "Unless you'd rather have me and Christopher, St George? We're used to your particular style of driving, and I'd hate for Miss de Vos to ruin those lovely shoes."

Johanna looked a bit less delighted at that, perhaps because they really were lovely, and probably expensive. Black leather—part suede, part patent—with a T-strap and a dainty silver buckle. If there was one thing I might find fault with, it was that they weren't small. Johanna did not have dainty feet. But she was a tall girl, so perhaps that was to be expected.

In any case, it really would be a shame for her to lose her breakfast all over them. Not so much for her sake as for the shoes'. It's hard to get stomach acid out of suede.

It was Gilbert Peckham who spoke up. "That's a capital idea." He smirked at Crispin, totally without bothering to sound like he meant it. "Sorry, old chap, but I should probably stick with my sister. Be the older brother, you know. I'm sure you understand."

"Oh, certainly." Crispin did sarcasm beautifully. "Wouldn't want her sitting next to my cousin as he drives down the road for the next hour without some sort of oversight."

Peckham had nothing to say to that, but Crispin didn't wait to hear it, anyway. "Hop in then, Darling."

At least he opened the door for me this time. I dropped my weekender bag at his feet and scooted past him into the back of the Hispano-Suiza. "Thank you, St George."

"My pleasure, Darling." I'm not sure either of us meant it, and the way he heaved the bag in after me certainly indicated that he wasn't thrilled about the way things had worked out. "Are you coming, Kit?"

"I'll go with Francis and Miss Peckham," Christopher said, which made Crispin blink and my mouth drop open.

"Christopher?" He was abandoning me? To spend an hour in the car with Crispin? *By myself?*

"Perhaps there's room for me after all, then?" Johanna asked brightly. Gilbert opened his mouth, but at this point there was little he could say, after he had insisted that his sister needed his chaperonage. "I would so much appreciate not being stuck inside the stuffy old saloon car on the way home. And your racing car..."

She let her fingers slide over the bright blue panel of the Hispano-Suiza in a prolonged caress, before she looked up and fixed Crispin with a limpid stare, "—is beautiful."

It was almost too blatant to be believed, and I wasn't sure whether to stare in horrified bemusement or burst out laughing. When Crispin's throat moved with a hard swallow, I decided to do neither, but rolled my eyes instead, violently enough that they almost disappeared into the back of my head. "Get a grip, St George. Unless you'd like me to slap you on the back so you don't choke on your tongue?"

The look he gave me wasn't very friendly, nor was hers. But she removed her hand from the motorcar, and he avoided her eyes when he got her settled in the passenger seat. And when he headed out of the courtyard and down the hill towards the village, the H6 was traveling fast enough that I didn't have to listen to any vapid flirtation from the front seat. Johanna may have tried, but the words were gone before they reached me. Once or twice, I thought I noticed Crispin looking at me in the mirror, but if he were trying to catch my eye, he must have thought better of it by the time I got around to looking back at him, because by then his attention had moved on. And that was perhaps just as well, since I would have been tempted to stick my tongue out, and then *he* would have had cause to call *me* immature.

All in all, the trip went as quickly as one could have hoped. Johanna had the sense not to try to touch St George, and as a result, we stayed on the road on the way there. We pulled up in front of the Dower House well ahead of the Crossley. (They had, in fact, got a late start, as Christopher shared with me later. Just as they were ready to leave, Gilbert had made an exclamation about having misplaced something or other—Christopher wasn't sure what; perhaps he had wanted a lavatory and was too shy to mention it—and had run back inside the Hall. It had been almost five minutes before he'd come back outside and they had got off. And Francis isn't the daredevil that Crispin is, or perhaps he simply lacks the latter's death wish, so they had proceeded at a more decorous pace, too. As a result, we had already been at the Dower House for fifteen minutes by the time they pulled up out front.)

By then, I had had a look around and got the lay of the land. The Dower House turned out to be a lovely two-story cottage in creamy stone, roughly one-third the size of Sutherland Hall. On the ground floor, there was a parlor, a small library, a study, a dining room, and a box room in addition to the entry foyer/reception room and a small water closet tucked away under the stairs. The kitchen and maids' quarters were below-stairs, of course, and I'm sure the chauffeur had his lodgings above the garage. Upstairs in the main house, there were five bedrooms, four of which were occupied, and two bathrooms, along with a dressing room attached to the dowager's chamber.

"I'm in with Constance," I announced, as soon as everyone had piled out of the second motorcar with their bags. "Christopher, why don't you and Francis take Crispin and see if the spare room is big enough for all three of you?"

I had halfway expected someone to object to that—perhaps Crispin himself, perhaps Johanna, or perhaps Francis, who wasn't a lot fonder of Crispin than I was—but no one did. And it was clearly the only reasonable solution. Crispin couldn't share a room with either Gilbert Peckham or, when he arrived, Laetitia Marsden's brother. He wasn't likely to survive the night in either scenario. I certainly wasn't willing to share with either Johanna or Laetitia, and no one, I was quite sure, would let me share with Christopher. Peckham wouldn't countenance putting Crispin in a room of his own, I assumed—too much opportunity for mischief that way, with Johanna or Laetitia (or both) tiptoeing across the landing in the middle of the night—and with nine of us and only five rooms, one of which was Lady Peckham's bed chamber, it was obvious that we'd have to double up. Gilbert could deal with Lord Geoffrey, and if Johanna and Laetitia murdered each other overnight, so much the better for everyone else.

We spent the afternoon exploring the house and wandering the grounds. I made Constance show me around, and of course Francis attached himself to us, and so did Christopher. We invited Crispin to come along, mostly to be polite, but he declined. He did look tired, so I couldn't very well quibble when he said he wanted to rest, not walk all over creation.

If he had an ulterior motive, he wasn't likely to get what he wanted. Gilbert Peckham stayed behind, too, jealously guarding the lovely Johanna, and I didn't think Crispin had a chance of getting anywhere close to her.

"You should have seen her caress the Hispano-Suiza earlier," I told the other three, who hadn't been close enough to see the shameless performance with their own eyes. "It was absolutely indecent. She stroked it, and then she looked up at Crispin when she told him how beautiful it was, in this very significant voice. I thought he was going to swallow his tongue."

Francis sputtered a laugh. "She isn't shy, is she?"

I shook my head. "Not at all. And good God... St George is supposed to be this great seducer, right, with a trail of broken hearts in his wake?"

Or if not that, at least a trail of women who maybe hadn't minded being used. I guessed I'd see how Laetitia Marsden felt later this evening.

"He turned as red as a schoolboy and looked like he had absolutely no idea what to do with himself. Or with her."

Christopher and Francis both chuckled, while Constance looked very prim indeed.

"Perhaps he prefers being the pursuer to being the pursued," Francis said. "Maybe his entire reputation comes from women chasing him."

"His title, you mean." But that was a possibility. Christopher had his own share of women trying to nail him down, simply because he was the grandson of a duke, and I'm sure

Francis had experienced the same. Crispin, as the actual heir to the title and estates, no doubt got it worse than either of them.

Although with the old duke dead, and Uncle Harold in that role now, things might get easier for both Christopher and Francis, who were now merely fourth and fifth in the line of succession, if anything should happen to Crispin before he could sire his own heir. That would take some of the heat off them.

And fire it up under Crispin, of course, but that wasn't likely to be my problem.

"At any rate," I said, "she seems to have made a dead set for him. It'll be interesting to see what happens once Laetitia Marsden shows up tonight, and which of them makes it out of that shared bedroom in one piece tomorrow."

"If he has any sense," Francis said, "he'll avoid them both. Although of the two, Lady Laetitia will make a much better match, if he's looking for one."

She would. Not only was she almost as lovely as Johanna, but she had a title and fortune of her own to bargain with, something Johanna did not have.

Then again, the lovely Miss de Vos hadn't given me the impression of being someone who'd take kindly to being shunted off to the side.

So yes, Francis had a point. Safer by far for Crispin to avoid them both.

"Let's talk about something else," I said. "I'm tired of discussing St George's shortcomings. Whose estate is that over there, Constance?"

I pointed in the direction of a large manor house, also in creamy stone, built up against a low ridge some distance away. It looked like an oversized, bloated version of the Dower House, with its many windows reflecting the afternoon sunlight.

Constance looked at it, and then back at me, apologetically. "I'm afraid that's Marsden Manor, Pippa."

Of course it was. I gave it a baleful look and turned the other way.

SIX

THE MARSDENS MADE their entrance just in time for supper, as the rest of us were waiting for the gong to sound.

The dowager Lady Peckham operated the Dower House on what was practically a skeleton staff. She had her chauffeur, of course, but he was still at Sutherland Hall with her and the Crossley. There was Cook, there was a kitchen maid, a single housemaid who handled both the bedrooms and the common rooms, and then there was Dawson the butler and Nigel the hallboy, plus a gardener, who shared the space above the garage with the chauffeur.

"None of us have help dressing," Constance confided as we were getting ready in her room before supper. "Mother had a maid, but she up and left a week ago, without so much as a by your leave."

I glanced up at her. I was in the process of putting on lipstick and powder at the makeup table, while Constance was leaning over me to adjust her fringe. "You're not serious?"

She met my eyes for a second in the mirror. "I'm deathly serious. She woke up one morning, I think it must have been

Wednesday, or perhaps Thursday—unless it was Tuesday; it wasn't Monday or Friday—and announced that she had to leave."

"Just like that? Without giving notice or any kind of warning?"

Constance nodded. "Mother tried to get her to stay another week so she could come to Sutherland Hall with us—she used to work for Lady Charlotte before I was born, and we thought she might want to see her old friends and attend the funerals—but she said no, something had come up and she had to go immediately. There was something about getting a phone call the night before, which Cook confirmed that Morrison took in the kitchen, but she said nothing to anyone about where she was going or why."

"That's strange," I said.

"Isn't it? It's no bother to me, honestly. She wasn't helping me anyway. But Mother and Johanna will have a hard time getting by without her."

"Serves them right," I said. "Why wasn't she helping you?"

Constance shrugged. "I suppose nobody thought there was any help for me?"

"That's silly. You're just as worthy of help as any of the other women in the household. And with the way Johanna looks, she could honestly do with monopolizing a little less of the maid's time and attention."

"She doesn't look like that without help, you know," Constance said. "Not that she isn't naturally beautiful. She is. That hair, and those eyes. But she doesn't look like that when she gets out of bed in the morning. It takes work."

"It takes work for all of us," I told her, as I blew myself a final kiss in the mirror before I spun the chair around to look at her. "That dress is so much more becoming than the one you brought to Sutherland Hall. I was worried they had taken all the color out of your wardrobe, but I guess it was just that one hideous tobacco-brown dress."

Constance ran a hand down the shimmering rose crepe satin gown she was wearing, looking rather pleased. It was quite a simple dress, with a deep V-neck that de-emphasized the roundness of her face, three layers of skirt—but no ruffles that added extra width—and a big droopy bow on one side of her hip. Because it was all the same color and fabric, it gave her a longer, slim line, and the color brought out the roses in her cheeks.

Unless it was the prospect of seeing Francis that was doing that, but if so, I wasn't going to comment.

"I think," she said apologetically, in response to my comment about the brown dress, "it was mostly because Johanna went to Wiltshire planning to snare either the Duke of Sutherland or his son, and she wanted to have every opportunity to dazzle without anyone dimming her glow."

"That's awful," I said. "Not only is it extremely grasping of her to go after Crispin that way, but Aunt Charlotte has barely been dead a week. Surely she must realize that Uncle Harold wouldn't be in a frame of mind to pick a new wife so soon?"

"To be honest," Constance said, "I'm not sure what Johanna realizes. She doesn't really think much about anyone but herself."

Of course she didn't. As if I couldn't have worked that out for myself without Constance's help.

"I really loathe her," I said.

Constance nodded. "You and every other woman who has ever met her."

"Except your mother, it seems."

"My mother was a great beauty in her day," Constance said. "I was always a disappointment to her. Not pretty enough, not glamorous enough, not sought-after enough. With Johanna, she got a second chance at bringing out a beautiful daughter. And Johanna is lovely to Mother. And to Gilbert. It's just me she doesn't like."

"And me," I said, jumping to my feet, "apparently. Probably because we can see through her. Shall we go down and give her some competition?"

"You, perhaps," Constance said, looking at my apple green silk with the diamante accents. "I'm no threat."

"Don't let Francis hear you say that." I tucked my arm through hers and pulled her toward the door. "It doesn't appear as if she wants him, but he hasn't looked twice at her in the past two days. He saw you in the courtyard that first day, and he hasn't looked away from you since."

She flushed, but there was a pleased smile curving her mouth. I squeezed her arm and added, "Happiness is the best revenge. If Johanna marries St George, she definitely won't be happy. The money and title won't make up for the fact that he's an awful person, and a womanizing bounder, to boot. But also, he doesn't love her, no matter how dazzled he is right now. So let's go down there and flaunt what she'll never have."

Constance nodded.

"Shoulders back," I told her. "Head high."

"Shoulders back. Head high. Just like at Godolphin."

We shared a grin as we headed down the stairs to the ground floor and supper.

IN LADY PECKHAM'S ABSENCE, Johanna had taken it upon herself to act as our hostess. She wanted to get the practice in, perhaps, or maybe she really felt that the duty was hers. It was quite remarkably rude to Constance either way, but no one seemed to think anything of it. Least of all Constance, who seemed relieved to be rid of the responsibility. "Let her do what she wants," she told me, as we made our way across the parlor to where Francis and Christopher were waiting. "It's not worth making a scene over."

It was worth it to me, or would have been worth it had I been the one snubbed, but as I wasn't, all I could do was follow Constance's lead. Which I did, but not without a scowl at Johanna, who of course looked absolutely exquisite in pale blue. Christopher had a similar dress, one he had worn to a drag ball the day before we'd been summoned to Sutherland Hall for the late duke's dressing down, and while he'd looked stunning when he left the flat that night—Christopher makes for a gorgeous girl when he's in full makeup and wig—I wondered if Johanna didn't in fact wear it a bit better.

That felt disloyal, however, and so I was scowling. Crispin, who was standing next to the vision in blue, noticed—as he would—and arched a brow at me as we passed. "Hasn't anyone warned you that that expression is enough to curdle milk, Darling?"

"You must have," I shot back, "I'm sure. It can't be the first time you've seen it."

"No, indeed." He looked me up and down, and then again. "Well, don't you look tart and crisp and good enough to eat?"

The look on his face was straddling the line between a sneer and a smirk, and I flushed angrily. "If you're suggesting that I look like an apple, St George...!"

The smirk—it was definitely a smirk by now—widened. "I'm merely suggesting that you look rather edible, Darling."

I narrowed my eyes. The dress was green. Apple green. But I'm tall, not short, and slim, not round, and for him to imply—

"What a beautiful dress," Johanna deigned to remark, as she put a calming—I assume it was meant to be calming—hand on Crispin's sleeve. He was in full evening kit, of course—black tie—and looked just as good as could be expected. Some people are born to wear evening kit, and the Astleys are among them. They're all remarkably good-looking—yes, even St George; I'm disdainful, not blind—and the stark black and white sets off their fair hair and fair complexion to advantage. Crispin's eyes are a cold gray instead of the warm blue of Christopher and Francis, but it didn't matter. He looked perfectly like the lord of the manor, and Johanna's hand looked right in place where she'd put it.

"I'm glad you think so," I told her, without bothering to sound like I meant it. "Yours is nice, too. Poiret?"

She inclined her head but didn't actually say anything. It was hard to guess whether she meant yes, it was a Paul Poiret, or no, it wasn't, but she'd like me to think it was. It didn't actually matter either way, since the dress was lovely and I couldn't care less whether it was a real Poiret or not.

"Excuse us," I told her, with a flicker of a glance at St George that ought to have dropped him dead where he stood. "We're going to join Christopher and Francis."

I didn't wait to be dismissed—who was she, who were *they*, to dismiss us?—just pulled Constance after me across the floor towards the corner where the Astley brothers were standing with Gilbert Peckham.

He gave his sister a surprised arch of an eyebrow—perhaps it was the first time he'd noticed her looking pretty, or perhaps it was simply the first time he'd looked at her in a while—and me a more thorough once-over. "That's a lovely dress, Miss Darling. Very becoming."

"Thank you," I said, through gritted teeth. "Let St George know when you have a chance."

Christopher smothered a laugh. "What did he say now?"

"Told me I look like a Bramley," I said, with a scowl over my shoulder.

Christopher and Francis both choked back startled laughs

at that, Francis a little less successfully than Christopher. Constance made a tiny protesting sound that resolved itself into clearing her throat when we all turned to look at her.

"What?" I demanded.

She flushed. "Strictly speaking, he said you looked good."

"Good enough to eat! I heard him. Edible, he said! Crisp and tart and—"

The Astley brothers smothered another round of laughter.

"That means you look good," Constance insisted, as if I wasn't fully aware of exactly what it meant.

"If someone else had said it, it would have been a compliment. When it's St George and I'm wearing apple green, it's an insult."

I threw another scowl over my shoulder at him. He didn't notice, of course. Just kept making cow eyes at Johanna.

And then someone new turned up in the doorway of the parlor, and Gilbert sounded pleased. "Looks like the Marsdens are here. Excuse me."

He moved away from us and towards the door, where a beautiful young woman stood, flanked by an extremely good-looking young man.

I had met Lady Laetitia Marsden before. Mostly in passing, since we're not friends and not likely to become so. She's deep into the very fast set of Bright Young People that Crispin spends his time with when he's in London, while Christopher and I, who are in London all the time—except when we're not, like now—stay more on the fringes of the fast crowd. When you live in London and there's a party going on almost every night, you tire of it a lot more easily than when you have to make the trip from Wiltshire—or Dorset—on occasional weekends when your parents aren't overseeing you too closely. Crispin spent more time at Sutherland Hall than he did in Town, and when he did come up to London, he made every minute count. So, I assumed, did Lady Laetitia.

She's a beautiful woman. Tall and slender, as dark as Johanna was fair, with shiny, black hair cut in a precise, angular bob, and eyes of the same bright blue as Christopher's. And her dress gave the Poiret a run for its money.

It might, in point of fact, have been a Poiret.

She was wearing black, and wearing it extremely well. Sheer chiffon at the top, then chiffon over crepe satin down to the dropped waist, where there was shiny satin the rest of the way, except for a flouncy overlay of chiffon that stopped well short of the skirt's hem. The whole thing was pinned with a bright pink cabbage rose at one hip. She was carrying an ostrich feather fan—black, of course—with elbow-length, black gloves, and her shoes were also black, with three dainty straps across the instep. The only things that were not black, were the sparkly earrings dangling from her lobes—with the way they sparkled, they had to be real diamonds—and the slash of hot pink on her mouth.

She surveyed the room with a bored expression. Until she saw Crispin, and then she gave a delighted little squeal and raced over to attach that pretty, pink mouth right onto his. And kept it there as the seconds dragged on. And on.

Her hand started on his cheek, before creeping up to his ear—she ran her finger around the outline of it—before curling around the back of his neck to keep him in place.

As the kiss went on, Johanna's expression grew stonier and stormier. Mine, I'm sure, grew sour. Francis looked like he wanted to burst out laughing, and Christopher was clearly embarrassed, probably on his cousin's behalf. Constance was just embarrassed, period. Her cheeks were as pink as Laetitia's lips, and she was averting her eyes from the—frankly disgraceful—display.

It was Lord Geoffrey, Laetitia's brother, who put an end to the show. Cheeks hot, he put a hand on his sister's shoulder and yanked. "For God's sake, Laetitia. Let the boy breathe."

The reference to Crispin as a boy was rather rude, I thought. He was a few years younger than Lord Geoffrey—three or four, maybe—but he's well past his majority.

However, Marsden's rudeness got the point across. Laetitia stepped back with a titter, and Crispin blinked his eyes open, looking dazed.

While Laetitia and Johanna stared daggers at each other, and while Marsden and Peckham exchanged guarded looks, I crossed the room and snatched Crispin's linen square out of his breast pocket and dragged it across his mouth before I dropped it into his hand. "Soul still intact, St George?"

"Seems to be." He closed his hand around the handkerchief.

It was my opportunity to smirk at him, so I took it. "The pink is quite becoming, actually. Who knew you'd look so good with lipstick on, St George?"

He glanced at me over the square of linen. "You knew, I imagine, Darling. You've seen Kit…" He hesitated, "Kitty that way often enough, haven't you?"

I had, now that he mentioned it. I just didn't usually consider how much they looked alike. Their personalities were so different that they didn't look alike to me. But yes, Crispin smeared with Laetitia's lipstick didn't look too dissimilar to Christopher smeared with his own.

"Let me know if you'd like to borrow my dress," I told him. "Apple green would be quite fetching on you, with your coloring. You'd look positively edible, too, I imagine."

And then I smirked. "Oh, wait…"

He shook his head with a wince. "Don't say it, Darling."

I sniggered. "I'll do you a favor, St George, and refrain. But do try to look a little bit less delicious, would you? The rest of us can only handle so much of what we just witnessed before we all sick up our supper."

I flounced off toward Christopher, Francis, and Constance again, leaving Crispin to stand there, still passing the handkerchief over his mouth, under the combined eyes of Laetitia, Johanna, Gilbert Peckham, and Geoffrey Marsden.

WE WERE an uneven number at dinner again, although Gilbert figured out the seating to his satisfaction, even if he—like Uncle Harold—took some liberties with the placement in order to do so.

He sat himself at the head of the table, just as Uncle Harold had done, and put Laetitia in place of honor at his right —as he should, as she was a female guest, and one with a title, which I didn't have. Johanna was at his left. That ought rightly be Constance's place, as a true daughter of the house, or perhaps mine, as the second female visitor, but Constance was on the other side of the table next to Francis, which I'm sure she liked better, and I was across from her, next to Christopher, which I certainly preferred.

Unfortunately—for Constance, I mean—she had to deal with Crispin as a dinner partner for the first course, since Peckham had placed him between Constance and Lady Laetitia, surely to get him away from Johanna. She had Geoffrey Marsden next to her. He was a viscount, too, of course, and couldn't really be shoved further down the table when neither Christopher nor Francis had a title, although I'm sure Gilbert would have preferred to put one of them next to Johanna. Someone who wasn't interested in her at all, and someone in whom she had no interest, either. I was next to Lord Geoffrey on his other side, and then Christopher was next to me. At least we made for a symmetrical crowd.

I won't bore you with a detailed synopsis of dinner. The food was passable and everything else excruciating.

Or perhaps I shouldn't say that. There were high points. Having Christopher to share my amusement with was one of them. Watching Constance and Francis coo on the other side of the table was another. Then there was Laetitia Marsden and her determined pursuit of Crispin, which had its moments of extreme hilarity. They were playing footsie under the table, or at least she was trying to play with him, and quite brazenly, too. He seemed a bit less inclined, I have to say, albeit without being rude about it. The third time he kicked my foot in his effort to get away from hers, I spoke up. "Footsie, St George?"

He flushed. "Sorry, Darling."

He actually seemed sincere, and sincerely put out, either because he'd had to apologize to me, or maybe just because Lady Laetitia's brazenness really was embarrassing to him. As such, I took pity on him and didn't employ the sarcastic comment I had planned to utter next.

Instead, it was Laetitia Marsden's eyes that narrowed on me across the table. "Have we met?"

She uttered it like a challenge. As in, how dare I get in the middle of her flirtation with my pseudo-cousin?

"We have," I told her blandly, "several times, although I wouldn't expect you to remember. As I recall, you were well marinated each time."

Crispin's lips compressed at that. I don't think it was laughter. Laetitia herself just stared at me for a moment, perhaps to see if she could determine whether I was joking or not. When I just looked at her placidly, she sniffed. "Well. I never."

"I know," I nodded, as condescendingly commiserating as I could. "Since you don't seem to remember me, I'm Philippa

Darling, Christopher's and Francis's cousin. My friends call me Pippa. St George calls me Darling, and won't stop, even with as many times as I've asked him to."

I gave him a lingering sort of look across the table, and added just a hint of what I thought might look like intrigue in the sweep of my lashes. Next to me, Christopher let out a hysterical snort, and across the table, Francis sputtered into his glass.

"You know, Darling," Crispin told me, completely straight-faced, "there are other things I'd like to call you, if you'd only let me."

Oh, no doubt. I abandoned the overblown coquetry in favor of grinning at him. "Perhaps some time when we're alone, St George. You wouldn't want to let that kind of language out in polite company."

At that point, Christopher gave up the fight and started laughing so hard he cried. Laetitia and Johanna exchanged a barbed glance of mutual incomprehension across the table, and the rest of us went back to our food. Crispin didn't kick me again after that. Perhaps Laetitia didn't try to trap him anymore, or perhaps he'd simply decided that he preferred to deal with her rather than with me.

SEVEN

I'D LIKE to say that the rest of the evening improved somewhat, but I'd be lying.

After dinner we retired to the parlor, where there was a gramophone and a stack of records. Gilbert Peckham put music on, and we danced the foxtrot and the Charleston and a few other of the popular dances. Johanna and Laetitia still tried to monopolize Crispin, of course, but since there were two of them and only one of him, it turned into more of the pitched battle Aunt Roz had predicted. And by now, Gilbert had realized what was going on with Francis and Constance, too, so he was glaring alternately at both Crispin and Francis.

Christopher is an accomplished dancer, so he and I had some fun, at least until Laetitia and Johanna caught on, and after that, whichever of them wasn't dancing with Crispin started to monopolize Christopher, as well. I ended up with Geoffrey Marsden, since Gilbert was too busy playing fire extinguisher to do anything other than glare at practically everyone else.

Geoffrey was not a particularly graceful dancer, and after

the second time he trod on my toes, he suggested that we should sit down. Gilbert mixed me up a cocktail at the bar cart —equal shares Bombay Sapphire, Calvados, and Apricot Brandy in a water glass with an orange peel twist; also known as an Angel Face—and then Geoffrey escorted me over to a sofa in a quiet corner, and sat down rather too close to me. I tried not to mind, because he was exceedingly handsome, just like his sister was exceedingly beautiful. Gorgeous face, smooth-shaven, with bright, blue eyes surrounded by thick, dark lashes, and jet-black hair that shone with brilliantine in the overhead lights.

No, the problem wasn't his looks. He had those, and in spades. And it wasn't that his personality was actually a prob-lem. He was pleasant enough, if rather boring. I'm used to talking to Christopher, who's clever and quick-witted, and to Aunt Roz, who is both of those things, as well. And much as I abhor St George in practically every way, I must admit that as a conversationalist he's first rate. One can't afford to let one's guard down for a second when speaking to him, or one will find oneself missing some sly, or snide, or downright wicked infer-ence, or an admittedly clever pun.

Marsden wasn't like that. His conversation was straightfor-ward, rather plain, and—yes—somewhat boring. But that wasn't the problem, either. I've been trained to put up with boring conversation. It's part of the price you pay for being among the upper classes. They're frequently boring. At least the older set.

No, the problem with Marsden was that he seemed to have got the impression, God knows where, that I was easy. He appeared to think that all he had to do was feed me a drink, and sit down next to me, and put his knee against mine, and then, as time went by, the rest of his thigh against mine, and as a result of all that, I'd let him pet me.

And I'm not easy. Far from it.

Now, I'm not a wet blanket. I'm not opposed to a little snuggle with the right man. But Geoffrey Marsden wasn't he. And he just wasn't taking the hint.

He put his leg against mine. I moved mine away.

He moved closer. I scooted an inch farther over toward the bolster.

He followed, and then put his hand on my knee.

I moved my knee out of reach, by folding it over the other knee.

As a result, my dress rode up. So did Marsden's hand.

At that point, I had the choice between making a scene, or at least getting up and walking away from him, or alternatively finding someone to rescue me, so I wouldn't actually have to offend him.

It should be said that I wasn't opposed to offending him. He was certainly offending me, with his uninvited, wandering hand. But I was a guest in someone else's home, and Marsden was a lord of the realm and a friend of the Peckhams. Unless I missed my guess, the Dower House was actually part of the Marsden estate, and Lady Peckham might have been a Marsden before she married Lord Peckham. It's been a long time since I consulted Debrett's, but I wouldn't discount it. So while part of me dearly wanted to impersonate a screaming meemie and puncture his eardrums, the other part thought it might be better to be a little more circumspect about the situation.

I looked first for Christopher. But he had been appropriated by Laetitia Marsden, who had him in a tight grip for the one-step, and his back was to me. Francis was dancing with Constance, and had managed to maneuver her to the edge of the 'dance floor,' where the light was a little less bright, and where they were circling slowly, not even in time with the music. Francis's lips were close to Constance's ear. Gilbert hadn't noticed yet, as he was too busy keeping an eye on Johanna, who was draped like a scarf around Crispin's neck.

St George didn't appear to be suffering, but he didn't look as enthused as one might have presumed, either. Perhaps the incident with Lady Laetitia had reminded him that there were other fish in the sea, and that he wasn't ready to settle down with just one woman yet. Or perhaps he was simply bored. I hadn't been impressed with Johanna's vocabulary any more than I was with Geoffrey Marsden's, and although she was certainly nice to look at, there's more to a romantic match than physical beauty.

At any rate, he looked over at me. He must have noticed the way I was squeezed into the corner of the sofa, and also the expression on my face—it was one he should be familiar with after years of seeing it directed at himself: I was ready to blow— and then he looked down and spied Marsden's hand on my leg. His eyes narrowed, and I saw a muscle tighten in his jaw.

At that point the song was winding down anyway, so he was able to stop dancing and extricate himself from Johanna without giving offense. Or rather, he was able to stop dancing, but Johanna wasn't willing to let go. She slipped her hand through his arm and clung, and he had no choice but to take her with him when he came towards me.

I don't know what I expected. I certainly didn't think he'd punch Marsden in the face. (Nor did he, which was probably a good thing, although I would have enjoyed it if he had.) I suppose I had expected some cross words, at least.

There were none of those, either. Instead, he simply stopped in front of me and put out a hand. "Would you care to dance, Darling?"

As far as getting me away from Marsden, it was brilliantly simple. I jumped to my feet, dislodging Marsden's hand in the process, and put my glass on the table. "Please, St George."

Johanna had to let go, of course, since she couldn't very well dance with the two of us. But as she was there, and physically unattached to anyone now, Marsden saw his own chance for a moment in the sunlight, and pounced. "May I accompany you on the dance floor, Johanna?"

"Delighted," Johanna said, sounding quite a lot less delighted than I would have expected, seeing as Marsden was a lord, too. Perhaps she preferred blonds, or perhaps the Sutherland fortune was bigger than the Marsden one. Or perhaps it was simpler than that: she had already tried to dance with Marsden, and he had stepped on her toes, as well.

At any rate, now I had to circle the floor with Crispin, which I hadn't done in years.

We'd all learned together, at eleven and twelve, before I went off to Godolphin and Christopher and Crispin to Eton. Aunt Roz and Aunt Charlotte had had a teacher in, and because Francis and Robert had been through it earlier and were now off at Eton themselves, it was just the three of us. As a result, I'd had to dance with both boys, and got twice as much practice as either of them did.

By now, they'd both caught up, of course. Christopher had his drag balls—I'm not sure whether he led or followed there, although I assumed he followed, as he were the one in the gown —and Crispin's Bright Young Set obviously liked to dance. And these weren't the dances we'd been taught eleven years ago, either. Back then, it had been the waltz, and the one-step and two-step, and the foxtrot. Now, of course, there was *Le Jazz Hot* and the Charleston, and Rudolph Valentino had even brought back the tango, which I sincerely hoped St George wouldn't want to attempt.

But at least I probably didn't have to worry about him stepping on my toes.

I put my hand in his, and my other hand on his upper arm,

where I could feel the muscle flex through the fabric of his jacket and shirt. And when he put his other arm around my waist with the hand flat against my lower back, he made sure he didn't hold me too close. It was surprisingly thoughtful of him, and to be honest, I was rather impressed that he had realized that after being pawed by Marsden, I might not appreciate someone else holding me tightly.

In fact, he even asked, "All right?" before setting us into motion.

I nodded. "Thank you."

"The pleasure was mine." The look he leveled on Marsden's back indicated that he meant it. "Should I take Francis away from Miss Peckham to punch him in the nose?"

"What do you mean," I asked facetiously, "take Francis? Won't you punch Marsden in the nose yourself, St George, to uphold my honor?"

"I would if you asked me to." He sounded sincere about it, too. Until he added, "Although I think Francis might hit harder. I thought that would be desirable."

"Now that you mention it."

We danced in silence for half a minute.

"No," I said, "I shan't need anyone to punch Marsden in the nose. If he's getting punched, I'll do it myself. I just didn't want to cause a scene, or I would have done it already."

Crispin smirked. It was even more annoying so close to my face. "There's the Darling we all know and love."

"Oh, sod off, St George," I said. "Would you let him put his hand on *your* knee without punching him?"

And then I added, "Oh, wait. You let Laetitia Marsden do worse than that earlier, didn't you?"

That eyebrow lifted again, and so did the corner of his mouth. "Jealous, Darling?"

"Frightfully," I said dryly. "You're everything I've ever dreamed of in a man, St George."

"Right." He flushed. "Anyway, it wasn't like I could punch her, was it?"

Perhaps not. But— "You might have done *something*, instead of just standing there looking like you enjoyed it. Not that it's any of my affair, of course. But this girl you claim to love might feel differently about it. Besides, you probably *were* enjoying it. What's not to enjoy, after all?"

I glanced around. By now Christopher had noticed that I was dancing with Crispin, and the expression on his face was one of cautious panic. I sent him a bright smile, but that only seemed to worry him more.

"She *is* quite lovely," Crispin mused, and I turned my attention back to him.

"Oh, quite. They both are. Johanna might be a bit more beautiful, truthfully, although I suppose that depends on taste. But Laetitia's title and fortune makes up for it, I assume."

He didn't answer, so I went on, twisting the metaphorical knife a little harder. "Neither of them would be hard on the eyes across the breakfast table in the morning. And either one would jump at the chance to drag you to the altar right now. Just think about it, St George. By Christmas you could be wedded and bedded—or should that perhaps be the opposite in Laetitia's case? Bedded first, and then wedded?—with an heir on the way, tied down for life."

He'd turned progressively paler as I went on, until he looked almost ill. Now he swallowed hard, like the prospect was nauseating. It nauseated me a bit too, so I found I couldn't blame him.

"You really are vile, Darling," he told me when he'd got his voice back.

I smirked. "Oh, am I? I'm not telling you anything you shouldn't already have worked out for yourself."

He nodded. "I'm aware. You just have this way of setting everything out in the least flattering terms possible, that makes me see the consequences and cringe."

"My job here is done, then. You can drop me off next to Christopher, if you don't mind."

"If *you* don't mind," Crispin retorted, "I'm going to drop you off next to Peckham instead, and beat a hasty retreat through the door. I need some fresh air."

"And a cigarette to settle your stomach?"

"That, too. But mostly just a few minutes where I'm not being pawed over by one girl or another."

Or a third, I supposed, if he included me. "Am I pawing at you, St George?"

"No, Darling, more's the pity. I was referring to Laetitia and Johanna."

"That's fine," I said. "I can handle Peckham."

"Then I'll see you later, Darling." He dropped my hand and unwound his other arm from around my waist, and the next second, he had vanished into the reception room before I had really noticed him move. I found myself standing next to Gilbert Peckham, who was looking at me with a puzzled frown, as if he had no idea where I had come from.

THAT WAS the end of the amusement for the evening. When both Laetitia and Johanna saw that Crispin had made his escape, they set up a hue and cry after him. I let them look, and made my own way over to Christopher, who had also escaped as a result of Laetitia's search for Crispin. He was standing by the bar cart mixing himself another cocktail, and when I appeared next to him, he arched his brows. "How did that happen?"

There was no need to ask what he meant. "Marsden put his hand on my knee," I said, "and tried to crowd me into the corner of the sofa. I thought about causing a scene, but I decided against it. I suspect the Dower House is on Marsden land, and it wouldn't do to offend the lord of the manor."

Christopher nodded.

"I couldn't catch your eye," I continued, "and Francis and Constance were off in the dark over there—" I flapped a hand toward the less-lit corner of the room, "—so I got Crispin's attention instead."

"And he came to your rescue?"

I nodded. "He was remarkably decent about it, too."

Christopher glanced at me. "You sound surprised."

"I am." I squinted at him. "You're not?"

"I'm not," Christopher said. "He was brought up partly by my mother, so he would have learned to respect women. And aside from that—"

"Respect women?" I cut him off, appalled. "You call the way he's running through every girl in London 'respecting women'?"

Crispin might have saved me from the advances of Marsden earlier, but that didn't mean I couldn't see his (many, many) glaring faults.

"He's not as bad as that," Christopher said. "It's hardly *every* girl in London. And besides—"

I popped my hands on my hips. "Oh, and because he leaves out the ones who are too unattractive, or not rich enough, or who have enough morals that they won't agree to do whatever he wants—"

"Pippa—"

"And I don't know why you persist in defending him, because you know as well as I do—"

"Pippa!"

"What?" I asked.

He nodded to something over my shoulder. I spun and found myself, of course, face to face with St George. Johanna was latched onto his arm, and Laetitia was standing nearby, scowling.

He arched a brow. "Dear me. I go outside for five minutes, and already you're off again. What is it this time, Darling?"

"It's you!" I said. "You're utterly despicable, St George."

He sighed. "I know, Darling. You've told me so before." He glanced at Christopher. "Perhaps you should take her up to bed, Kit. She seems a bit overwrought."

"I'm not overwrought," I told him, "you absolute git—"

But Christopher nodded and grabbed my arm. "He's right, Pippa. It's time for bed."

"It's *not*—"

It was barely eleven. Hardly the shank of the evening. But by then, I was halfway to the door, propelled by his hand at my elbow, and Christopher had his head bent and was talking to me. "You're causing a scene, Pippa. You don't want to do that, not in front of Laetitia and Johanna. Not to mention Francis. You falling apart would not be good for Francis, and you know it."

"I'm not going to fall apart," I said, but I felt tears prickle at the back of my eyes, and Francis was watching me from the corner of the room where he was standing with Constance, his eyes worried. I tried to send him a reassuring smile, but I'm not sure how successful I was. I'm afraid it probably looked more like a grimace than a smile.

Then we were outside in the foyer, or reception room as

they called it at the Dower House, and on our way to the stairs. "I'm just put out with St George," I said, blinking hard.

"You're always put out with St George, Pippa." Christopher's voice was warm, and so was his hand on my back through the dress. "And I doubt it's Crispin so much as it was the incident with Marsden. And I suppose having Crispin actually be kind and considerate."

I sniffed. "That would be enough to discomfit anyone."

Christopher nodded, but I could tell it was just to humor me. "It's been an uncomfortable evening all around. An uncomfortable few days, to be honest."

Yes, it had. "There are entirely too many predators at this party."

Christopher nodded. "Johanna and Laetitia both pursuing Crispin. Marsden putting moves on you. And Peckham looking at Crispin and Francis like he'd like to murder them in their sleep."

"I don't know why I'm so distraught," I confessed as I sniffed back another tear. "Nothing happened to me. What Laetitia did to St George was certainly worse. Marsden was just a bit too persistent—he didn't even ask first, and I have no idea where he got the impression that I would welcome that kind of advance..."

"From that look you gave Crispin at the dinner table," Christopher said promptly as he nudged me towards the door to Constance's room. "I thought I was going to die laughing when you fluttered your eyelashes at him and said, 'sometime when we're alone.' Like you ever do anything but bicker when you're alone together!"

"We bicker when we're not alone together, too. All we ever do is bicker."

Those things he'd like to call me—the remark which had

prompted the 'sometime when we're alone' response—weren't likely to be pet-names, after all.

Christopher shrugged. "It's not all you do. You just spent a pleasant couple of minutes dancing."

"And bickering," I said.

"Perhaps. At any rate, I'm sure that's where Marsden got the idea. If you amuse yourself with Crispin when he isn't amusing himself with other girls..."

"Disgusting," I sniffed.

"I know, Pippa. Marsden isn't very bright, is he?" He pushed the door to Constance's room open and nudged me inside. "Here we are."

Once past the door, he glanced around, at the light blue walls and muslin curtains and soft, pale coverlet. "This is quite lovely, isn't it? Very girlish and pretty. Peaceful."

He turned back to me. "Yes, I know quite well that you'd never put up with something like that. If you were involved with Crispin, and he'd allowed Laetitia to kiss him that way, they'd both be dead now."

They absolutely would. Or at least I'd no longer be involved with him, and he could console himself with the woman he'd been stupid enough to kiss in front of me.

"St George would need a complete personality change before I'd consider having anything to do with him," I said, "and I doubt I'd do it then. Although he was surprisingly decent earlier. A pity it didn't last longer."

"That was your own fault, Pippa," Christopher said. He isn't one to pull punches when he thinks I need to hear something. "When he went outside, you were on good terms. By the time he got back, you had worked yourself up over his supposed lack of respect for women."

"He doesn't..."

"He respected you," Christopher said. "That's all you need concern yourself with. Crispin's other habits are his own."

I supposed that was true. "He just bothers me. A lot."

"I know, Pippa. For what it's worth, you bother him, too."

"I'm sure I do." At least that was something I could take pleasure in. If he got on my nerves, I knew I got on his equally. "Thank you for walking me up, Christopher."

"It was my pleasure, as always. Are you all right now?"

"I was all right down there," I said. "But you're right, I should go to bed. I think the incident with Marsden upset me more than it should have." On top of everything else that had happened to annoy me. "Hopefully, after some sleep, I won't want to murder St George when I see him tomorrow morning. Or Marsden, either."

"I'll see you at breakfast, then." He dropped a kiss on my temple. "Sleep well, Pippa. And lock your door, in case Lord Geoffrey gets ideas about coming upstairs."

"I don't see how I can," I protested, "when I'm sharing with Constance and she isn't up yet."

We both eyed the door, which had a big, old-fashioned, iron skeleton key sticking out of the keyhole.

"I can lock the door from the outside," Christopher suggested, "and bring the key downstairs and give it to Constance."

I eyed him. "You'd come and rescue me if there was a fire, wouldn't you?"

"Of course I would. So would Francis. So would Crispin."

I nodded. And it says something about how rattled I still felt that I would rather be locked in with no way out than risk someone else—specifically Lord Geoffrey—making his way into my room while I was asleep. "Yes. Please do that. Just let me visit the lavatory and brush my teeth first."

"Take your time," Christopher said and leaned against the

wall. "When I'm up here, I'm not down there dancing with one of them."

He smiled brightly. I scurried across the hall and then back two minutes later. "I'm ready."

"Then I'll see you in the morning, Pippa. And don't worry, no one's going to get in. If Constance won't take the key, I'll come back myself, and spend the time with you until she gets here."

"That'd be one in the eye for Marsden, wouldn't it?" I shook my head. "I know I'm being a ninny, Christopher..."

"You're not a ninny," Christopher said. "Marsden was being objectionable, and you have every right to be upset. Just because you're a thoroughly modern girl in 1926, doesn't mean anyone has the right to touch you without your permission. Now go to bed before I become cross with you. Good night, Pippa."

"Good night, Christopher," I said, and waited for the sound of the key in the lock before I removed the apple green dress and my underthings and crawled into the bed. We hadn't discussed which side Constance preferred to sleep on—she might be a bed-hog who preferred the middle, and if so, I assumed I'd find out—but if she didn't like me being on the right, she could tell me to move. I dropped my head on the pillow and closed my eyes.

The key in the door woke me a bit later, but it was only Constance. "I'm sorry," she whispered.

I raised myself up on my elbows. "I'm the one who should be sorry. I'm not usually such a goose."

She didn't say anything for a few minutes, just busied herself taking off her dress and hanging it in the wardrobe before rolling down her stockings.

"It was Lord Geoffrey," she said eventually, without looking at me, "wasn't it?"

I nodded, although I didn't think she could see me in the darkness of the room, so I said, "Yes. He put his knee against mine, and then his whole leg against mine, and then he put his hand on my knee and moved it up my leg under my skirt..."

"He does those kinds of things," Constance said. "And because he's a viscount, everyone lets him get away with it."

I had let him get away with it, too, which was galling. "Perhaps I should have made a bigger fuss."

"It wouldn't have mattered." She pulled the counterpane back on the other side of the bed. "He knows he's not supposed to. He does it anyway. And everyone else knows he's doing it and doesn't say anything."

She crawled under the blankets and let them flop back down.

"Am I all right on this side of the bed?" I asked.

"Of course." She turned on her side, toward me. I could just make out the shine of her eyes in the dark. "I'm sorry that happened in our house, Pippa."

"It wasn't your fault," I told her. "You were dancing with Francis."

"I should have been paying attention."

"If anyone should have been paying attention, it was your brother." But he had been too busy scowling at Johanna and Crispin to keep an eye on his other guests.

Constance didn't say anything to that, and I added, "At any rate, St George came and rescued me. It all turned out fine. I was just a bit rattled afterwards, that's all."

"Well, the door is locked from the inside," Constance said, "and we're safe, so let's try to get some sleep. Gilbert was talking about croquet in the morning."

Croquet? "Really?"

Was it a good idea to let this group loose with croquet

mallets? Speaking only for myself, I'd be quite tempted to 'accidentally' break Marsden's kneecap if he came too close to me.

Constance shrugged, or tried to. It's hard to do, lying down. "That's what he said."

"On his head be it, I guess."

She nodded, and yawned. "Good night, Pippa."

"Good night," I said, and let her go to sleep.

I DID TRY to sleep myself, too. But there was activity outside on the landing—Christopher and Francis using the loo before bed—and before long it was borne in upon me that I might need to visit the facilities myself, before I could sleep again. I'd had several cocktails downstairs, and by now they had caught up to me. If Constance hadn't woken me, I might have slept through until morning—or perhaps not—but since I was most definitely awake now, and not likely to become otherwise until I had relieved myself, I waited until the door shut behind Christopher or Francis, and swung my legs out of bed.

The landing was quiet, and I scurried across to the water closet on bare feet while I registered, faintly, the presence of raised voices from below. It sounded as if an argument had broken out in the parlor.

By then I was on the other side of the landing and could close the door behind me and shut the voices out, so I did.

And I do recognize, just to mention it, that it's rather unorthodox, in a narrative like this, to make so much out of a visit to the lavatory. I wouldn't mention it if something hadn't happened while I was in there.

As already mentioned, with the door closed I could no longer hear the raised voices from downstairs. I could hear, and feel, the closing of the parlor door—the one leading from the back of the Dower House onto the terrasse—when someone pushed it open and then slammed it back into the frame. There was an irate scream from below, to go along with someone's escape, but I couldn't make out the words, just that the voice sounded female.

At that point, I was in a position where I could get up, so I turned out the light and squeezed my way over to the window, between the toilet and the sink, and peered out.

It took my eyes a few seconds to adjust to the change in lighting, and then a few more to find the figure I was looking for among the hedges and bushes and other dark and lumpy things in the garden. Tall, dark, clearly male—wearing an evening suit, not a dress—and with the faint light of the quarter moon shining on a head of white-blond hair.

Crispin Astley, Viscount St George.

Not only was he the only one of the men left downstairs who had fair hair—Lord Geoffrey's hair was the same shiny black as his sister's, and Peckham's a shade or two lighter than Constance's, still solidly brown—but I recognized the set of his shoulders and the tilt of his head.

He stalked across the grass until he was brought up short by the stone wall at the back of the garden, and there was clear frustration in his posture and in the way he was glancing over his shoulder at what I assumed was the parlor door. He even kicked the wall once, for good measure, before digging in his pocket for his cigarette case and lighting up.

Then something else happened downstairs, and he swung back around to face the house. The moon illuminated a triangle of white shirtfront as a figure came pelting out of the shadow of the house and onto the terrasse.

Pale blue dress, gold hair. Johanna.

She hesitated for a moment at the edge of the flagstone, and then must have figured out where he was, because she loped that way, hair bouncing and scarves fluttering on her way across the grass. And she didn't stop until she had flung herself at him.

His arms were a little slow in coming up to catch her, so it must have been unexpected. But by then her mouth had fused to his—it was almost as bad as when Lady Laetitia had done it in the parlor earlier, except less calculated and more clumsily passionate, which might just make it worse, actually. At any rate, at least she didn't do it in front of an audience. The cigarette went flying, an arc of tiny red through the darkness, as Crispin bent to the task.

I stepped back from the window as my nose wrinkled.

Really? Two of them in the same evening? Had he no shame whatsoever?

I WANDERED BACK to bed after that, and fell asleep eventually, and it was later—I don't know how much later, as it was too dark to see the hands on the small ormolu clock on top of the tallboy—when I woke up to the sound of footsteps outside the room.

I can't tell you who was walking, where they came from or where they were going. I can't even tell you whether they were male or female. The footsteps didn't click particularly, which might indicate that there weren't heels involved, but who really knew?

What I can say, is that they slowed for a moment in passing our door, as if whoever was out there had contemplated trying the knob, or perhaps just hesitated to think about who was sleeping inside. But no one tried to get inside, and after a second or two, the footsteps moved on. Then a door closed somewhere else on the first floor, and everything was silent.

I thought about slithering out of bed again, to see whether I could spy a light under someone's door. But it was late and I was tired, and still rattled enough about everything that had happened today not to want to risk running into someone who was up to no good.

It might be St George coming back from the garden, and while I would love the opportunity to twit him about what had happened outside, there is just something very lowering about having to admit to spying out the water closet window.

Or worse, it might be Marsden wandering around, looking for fresh prey, and the very last thing I wanted was to come face to face with an amorous Lord Geoffrey in the dark, in my pyjamas and bare feet, and with no one else awake who could save me if he decided to pick up where he had left off earlier.

And yes, if he did that I could absolutely defend myself. I had been constrained by good behavior in the parlor earlier. I hadn't wanted to make a scene. If someone tried to grab me on the dark landing, I'd absolutely make a horrendous fuss and wake the whole house while I was at it.

But that didn't mean I wanted to, for my own sake as well as everyone else's. So I ignored the footsteps and turned over on my other side and closed my eyes and willed myself back to sleep.

EIGHT

I WAS the first one up the next morning, and the first one down to breakfast. Not surprisingly, perhaps, since I'd also been the first one to bed.

I made myself comfortable in the dining room, with a cup of coffee, and eggs and bacon and a piece of toast. "No newspaper, Dawson?"

The butler shook his head. "No, Miss Darling. The strike is ongoing."

Of course it was. The general strike had been in the offing for a while, but it had started officially two days before Christopher and I came down to Sutherland Hall for the funerals. The Miners' Union wanted higher wages and better work conditions, and going by the inconveniences the newspapers were describing, who could blame it?

On the other hand, the mine owners were citing diminishing returns, and with Germany now sending free coal to France and Italy as part of their war reparations, it was difficult to blame the mine owners, too.

Then a lot of other industries had joined in, and as a result, now a lot of things were at a standstill. Ironworkers, dockworkers, and the railway were included in the strike in addition to the newspaper industry, so if things went on for much longer, Christopher and I would have a difficult time making our way back to London after the weekend.

I picked at my eggs in annoyed silence, since there was nothing else I could do.

The others trickled in slowly. First came Gilbert Peckham, who looked rather the worse for wear, especially considering that most of his evening had consisted of minding the gramophone and keeping an eye on everyone else.

But perhaps he had become more involved in the festivities after I had gone upstairs. His eyes were bloodshot and his face haggard, like it had been quite a late night, and a not very pleasant one. He dragged himself through the door, and gave me a short nod but no greeting. Then he poured himself a cup of coffee, loaded up a plate with eggs and bacon, and tucked in, still without speaking.

Geoffrey Marsden was next. He bounded into the dining room as bright-eyed and bushy as if he hadn't spent the evening drinking cocktails and feeling up unsuspecting young women. He nodded to Peckham, smiled warmly at me—as if I hadn't been the young woman he'd been feeling up last night—and went to the sideboard, where he filled up a plate, before sitting down across the table.

I devoted myself to my own plate. I didn't want to acknowledge Marsden's existence, let alone have a conversation with him—certainly not about the general strike, a subject on which he was unlikely to be able to keep up his end of the discussion anyway—so I pretended he wasn't there. It wasn't easy. For being a well-trained member of the aristocracy, he ate very loudly. And his foot kept nudging mine under the table.

A double set of footsteps on the stairs heralded the arrival of Christopher and Francis. The latter gave the dining room a comprehensive glance as he entered, and he seemed disappointed not to see Constance. Christopher just grinned at me. "Hullo, Pippa. All right this morning?"

"Right as rain," I said, with a glance across the table at Marsden. "Couldn't be better."

Christopher nodded. "I'll keep you company. Just let me fill a plate, and I'll be right there."

He headed for the sideboard. Francis was already loading up, and when he arrived back at the table, he took the chair to one side of me. Christopher took the other, and Marsden's foot withdrew.

"No St George?" I asked Christopher.

It was Francis who answered. "He was the last one out of bed this morning as well as last into bed last night. The poor beggar's being run ragged."

"He could easily put a stop to it," I said callously. "If he doesn't want to be pursued by all and sundry, he could simply say no."

"I don't imagine it's that easy," Christopher said gently, "do you?"

I rather thought it was, actually. St George was a man. He had some say in what happened to him. Unlike me with Lord Geoffrey, he could have simply removed Laetitia's hand from behind his neck and her lips from his, and then he could have stepped away from her. And the same with Johanna in the garden later. It might have upset either or both women, of course. Might even have hurt someone's feelings. But he was the one with the power. He didn't have to put up with the aggression if he didn't want to. Since he did put up with it, I assumed he did.

Want it, I mean.

Although I didn't articulate any of that, because Francis added, "Here he is now."

And there he was. Footsteps on the stairs and across the floor of the reception room, and then St George's form in the doorway to the dining room.

Like Francis, he looked around the room before he entered. Unlike Francis, it was more wary than expectant. And when he didn't find what he was looking for—whether it was Laetitia or Johanna—his shoulders sank a centimeter or two and he stepped through the doorway. "Good morning."

"St George," Peckham grunted. It was quite a rude greeting, especially to a guest in one's home, but to give him the benefit of the doubt, perhaps he was just terribly hung over and couldn't muster anything more enthusiastic.

Crispin gave him an arched brow, but didn't comment.

"St George." Lord Geoffrey showed all his teeth in a bright grin. This time it was Crispin who grunted a noncommittal greeting. Perhaps he was still annoyed about having had to rescue me yesterday, or perhaps he was irritated with Lady Laetitia for some reason, and the feeling transferred to her brother.

He had spoken to both Christopher and Francis upstairs in their shared room, of course, so they just got short nods. Then there was only me left to greet. I got a flash of gray and a brief, "Darling."

"St George," I smiled sweetly. "You look rough."

"Thanks ever so, Darling."

He headed for the sideboard. Marsden eyed me across the table. So did Peckham.

"What?" I asked.

They both shook their heads and went back to breakfast.

I turned to Christopher. "There's no newspaper again this

morning, so the general strike is still ongoing. We might find it hard to get home after the weekend."

"The roads are open," Peckham pointed out, "and both St George and Mr. Astley—" He glanced at Francis, "brought cars."

"Christopher and I share a flat in London," I explained, since I hadn't meant—obviously—the difficulty of getting back to Sutherland Hall from here. I wasn't stupid, so I remembered that we had, in fact, got here by road.

Peckham stared at me, mouth open. Marsden looked from me to Christopher, and then to Crispin. And back at me. "I thought—"

"No," Francis told him, with amusement in his voice. "You read that one wrong, old chap. Kit and Pippa live together. Crispin and Pippa—"

"—are just friends," Crispin said, bringing his plate back to the table and putting it down next to Peckham, across from Francis. "Isn't that right, Darling?"

Friends? Surely that was stretching the point a bit? "I don't know, St George," I said, squinting at him, "is it?"

For some reason, his cheeks flushed pink. "Well, of course, Darling, if you'd rather I—"

"For God's sake, St George," I cut him off, as Francis burst into laughter next to me, "if you would like to claim me as a friend, then I suppose we are friends. We've certainly known each other long enough. And it's been explained to me—quite recently, in fact—that when I dropped down into the middle of the family, I accidentally took away *your* best friend, and then I claimed him for my own, and if that's the case, then I'm sorry, St George."

He didn't say anything, just stared at me. I added, "That was an apology, in case you didn't recognize it. So yes, St George, if you'd like to be friends, then we're friends."

There was a moment of ringing silence, only interrupted by Francis's sputtering. Christopher was almost preternaturally quiet, eyes on his plate, while Marsden and Peckham both looked from me to Crispin and back in silence.

Eventually he nodded. "Very well, Darling. Friends it is."

"Friends," I told him. "Shall we shake on it?"

"Better not. This jam is sticky."

Of course.

"At any rate," I told Peckham, "Christopher and I live in London. We may have to stay at Sutherland Hall until the strike blows over. I suppose it wouldn't be the end of the world..."

At least we'd have our own private rooms there, unlike here. And no Geoffrey Marsden to contend with, not to mention Lady Laetitia and Johanna.

"Or you can come back to Beckwith Place with us," Francis suggested. "Spend some time with Mum and Dad before you go home. We haven't seen much of the two of you since you moved out."

I supposed we could do that. I missed seeing Aunt Roz and Uncle Herbert, too.

"Or I can take you up to London in the H6," Crispin offered. "I'd enjoy a trip up to Town."

No doubt. He hadn't had a chance to let down his hair for almost two weeks since his mother died. He must be suffering from withdrawal.

Or must have been until this weekend, at any rate. With what was going on here at the Dower House right now, going up to Town was superfluous.

"Kind of you to offer, St George," I said, "but I think Uncle Harold would likely have something to say about that idea. Not to mention Lady Laetitia. And Johanna. And perhaps the woman you keep insisting you're in love with. And that girl with the baby, who showed up at Sutherland House two months ago..."

There were twin sighs from each side of me. "Here we go again," Francis said.

Christopher sniggered. "The truce lasted less than a minute this time. Might be a record."

Crispin rolled his eyes. "Mind your own, Darling. If I want to go up to London, I can go up to London. I am of age. My father doesn't run my life."

"Could have fooled me," I told him, considering the conversation—more like a shouting match—Christopher and I had overheard at Sutherland two weekends ago.

Crispin ignored this magnificently. "I already told you. The girl with the baby was a fraud. I'd never seen her before in my life."

"A likely story," I told him. "You probably just got so drunk one night that you didn't realize who she was when you bedded her."

His cheeks were pink again now, and so were the tips of his ears. "I don't get tight and go to bed with random women, Darling!"

"So you say," I jeered.

"Because it's the truth! I didn't know the girl with the baby, and it was absolutely not mine."

A scuff of a shoe in the doorway brought us both up short, and turned everyone's heads around, not just Crispin's and mine. He tensed, and then relaxed again when he realized it was only Constance.

Not that I imagined his feelings about either Laetitia or Johanna mattered at this point. If Geoffrey Marsden had any sway over his sister, and if Gilbert Peckham had any say over his mother's ward, neither of them—Marsden or Peckham— were likely to let their women marry someone like St George after the revelations that had just come out. I might actually believe him when it came to the girl with the baby—he certainly did seem sincere in denouncing her—but I was willing to bet that both Peckham and Marsden had him scratched off the list of potential suitors on the strength of it. In fact, Peckham looked quite nauseated by the whole thing.

But in any case, it was Constance in the doorway, not someone Crispin cared about. "Girl with a baby?" she asked as she made her way into the room. "Dear me. Good morning, Pippa. Gilbert. Lord Geoffrey. Lord St George. Mr. Astley. Francis."

The last was accompanied by a small, secretive smile. Peckham glanced from Constance to Francis and back, but refrained from comment, beyond, "You slept late, Connie."

"Late evening," Constance said, as she made her way to the buffet. "And I'm not as late as Laetitia or Johanna."

This was blatantly true, of course. Neither of them had joined us yet.

It was possible they were engaged in girl talk upstairs, I supposed. Sharing experiences of St George in their shared bedroom. Tips and tricks for how to seduce Crispin Astley, Viscount St George.

Or—since I had received the impression that they were pretty firmly opposed to one another—perhaps they were just taking their time getting ready. Considering the competition going on between them, they each had incentive to outdo the other in loveliness. So perhaps they were just upstairs preparing to make their entrances, each in an effort to outdo the other for Crispin's attention.

Constance sat down next to her brother on the other side of the table. "There's a girl with a baby?"

"She showed up at Sutherland House in London a few

months ago," I said, "with a baby she said was St George's. He says it's not."

"It's not!"

"Here we go again," Christopher muttered, and addressed Constance. "We don't know who the girl was. Or whose baby it is. If my cousin says he doesn't know her, then he doesn't know her. Crispin—"

He looked at me severely before turning his attention back to Constance, "is not a liar."

"Fine," I said, with a grimace.

"Delighted to have your support, Darling." Crispin devoted himself to his breakfast, and to the peace and quiet that would no doubt be shattered once Johanna and Laetitia made their way downstairs to join us.

I engaged Christopher and Francis in conversation about the general strike. Marsden seemed amazed—unflatteringly so—that I understood enough about what was going on to converse about it, which probably meant that Lady Laetitia was just as dim as her brother. Peckham, on the other hand, did contribute a few comments. Crispin joined in, too, eventually, and so did Constance, which seemed to amaze Marsden even more.

We were about to abandon the dining room for the lawn and the croquet mallets when Lady Laetitia finally made her entrance. And whatever she'd been doing upstairs, it had obviously been worth it. She floated through the doorway into the dining room in an afternoon frock of unparalleled loveliness. Black, like yesterday's gown—and like her shiny cap of hair—it had a thin, pink stripe on the bottom of the skirt and sleeves, a wide pink sash around the dropped waist, and a circle of pink flowers with green leaves around the top. The sleeves were tight around her upper arms and fluttered out below the elbows.

Paired with a scoop neck that showed her chest to best advantage—there was what looked like a diamond nestled into the hollow at the bottom of her throat—she was simply astonishing.

As I sat there in the twill skirt and jumper I had put on in preparation for lawn croquet, I felt very much like a little girl, outdone and outclassed by the grown women.

Really, I had no designs on St George, but if I had had, how is one supposed to compete with someone who looks like that?

She descended on him with cries of greeting and gladness, and although she didn't go to the lengths to which she had gone upon first setting eyes on him yesterday afternoon—the logistics may have been too difficult, with him sitting at table in the wrong position for a passionate kiss—she did lean down and buss his cheek.

"Good morning. Did you sleep well?"

She kept a hand on his shoulder while she straightened, quite as if she had already laid claim to him. Crispin looked mildly uncomfortable, and it only got worse when I arched my brows at him across the table. There was a smear of lipstick on his cheek, that same hot pink color as yesterday, and I eyed it for long enough that he noticed, because he snatched up his napkin and rubbed his cheek vigorously.

"Getting a late start," Geoffrey chided his sister jovially, just as Gilbert had nettled Constance earlier.

Laetitia tossed her head so the sharp points of her bob swung at her cheeks. "Not as late as some."

When none of us said anything in response, she added, "It doesn't look like Johanna is down yet, either."

Doesn't look like...?

"Don't you share a room?" I asked.

She looked at me blankly, as if one of the pieces of furniture had spoken up. It went on for long enough that Marsden finally prompted, "Letty?"

She turned to him, with another flip of her hair. "She didn't come to bed last night. Other plans, I assume."

The very possessive hand on Crispin's shoulder made it look like fear that the plans had been with him, and she was hoping he would assure her otherwise.

When he didn't, I asked, "Does anyone know where she is?"

No one did, or at least they didn't admit to it.

"Did anyone see her after the party broke up last night?"

No one had, at least not anyone who wanted to admit to it.

"St George?" I prompted, since I knew for a fact that he'd seen her outside in the garden.

He shook his head. "I spent the night with Kit and Francis. You can ask them."

Christopher nodded. "I was still awake when he came in."

"If she's not in her own room," I said, "and she's not in St George's bed, can anyone think of anywhere else she might be?"

"Darling..." Crispin sounded pained. "Must you?"

"Clearly, St George. Why would you assume otherwise?"

He didn't answer, and there was a pause. "Out walking?" Marsden suggested.

Johanna was hardly the type to indulge in a bracing walk the morning after a party—not that it was early anymore: it was almost noon—but no one pointed out the obvious.

"If she's not walking?" Were there horses? Bicycles? Or did she know how to drive a motorcar, so she might have taken one of them out?

"I hardly think it's a matter for concern," Laetitia said impatiently. It was clear that she didn't like for the conversation to be about her rival and not herself. Her hand was still on Crispin's shoulder and he still looked a bit uncomfortable over the blatant display of ownership. "It's not as if anything's likely to have happened to her. She's probably just off somewhere, sulking."

After what I'd seen through the window last night, it didn't seem as if she'd have any reason to sulk, but what did I know?

"So no one here has seen her since last night," I said. "Dawson?"

The butler shook his head. "No, Miss Darling."

"Can you ask the other servants whether any of them have seen her this morning?"

He glanced at Gilbert, who looked blank, and then at Constance, who nodded. "Please, Dawson."

"Right away, Miss Constance." He removed himself.

Laetitia huffed, and finally took her hand off Crispin's shoulder. "This seems like a big to-do about nothing."

Of course it did, to her. She wasn't the one who had found two different people dead in their beds two weekends ago.

"If she's down in the servants' quarters sleeping off a night of excess, we'll all be very happy," I told her, "but in the meantime, I'm going to look for her."

I pushed my chair back.

"I'll come with you," Christopher said, and did the same.

"I'll stay with Constance," Francis said. "We'll look around the ground floor."

"Dawson will speak to the servants," Constance added, "and, I'm sure, look around below stairs. If you two will do the first floor, that should be the whole house. If she isn't inside, I suppose we'll have to check the garage and garden next."

"Did anyone see her come in from the garden last night?"

No one admitted to having done so. And no one asked me how I'd known that Johanna had been outside after I myself had gone up to bed, either. But I noticed Crispin's eyes on me, so at least he was wondering, even if he didn't actually say anything about it.

When he made to push his chair back from the table, I shook my head. "Stay here."

If what I feared had taken place, and something had happened to Johanna, Crispin was the very last person who should be looking for her.

I took Christopher's arm instead. "We'll be back down in a few minutes. Don't go anywhere."

We headed out of the dining room and toward the stairs.

NINE

WE FOUND her in Lady Peckham's bed.

I won't bore you with a detailed recounting of the time or ratiocination that led up to the discovery. Johanna obviously wasn't in Constance's room, since she or I or both of us had been in there until Constance came down for breakfast. And she equally obviously wasn't in the room Christopher had shared with Crispin and Francis, since they'd all been there together.

"Just so there is no question," I said as we made our way up to the first floor landing, "when St George said he was with you and Francis all night...?"

Christopher slanted me a look. "He was with me and Francis. Not immediately. He came in perhaps twenty minutes after we did. Perhaps a bit longer. But I was still awake when he did. We spoke. And he didn't leave the room again after that. I would have woken up if he had. And he was still in the room with us this morning."

I nodded. I hadn't expected anything different, but it was good to have it confirmed. "That leaves Gilbert Peckham's room, that he shared with Marsden, and Johanna's room, that I guess only Laetitia slept in."

"And Lady Peckham's room," Christopher said. "Which is really the most likely place if she's up here. There was at least one person, sometimes two or even three, in all the other rooms last night. I'm sure we've all visited the loo at some point this morning, so we know she isn't there. It's either one of the closets, or Lady Peckham's bed chamber. Or she isn't upstairs at all."

Yes. If she was on one of the sofas in the parlor, Francis and Constance would find her, and if she was below-stairs with the servants, then Dawson would see her. Or, I suppose, she might be in the carriage house with the gardener. None of us knew whether he was young and good-looking and whether she might have been carrying on an illicit affair with him behind everyone's back.

But she hadn't. Or if she had, it wasn't where she had spent the night. That became obvious as soon as Christopher pushed open the door to Lady Peckham's room.

I guess I should call it the Dowager's Chamber, actually, since there ought to be a Dowager's Chamber in the Dower House in the same way that there's a Duke's Chamber and a Duchess's Chamber at Sutherland Hall.

Anyway, Christopher opened the door to Lady Peckham's room and we saw Johanna lying on the bed.

We caught our breath at the same time, and I saw Christopher's hand go white around the doorknob.

"Johanna?" I ventured. "Miss de Vos?"

There was no response, of course. Nor had I expected one, but you have to try, don't you?

It was really quite clear that she was dead, even in the low light with the drapes closed. Her dress—the same lovely garment she had worn to the parlor last night—was twisted around her limbs, baring her legs up to mid-thigh, and her face was dark and mottled, with her tongue sticking out. The fringed scarf that went with the dress was wrapped around her throat, trying, but not quite succeeding, in covering the purple bruising, and the long string of pearls that had draped her chest was broken, with pearls strewn everywhere. Her eyes were fixed and bloodshot, and a thin line of red, like a cut or perhaps a scratch, ran horizontally along one side of her neck. Perhaps her killer had scratched her with a fingernail.

My mind flashed to Lady Laetitia's hand on Crispin's shoulder in the dining room earlier, and the polished, pink center of each nail, with the unpainted, bright white tip and half-moon crescent at the base.

"Strangled," Christopher said, in what was practically a whisper.

I nodded, swallowing back a combination of nausea and panic. This was so much worse than seeing His Grace, Duke Henry, or Lady Charlotte, after their respective deaths. They'd both had an air of peace, tucked up in bed with the blankets drawn up to their chests and their faces calm.

Johanna didn't look peaceful. Her bruised skin and blood-shot eyes spoke of a violent assault, nothing tidy or calm.

I took a step back from the bed, and then another. Christopher followed. When we were out on the landing, I told him, "Get the key from the door."

My voice shook, and I tried to firm it as I added, "We should lock the room so no one else can go inside."

"I don't think Peckham's going to appreciate that, Pippa."

"I don't care what Peckham thinks," I said fiercely. "The police will appreciate it."

Christopher nodded, and locked the door. Holding up the key, he turned to me. "What do you want me to do with it?"

Not give it to Gilbert Peckham, certainly, even if, with his mother gone, he was the man of the house.

Then again, I didn't want to be responsible for it, either. Nor did I want Christopher to be, or Francis. Or—especially under these circumstances—Crispin.

There was Constance, of course. After Gilbert, she was perhaps the next most logical choice. But Johanna had been murdered, and Constance had made no secret of how much she had disliked the other woman, and giving the key to the room to someone who would surely turn out to be a suspect in the eyes of the police...

"Let's take it downstairs and give it to Dawson," I said. "He can deal with it."

Christopher nodded. "Let's do it before we break the news to the others. That way, Gilbert can't take the key."

He could still demand it from Dawson, being Dawson's employer—or at least the son of Dawson's employer—but I hoped he'd see sense and wouldn't try.

And speaking of Dawson's employer... "We have to contact Sutherland Hall and let Lady Peckham know. She might want to come home."

"Dawson first," Christopher said. "Then the police. Then Sutherland."

"You should phone Tom," I told him as we made our way towards the stairs. "Let him know what's happened and ask him to come here."

He gave me a look. "You don't just phone Scotland Yard and ask them to stop by, Pippa."

"You do if you have Scotland Yard's private number, and Scotland Yard has saved you from being arrested before."

He flushed. "I don't have his private number, Pippa, all right? He knows where to find me, but I don't know how to get in touch with him."

"Maybe we could ring up Scotland Yard in London and ask for him?"

"No," Christopher said. "There are rules for this."

He didn't specify whether the rules applied to murder and to calling in Scotland Yard, or whether they applied to young men who may or may not have a fondness for one, romantic or otherwise.

"Enlighten me," I suggested as we pushed open the green baize door in the hallway and began our descent to the below-stairs.

"When something happens, you contact the local constabulary. They bring in the chief constable for the area, and he decides whether to call in Scotland Yard."

"Which they will certainly do, seeing as this was Lady Peckham's ward in Lady Peckham's bedroom."

"But there are still rules," Christopher said, and stopped in the doorway to the kitchen. "Dawson."

"Mr. Astley." Dawson straightened and turned. He looked at Christopher's face, then at my face, and then at the key in Christopher's hand.

"She's in your mistress's chamber," Christopher said, holding out the key. "Dead on the bed."

Cook, a round-faced woman who looked to be in her fifties, squeaked, and the kitchen-maid, who was surely younger than I was, turned pale.

"We locked the door," Christopher added, "so no one else can go in while we wait for the police. You should phone them."

Cook squeaked again, and pressed the flat of her hand against her chest.

Dawson reached out slowly and took the key. "How?" He had to clear his throat before he could get the single word out.

"It looks like she was strangled," I said, "but we're hardly professionals. That's why you need the police. And probably the local doctor."

He nodded. "Lady Iris—"

"My mother is at Sutherland Hall," Christopher said. "Lady Herbert Astley. I propose I call her once you've arranged everything with the police, and let her break the news to your employer. Then Lady Peckham can decide whether to come home today, or not."

"The mistress will want to come home," Cook said. "Loved the young miss, she did."

It had certainly seemed so. That didn't mean she'd want to drive home to a murder investigation that centered on the dead body of her ward discovered in her own bed.

"We haven't told any of the others," Christopher said to Dawson, "but I don't see any way around that. That's why I want you to have the key. If Peckham—Gilbert—comes and asks you for it—or anyone else, for that matter—don't give it to them. The police will want the crime scene preserved."

Dawson nodded. "I'll ring them up right now. The village isn't far. Someone should be along shortly."

"We'll go back to the dining room," I said. "We'll break the news and then keep everyone there while we wait. If you could bring the bar cart over from the parlor after you've phoned the police, I think we would all appreciate it."

Dawson nodded, and excused himself to go over to the kitchen extension to ring up the local constabulary while Christopher and I made the climb back up to the ground floor. It was surprisingly difficult, and took more effort than a dozen steps of a staircase ought to take.

"Well?" Peckham asked, a bit belligerently, when we came back through the door. "Connie and Mr. Astley searched the entire ground floor, and there was no sign of her. Dawson hasn't come back upstairs, so I assume she wasn't below."

I glanced at Christopher. He looked at me, visibly ceding the responsibility. I sighed, but did my duty. "I'm sorry to be the bearer of bad news, Mr. Peckham, but I'm afraid Miss de Vos has met with an accident."

Gilbert opened his mouth, but no words came out. Constance, however, made a little noise that caused Francis to glance at her and then scoot his chair closer. Meanwhile, Laetitia looked politely unfazed, or perhaps just disbelieving. In the time we'd been gone, she had seated herself next to Crispin, whose eyes were fastened on my face with a mixture of dread and a horrible certainty.

"An accident?" Marsden said, and when I looked at him, I saw that his brows were drawn together in what looked like confusion. They were exquisite brows, just like the rest of him, and he looked marvelous even when he was nonplussed by something that should have been quite obvious.

"She's dead," I said plainly. "And no, it didn't appear to have been an accident. That was what we call a polite euphemism."

Marsden gaped. "Did you say she's dead?"

If he was guilty, it was a masterful display of dumbfounded ignorance.

"She's dead," I confirmed. "Strangled. In Lady Peckham's bedroom. We took the liberty of locking the door and giving the key to Dawson. He's phoning the police as we speak."

Gilbert blinked. Cleared his throat and tried again. "I want to see her."

"The police will want the crime scene to be as undisturbed as possible," Christopher told him.

Everyone winced at the mention of a crime scene, although I would have assumed the word 'strangled' would have given adequate warning that this was a crime. Peckham didn't relent, however. "With Mother gone, I'm—"

"A suspect," I said bluntly. "We all are. None of us can go back into that room. That's why we gave Dawson the key."

"Well, I never!" Laetitia sniffed. "How can you possibly suggest that I would do anything to harm dear Johanna?"

It was so blatantly disingenuous that we all just stared at her.

"Letty..." her brother said, pained.

Laetitia tossed her head. "Fine. But if she was strangled... I'm not strong enough to strangle anyone."

"I don't know much about it," I told her. "But it looked like she was strangled with her scarf, and I imagine you'd find that easier than using your hands."

Laetitia turned pale, and so did Constance.

"Pippa..." Francis protested.

I nodded. "Sorry. I'm upset."

"We're all upset," Gilbert said, and sounded petulant. "Who are you to take charge and tell us these things?"

I turned to him. "I'm nobody. I'm one of the two people who found her, but apart from that I'm nobody. I wish she wasn't dead, and I wish I hadn't seen her, and I wish we didn't have to talk about it anymore. But I assumed you'd want to know. If you didn't, then I apologize."

There was a moment of silence while no one said anything. Then Crispin opened his mouth. "Sit down, Darling." He glanced around the dining room. "Maybe we can find something—"

"Dawson's fetching the bar cart," Christopher said, dropping onto the chair next to me, "as soon as he's called in the local police."

Crispin nodded. "I think we can all do with a drink."

There was a murmur of agreement around the table. I'm normally not one to imbibe before three, especially not on a morning following a party, but we'd done it at Sutherland Hall two weeks ago, so there was no reason we couldn't do it here. It was definitely needed.

"What was she doing in your mother's room?" Marsden asked.

The question was directed to Gilbert, I think, or perhaps to Constance, but again the words fell out of my mouth without thought. "Isn't it obvious? She didn't want to share a room with Lady Laetitia. Lady Peckham's room was empty. Why not go there?"

"So who of us knew where she was?" Marsden asked, looking around at everyone.

It was another blatantly obvious question, and not one he was likely to get an honest answer to. If no one would admit to having seen Johanna after she went out into the garden last night, no one would admit to knowing where she'd gone to spend the night.

"I knew she wasn't in her own room," Laetitia said, "although I didn't stop to think where she might be instead."

The way she very carefully avoided looking at Crispin gave the lie to that assertion. She had thought Johanna was with him, and had been determined not to dwell on it.

"I went up to bed long before the rest of you," I said. "I have no idea what anyone else did after that."

Except for those moments in the water closet, of course, and the embrace I had spied through the window.

Although if Crispin had gone to Lady Peckham's room with Johanna after the scene I'd witnessed in the garden, things must have turned sour very quickly. Christopher had told me that Crispin had come into their shared bedroom twenty minutes or so after him and Francis. Take off the time they had been in there while he'd been outside the garden, and you were left with... what? Fifteen minutes? Ten?

That might have been enough time to kill someone if he

had wanted to. He would have had to be very quick about it, though. And the scene I had witnessed hadn't looked like it would turn to violence that fast.

I eyed him across the table. He didn't look any guiltier than he normally did, which is to say not at all. Then again, I've never had the impression that he has much of a conscience. That was why I had been able to convince myself so thoroughly, on so little evidence, that he had killed his grandfather and his grandfather's valet two weeks ago.

Which, of course, he hadn't. And he probably hadn't done this, either. Why would he? He had two beautiful young women fighting over him. Why ruin the fun by killing one of them?

He looked up and caught me staring, and met my eyes for a moment. After a second, he smirked. "Penny for your thoughts, Darling?"

"Just wondering whether you retired to Lady Peckham's room with Johanna last night," I said.

Next to him, Laetitia stiffened, and both her brother and Gilbert Peckham turned to eye him suspiciously.

If he noticed, it didn't bother him. One eyebrow arched, but his voice was perfectly calm when he told me, "I didn't."

I nodded. I didn't think he'd admit to it even if he had, so this was nothing I hadn't expected.

A rattle outside the door heralded Dawson with the bar cart. "Gentlemen," he intoned as he pushed it through the door. "Ladies."

Peckham sprang to his feet. "Dawson. Astley says you have the key to Mother's room—"

"I'm sorry, Mr. Gilbert." Dawson didn't even look up at him, just kept pushing the cart across the floor.

"But with Mother gone..."

"The police," Dawson said, "gave clear instructions that the room was to be kept closed and locked."

He pushed the cart to a standstill and straightened. And relented just a bit as he did it. "I'm sure you'll get to see her before she's taken away, Mr. Gilbert."

Peckham flushed and dropped back onto his chair. Dawson turned to Christopher with a nod. "Mr. Astley. The police have been phoned and are on their way. You can ring up your mother now, if you want."

Marsden and Peckham both looked over at that, and Marsden sniggered. "You're phoning your mother, Astley?"

The inference—*what kind of man are you, to call your mother when the going gets tough?*—was there, and clear.

"I'm contacting my mother," Christopher said coldly, "at Sutherland Hall, so she can break the news to Lady Peckham. I'm sure she'll do it more gently than the police would."

There wasn't much Marsden could say to that, of course, and he didn't try, although he did look a bit chastened. The corner of Crispin's mouth twitched, like he wanted to smile but was refraining. Deliberately.

"I'll go with you," I told Christopher as he pushed his chair back.

"To the telephone?" This was Marsden again, of course. "Are you going to hold his hand while he holds the ear piece?"

"I'll hold anything he needs me to hold—!" I began, but before I had the chance to go on, Crispin had done it for me.

"I wouldn't recommend getting on Darling's bad side, Marsden," he said languidly. "Much better to keep your mouth shut than antagonize her. She never forgets a slight, and never lets you forget that you slighted her. And after last night, you're already on thin ice."

"Thank you, St George," I said, although it wasn't what I'd call a compliment. Or at least not a very nice one.

He grinned. It wasn't a very nice grin, either. "Don't mention it, Darling. Much as I'd enjoy watching you eviscerate Lord Geoffrey, we've already had one murder here this weekend. That's probably enough."

Probably. Although eviscerating Lord Geoffrey did have its appeal.

At that point, Christopher was almost to the door, so I scurried after. Not quite quickly enough to miss the exchange that took place next, however.

"I had no idea you were so whipped, St George," Marsden said, with a decided sneer to his tone.

"What, by Darling?" Crispin made a noise that might have been a derogative snort, but sounded more like suppressed laughter. "We all let Darling whip us. It's easier than the alternative."

Francis made a little humming sound. It could have been agreement, but sounded more like amusement, as well.

"Needs a good shagging," Marsden commented, "to show her who's boss."

My cheeks flushed a deep red, and I thought about turning around and launching something at him—how dare he talk about me like that?—but there was nothing in range that I could throw, and anyway, the conversation went on.

"I'd give half my inheritance to watch you try to show Darling you're boss," Crispin commented, although his voice was tight.

Francis added, "I wouldn't go there if I were you, Marsden. Not only will you have Pippa to contend with, and she's quite enough all on her own, but you'll be dealing with us, too. As St George said, much healthier for you to keep your mouth shut. Not to mention your hands to yourself."

Someone must have informed Francis about what had

happened in the parlor last night, it seemed. He clearly didn't approve.

By then I was through the door and could close it behind me, so I did, with a bit more of a slam than I intended. It felt good to relieve some of my spleen, so I wasn't about to apologize for it.

Christopher had made it to the telephone table in the reception room and had the receiver up to his ear while he was speaking into the mouthpiece. "Operator?"

I headed across the floor to him as he continued, "This is the Dower House in Marsden-on-Crane. I need you to put through a call to Sutherland 14 in Wiltshire. I'll wait."

He leaned against the wall next to the table, receiver to his ear and ankles crossed, while on the other end of the line, the operator must be trying to make the connection to Sutherland Hall.

"Sounds like someone's coming," I said, since my ears had caught the sound of an engine outside.

"Probably the police," Christopher answered.

"I know Dawson said the village is close, but surely that's very soon?"

"Maybe the village is *very* close." He shifted his weight as the motorcar stopped outside the front doors and the engine fell silent.

I peered in that direction, but couldn't see anything through the wood of the door. "I guess I should go and open the door for them."

Christopher nodded. "Might as well. If we know they're here, there's no reason to wait until they knock."

"No answer at the Hall?"

"It's ringing on the other end," Christopher said. "No one's picked up thus far."

I nodded, as the slamming of a motorcar door drifted in from outside. "I'll get the door. Spare Dawson the trouble."

"Please." Christopher bent over the telephone table again, so he could speak into the mouthpiece of the phone. "Tidwell? This is Christopher Astley, phoning from the Dower House in Dorset. Is my mother around?"

Tidwell must have had plenty to say—probably an explanation for where Aunt Roz was and why he couldn't immediately call her to the phone—because Christopher straightened again to listen. I could hear Tidwell's voice as a faint quacking through the earpiece Christopher was holding to his ear.

The quacking faded as I got closer to the front door. I undid the lock and pulled the door open. And found myself face to face with a well-built young man in a tweed suit, with clear hazel eyes under the brim of a Homburg.

My mouth dropped open.

"Good afternoon, Miss Darling," Detective Sergeant Thomas Gardiner of Scotland Yard said.

TEN

OVER AT THE TELEPHONE TABLE, the earpiece went clattering as Christopher swung around. The he scrambled for it again, while he bent to address the mouthpiece. "Listen, Tidwell. Detective Sergeant Gardiner just walked in. I'll ring you back if I need to talk to my mother."

He cradled the earpiece without listening to what, if anything, Tidwell had to say to this announcement. His cheeks were hot pink when he turned back to us. "Thomas."

"Kit." Tom Gardiner looked around the reception room before turning back to him. "I need to see Gilbert and Constance Peckham."

I furrowed my brow. "Why just them? Surely we're all suspects? We were all here, weren't we?"

Tom looked just as confused as I felt. "Here? What's happened here?"

"Johanna de Vos is dead," I said, "although I get the impression that isn't why you've come."

He shook his head. "I have to notify the Peckham siblings that their mother is dead. And ask some questions."

There was a pause while we all took some time to realign our expectations.

"Lady Peckham is dead?" Christopher said.

Tom nodded. "Johanna de Vos? That's the ward, correct?"

"Was," I said. "Not only was she an adult, and had been for years, but she was strangled overnight, and thus is no more. We thought you were the police."

"I *am* the police."

"The local police. Dawson called them."

"The butler," Christopher added, as if it mattered.

Tom glanced over his shoulder, at the door and the hypothetical police that wasn't there yet. "I'll talk to them when they get here. But given that Lady Peckham also passed last night, I'll go out on a limb and say it'll be Scotland Yard's case."

No doubt. When two people in the same household die in the same night, even if they're miles apart when it happens, it makes sense to treat the cases as connected, at least until you've proven that they're not.

"What happened to Lady Peckham?" I asked, but Tom shook his head.

"Just lead me to Mr. and Miss Peckham, if you please, and we'll get it all out of the way at once."

"Dining room," Christopher told him, gesturing to the door. "We were having a late breakfast when we realized that Johanna had never come down, and then, when we found her, we locked the door and kept everyone in the dining room."

"Who found her?" Tom looked from Christopher to me and back as we made our way towards the door to the dining room. "You two?"

"By happenstance. We checked the upstairs. Francis and Constance looked around the ground floor, and Dawson asked the staff."

"Any trouble last night?"

"Let me count the ways," Christopher said, but by then we had reached the door to the dining room. "Perhaps later will be better."

He opened the door instead of going on. "Gentlemen, ladies. This is Detective Sergeant Thomas Gardiner from Scotland Yard."

There was a moment of silence while everyone looked at Tom. Gilbert Peckham appeared concerned. So did Marsden. Laetitia assessed him the way she probably did any young man —or any man, young or old—who crossed her path: for looks, money, and the likelihood of a title. Constance blinked, and the rest of us, of course, all knew Tom and had seen him quite recently.

"That was fast," Francis commented, and Tom shook his head.

"Coincidence. Hello, Astley. St George." He nodded to them. Geoffrey Marsden and his sister must be strangers to Tom, because he contemplated them for a moment, but without greeting them, before he turned his attention to Gilbert and Constance. "Mr. Peckham, Miss Peckham. I'm afraid I have unwelcome news."

Constance immediately turned pale. Gilbert flushed. "Worse than Johanna being dead?"

Tom looked at him for a second, perhaps to try to determine whether the death of his mother would strike Gilbert as more or less bad than Johanna's death.

"It's your mother," he said finally. "I'm sorry to say she ingested something that proved fatal last evening. She was found lifeless in bed this morning."

Constance's eyes filled with tears, and she turned to Francis, wordlessly. I'm sure he would have liked to have put his arms around her, but not only were they in public, they were on two separate dining chairs. The best he could do was reach out and put his hand on top of hers, and then pass her his pocket square when the tears overflowed.

"What?" Geoffrey Marsden said blankly.

Tom turned to him. "I'm afraid I haven't the pleasure...?"

Marsden stuck his chest out. "I'm Geoffrey Marsden. This is my sister Laetitia. We're cousins to the Peckhams. This house is Marsden property."

Tom nodded. "I'm sorry to have to tell you that your relative, Lady Peckham, died overnight. We suspect a fatal dose of Veronal."

Francis started, and so did Constance. Gilbert's jaw dropped. "Veronal?" he repeated.

"My mother wouldn't take her own life," Constance protested. "She was only forty-seven, and healthy. She had everything to live for. And Veronal..."

She flicked a glance at Francis and then away again. "It's a sleeping draught, isn't it? She didn't have trouble sleeping."

"At this time, we're not excluding the possibility of suicide," Tom said, "but it's more likely to have been an accidental ingestion. The substance was mixed with her own medicine. She had intestinal issues?"

Constance nodded. "She called them her tummy troubles." Her voice shook. "She'd eat something that didn't agree with her, and then she'd have to take a dose of her medicine to feel better."

"So a curative medicine," Tom said. "Not a preventative."

"If you mean that she took it after she was feeling ill, then yes."

Yes. I could picture it clearly. Supper with Uncle Harold, and with Aunt Roz and Uncle Herbert. Mrs. Sloane, the cook at Sutherland Hall, doesn't spare the rich ingredients. There'd be butter and cream, and perhaps truffles and sweetmeats. Indigestion might have crept up on Lady Peckham after supper, and before bed she had taken a dose of what she thought was her stomach medicine. And instead, she had ingested a fatal dose of sleeping draught and had drifted off, all alone, away from her son and daughter and the young woman she had loved like her own child, never to wake up this morning.

It was rather sad. Although if nothing else, it sounded as if it would have been a peaceful way to go. Not like the one Christopher and I had seen upstairs.

And she had been spared the knowledge that her beloved ward had been strangled, and in her own bed. That was something to be grateful for, anyway.

"Her fingerprints were on the bottle and the stopper," Tom said, "as well as on the waterglass beside the bed. There's every reason to think she gave it to herself."

Gilbert looked relieved at this statement. Perhaps he didn't realize that it in no way meant that his mother hadn't been murdered. It just meant that whoever had murdered her hadn't poured the poison—or medication—down her throat him- or herself.

Or—if Tom was right and it was an accident—Lady Peckham might have, for one reason or another, decided to take a sleeping draught last night, even if she usually didn't, and because she usually didn't, she accidentally gave herself an overdose.

"Where did the sleeping draught come from?" I asked.

"Chief Inspector Pendennis and Detective Sergeant Finchley are still figuring that out," Tom answered.

I glanced at Francis, whose supply of Veronal had been responsible for Aunt Charlotte's demise two weeks ago. He was pale and looked ill.

There was a moment of silence into which Constance dropped a simple, yet devastating, sentence.

"My mother's dead," she said, her voice small, and I was

reminded, forcibly, of sitting in the library at Sutherland Hall a week and a half ago, as Crispin said those same words, with the same inflection and the same lost expression on his face.

I moved over and sat down next to Constance, and took her other hand. Crispin looked at me across the table, but he didn't say anything. Perhaps he remembered, too.

And then there was a knock on the front door, and a moment later, Dawson's measured steps across the tile floor of the reception room.

"The police," Gilbert said, raising his head like a pointer on the job.

"I'll go deal with them." Tom headed for the door. "Don't go anywhere."

He vanished into the reception room. By now, Dawson had admitted the local constables and we heard Tom greet them and introduce himself. At that point I stopped paying attention to the conversation—I could guess what it was about—and turned to Constance, whose hand I was still holding.

"I'm so sorry for your loss, Constance. You too, Mr. Peckham."

Francis nodded. "Condolences all around, Peckham." He patted Constance's hand. She sniffed into her—or rather his—handkerchief.

"This is just so very hard to believe," Gilbert said. "First Johanna and now Mother. Both on the same night. It's almost as if Mother knew, isn't it?"

There was a pause of—if you'll excuse the turn of phrase—dead silence.

"Knew?" Constance repeated, a little shrilly. "Knew what? That Johanna would also die last night?"

Gilbert shrugged, somewhat sheepishly. "You have to admit it's quite a coincidence."

"I don't see how it can be anything else," I told him, "unless you're suggesting that your mother sensed Johanna's death was imminent, and decided to end her own life in solidarity."

He didn't say anything, and I added, "Because if you'll excuse me, that sounds like a lot of rot. I'm sure your mother cared about Johanna—she certainly seemed to—but she still had you and Constance."

"She liked Johanna better," Constance said with a sniff. The sniff could have been sad or indignant, depending.

"That may be," I told her, because I had certainly got the impression that the late Lady Peckham had been fonder of her pretty ward than of her natural daughter, "but that still doesn't explain how she could have possibly known that Johanna, all the way in Dorset, was dying last night. Johanna's death didn't look planned to me, so Lady Peckham couldn't possibly have known that it was going to happen."

"All I said," Gilbert grumbled, "was that it was strange that it should happen this way."

He had done a bit more than that. It seemed, to me at least, that he had suggested the presence of some sort of supernatural knowledge on Lady Peckham's part, which was plainly ridiculous. We were almost halfway through 1926, more than halfway through this thoroughly modern decade. We didn't believe in ghosts and supernatural woo-woo anymore.

Besides, chances were that Lady P had ingested her fatal brew before the party broke up in the parlor of the Dower House anyway. Our family members at Sutherland Hall keep earlier hours than we had done last night. They would have been in bed by midnight, if not sooner. By the time Johanna kissed Crispin in the garden, Lady Peckham had certainly been asleep, if not actually dead.

At this point, Tom came back into the dining room, followed by a young constable from the nearby constabulary, and took over the proceedings.

"We'll start with an overview of last night and this morning," he told us, "while we wait for my colleagues to arrive from Sutherland Hall. Constable Collins here is going to take notes. Just pretend you don't see him."

He nodded to Collins, who took himself off to the far corner of the room where he pulled out a pencil stub and a notebook and pretended to blend into the wallpaper.

"I know who you are, of course," Tom continued, "but if you would introduce yourselves and explain how you came to be here, for the record?"

It sounded nice and polite, with a question mark at the end, but it wasn't a request. We went around the table, gave our names and addresses, and explained what we were doing at the Dower House.

"Philippa Darling," I said, when it was my turn. "I went to Godolphin with Constance. When she and her family came to Sutherland Hall for Lady Charlotte's funeral on Wednesday, she mentioned the house party and invited us all to come."

"When you say 'us all'...?"

"Myself," I said, "Christopher Astley, Francis Astley, and especially Lord St George."

Tom glanced at him and back at me. "Why especially St George?"

"Constance made it clear that her mother was hoping to matchmake. Crispin has the title and most of the money."

I avoided looking at Crispin when I said it, since this was something I had thrown in his face many times before, most of them in the heat of an argument. He knows that women pursue him because of his title and fortune—how could he not know it, with as many times as I've pointed it out?

Where we disagree, is whether that's the sole reason that they pursue, or whether it's just a contributing factor. Crispin insists that he has other things to recommend him. I tell him that he doesn't. (Of course he's also quite good-looking and can be very clever, even if he has a terribly sarcastic tongue to go along with that quick mind. I just don't see why I should take pains to mention any of those attributes, since he's conceited enough already.)

But on this particular occasion, I felt no need to rub his face in Lady Peckham's pecuniary attitude. He might even have believed that his connection with Johanna was different, and who was I to take that away from him?

"Tell me about last night," Tom said when we had finished the introductions and Collins's pencil had stopped scratching across the page of the notebook.

We looked at one another, to see who would go first. When no one else spoke up, Lady Laetitia did. "My brother and I arrived in time for supper. We live just across the valley..."

She waved a languid hand, although unless my sense of geography failed me, I thought Marsden Manor was actually located on the other side of the Dower House than the one she was indicating.

"And you were planning to stay the weekend? When was that decided?"

"Oh." She looked vague. "Aunt Iris asked us earlier this week. Before she and the others went to Sutherland Hall. She mentioned that Lord St George might be coming..."

She fluttered a look at Crispin under her lashes. He looked uncomfortable.

"You and St George are old friends," Tom said. It was a statement of fact, not a question.

Laetitia stopped. She looked at Crispin, then at me and Christopher, and then at her brother before she looked at Tom again. Finally she said, "Yes?" with a sort of vague uncertainty that made it sound like she wasn't certain at all.

"You spent some time together in London earlier this year. At Sutherland House, back in January."

Laetitia blinked, as if she couldn't imagine how he would know that. The look on Crispin's face was horrified.

"Grimsby's notes," I told him, and he transferred the horrified look to me.

"Good God, Darling. Just how detailed were these notes?"

"Quite detailed." I smirked. "The staff at Sutherland House had no qualms about telling Grimsby everything they'd seen and heard, and your mother apparently had no qualms about sharing it with me."

I had the pleasure of seeing the color drain out of his cheeks. "My mother?" he choked. "Told you about this?"

"Remember that envelope I gave to Tom two weeks ago at Sutherland Hall, that you refused to believe contained a record of my movements? You made some quite uncouth comments, as I recall."

He didn't respond to that, and I added, "Your mother tore the pages about you out of Grimsby's notebook and left them in my room." Along with the pages pertaining to me and to Christopher.

I had dutifully passed it all on to Scotland Yard, of course. After committing it to memory.

Crispin's jaw dropped. "She gave you information about *my* affairs? My mother gave *you* information about my affairs? My *mother?*"

"Every woman you've brought to Sutherland House in the past year and a half," I confirmed. "How did you think I learned about the girl with the baby?"

"I have no idea." Crispin sank back against the chair looking wan. "Good God. If Grimsby wasn't already dead, I'd kill him myself."

"Not the kind of thing you want to say in front of Scotland

Yard," Tom told him dryly, but without making it sound like he thought a whole lot of Crispin's confession.

"Besides," I told him, "you told me about Lady Laetitia yourself, remember? Not a conquest, you said. It was more that—"

"Yes, Darling." He interrupted me so quickly that I'm sure we all got the idea that there was something I was about to blurt out that he didn't want me to say. "Thank you. I remember."

Laetitia, not a lot smarter than her brother, certainly not smart enough not to ask, flapped her eyelashes at him coquettishly. "What was it you said about me, St George?"

He squirmed. Glanced at me, looked away. Flicked a glance at Christopher, who had also been present for that particular conversation two weeks ago.

"Might as well tell her," I said, as I fought back laughter. "She's just going to keep asking until you do."

"Fine." He gave her his best soulful look. "I told them that you're not one of my conquests—Darling can be very crude in the way she puts things—but rather, you conquered me."

"Oh!" Laetitia looked transported with delight. Her brother looked like he'd eaten something rancid. Christopher glanced over at me, and it was clear he was trying hard not to laugh.

"Masterful, St George," I said dryly when I had conquered my reflexive desire to gag.

"Thank you, Darling." The look he gave me said clearly that he didn't appreciate having been pushed to make this confession at all.

"If we can just get on with it?" Tom suggested, in the tone of one sorely put upon. "Try to keep the detours to a minimum, if you please. So you and your brother arrived." He turned back to Laetitia. "You greeted the people who were already here, including St George, whom you know well."

She nodded, and a shade of discomfort crossed her face. I

was happy to see it, since it seemed like the least she could do, really.

"You had supper. And after supper...?"

"Drinks and dancing in the parlor," Laetitia said promptly. "Gilbert manned the gramophone. Constance danced with the elder Mr. Astley. I danced with St George—" She lowered her lashes demurely, "and the younger Mr. Astley."

Tom glanced at Christopher—he shrugged—before turning his attention to me. "What about you, Miss Darling?"

"I danced with Christopher," I said, "and Lord Geoffrey, and at one point with St George."

This was not the time and place to bring up Marsden's foray up my leg, I decided. I'd confide his liberties to Tom later, since they might have some bearing on what had happened to Johanna—or not—but it was better done privately.

"What about Miss de Vos?" Tom asked.

There was that moment of dead silence again. When no one else spoke up, I did. "She danced with Crispin and Christopher and at least once with Lord Geoffrey."

"And at the end of the evening?"

"I went up first," I said, and avoided looking at everyone. "Christopher walked me to my room and waited while I brushed my teeth. Then he went back downstairs."

The fact that he'd locked me in and taken the key to give to Constance, and the reason why it had been necessary, was something we could also tell Tom later.

I got the feeling that he could sense there was more to it than what I had articulated, but he simply nodded. "Anything to add to that, Kit?"

Christopher shook his head. "It was early. Just after eleven. I spent another hour, hour and a bit, in the parlor. By then Constance—Miss Peckham—was tired, so Francis and I walked her to her room, which was also Pippa's room—they were sharing—and then we retired to our own."

"The two of you shared a room? You and your brother?"

"The three of us," Christopher corrected. "Francis, Crispin, and I. Nobody wanted to invade Lady Peckham's bed chamber, so we doubled and tripled up in the other rooms. Pippa stayed with Constance, and Lord Geoffrey with Mr. Peckham. Lady Laetitia was in Miss de Vos's room."

Tom eyed Laetitia for a moment before he asked, "But Miss de Vos was found in Lady Peckham's bed, you said?"

Christopher nodded.

"So she didn't come to bed last night?"

Laetitia shook her head, which may or may not have been the truth. They might simply have avoided one another completely—Johanna had still been wearing her evening dress when we'd found her, so she might have gone directly to Lady Peckham's room when she came upstairs—or there could have been a big fight in Johanna's room first, before she stormed out and across the landing. But if so, it must have been done in whispers, since none of us had heard anything of it.

Or at least I hadn't. Someone else might have heard, but was keeping mum about it.

Maybe it had been Johanna I had heard outside on the landing later in the night. Maybe she had hesitated outside our room, wondering whether to knock or not.

If she had, might she be alive now?

Almost certainly, I thought. Although it might not have been her at all. Instead, it might have been her murderer, going back to his—or her—own room after committing the murder.

"Very well," Tom said. "Let us go back for a moment to the end of the evening. It was twelve, twelve-thirty. Miss Darling had gone up shortly after eleven. The Astley brothers walked Miss Peckham up and then they went to their room. Lord Geoffrey and Lady Laetitia, Mr. Peckham, Lord St George, and Miss de Vos were left downstairs, I assume?" He looked at them, one after the other. "What happened next?"

Peckham and Marsden looked at one another. Then Marsden looked at his sister, and at Crispin. Peckham looked at Crispin. Finally, Laetitia looked at Crispin.

Crispin didn't look at anyone, but kept his eyes on the centerpiece of multicolored tulips in the middle of the table.

"The ladies got into a row," Peckham said sourly. "Over St George."

ELEVEN

CRISPIN FLUSHED, all the way to the tips of his ears, and I rolled my eyes. Of course Laetitia and Johanna had got into a row over him. It had been inevitable. The only surprising thing was that they'd done it with an audience, and not in the privacy of their own shared room.

One of them must have pushed the other to the limit of her patience, I assumed, and so she had blown. The only question was who. Or rather, which.

I prepared to wallow in the tale. Until, disappointingly—

"I can get the details of that later," Tom said, which was quite considerate of him, actually. Having to recount the scene in front of a crowd in which half the people hadn't been present, would be quite embarrassing, not just for Lady Laetitia, but for Crispin. I had to commend Tom for his sensitivity, even if I dearly wished I could hear every gory detail for myself. There was sure to be years of torment for St George in this story, and now I would miss it.

Unless I could talk Tom into sharing his notes with me

later. I didn't think it was likely, but it would perhaps be worth the effort to try.

At any rate, Laetitia and Crispin both looked relieved at the prospect of not having to rehash the scene in front of an audience, and Tom went on. "What happened after the quarrel?"

"I went up to bed," Laetitia said.

"Alone?"

Laetitia nodded, her line of white teeth sunk into her lower lip. "I was embarrassed. All I wanted was to be alone."

She glanced at Crispin under her lashes, and while he didn't look up and meet her eyes, he must have sensed it, because I saw him twitch.

"Very well," Tom said. "So Lady Laetitia went up to Miss de Vos's room. That leaves four of you in the parlor. What did the rest of you do?"

"I went outside in the garden," Crispin said. "I wanted a fag and some peace and quiet."

He probably hadn't meant for it to sound quite as callous as it did, but Laetitia flinched. Francis managed to suppress most of a bark of laughter, but there was enough left that Crispin shot him a look. Francis chuckled and raised both hands in the universal sign of surrender. "Sorry, old chap."

"Behave yourself, Astley," Tom told him, but without any heat. "St George."

Crispin looked at him.

"Did you see anyone else while you were in the garden?"

Crispin shook his head. I opened my mouth to call him on the lie, that he had most certainly seen Johanna, and not just that, but had embraced and kissed her, but then I closed my mouth again. Maybe there was a reason he didn't want to admit it, and it wasn't because he had committed murder. While my first instinct was always to believe the worst of him, maybe I ought to stay my hand and learn a little more first.

There were, after all, things I hadn't come out with in this group of mixed company, too, but that I planned to tell Tom later.

"How long were you out there?" the latter wanted to know.

"Long enough to smoke a cigarette and kick the fence a few times." Crispin still kept his eyes down, perhaps afraid that one of us who knew him well would be able to read the lie on his face. I don't think I would have done if I hadn't known he was lying, however. He looked embarrassed, certainly, but not like he was holding anything back.

Tom turned to Christopher, who said, "He came up some twenty minutes after Francis and myself."

"It wasn't a long, drawn-out scene in the parlor, then?"

"A matter of a few minutes," Peckham said with a sneer he couldn't quite hide, "but quite shrill."

Lady Laetitia's lower lip quivered.

"So you went from the garden up to bed, St George. Did you reenter the house through the parlor doors?"

Crispin shook his head. "I went around to the front. I didn't know what might be going on in the parlor, or who was still there, and I didn't want to instigate another row if I could help it."

"Did you see anyone on your way through the house?"

"Peckham was still in the parlor," Crispin said, with his eyes on the tulips. "So was the butler. I saw them through the open door. I didn't see anyone else."

"And when you got upstairs?"

"Kit was awake." He slanted a look at his cousin. "He asked me whether everything was all right. I said yes. That's it."

"And you stayed in your room for the rest of the night?"

Crispin nodded. So did Christopher.

"Lord Geoffrey." Tom turned to him.

"Went upstairs after St George went outside," Marsden

grunted. "Looked in on my sister, you know, to make sure she was all right—"

Laetitia sniffed, either because she'd obviously not been all right, and it was ridiculous that he'd think she would be, or perhaps simply because she was touched that he'd thought of her enough to check in the first place. With what I knew of Marsden, it could easily have been either.

"And was she?" Tom asked dryly, as if his thoughts had gone along the same path as mine.

"Right as rain," Marsden said, in a display of obliviousness that was frankly stunning. "In her room taking off her face, getting ready to go to sleep. I asked if she needed anything, she said no, and so I went to bed, too."

"You were sharing a room with Mr. Peckham?"

Marsden nodded.

"When did he come upstairs?"

Peckham opened his mouth to tell him, but Tom waved him to silence.

"No idea," Marsden said cheerfully. "I dropped off as soon as my head hit the pillow. Always do, you know. I took an aspirin to ward off the hangover this morning, lay down, and that was it."

"And you didn't hear Mr. Peckham come in, or anything from outside your room?"

Marsden shook his head.

"Very well," Tom said. "Mr. Peckham?"

"I was the last one out of the parlor," Gilbert said. "I turned off the gramophone and spoke to Dawson, to tell him that several of the party were still outside, so don't lock the doors yet."

"Several?"

"St George went out for his gasper," Peckham said. "And

when Lady Laetitia booked it upstairs, Johanna ran outside, too."

"Miss de Vos also went into the garden?" Tom glanced at Crispin, who was still eyeing the centerpiece and didn't look up to meet Tom's eyes.

Gilbert nodded. So did Marsden, confirming it. "I assumed that was the reason she ran out," he added. "Because he was out there."

Lady Laetitia whimpered at the sound of this, and I found myself torn between reluctant sympathy—it must be terrible to be so gone over a man that you'll whimper when he doesn't want you—and irritation, because title and money aside, this particular man really wasn't worth this level of devotion.

Although he heard it and it made his shoulders twitch, so at least that was something.

"St George?" Tom prodded. "Do you want to change your story?"

Crispin shook his head. "It happened the way I said. I smoked a fag and came back inside. I didn't see anyone except Peckham and the butler. They were still in the parlor when I walked past."

"I didn't see him," Peckham said, "but that doesn't mean it didn't happen."

"Does it matter?" I wanted to know. "We know he came upstairs twenty minutes after Christopher and Francis. Everyone came upstairs eventually. Even Johanna. She wasn't killed in the garden."

"How do you know?" someone asked. It wasn't Tom, and none of the Astleys would have asked such a stupid question. Certainly not Christopher, who had seen the body along with me.

My money was on Marsden, who was rather prone to asking stupid questions.

"Because," I said, "no one would strangle a woman in the garden and then take the trouble to carry her body into the house and up the stairs to the Dowager's Chamber. Certainly not with everyone else still awake and walking around. It would be much easier just to leave the body on the grass if it happened that way."

"He might do it if he was the only one who had gone into the garden, and we all knew it," Marsden said. It was definitely Marsden this time, and he accompanied the statement with a cold look at Crispin.

Payback for making Marsden's sister cry, I guessed.

Unless Marsden had killed Johanna and was trying to shove suspicion onto someone else, of course.

Crispin looked at Marsden for a moment, and then he said, "Much as it pains me, I have to agree with Darling. It would have been stupid to carry the body inside when I could have left it in the garden."

"Maybe you're stupid," Marsden said belligerently, and caused Crispin's lip to twitch with amusement.

"Much as it pains *me* to say it," I answered, "he's really not."

Crispin inclined his head. "Thank you, Darling."

I flicked a glance at him. "Don't mention it. I think we should probably all just leave the detecting to the professionals. Tom—Detective Sergeant Gardiner—and his colleagues will figure out who killed Johanna. We'd just get in the way."

It was Tom's turn to twitch with suppressed laughter. He didn't know me well, but he knew well enough that I had spent quite a lot of time two weekends ago thinking about who might have killed the late duke and his valet. Staying out of the way isn't really my forte.

However—

"Thank you, Miss Darling," he told me, keeping a mostly

straight face. "On that note, I think I have the general timeline of the evening straight. It's time for individual interviews. Is there another room I could use for those, Mr. Peckham?"

"There's the parlor," Gilbert said, but Tom shook his head.

"Since you spent the evening in there, I think it's best if we leave that room undisturbed until I've had a chance to look at it."

"The library?" Constance suggested diffidently.

Tom nodded. "Thank you, Miss Peckham. Miss Darling, Kit, if you'll come with me? The rest of you stay here with Collins."

From the glances into the recesses of the room, it was quite clear that several people had forgotten the existence of Constable Collins and his notebook. I wondered how long it would take them to forget it again once we'd walked out.

"WHERE?" Tom asked when we were outside in the reception room. I indicated the door to the library, and we headed that way.

I'd been inside the library yesterday, looking to see whether there was anything of interest I hadn't read. There'd been a copy of *The Moonstone*, and several early novels by P.G. Wodehouse, but no recent detective fiction. Neither Gilbert nor Constance had struck me as big readers, nor had Lady Peckham herself. And there was nothing at all in the Dutch language, so if Johanna had had books in her native tongue, she must have kept them in her bed chamber.

We settled around the library table in the middle of the room, with Christopher and me on one side and Tom on the other. He pulled out a notebook and pencil of his own, that looked exactly like the ones Collins had been using in the dining room. They must be standard issue in the police forces.

"Before I start asking questions," Tom began, "is there anything you want to tell me that you didn't feel comfortable mentioning in front of the others?"

"There's Marsden," Christopher said.

"Lord Geoffrey? What about him?"

"Last night, during the dancing, he made a nuisance of himself with Pippa." Christopher slanted a look my way. "He touched her, crowded her into a corner of the sofa. Crispin had to rescue her."

Tom looked surprised. "St George did?"

"He was the one whose attention I could get," I said. "Francis was dancing with Constance, and seemed quite distracted..."

Tom nodded. "They appear quite taken with one another."

"—and Christopher was dancing with Lady Laetitia."

Tom turned the look on Christopher, who flushed.

"St George was dancing with Johanna, but he was facing me, so he noticed that something wasn't right. He came over and asked me to dance. Marsden ended up inviting Johanna to accompany him around the floor instead."

"And did she say yes?"

"She said she'd be delighted, although she didn't look it."

And after that, for the next few minutes, I had been preoccupied enough with Crispin that I hadn't really noticed what anyone else was doing. Keeping up with him verbally takes such effort that it doesn't leave much room for worrying about anything else. But I did think I had seen glimpses of Johanna and Marsden revolving slowly around us as the music played.

"Then what happened?" Tom asked.

"Crispin went outside for a cigarette and some peace and quiet."

"Again?"

"This was almost two hours before the end of the party.

And Laetitia and Johanna had taken turns monopolizing him all night. He had been dancing nonstop since supper."

Tom didn't say anything, and I added, "As soon as they noticed that he'd escaped, they ran after him, anyway, so he didn't get much time to himself. I went over to talk to Christopher, and then Crispin showed up again just a few minutes later and was his usual sarcastic self."

"And that's when Kit walked you upstairs?"

I nodded. "I was a bit rattled, I suppose, and I also didn't want to give Lord Geoffrey another chance to come at me."

"I would have stayed with you—" Christopher began, but I shook my head.

"It would have been like before, and you know it. As soon as Laetitia and Johanna discovered that you could dance, you were almost as popular as Crispin."

Tom hid a smile at that.

"They would have kept you busy," I added, "and Francis would have stayed with Constance, and Peckham would have stayed by the gramophone, and I would have had to deal with Marsden by myself. So I went upstairs and to bed instead. Christopher locked me in and gave Constance the key, that way Marsden wouldn't have been able to come inside my room even if he'd wanted to."

"And did he want to?" Tom asked.

I shook my head. "Not as far as I know. I think he stayed downstairs—"

Christopher nodded.

"—and nobody else tried to enter my room until Constance came up an hour and a half later."

"And you walked her up?" Tom asked, with a glance at Christopher, who nodded.

"Francis and I did. I wanted to go to bed anyway. Both the

ladies were getting agitated, and I wanted to get away before the screaming started."

"Then you weren't there for the big disagreement?"

Christopher shook his head. "I didn't even hear it begin. The first I knew of it was when I heard one of the doors downstairs close with a slam, and then someone screamed, 'Come back here, you coward!'"

Oh, really? Was that the shriek I hadn't been able to make out while in the loo?

Tom's lips twitched. "No joke?"

"Not at all. I went to the window, and saw my cousin stalk away across the lawn. I don't know which of the ladies screamed at him, though."

"I thought they were arguing with each other," I said, with an indelicate snort.

Christopher glanced at me. "I'm sure they did that, too. But someone probably thought it would be a clever idea to challenge him to make a choice between them, and that wouldn't have gone over well."

Clearly not.

"But Lady Laetitia was in the past, surely," Tom said, "and Johanna was the new blood."

"I got the impression that Lady Laetitia didn't want to be in the past," I told him. "When she and her brother arrived yesterday, she greeted St George like she thought she had a current claim on him."

"Or at least like she wanted the rest of us to think she did," Christopher added.

I glanced at him. "Just Johanna, surely?" Why would she care what the rest of us thought?

"Johanna and you," Christopher said. "I doubt she considered Constance to be proper competition."

"But she thought I was? Who would consider *me* as competition for St George's title and fortune?"

"Anyone who's heard him call you Darling, I imagine," Christopher said.

I shook my head. "Don't be ridiculous, Christopher. It's my name."

In a manner of speaking, anyway. What it is, is an Anglicization of my German surname of Schatz, since 1914 wasn't a good time to arrive in England with a German surname.

"Besides," I added, "surely everyone can tell that he just uses it because he knows it irritates me."

"I wouldn't be so sure," Christopher answered. "And you must know that you're not helping your case when you behave as you did on that particular occasion."

"What do you mean? How did I behave?"

Tom looked interested in the answer, too. I most definitely was, because as far as I could recall, I had behaved in a perfectly rational manner.

"You stalked across the floor to him, snatched his handkerchief out of his pocket, and used it to wipe her lipstick off his mouth."

"I did not!"

"Did so," Christopher said.

I eyed him, since there was some truth to what he said. He had the movements right, if not the implications of them. "I may have crossed the floor and reminded him that he had a pocket square on his person and lipstick on his face. I won't say I didn't. I may even have taken said pocket square out of his pocket and used it on him. I did not, however, do it in what you make sound like a very possessive manner. I do not feel possessive towards St George."

Christopher arched his brows.

"I don't! What she did was inappropriate. Completely and

utterly appalling. To subject us to it—to subject *him* to it!—was inexcusable, especially in front of us all. She didn't even wait for permission, just waded right in! What if he didn't want to kiss her? Just because he's a man doesn't mean that kind of thing is acceptable! And aside from that, he looked ridiculous."

"I'm not arguing," Christopher answered. "I'm simply pointing out that someone who doesn't know you well could misconstrue something like that as jealousy on your part."

"Eurgh!"

"And then, when he abandoned Johanna in the middle of the dance floor to remove you from Marsden—"

"He didn't abandon her," I said. She hadn't allowed him to.

"He stopped dancing with her to approach you. Specifically, to take you away from what might look like a romantic tête-à-tête with Marsden in the corner of the sofa..."

"Romantic?" My voice rose, into a range only decipherable by bats. "You call what happened to me *romantic?*"

"Naturally I don't," Christopher said. "But for someone watching, that could also be construed as an attachment, this time on Crispin's part."

"Don't be ridiculous." It struck me that I had used that particular word quite a lot in this conversation, but really, what other word would be as apt? "That's ludicrous, Christopher. St George doesn't like me any better than I like him, and you know it. The only reason he stopped dancing with Johanna—who was still clinging to him like a vine when he asked me to dance, by the way—was because I managed to catch his eye while he was dancing with her. If I hadn't, he wouldn't even have noticed what was going on."

Christopher muttered something. It might have sounded like, "Don't be too sure," or perhaps, "That's what *you* think," but since it couldn't possibly have been either, I pretended I hadn't heard it.

"At any rate," I told Tom, "they fought over him all evening. If Laetitia thought their affair was in the past, she showed no signs of it."

"But neither of you saw either of them after you left the parlor last night?"

Christopher and I both shook our heads. I did it with a smidgeon of guilt, because I liked Tom, and I knew I was helping Crispin lie to Scotland Yard. I did it nonetheless.

Tom already knew that Johanna had run into the garden after Crispin last night. Whether they'd kissed or not didn't really make a difference. Did it? She hadn't been murdered until later. And Crispin might just have wanted to keep the encounter from Laetitia while we were all sitting around the dining room table. Once they were in the library alone, he might tell Tom all about it.

And if he didn't, I could always tell Tom about it myself later.

"I know you already told me about finding Miss de Vos's body," Tom said, "but go through that again, for the record."

We went through it again, while Tom asked questions we mostly couldn't answer, since neither of us had really noticed much but the fact that Johanna was dead.

"Just go look at her yourself," I told him eventually. "She'll look exactly the same as she did when we saw her. We didn't touch anything. It was clear from the start that there was nothing we could do for her. So we locked the door and gave Dawson the key,. No one will have been in the room since then."

Tom nodded. "Anything else you think I ought to know?"

Christopher shook his head.

"I heard someone out on the landing in the middle of the night," I said. "It was after Constance came up to bed. I was restless, and woke up a few times. Once, it was because I heard steps outside the door. No one touched the knob or tried to get inside. But I heard someone walk past the door and hesitate, then continue. And the sound of a door closing somewhere else on the landing."

"You didn't get up to see who it was?"

"I didn't think it was any of my business if St George was creeping around going to or coming from an assignation," I said. "And just in case it was Lord Geoffrey, I didn't want to come face to face with him in the darkness outside my room."

"Any idea of the time?"

"After two but before dawn. I had fallen asleep again since Constance woke me. I don't think I can be more specific than that."

"I'll just have to figure out who might have been out of bed at that hour," Tom said and made a note. "Anything else?"

I couldn't think of anything else. Not that I was willing to share, anyway. "I don't suppose you can tell us anything about what happened to Lady Peckham?"

"Right now," Tom said, "you know as much as I do. The others may have discovered something since I left, but as soon as we learned who she was and that you were here, I volunteered to come down ahead of the others and get started."

"You think one of us did it."

Or perhaps not one of us, specifically. Neither Christopher nor I had any reason to want Lady Peckham out of the way. But one of the people who lived in this house.

"I don't think anyone still left at Sutherland Hall would have had a motive for wanting her dead," Tom said. "Not your parents, certainly. Unless you think your Uncle Harold is emulating Doctor Crippin and doing away with his wives and prospective wives all of a sudden?"

Christopher shook his head. So did I.

"It's logical to look at the people who knew her best. The

medicine bottle was one of her own. The Veronal might have been added at Sutherland Hall, or it could have been done here. It depends on the last time she took a dose of it. For all we know, the Veronal could have been in the bottle for weeks. Tell me about Lady Peckham's relationship to her children."

I looked at Christopher. He looked at me.

"We don't know them well—" I began.

"You went to school with Miss Peckham, didn't you?"

"Five years at Godolphin in Salisbury," I confirmed. "The same five years that Christopher and Crispin were at Eton."

Where Tom had also been, although it had been his last year when it was their first. He was twenty-seven or so now, the same age as my late cousin Robert.

"And since?"

"I haven't really seen her since. We weren't close. She was very shy and retiring, and I—"

"Wasn't," Christopher said with a grin.

Well, no. "And besides," I told Tom, "it's always been Christopher and me against the world, you know? Once we left school, we started spending all of our time together. There wasn't really room for anyone else."

Including Crispin, who had no doubt felt the loss and who was, also no doubt, still holding it against me.

"But Constance came to the funerals?"

"Lady Peckham came to the funerals," I corrected, "and brought her family. She had been a close friend of Aunt Charlotte's when they were younger, Constance told me. And with Uncle Harold a widower, and Crispin eligible, and the other two Astleys there, it must have seemed like a golden opportunity to do some matchmaking."

"She was trying to get her daughter and her ward married off?"

"And herself," Christopher said, "unless she stayed behind to console Uncle Harold out of the goodness of her heart."

His tone was cynical.

"Certainly not," I said. "With the way she neglected Constance in favor of Johanna, I didn't get the impression that she had much of a heart to speak of. And it seemed very much like she was eyeing Uncle Harold for herself."

"Miss de Vos for St George, then?" Tom guessed.

"I'm sure she would have been thrilled had either Constance or Johanna managed to snag Crispin," Christopher said, "but Constance never had a chance. Not only is she not remotely his type, but Johanna made a dead set at Crispin the moment she laid eyes on him."

"How serious do you think she was?"

"Oh," Christopher said, "I'd say she was quite serious. So was her mother."

I nodded. "Constance told me that her mother had big plans for all three of her children. Or her son and daughter and her ward. She paraded Johanna in front of both Crispin and his father like she was showing a Best Champion Greyhound at Crufts."

Christopher smothered a laugh. "Or a collector's item they could have for the right price."

Tom arched a brow. "The right price being the Sutherland title?"

Christopher and I both nodded.

"I understand she was quite lovely," Tom said.

Christopher merely shrugged, since she obviously hadn't been his type. I said, "She was stunning. Quite as beautiful as Lady Laetitia. Maybe even a bit more so. Fair, with golden hair and big, blue eyes."

"And St George seemed to like her?"

"What's not to like?" Christopher wanted to know, rhetorically, and I nodded.

"She went after him like a fox after a rabbit. Flat out. And he's fairly susceptible to beautiful women, anyway. She was a few years older, maybe twenty-four or -five, and there were times she had him looking as dazzled as a schoolboy."

"And Lady Peckham had no problems with that?"

"She seemed thrilled," I said, with a glance at Christopher. He nodded.

"What about Francis and Miss Peckham? Was that a problem?"

"I'm not even sure Lady Peckham noticed anything going on," I said honestly. "Compared to Johanna, I got the impression she paid Constance very little mind."

"Would she have objected?"

Christopher and I exchanged another look. "I can't imagine why," Christopher said. "We're not in the direct line, nor are we exceedingly wealthy, but Francis is third in line for the title, after Crispin and Dad, and we're not poor. I don't see why Lady Peckham would have minded a union between Francis and Constance."

"Francis's drug use isn't widely known..." I began, since Lady Peckham might have objected to that, had she known about it. And then I stopped when Tom winced. "What is it?"

"Francis had a large bottle of Veronal in his room two weeks ago, when we did our search for Grimsby's notebook pages. That was where Lady Charlotte got the sleeping draught that killed her."

I nodded. So did Christopher. "But Francis had no reason to want to get rid of Constance's mother," he said.

"Not even if she objected to his courting her daughter?"

"Not after three days' acquaintance," I said. "He seems rather smitten with her, but it's only been three days. And as I said, I'm not sure Lady Peckham even noticed. She was so busy watching Johanna vamp Crispin and Uncle Harold."

Tom nodded. "It seems far-fetched, but I have to ask."

"Of course. But I don't think Francis had anything to do with it. For that matter, I haven't noticed him indulging in anything but alcohol so far this trip. I think perhaps Aunt Charlotte's death scared him off the Veronal, at least for the time being."

"If I remember correctly from two weeks ago," Tom said, "your cousin knew about Francis's drug use?"

"Crispin, you mean?" Not my cousin, but yes, he was the one who had told me about it. "He had no reason to want to do away with Lady Peckham, either. She was thrilled about him and Johanna."

"If he felt like he was being pushed into it?"

"He didn't," I said, since he'd given me the impression that he was quite happy to be vamped. "But even if he did, all he would have had to do was say no. They couldn't force him."

"Then let's leave it here," Tom said, "and move on."

TWELVE

MOVING on meant sending Christopher and me back to the dining room with the directive to dispatch Francis to see him. This we did, and I took Francis's place next to Constance, who was still trying to cope with the sudden news of her mother's demise.

"I can't believe she's gone," she said, certainly not for the first time, because Lady Laetitia rolled her eyes.

"Give it a rest, Constance. We all know that you and your mother were on bad terms the past few years."

"We were not on bad terms!" Constance protested. "I loved my mother!"

"But you didn't like the way she fawned over Johanna."

Constance flushed. "Of course I didn't. Would you have?"

Laetitia didn't answer, which certainly meant that no, she wouldn't, and furthermore, she hadn't liked the way Johanna had fawned over Crispin, either.

"But I loved her," Constance insisted. "I certainly wouldn't have wanted her dead!"

"You might have wanted Johanna dead, though."

Constance stared at her for a moment, mouth open and working, before she closed it again, apparently unable to find anything to say.

"Constance didn't leave our room last night," I said. "So whether she wanted Johanna dead or not—and I wouldn't have blamed her, to be honest; Johanna was a cow—Constance didn't have the opportunity to kill her. When she came upstairs, Johanna was still alive. Downstairs. Arguing with you —" I pointed at Lady Laetitia, "over him." I indicated Crispin. "And while we're on the subject of cows—"

"Now, now, Darling," Crispin interjected. His face was solemn, but I could hear the undertone of laughter in his voice.

I flicked a glance at him. "Sod off, St George. You know as well as I do that it was a terrible thing to say to someone who has just lost her mother."

Crispin had nothing to say in response to that, so yes, he absolutely knew it.

"And if we're going to discuss people who would have wanted Johanna out of the way," I continued, turning back to Laetitia, "I'd say you—"

"Now listen here," Marsden began.

I ignored him in favor of his sister. "You were the only one of us who had a room to yourself. You could come and go as you pleased. All the rest of us shared with someone, who would have heard us leave and come back in the middle of the night. You had the best opportunity to kill her, and probably the best motive for wanting her dead."

Laetitia gaped at me. "Well, I never..."

"If you don't like someone accusing you," I told her, "then you shouldn't accuse anyone else."

Silence reigned after that. Constance made an effort to get her tears under control, while Gilbert just looked wan and pale on the other side of the table. Whatever Lady Peckham had been to the Marsdens—aunt? Second cousin?—neither of them seemed affected by her death, or even by that of Johanna.

Francis came back fairly quickly. He had been so preoccupied with Constance last night that he probably hadn't noticed much of what was going on with the rest of us, and so he didn't know anything that could help Tom. As for his having had anything to do with Lady Peckham's demise, the idea was ludicrous, although I imagined Tom had probably brought up the question of Francis's Veronal. Whatever the answer had been, Francis didn't look discomfited by it. He took my place next to Constance, and I moved to sit beside Christopher while Francis informed his cousin that his presence was requested in the library next.

Crispin looked resigned but not worried when he got to his feet and headed out.

The door shut behind him. A moment passed, and then Gilbert Peckham and Geoffrey Marsden exchanged a glance. "It has to be him," Marsden said, "don't you think?"

Laetitia sucked in a breath. Peckham nodded, eyeing Crispin's nearest and dearest sitting on the other side of the table as if assessing us.

"I beg your pardon?" I said, while Francis began, "Listen, you—"

"Did you just accuse my cousin of murder?" Christopher wanted to know.

Peckham looked apologetic. "He's the one with the motive and opportunity, wouldn't you say? The two of you—" meaning Christopher and Francis, "went up to bed together. He stayed behind. And I know he said he didn't see her, but they were both outside in the garden. He could have talked to Johanna and arranged an assignation in my mother's room later."

He could have. Of course he could. I'd seen them together,

and the kiss could absolutely have culminated in an agreement to rendezvous in the Dowager's Chamber once everyone else was in bed.

"He might even have walked in with her," Peckham added. "He says he saw me in the parlor, but I didn't see him. For all I know, Johanna was with him."

I supposed she might have been. If no one had seen Crispin come in and go upstairs, he could have been with anyone.

Or alone, as he claimed.

And then Peckham drove the knife home with a final question. "Who else would she have let into her bedroom last night, but the man she wanted to marry?"

There was a moment of silence while I—while we all—pondered that extremely salient point.

"I don't believe it," Francis said eventually.

I shook my head. "Nor do I. And besides, if there was truly only twenty minutes between the time Christopher and Francis went upstairs, and when Crispin came into the room they shared, there was no time for him to kill anyone."

You'll surely have gathered by now that I don't have a terribly high opinion of St George. There isn't much I wouldn't believe him capable of. But to strangle a woman in cold blood, a woman he had just been kissing, and then to walk from where he had killed her directly into his bedroom, where two of the people who knew him best in the world were waiting, and not give away an inkling of what he had done? No, I couldn't talk myself into believing him capable of that.

Besides, the kiss in the garden hadn't looked as if it would turn to violence in the blink of an eye.

"Perhaps the assignation was for later," Marsden suggested, with a sideways look at his sister. "Perhaps he went upstairs, waited for you both to fall asleep, and then went across the landing to Lady Marsden's room, where he killed Johanna."

"You can't be serious, Geoffrey," Laetitia said.

I nodded, even as it galled me to have to agree with her. "Christopher would have heard him leave. He's a light sleeper."

"You would know," Marsden said, which I decided not to dignify with an answer, mostly because I didn't want to descend to his level.

Christopher, however, narrowed his eyes. "What's that supposed to mean?"

Marsden looked at him down his nose. "You and Miss Darling share a flat, I thought?"

"Oh," Christopher said. "Yes. We do."

Marsden nodded. "There you have it."

There was nothing much one could say to that, either. I could hear the insinuation, of course, and so could Christopher—so could anyone present—but anything I might say would only make Marsden think worse of both of us.

"At any rate," I said, "there are people here with better motives and opportunities for murder than St George."

I didn't eye Lady Laetitia when I said it, but I didn't have to. She tossed her neck. "I had no reason to kill her, you daft cow. I'm Lady Laetitia Marsden. She was a penniless refugee from the Continent with no title and no money. Do you really suppose he'd choose her over me?"

"He'd already had you," I said, stung a little in spite of myself. Not that I wanted St George, but *I* was a penniless refugee from the Continent too, and at some point I expected I would want someone to want me, even if it wasn't someone of St George's social standing. "Maybe he just wasn't impressed."

Her eyes narrowed. "I suppose you think you could do better?"

Me? I started laughing. "Dear me, no. I have no interest in St George. You're welcome to him. I told Johanna the same."

"Kind of you, Darling," Crispin drawled from behind me,

because of course he came back into the dining room just at this moment, "but you do know that I'm not actually yours to dispose of, don't you?"

"Of course I know," I said. "Good Lord, St George, it's not as if I've deluded myself into thinking that your need to call me by my last name is actually a cover for any fonder feelings on your part. I'm not stupid, you know."

"Of course not," Crispin said and sat down. "Very well, then. Your turn, Marsden."

Lord Geoffrey pushed to his feet and ambled out.

"I see you're still walking around," Peckham told Crispin, who gave him a look down the length of his nose.

"As opposed to being carted off in handcuffs, I suppose?"

"He and Lord Geoffrey have decided you're guilty of Johanna's murder," I told him.

He shot me a look. "Of course they have. I suppose they think I did it in the five minutes between the time I went upstairs and the time I went into the bedroom where Kit and Francis were?"

"Something like that," I said.

He nodded. "Very good. I'll just wait to be arrested, then."

He kicked back in his chair, rested one ankle on the other knee and folded his hands across his stomach, with every appearance of being at his ease.

Marsden's interview didn't take long, and then it was Laetitia's turn. By now, the conversation in the dining room was down to single syllables and long drawn out silences between most of us, and private murmurs between Constance and Francis.

Laetitia looked pale and drawn as she made her way back, and she avoided looking at Crispin. I don't think he cared, because he wasn't looking at her either, just kept his eyes on the tulips.

"Your turn, Constance," Laetitia said, and took her seat. Constance removed her hand from Francis's with the air of someone going to the gallows.

"Don't worry," I told her, surmising that this would be her first interview with a representative of Scotland Yard. "Tom is perfectly lovely."

Marsden sneered. "First name basis?"

"Friend of the family," Crispin said without looking up. "We all knew him at Eton. Close friends with my cousin Robert."

"And where is Robert?" Marsden made a point of looking around the table.

"Somewhere in Belgium," Crispin said. "He went over in 1917 and didn't come back."

His eyes, when they flicked up and fastened on Marsden across the table, were like chips of ice. I didn't blame Marsden at all for flinching.

"My condolences," he muttered.

"Thank you," Francis said, while Crispin said nothing, just lowered his gaze to the flower arrangement again.

By that point, Constance had disappeared through the door into the reception room and we fell back into silence. By now, none of us had anything to say to anyone else. Or rather, I would have liked a conversation with Crispin, but not with an audience, and I could have spoken to either Christopher and Francis, but I didn't really want to do that while Marsden and Laetitia could hear what I was saying, either. I imagined the others probably felt the same.

So we sat in silence and waited to be dismissed. Constance came back and nodded to her brother. He went out while she sat back down beside Francis.

At the end of the interview with Gilbert, Tom accompanied him back into the dining room. "The police have finished searching your rooms—"

Laetitia opened her mouth in shock, so she must not have realized that that was going on while we were sitting here. Tom ignored her, and so did everyone else.

"—and you're free to go about your business, but no one is to leave the Dower House without permission. I'm afraid I'm going to have to ask those of you who are visiting to stay on until we have a better idea of what's going on."

Marsden grimaced. Peckham looked wooden. The rest of us nodded, having been through this at Sutherland Hall just a few weeks ago.

"Collins and I shall start to process the crime scene."

He nodded to the young constable, surely no older than Christopher or Crispin, who tucked away his notebook and pencil and got to his feet. I had forgotten he was there again, and I daresay I wasn't the only one.

The two of them left the dining room, and left the rest of us to stare blankly at one another.

"Anyone for lunch?" Peckham wanted to know.

No one took him up on the offer.

"Cocktails in the dining room at five, then. Or tea for those who want it."

He walked out, perhaps to deal with his mother's passing in private, or perhaps to see if he could talk Tom into letting him see Johanna. I glanced at Constance. Francis had her by the hand and was murmuring things to her bent head. She looked like she was in good hands, so I turned to Crispin and tucked a hand through his arm.

"Walk in the garden with me."

It wasn't a request, and I'm sure he could hear it, because all he did was nod.

Everyone in the family knows that I don't seek out St

George's company for anything but the most compelling of reasons. As a result, Christopher and even Francis looked at me as if I'd grown a second head.

"You're welcome to accompany us," I told them both. "We're not planning to do anything illicit."

Crispin murmured something, but I decided I didn't care to know what it was, so I didn't ask him to repeat it.

Francis declined in favor of staying with Constance, but Christopher followed behind us when I tugged Crispin out of the dining room, across the reception room, and out the front door.

"What's going on?" Christopher asked when we were down the steps and far enough away from the house that no one could overhear.

I glanced at him over my shoulder. "I want to know why your cousin was lying to Tom earlier."

"I didn't lie to Tom," Crispin said, and twitched his arm out of my grasp.

I scowled at him. "You most certainly did. You saw Johanna in the garden after you went outside last night, and you denied it."

He flushed. "Are you a witch, Darling? How could you possibly know that?"

"I saw you through the window," I said.

"Your room is on the front of the house!"

"The lavatory window, if you must know. It overlooks the back garden. I saw you storm out of the parlor and onto the lawn—"

Christopher nodded, since he had seen the same thing. "Which of them called you a coward as you ran away?" he wanted to know, his voice uneven with laughter. Crispin shot him a look of concentrated dislike, but didn't volunteer a name.

"And then, a minute later," I continued, "I saw Johanna

come running out and fling herself at you. It looked quite romantic."

He looked at me down his nose. "Been reading Austen, have you, Darling?"

"Hull," I said, more to shock him than for any other reason. While *The Sheikh* had been a titillating read when I was sixteen, these days I much prefer a good detective novel.

"That's appalling."

I shrugged. "My reading habits are none of your concern, St George. Nor are your amatory habits any of mine. Except Johanna's dead, and you lied about it."

"I had nothing to do with her being dead!"

"You had something to do with her in the garden," I said, "and instead of admitting it, you said, several times, that you didn't see her after you left the parlor."

"Would you admit to a snuggle with a girl who ended up dead, Darling?"

"I wouldn't admit to a snuggle with any girl, but that's beside the point. You're prevaricating, St George. You were there, she was there, and you won't admit it."

We were coming upon the low stone wall where he'd stood last night, at the edge of the garden, and I took a seat on it and crossed my ankles. Christopher sat down next to me, and Crispin looked around.

"This is where you were standing last night," I told him. "And up there—" I pointed, "is the lavatory window. I had quite a good view, as you can see. It was dark, of course. But the moon was out. A quarter moon, admittedly. Not full. But it was clear..."

"Fine!" He slashed a hand through the air. It came nowhere near me, of course. He wasn't actually trying to strike me, just make me stop talking. "Good Lord, Darling, do you ever shut up?"

"Rarely," I said.

He took a breath. In through the nose, slowly. Out through the mouth, equally slowly. Then he pulled out his cigarette case and offered it around. Christopher and I both took one—we might as well, if they were on offer—and Crispin did, too, before he tucked the case back inside his jacket pocket. After everyone's fag was lit, he took in a mouthful of smoke and blew it out again before he said, "What is it you want me to say, Darling? You heard about what happened in the parlor."

"Not in the detail I would have liked," I said, "but yes. Enough to get the general idea."

"One of them called you a coward," Christopher added. He had one knee draped elegantly over the other with his elbow planted on it and the cigarette in his hand. "I assume it was Lady Laetitia, if Johanna was the one who ran after you. Is it safe to assume that one or the other wanted you to declare yourself, and you refused?"

Crispin glanced at him and then at me. "I'm not discussing this. Not in front of her."

"Don't mind me," I told him. "I already don't think much of you, St George. Whatever happened, I don't imagine it's going to make me think less."

He bared his teeth. "I don't care what you think of me, Darling. But I'm not baring my soul in front of someone who'll only get a good laugh out of it."

"I wasn't aware you had a soul," I said.

"Yes, you were. You asked me yesterday whether it was intact. You must have assumed there was one there to begin with."

I sighed. "Fine. If I promise I won't laugh at you, will you tell us what happened?"

"No," Crispin said. "There is nothing you can offer me that would make me risk showing feelings in front of you."

"I'm not that bad," I protested. "But fine. How about this? You tell us, and I won't tell Tom you lied to him."

He arched a brow. "Blackmail."

I shrugged. Christopher chuckled. "You might as well get it out, old chap. You know how she gets."

"Oh, I know exactly how she gets," Crispin said. "Fine, then. Johanna came after me into the garden to tell me she loved me."

He stopped. I waited, but when he didn't say anything else I arched my brows. "That's all?"

"What do you mean, all?" He threw his hands up. "Yes, that's all! Do you think women regularly throw themselves in my arms and declare their undying love?"

In a word, yes. "With as many women as you have on your string, I assumed it happened rather a lot."

"No," Crispin said. "That's the point. I don't want what I do to be about love. I want—"

He stopped, right before he might have said something interesting.

"Don't mind me," I invited. "Do go on."

He growled. "You're awful, Darling. You're enjoying this, aren't you?"

"Of course I am. What's not to enjoy?"

He didn't answer, and I added, "Come now, St George. It can't be the first time some woman has told you she loves you."

"Believe it or not, Darling, it happens less frequently than you'd think. Mainly because I make very sure whatever I do won't descend to that level."

He sucked on his cigarette, hard enough that his cheeks appeared hollow. I had ignored mine in favor of talking to him, and it had mostly burned away already. I dragged the tip of it across the stone wall to put it out, and tossed it outside the garden wall where I could forgot about it.

"What happened with Johanna?" Christopher wanted to know. "If it normally doesn't descend—or ascend—to that level?"

Crispin glanced at him. "She wanted to get married, what else?"

"And you don't?"

"I didn't want to marry *her*," Crispin said. "I'd get married if my father would let me marry who I want to marry. Since he won't, no, I don't want to get married."

"I thought you seemed rather taken with Johanna," I told him, swinging my feet. "You certainly thought she was beautiful."

"Anyone would think she was beautiful," Crispin said. "The world is full of beautiful women. That doesn't mean I want to marry them. Not when I knew she would have professed the same feelings to any man with a title and fortune."

"She didn't mean it?"

He snorted. "Of course she didn't mean it, Darling. It had been two and a half days. Nobody falls in love in two and a half days."

"Francis seemed to," I said.

He shook his head. "Francis is delighted that someone prefers him to me. Constance is delighted that someone noticed her instead of Johanna. They're not in love. Not yet, anyway."

"That's appallingly cynical," I told him, while Christopher choked on a laugh. "You should be happy for your cousin. And also, could you possibly be any more conceited? *I* prefer Francis to you, for your information."

He rolled his eyes. "I'm well aware of it, Darling. The only people who prefer me are the ones who want the Sutherland title and fortune."

There was a moment of silence after that rather bald statement. I didn't know quite what to say, because I had told him that, or something similar, rather a lot of times over the years. I did hate to hear the words thrown back at me, though. It was one thing for me to say it, particularly in the midst of a quarrel, but quite another for him to repeat it, especially when it sounded as if he actually believed it. Up until this moment, I hadn't realized he did.

"I'm sure that's not true," I said.

He smirked. "Guilty conscience, Darling?"

It was frankly appalling how well he could read me. "Not at all," I said robustly. "We both know you have other things to recommend you than the family title and the family money. Besides, aren't you waiting for this girl your father won't let you have. Or...?"

"No, Darling. It wasn't Johanna. She wouldn't have been any more acceptable to Father than—"

He caught himself just in time, and bit back what I assumed would have been the girl's name. I arched my brows in invitation, but he didn't continue.

"And it isn't Laetitia, either," he added after a few seconds. "Father would have been delighted to hand me over to her, I'm sure. She has a title and a fortune of her own, and if it isn't quite up to the Sutherland standard, it's nothing to sneeze at."

"Well," I told him, "after this weekend, I think the Marsdens might think twice before they approve of giving Lady Laetitia to you."

"I'd say so," Christopher agreed. "When you brought up that girl with the baby earlier—always the girl with the baby, Pippa!—Peckham looked ready to vomit, and Marsden wasn't much better."

"Serves him right," I said. "If he hasn't got some woman with child himself already, it hasn't been for lack of trying. Him and his wandering hands."

I turned back to Crispin. "At any rate, St George, you're well out of it. Lady Laetitia is a cow, and you'd spend your life cleaning up her brother's indiscretions, insofar as they could be cleaned up. And as far as Johanna goes..."

He looked resigned. "What about her?"

"She came into the garden to tell you that she loved you. She softened you up by kissing you, and then she angled for a marriage proposal. I assume, when you didn't offer one, she brought up the possibility of marriage herself?"

He nodded. "It got ugly for a minute or two. She cried, and then she begged," he winced, "and when that didn't work, she started to threaten."

"Threaten what?"

"To lie," Crispin said, "and say that I had ruined her so I'd be forced to marry her."

"Ruined her? She'd say you'd taken her to bed, do you mean? Had you?"

They both stared at me. "Pippa!" Christopher exclaimed, shocked that I'd asked, while Crispin merely looked appalled, whether about the question or the idea.

"No, Darling. I'm not in the habit of bedding women at Sutherland Hall. Certainly not on the evening before my mother's funeral. I keep my flirtations, when I have them, in Town."

"Is that what you call them? Flirtations?"

He gave me a crushing look. "I told Johanna to do her worst, and then I left her in the garden and went inside. I didn't see her again. I certainly didn't kill her. I didn't want her dead. I just didn't want to marry her."

His voice finally took on some emotion, and he added, "Good Lord, Darling, don't you know me better than that?"

"I didn't think you'd strangled her," I said. "I just wanted to know what happened."

He nodded. "Well, now you do. May I go?"

I nodded. And sat next to Christopher on the wall and watched as he stalked away around the corner of the house. A moment later we heard, faintly, the slam of the front door.

THIRTEEN

"SOMETIMES I WONDER ABOUT YOU, PIPPA," Christopher told me.

I took my eyes off the spot where Crispin had disappeared and turned back to him. "What do you mean?"

He gestured to the house, and by extension, to his cousin. "You've known him more than half your life. You've known him as long as you've known me. And you made a good case, last month, for why and how he might have killed Grandfather and Grimsby. I didn't really think he had, but it all made sense, at least. But this? How could you possibly think my cousin could have strangled a young woman who never did him any harm? Don't you know that he isn't like that?"

"Of course I know that," I said, since I had come to the same conclusion myself earlier. "I just wanted to know what happened. And to rub his nose in it, I suppose. You know St George and I have never got along."

"You get along just fine in your own way," Christopher said severely. "You call it not getting along because all you do is bicker, but in truth, the two of you get on like a house on fire."

"Is that supposed to be a good thing?"

He rolled his eyes, and looked disconcertingly like his cousin for a second. "You enjoy the bickering. If he stopped twitting you, you'd miss it."

"I would not," I said, offended. "I would like nothing better than for St George to leave me alone. I can't believe you're defending him, Christopher."

"He lost his mother and grandfather less than two weeks ago," Christopher said. "Today he lost Johanna. And no, he mayn't have been serious about her, but that's still a lot of death. He's not without feelings, you know. People think I'm the sensitive one..."

Because he comes across as softer and more open and less abrasive than his cousin. I nodded.

"—but Crispin developed that sharp tongue for a reason." He slanted me a look. "I had Mum, Dad, Francis, Robert, and you. Who did he have?"

He'd had Uncle Harold, who had never seemed to care much, and Aunt Charlotte, who'd cared too much, and Christopher, until I took him away.

And he'd had me, always giving back as good as I got.

I grimaced. "You're saying I have to apologize again, aren't you?"

"No," Christopher said. "Too much of that, and it'll lose its effectiveness. Just try to be a little nicer to him, if you can. Don't go out of your way to be hurtful."

"I don't—" I began, and then I stopped with a sigh, because yes, sometimes I did do my best to hit where I knew, or hoped, it would sting. "I'll try."

"Thank you, Pippa."

We sat in silence for a moment.

"I suppose we just forget all this, then," I said, "and pretend we're having a jolly holiday at the Dower House until we can leave?"

"I don't think we can," Christopher answered. He eyed the house pensively. "Someone in there is a murderer. It isn't you or me or Crispin—or Francis; he was in our room all last night, too, and he had no motive—but what if it was Marsden and he comes after you next?"

"He'd have no reason to come after me," I protested, even as a tendril of fear made its way down my spine. I remembered Marsden's hand on my knee, and shivered.

Christopher glanced at me. "We have no idea what his reason might be. Perhaps he just likes to strangle women. Perhaps he made a play for her after she came in. Peckham was downstairs with the butler, Crispin said, so Marsden was alone upstairs—"

"Unless he was with his sister."

"But if he wasn't with Laetitia, then he was alone. He could have met Johanna coming up, and noticed that she was crying, and he could have decided to console her after Crispin rejected her, and when she said no, he strangled her. Maybe he's someone who doesn't like to be told no."

"It's a good thing I didn't reject him to his face last night, then."

Christopher nodded. "Be very careful not to be alone with him from now on."

"I was going to do that anyway," I said. "I wasn't worried about being murdered—" although perhaps I should have been, "—but I didn't fancy being backed into a corner and mauled, either."

"We'll make sure that doesn't happen," Christopher promised.

I arched my brows at him. "Who are we?"

"Well, there's me and Francis. And Crispin, I suppose. And Tom..."

"Detective Sergeant Gardiner is working. And Francis had better stick with Constance. If Marsden would go after women indiscriminately, she might be in danger, too."

Christopher conceded my point. "Perhaps I'll talk to Francis and Crispin and make sure someone is always with one of you. We can swap off."

"What about Laetitia?"

He squinted at me. "Marsden isn't likely to go after his own sister, surely?"

Not in the romantic sense, certainly. Unless their relationship was something quite different from what I had pictured. "I was thinking more that she'll try to monopolize Crispin's time now that Johanna is gone."

"Do you really think so? After last night and this morning, he must have lost some of his luster, don't you think?"

"He's still the Viscount St George with the Sutherland name and fortune," I said. "And she seems inexplicably attached to him."

"That's disturbing," Christopher said. I nodded. "Then I suppose Francis and I will deal with Constance and you."

"Or perhaps all three of you can deal with all three of us. We don't know that it was Marsden, after all."

"If it wasn't Marsden, it was Peckham," Christopher said, "and if so, I suppose he might attack Laetitia, although I have no idea why he would."

"Maybe he's someone who likes to strangle women."

Christopher sent me a jaundiced look, but said, "Perhaps we should all just keep an eye on all of the women."

"That should make Laetitia happy, anyway."

"And Marsden less so, I imagine. I didn't get the feeling that he likes Crispin much."

"Hard to blame him for that," I said. Christopher gave me a look of accusation which I answered with a tilt of my chin. "I'm not being unkind, Christopher. Think about it. St George brought Lady Laetitia to Sutherland House in January. I'm sure they spent the night together. It's not unreasonable that a doting brother might object to that. Especially when it's someone with Crispin's reputation. If it had been me, wouldn't you have been upset?"

"I would have wanted to kill him," Christopher growled. "Although in this case, I blame Laetitia as much as I do Crispin. If anyone seduced anyone in that scenario, it was probably she."

Not impossible at all, actually, given her behavior. "And then there's the possibility that Laetitia herself strangled Johanna. But if she did, at least Crispin ought to be safe with her."

"Tom will figure it out," Christopher said. He got to his feet and brushed off the seat of his flannel bags. "Walk a bit?"

"We might as well." I tucked my hand through his arm. "There's nothing else to do, after all."

"We could try to find proof."

I glanced up at him as we meandered along the stone wall. "How do you imagine we do that? If there's proof anywhere, it'll be in Lady Peckham's room, don't you think? And if it is, Tom will be the one to find it."

"I suppose." He sounded dissatisfied. "It's galling, having to sit here like a potted plant while someone else does all the detecting."

"You could ask Tom how to get a job with Scotland Yard," I said. "Become a detective sergeant yourself."

"I don't think they'd want the likes of me, do you?"

He didn't look at me when he said it, just eyed the vista of Dorset fields and trees, with Marsden Manor off in the distance.

"Why on earth wouldn't they... oh."

He nodded. "They know, you know. Or at least Tom knows, so I assume it's somewhere in the files for Grandfather's murder. And Grimsby's."

What they knew, of course—or what Tom knew, at any rate—was what Crispin had hinted at last night. Christopher's alter ego, Kitty Dupree, with her pretty evening gowns and black wig and propensity for going to drag balls. With the buggery laws still in effect, and the London constabulary cracking down on homosexuals consorting in dance halls, Christopher was right: Scotland Yard wasn't likely to want someone like him in their ranks.

"I'm sorry," I said.

He shrugged, a little jerk of his shoulders. "I daresay I wouldn't be very good at it, anyway."

"You could become a private investigator. Like Poirot."

He started laughing. "I hardly think so, Pippa. Perhaps I'll just help you write detective stories and live off the money you make."

"That seems fair," I agreed, leaning my head against his shoulder for a moment. "You're mostly supporting me these days, anyway. If I ever make any money of my own, it seems right that I should do the same for you."

"There's plenty of Astley money to support us both." He dropped a kiss on the top of my head. "As far as my mother goes, you're the next thing to a daughter. Don't worry. We'll be just fine, the both of us."

"Good to know," I said.

"And if something happens to me, Crispin will take care of you." There was amusement in his voice.

"When hell freezes over," I said, my face twisting as I tried to imagine myself the unmarried spinster cousin adjacent to St George's marriage to someone like Laetitia Marsden. "I'd rather be the maiden aunt to Francis's and Constance's children."

Christopher made a humming noise. It sounded like disagreement.

"Besides," I told him, "you are not allowed to go anywhere. One of these days, if no one else comes along, I might decide to marry you. We can live out our lives in separate bed chambers."

"If no one else comes along, I might take you up on that," Christopher answered. "It would solve a lot of problems. Although I had my heart set on a bachelor lifestyle, you know."

"I wouldn't interfere with your lifestyle, Christopher. But if I turn thirty with no prospects, I'd rather marry you than someone I don't like. I don't have it in me to chase a title and money."

"It's a good thing you won't have to," Christopher said, and gave my arm a squeeze.

THE REST of the Scotland Yard detectives—Chief Inspector Pendennis and Detective Sergeant Finchley—arrived in time for tea, but of course they didn't take the meal with us. They got busy in Lady Peckham's bedchamber while the rest of us sat around the dining room table, the parlor still being off limits.

Tom had brought his photography equipment, and had already spent the afternoon taking pictures of everything of interest upstairs and down, but Ian Finchley is the Yard's fingerprint expert—or at least that was his role with Inspector Pendennis's team—so he got busy covering every surface in the parlor and in Lady Peckham's chamber with fingerprint dust. We all had to roll our fingers on an ink pad and then again on a piece of paper for comparison. Those of us from Sutherland Hall had been through the same ordeal two weeks ago, so it was old hat for us, but Lady Laetitia didn't seem to like the process at all, and Constance's brother complained bitterly about the ink on his stubby fingers.

"Shut up, Peckham," Francis said finally, bluntly. "They're trying to find out who killed your mother and her ward. The least you can do is not whinge about it."

Gilbert flushed, but stopped complaining.

"Tea?" Constance asked sweetly, handing him a cup and saucer. Like everyone else's, her fingertips were black with ink she hadn't been able to scrub off.

Gilbert muttered a thank you, took the tea, and promptly put it down. "How long can we expect this to go on?"

"Scotland Yard's presence? They stayed at Sutherland Hall until they'd solved both murders. Day and night. It took several days."

"Good God." Gilbert eyed the bar cart. "Anyone else for a brandy?"

Constance looked shocked, but Laetitia nodded eagerly. "A cocktail for me, please."

"Miss Darling?"

"No cocktail, thank you," I said. "Although I'll have a splash of brandy in my tea."

Gilbert nodded and set the bottle of brandy on the table. Francis picked it up and poured a tot into my cup as well as into Constance's. "Anyone else?"

As at Sutherland Hall, all the men decided to forego the tea altogether in favor of alcohol. And Laetitia got her cocktail, which she sipped, looking alluring. She was still eyeing Crispin, I noticed, so the revelation about the girl with the baby hadn't done any more to cool her ardor than the possibility that he might be guilty of murder.

Or perhaps she just knew him better than I did, and had realized he wasn't likely to be guilty of either.

"When will we be allowed to leave?" her brother wanted to

know.

"Not until they've solved the case, I imagine," I told him. "We were all stuck at Sutherland Hall until the bitter end."

Crispin flinched, and I added, "Sorry, St George." I truly hadn't meant to be flippant about his mother's demise. Half the time, it seemed like I hurt him without even trying, just by not thinking before I spoke.

"Don't mention it, Darling." He tilted his head back and took a deep swallow of brandy.

"At Sutherland," Francis said, "they arrived on Sunday afternoon and departed again on Wednesday. You should expect them to be here a few days, at least."

Although at Sutherland, we had woken up on Tuesday morning to a suicide and a written confession, which had speeded things up considerably. Here, if no one confessed and the solution wasn't obvious, it might take longer.

Or, if the case was simpler, perhaps less time. It wouldn't do to either under- or overestimate, I thought.

"Better prepare for a few extra days' company, at least," I told Gilbert, who winced and went back to the bar cart to refresh his glass.

Constance looked concerned. "We don't have enough rooms at the Dower House to put up three gentlemen from Scotland Yard."

"I'm sure they won't expect you to put them up," I told her. "They stayed at Sutherland Hall because it was easy to make up three empty rooms. But if you don't have the space here, they'll just have to go somewhere else to sleep. I'm sure there's an inn in the village, isn't there? Or a pub that lets rooms? Or perhaps there's something over the garage? I'm sure they're not picky."

Tom had been in France during the war, so I knew he had dealt with worse. And Finchley was older than Tom by a year or two, so had probably served on the Continent, too. They wouldn't be bothered by uncomfortable sleeping arrangements, I was sure.

"I should talk to Dawson," Constance said. "Please excuse me."

She got to her feet and scurried out. Marsden watched her go with a smirk. "Bit uptight, your sister, Peckham. Someone should show her a good time, loosen her up a bit."

Beside me, Francis bristled. "Stuff it, Marsden. This isn't the time for your games."

Marsden bristled back. "Mind your own, Astley. It's none of your affair what—"

"Both of you mind your own," I snapped, and returned my cup to the saucer with a click that echoed around the table. "Constance lost her mother today, in case you've forgotten. She has a house full of guests she can't get rid of, and the police to deal with. Either say something helpful, or nothing at all."

Neither of them said anything. Francis looked chastened and Marsden belligerent. Christopher and Crispin looked down at the table with identical smirks.

"Laetitia," I said.

She looked up, startled. Perhaps I was supposed to have used her title. "You said you and your brother are related to the Peckhams, is that correct?"

She nodded.

"If Constance can't find accommodations for the men from Scotland Yard here at the Dower House, is it possible that there's room for them at the Manor?"

"Did you let them know what's happened, Letty?" Marsden wanted to know.

Laetitia nodded. "I rang up Mummy and Daddy. Daddy said he'd speak to the commissioner and get us permission to leave."

Of course he had. I refrained from rolling my eyes, but only barely.

On the other hand, if Laetitia and Geoffrey got permission from the commissioner—surely the commissioner of Scotland Yard?—to leave the Dower House, there might be room for the detectives here after all. The room Laetitia had been sharing, or should have been sharing, with Johanna would be empty, at least.

Of course, if either of them was a suspect—and to my mind they both were, at least in Johanna's murder—I doubted Pendennis would allow them out of his sight. They were both, as had been pointed out two weeks ago at Sutherland about the rest of us, well-off individuals who wouldn't have any problem, in the parlance, 'doing a runner.'

So commissioner or no commissioner, I had a feeling that Letty and Geoffrey would be stuck with us for the duration, and we with them.

Constance came back after a few minutes and took her seat behind the teapot. "Would anyone like another cup?"

I was still sipping my first, so I thanked her no. Everyone else was drinking alcohol, so they said no, also. Constance transferred a cucumber sandwich onto a place and bit into it, delicately.

"What are the coppers up to?" Marsden wanted to know.

Constance chewed as quickly as she could and swallowed, clearing her throat. "They're still processing the crime scene, and the rest of the upstairs. And I think Tom—Detective Sergeant Gardiner—and the young constable are talking to the staff."

"Maybe the butler did it," Marsden said, with an inane chuckle.

"I'm sure the police are investigating the butler," I said. "And the gardener and chauffeur—" who had been at Sutherland Hall with Lady Peckham, so couldn't possibly have killed Johanna, although I supposed he might be on the hook for Lady P, "—and the hallboy."

"No one had any reason to want my mother dead," Gilbert said firmly. "It must have been an accident. She got her hands on a bottle of Veronal somehow. Perhaps she needed help sleeping while away from home, or perhaps she simply mistook it for her own medicine and gave herself too much. But she wouldn't have harmed herself deliberately, and no one had any reason to want to harm her."

Constance nodded fervently.

"Be that as it may," I said, since it was at least possible he was right, "Johanna's death was no accident. Someone killed her deliberately. The police have to go through every room and everyone's belongings to see what, if anything, pertains to her death. And I'm sure that includes all the servants' rooms, as well."

There was a moment of silence.

"Well, I'm going to make sure Daddy complains to the commissioner," Lady Laetitia said. "If so much as one of my silk stockings goes missing—"

"They don't care about your silk stockings," I told her. "At least not unless you used one to strangle Johanna. I don't suppose you did?"

She stared at me.

"Then you have nothing to worry about. Anybody who didn't kill Johanna has nothing to worry about. So just sit back and wait for the detectives to finish. And eventually they'll let you go home."

I reached for a scone and put it on my plate. And then I reached for the jam and the clotted cream and put that on my plate, as well. And this, of course, was the moment when the door opened and Inspector Pendennis walked in.

FOURTEEN

THE CHIEF INSPECTOR from Scotland Yard is a stocky man in his late fifties, with shrewd eyes and a face like a bull-dog. He surveyed us all in silence for a moment—several faces evinced expressions of guilt, I noticed, but it was probably due to the brandy and not anything to do with either death—and then he focused on Crispin. "Lord St George. If I may have a word?"

Crispin swallowed and nodded. "Of course, Chief Inspector."

The legs of his chair screeched across the floor when he pushed it back, and several of us winced. If Pendennis noticed, he gave no sign of it. "Mr. Peckham?"

Gilbert jerked to attention.

"We're just going to continue to use your library for our business, if that suits."

Like the invitation for Crispin to come in for a chat, this wasn't a request. Gilbert gulped and nodded. "Of course."

"Thank you, sir. This way, my lord."

He nudged Crispin towards the door. They passed through

into the reception room, and the door shut behind them. Peckham and Marsden exchanged another significant look.

"The first one the chief inspector wants to talk to," Marsden muttered, and Peckham nodded.

I rolled my eyes and turned back to the scone. Christopher looked worried, I noticed.

The door opened again just a few minutes later, and Constable Collins stuck his head in. "Miss Darling?"

From the way his eyes flicked between me, Constance, and Laetitia Marsden, I guess he hadn't paid enough attention in the dining room earlier to know which of us was which. Too busy writing down the conversation verbatim, perhaps.

"That's me," I said brightly, while Peckham and Marsden exchanged another of those looks.

"Inspector Pendennis's compliments, miss. He wonders if you could spare him a moment of your time."

"Of course." I got to my feet. Every eye in the room watched me as I walked to the door. A few were speculative—Marsden and Peckham, mostly. Some were worried: Constance and Christopher. Francis looked, strangely, almost amused, while Lady Laetitia was staring daggers at my back. Had looks been able to kill, I would have buckled at the knees on my way to the door.

I guess perhaps she thought Crispin had asked for me. What was much more likely, of course, was that I was just next in line for some clarifying question or other the inspector had after going over the interviews Tom had already done.

The young constable walked me across the reception room to the library, knocked once, and pushed the door open. "Miss Darling, sir."

"Thank you, Collins," Pendennis grunted. "You can go on up and help Finchley with the rest of the fingerprints."

"Thank you, sir!" Collins ran off as if this was a real treat, and not, as I would have assumed, a rather tedious aspect of his job.

"Come in, Miss Darling. Close the door behind you."

I walked in and closed the door behind me. And crossed the floor to the same table where I had sat with Christopher earlier, across from Tom. Now it was Crispin who sat in the chair I'd been sitting in earlier, like a pale distortion of Christopher. Lighter hair, colorless eyes, pale skin.

Quite pale, in fact. Rather worryingly so. I frowned at him, but he didn't try to communicate anything to me, which was probably for the best, seeing as Pendennis was sitting there on the other side of the table turning a pen over in his hand.

He was rather deliberately perusing a piece of paper that was on the desk in front of him. But I didn't doubt that he was aware of every breath Crispin took.

And mine as well.

So I smiled brightly and took the chair next to Crispin. "Inspector Pendennis. It's nice to see you again, even if the circumstances aren't any better than last time."

"Miss Darling." Pendennis didn't waste time with niceties. "What can you tell me about this?"

He whipped it out like a conjurer, and spread it in front of me on the table.

I blinked. It was a square of fine linen, wrinkled and stained, with a set of initials embroidered in the corner. CAH.

"It's a man's handkerchief," I said.

Pendennis nodded. "Whose?"

I glanced sideways at the man who sat silently next to me. "His."

There was absolutely no point in lying about it, since anyone in the house would have been able to identify this particular handkerchief. "The A is for Astley, the H for Henry. Christopher's handkerchief would have the monogram

CAN, the N for Nicholas. Francis would have had an F, of course."

Pendennis nodded. "Is that the only reason you know that it belongs to the viscount?"

I shook my head. "I saw him use it yesterday. We all did. The pink smears all over it are from Lady Laetitia Marsden's lipstick, which she got all over his mouth before supper."

Crispin looked rather wooden over that statement. So, in point of fact, did Pendennis. "Tell me about that," he said.

Crispin shifted on his chair. I slanted him a look before I asked the inspector, "Surely you've read the statements? She arrived with her brother in time for supper, and when she saw St George, she squealed with delight and then ran across the room and attached her lips to his face like a succubus. Her brother had to remove her, forcibly, when it had gone on for long enough that there started to be concern for his ability to breathe."

"I see," Pendennis said solemnly, but not without a twinkle in his eye.

I nodded. "It was frankly appalling. You ought to have stopped it yourself long before it got to that point, St George."

He arched a brow. "Apologies, Darling. I didn't realize it bothered you."

"Well, you should have. It bothered all of us. The whole thing was horrifically embarrassing. Poor Constance was as red as a beet."

"What happened next?" Pendennis wanted to know.

I flicked Crispin another look. "I ascertained that St George's soul was intact and informed him that he had lipstick all over his face. He used the pocket square to remove what he could of it."

It was semi-permanent lipstick, so there had still been hints of it about his lips several hours later, when we'd been dancing together in the parlor.

"Did you see what he did with the handkerchief after that?"

I hadn't been paying attention, to be honest. But—

"Put it in your pocket?" I asked Crispin. "It wasn't suitable for displaying anymore, so I assume you crumpled it up and stuck it in your jacket pocket? Or trousers?"

He nodded.

"This smear right here," Pendennis said, pointing to a streak of color that was rather more red than pink, "can you tell me where that came from?"

Not Laetitia, obviously. And not me. Certainly not Constance. And it wouldn't have been there before last night. Crispin would never put a used pocket square in his dinner jacket before supper.

And contrary to what you might be wondering: no, it wasn't blood. Just more lipstick.

"Johanna?" I suggested. "She wore red lipstick last night, didn't she?"

"Did you see her kiss Lord St George at any point?"

Crispin winced. But really, what was the point of lying?

"Yes," I said. "After the dancing and the row—you heard about the row, I assume?"

Pendennis nodded.

"After the row, Lady Laetitia ran upstairs to her room. Crispin—Lord St George—went out into the garden, and Johanna followed him."

"That's not in the statement you gave," Pendennis told Crispin sternly. And turned his attention to me. "Nor in yours, Miss Darling."

"I saw them from the upstairs loo," I said. "I'd gone up early —to avoid Marsden, you know—and then Constance knocked me up again when she came in. But I had to wait until Christopher and Francis were both done in the washroom. By the time I made it there, the quarrel below was over, and I heard the door downstairs bang shut and saw St George walk into the garden. So did Christopher, from his room. Saw it, I mean. But he must have looked away before Johanna showed up. I hadn't."

And that made it sound as if I'd been standing there staring at Crispin for an interminably long time. In actuality, it had probably been a minute or two.

"And Miss de Vos kissed him?"

I nodded. "As far as I could tell from the upstairs lavatory. I was rather a long way away, and it was dark, but it looked like she did approximately the same thing Lady Laetitia had done earlier. Flung herself at him and latched on."

"Lord St George?"

Crispin nodded, cheeks hot and lips compressed.

"Then what happened?"

"I pushed her away," Crispin said. And glanced sideways at me. "That time, I pushed her away."

"Even though you were alone and there was no one watching?"

"Miss Darling was watching," Crispin said bitterly, "although I didn't know that until this afternoon. And there were still people in the parlor when I left. For all I knew, Laetitia was standing there looking at me. Her brother, too. And I'm not stupid, Inspector. I knew she was only interested in my title and money. For all that she claimed otherwise, those were what she wanted."

Pendennis nodded. "So the handkerchief?"

"I took it out of my pocket and used it to wipe my mouth. Then I..." He hesitated. His gaze dropped to the surface of the table. "I thought about throwing it to the ground to make a point. But instead, I shoved it at Johanna and told her to wipe her face. She was crying, big crocodile tears, still trying to convince me that she loved me, and I was disgusted by it."

"And she took the handkerchief?"

Crispin nodded. He was blushing, cheeks hot with embarrassment, and he resolutely refused to meet Pendennis's eyes. "I didn't give her a choice, really. I pushed it into her hand and walked away. And left her standing there."

"Was it still on her when she went inside?" I asked Pendennis. "Is that why you're asking about it?"

It hadn't been outside by the wall this afternoon, although I suppose we had had other things on our minds than looking for it, too.

The chief inspector hesitated for a moment before he nodded. "It was on the bed in Lady Peckham's room. The crime scene."

I felt all the color drain out of my cheeks. "I didn't notice it."

"I imagine you had other things to think about," Pendennis said simply. "But it was in the bedclothes. And so was this."

He conjured up something small and shiny that he placed on top of the handkerchief. Crispin and I both leaned forward. "A cufflink?"

Pendennis nodded. "Yours?" he asked Crispin, who made a face.

"It looks rather like one of mine."

"Can you tell me how it got there? Next to the body?"

Crispin shook his head. "I wasn't there. I left her outside in the garden and went to my own room. My cousins were there. They can tell you."

"Did you wear it yesterday?" I asked Crispin. "Do you have more than one pair?"

He looked at me as if I were some poor waif who had just crawled out of a tenement house in Southwark. "Of course I have more than one pair, Darling. No one has just one pair of cufflinks."

Pendennis's expression twitched. Maybe *he* had only one pair of cufflinks. Or perhaps he simply thought Crispin's offense over it was humorous.

"Of course not, St George." My voice was dry. "My apologies for suggesting that you might be so economically disadvantaged as to only possess one pair. Was this the pair you wore yesterday?"

He shook his head. "That's the set with the onyx. I wore that the day of the funeral."

"The day before yesterday," I told Pendennis. "We were still at Sutherland Hall then."

I turned back to Crispin. "Could they have been in your pocket and got tangled up with the handkerchief? Or did Johanna perhaps undress you after the funeral and decide to hold onto one as a keepsake of a lovely moment?"

"Don't be crude, Darling." His cheeks turned pink. "Johanna did not take my cufflinks off, nor any of my other clothing, after the funeral or at any other time. I already told you that. I have had no intimate relations with Johanna de Vos. Ever."

"Just kisses," I murmured. Saccharinely.

"I can't help that, Darling! *She* kissed *me*!"

"Of course she did," I said. "I have no idea how you've managed to get a reputation as such a consummate seducer, St George. From what I've observed this week, you hardly have to lift a finger."

A clearing of a throat brought me back to myself, and Crispin and I both looked at Pendennis. I felt my own cheeks flush. "Sorry, Chief Inspector."

"Don't mention it," Pendennis said. And added, "I mean that. Please don't mention it again. Lord St George..." He turned to Crispin, "you can't tell me how this cufflink came to be next to Miss de Vos's dead body?"

Crispin shook his head, the heat in his cheeks fading at the reminder that Johanna was dead and he was a suspect. "No, sir."

"When was the last time you saw it?"

"If it's mine," Crispin said, "the last time I remember seeing it was when I put it on before the funerals on Thursday morning. I must have taken them off again later, but I don't remember that."

He looked lost. Normally I would have twitted him about his memory loss, but seeing as it had been the evening after watching his mother's coffin being lowered into the ground, I thought perhaps I could forgive him a moment or two of inattention. He had been in terrible shape by the time we got back to Sutherland Hall that night.

"Did you bring this set of cufflinks with you to the Dower House?" Pendennis asked.

"I may have. But I didn't pack my own bag. My father's manservant at Sutherland Hall did that."

Pendennis nodded and made a note.

"If you did," I commented, "the other one ought to be here somewhere. In your room. With your other luggage. Or in the pocket of your dinner jacket, if that's where this one came from."

Pendennis looked at me, blandly.

"Or perhaps it isn't yours at all," I added. "It doesn't have your initials on it. Maybe it belongs to someone else."

Both Geoffrey Marsden and Gilbert Peckham had the means to afford onyx cufflinks, I assumed. And so did Christopher and Francis, of course, but they wouldn't have been in Lady Peckham's room with Johanna last night, either.

"Or maybe you're right." Crispin glanced at me. "Maybe it

was in my pocket and got tangled up with the handkerchief, and Johanna had them both when she went into the Dowager's Chamber."

"Well, then the other one should still be there," I said.

Pendennis looked inscrutable. "The final thing. What can you tell me about this?"

He put a small piece of writing paper on the table in front of Crispin. It had a couple of lines of handwriting on it. I leaned closer, close enough that my shoulder brushed his, to get a better view, and he slanted a look at me, perhaps not entirely thrilled that Pendennis had put this in front of both of us and not just him.

C, it said, or perhaps the first letter was a G. The handwriting was curly enough, girlish and loopy, that it was difficult to be entirely sure.

Come find me after everyone is in bed. J

The J was unmistakable, anyway. It wasn't an L or a C or—most certainly not—a P. Or at least one would have to squint most grievously to turn it into any of those.

"Johanna," I said.

Pendennis nodded. "We have confirmed that it is her handwriting."

It looked like something a twelve-year-old girl might have penned. A twelve-year-old girl who had not been educated at the Godolphin School for Girls in Salisbury.

"Who confirmed it?"

"Mr. Peckham," Pendennis said. "And it matches the other notations in her room."

"Where did it come from?" There was no date on it, and no names, just initials.

"It was found in the pocket of the jacket Lord St George wore to dinner last night."

There was a beat of silence.

"You already checked the pockets of his jacket?" I asked.

Pendennis nodded.

"Was there a second cufflink there?"

"There was," Pendennis confirmed.

"So he must have taken them off Thursday night and put them in his pocket, and then Johanna—"

"I wasn't wearing black tie to the funeral, Darling," Crispin interjected. "Etiquette dictates a black mourning coat."

I turned to look at him. "So on Thursday, you wore a black mourning coat with onyx cufflinks. On Friday night, you wore black tie with another set of cufflinks..."

"Pearl," Crispin nodded. "With matching studs."

I rolled my eyes. "Of course. But somehow, the pair of black onyx ended up in the pocket of your dinner jacket, where one of them got tangled with your handkerchief and wound up in bed with Johanna, while the other was still there along with this note for an assignation?"

"So it seems," Crispin said.

"That doesn't make any sense." I turned to Pendennis. "I think you ought to ring up Sutherland Hall and see if St George's onyx cufflinks are there. Because if they are, this set belongs to someone else."

Pendennis looked at me. Impassively. And then he turned to Crispin. "About the note?"

Crispin shook his head. "I've never seen this before. There was no need for her to pass me notes. We danced at least ten dances last night. If she had wanted to make an assignation, she could have done it then. Or in the garden, later."

"It's not dated," I pointed out. "And I'm not sure that's even a C at the beginning of it. It might be a G. Marsden's first name is Geoffrey. Peckham's is Gilbert."

They both looked at me.

"Well, they are," I said. "Look at it. It might be a G. Her

handwriting is excessively curly. And even if it is a C, she danced with Christopher last night, as well. And there's Constance. Maybe she wanted to talk with her sister about everything that had happened."

"I didn't get the impression that her relationship with Constance was anything like yours with Kit, Darling," Crispin said dryly, as if he hadn't realized that I was trying to help him. "And it's hardly likely she'd arrange an assignation with him, is it?"

"Maybe she thought, if she couldn't have you, he'd make an acceptable substitute."

Crispin didn't dignify that inanity with an answer, just rolled his eyes.

"Don't roll your eyes at me," I told him. "If she told you the truth, and she really did want you and not just your title and money, she could have done a lot worse than Christopher."

"She wasn't telling the truth, Darling. It was all about making an advantageous match. And Christopher wouldn't be interested in her even if she were telling the truth."

"She might not have realized that—" I began, and was interrupted by Pendennis.

"You shared a room with Miss Peckham, Miss Darling." I abandoned Crispin to attend to him. "Did she leave your shared room at all last night?"

I shook my head. "Not that I noticed, and I think I would have. We slept in the same bed, and I was awake rather a lot. I woke up when she came in, and I think I would have woken up if she'd tried to leave again, too."

And it was a good thing that I could tell him all of that with a clear conscience, because out of everyone here, Constance seemed to have the strongest motive for murder. Lady Peckham's demise might have been—most likely was—a tragic accident, but if someone had deliberately arranged for her to get a fatal overdose of Veronal, Constance was surely high on the list. She was familiar with her mother's health, and knew about the medication Lady Peckham might need to take. Her mother had ignored her in favor of Johanna, which must have been both painful and infuriating.

And then there was Johanna, who had taken Lady Peckham's attention away from Constance, and who had seemed to go out of her way to make Constance feel (and look) drab and unwanted. I could well imagine how any man Constance might ever have looked at with interest had been knocked flat by the lovely Flemish girl.

I hadn't been fond of Johanna, and I had known her for less than three days. Constance's well of animosity must have been fathoms deep after years of the same.

So no, of everyone present, I didn't particularly want to point a finger at Constance. Not any more than I wanted to point one at Christopher or Francis, anyway.

Or at Crispin. Cufflink or no, there was no part of me that could reconcile the man sitting next to me with what had been done to Johanna de Vos.

"My money is on Laetitia," I said. Crispin made a protesting sort of movement, but he didn't end up saying anything. "She had Johanna's room to herself, so nobody would know if she left it and went into Lady Peckham's room, and she wouldn't have known that St George turned Johanna down in the garden. Her room faced the front of the house, like mine and Constance's, so she couldn't have seen it for herself. I was in the lavatory, so she couldn't have been there. To her, Johanna was still a rival. She had motive and opportunity, and I think we all had means. Ergo, I think Laetitia Marsden did it."

Pendennis didn't respond. "Is there anything else either of you can tell me about this note? Or the handkerchief or cuff-link? Or anything else?"

I shook my head. Crispin did, too.

Pendennis nodded. "Don't go anywhere, Lord St George."

"Wouldn't dream of it, Chief Inspector," Crispin said, and while I'm sure he was trying to sound suave and insouciant, he only came across sounding snotty and young.

"Even if we leave here, you know where to find us," I told Pendennis, and took Crispin's arm before he could attempt to get away. "But we're not going anywhere. Neither of us had anything to do with this. We'll be around."

Pendennis nodded. "Find me Laetitia Marsden, will you, Miss Darling? I sent Collins upstairs, so there's no one else to send."

"My pleasure, Chief Inspector," I said brightly. "I'm already looking forward to it."

I tugged Crispin behind me out the door before Pendennis could muster up a response to that.

FIFTEEN

NOTIFYING Lady Laetitia that Chief Inspector Pendennis requested a moment of her time was everything I had hoped it would be. She paled, turned to her brother with an expression of panic on her face, and quavered, "Geoffrey?"

"Buck up, Letty," Marsden advised, as if this was nothing to worry about. Laetitia grimaced, but got to her feet and made her way across the floor.

I stepped politely out of the way to let her through. "Good luck."

She shot me a look, but it was more terrified than haughty, so I just smiled sweetly. Her gaze snagged for a second on Crispin, half hidden behind me and the door I was holding open, but she didn't say anything to him, and I'm not sure he even realized that she was looking at him.

"Christopher," I added, as Lady Laetitia moved across the reception room floor as slowly as an aristocrat headed for Madame Guillotine.

Christopher jumped up and ran for the door. Happy for an

excuse to leave the room, I expect. Francis arched a brow in our direction, but I shook my head at him. Nothing for him to worry about. He nodded and went back to whispering to Constance.

"Garden," I told Christopher. "Pendennis doesn't want you. I do. You too, St George."

They both fell in behind me as I swept toward the front door. On the other side of the room, Laetitia had finally reached the library door and was knocking timidly. "Enter," Pendennis's voice came from within.

And then we were at our own door, and through, and back outside the Dower House just in time to see Lady Peckham's Crossley make its stately way towards the garage. The motorcar and chauffeur must have been released from Sutherland when the police left, but had probably waited while Aunt Roz packed up all of Lady Peckham's belongings and sent them back to the Dower House.

"What's happened?" Christopher wanted to know as we made our way around the corner of the house and into the gardens yet again.

I tucked my hand through his arm. "Someone is trying to frame St George for murder."

Christopher shot a started look at Crispin. "Truly?"

"It seems that way."

I shot him a look that was a lot less startled. "What do you mean, it seems? It *is* that way. Although you may know something about it that I don't, I suppose, and perhaps it isn't actually a setup at all."

He rolled his eyes. "I didn't kill her."

"I'm glad to hear it," I said. "Although I didn't think you had."

"You thought I had last month."

"That was different. There were good reasons why you might have killed Grimsby and your grandfather. There's no reason at all to think you would strangle a young woman whose only crime was wanting to be your wife."

He grimaced. So did Christopher.

"At any rate," I said, "what makes you argue the fact that someone is framing you?"

"Because it could all be very innocent."

"I don't see how."

He shook his head. "No, listen. I gave the handkerchief to Johanna in the garden. The cufflink could have been attached to it. I'm not sure exactly how—"

"Cufflink?" Christopher asked.

I waved him down and concentrated on answering Crispin's obviously inane argument. "I'm not sure, either, since that makes no sense—"

"What cufflink?" Christopher persisted.

I turned to him. "A cufflink of St George's—"

"The onyx," Crispin said, as if Christopher would know the difference, or care.

"—or at least a cufflink that's identical to one of St George's, wound up in bed with Johanna's body."

Crispin flinched at the baldness of the statement.

"Ouch," Christopher said.

I nodded. "The problem is that he wasn't wearing that pair last night. He wore them on the day of the funerals, but not since. We're not even sure they made it here from Sutherland Hall."

"They must have made it here if one of them ended up in bed with Johanna," Christopher pointed out. He turned to Crispin. "Is this the same handkerchief that Pippa...?"

Crispin nodded.

"With your initials on it."

"Yes. With my initials on it. The same handkerchief that Darling whipped out of my pocket last night before supper."

"The one with both Laetitia's and Johanna's lipstick all over it," I added. "I'm reserving judgment on the cufflink—I think it could be someone else's—but there's no question about the handkerchief."

"And it was in bed with the body?"

Crispin and I both nodded. "But as he said, that's easily explained," I added. "He gave it to Johanna outside in the garden. She probably took it inside herself."

"Then the cufflink would have fallen off along the way," Christopher said, "wouldn't it?"

"Most likely it would. If it was there in the first place, which isn't likely. So the cufflink must have been planted."

"Can you prove you weren't wearing those cufflinks yesterday?" Christopher wanted to know, and Crispin shook his head.

"Not unless someone happened to notice my cuffs. You're an observant sort, Darling. I don't suppose...?"

"I may be observant," I said, "but I'm not in the habit of staring at your hands, St George. You'd be better off asking Lady Laetitia. You kept your jacket on all night, I do know that much. You wore it through dinner, and when I danced with you, and in the garden with Johanna. I don't see how anyone could have seen your cufflinks."

"They matched my studs," Crispin said. "As they are supposed to do. Did you happen to notice my studs, Darling?"

"I'm afraid I didn't, St George. I'm not in the habit of staring at your shirtfront, either."

Although I had been face to face with that shirtfront more than once over the course of the evening, and the onyx would have stood out against the white fabric much more so than the pearls he claimed he had worn. The fact that I hadn't noticed his studs argued for the pearls over the onyx. It was hardly evidence, however.

"The handkerchief could have got into the Dowager's Chamber with Johanna. But the cufflink must have been planted. And so was the note, obviously."

"Note?" Christopher asked, while Crispin said, "Not necessarily, Darling."

"A note inviting St George—or someone else, but the police found it in his pocket, so they're making assumptions—to come find Johanna after everyone else was in bed."

Christopher winced and I turned to Crispin. "What do you mean, not necessarily?"

"She could have slipped it in there herself, couldn't she? She had plenty of opportunities."

Yes. But— "Why would she bother, if you were right in front of her and she could just tell you—or to be polite, ask you —to meet her? Why put anything in writing?"

"Perhaps she didn't want anyone to overhear?" Christopher suggested. "There wasn't much privacy in the parlor last night. Plenty of other people around."

"Privacy enough that Geoff Marsden could practically assault me on the sofa, and nobody noticed."

"I noticed," Crispin said.

"Yes, thank you, St George. Even if she hadn't wanted to come out with the invitation in the parlor, she could have asked in the garden later."

I twisted my voice into an approximation of Johanna's breathy alto. "'I slipped a note into your pocket earlier, St George. Read it and tell me what you think.' Did she say anything like that?"

"She didn't get a chance," Crispin said. "She rushed at me, kissed me, told me she loved me and wanted to marry me. And I told her not on her life." He shuddered.

"Bad luck, old chap," Christopher told him, with little sympathy and a bracing slap on the shoulder. "You couldn't have known."

"Of course not," I said briskly. "It's not as if one can go through life avoiding saying such things just in case someone happens to be murdered. At any rate, if Johanna didn't slip the note into your pocket, someone else did, and probably to make you look guilty. I suppose it really was from Johanna? It was signed with what looked like a J, but none of us know what Johanna's handwriting looked like, do we, and..."

"Pendennis said Peckham had confirmed the handwriting," Crispin said. "I would have expected my name instead of an initial, though. Or nothing at all, actually. Why compromise yourself that way when you're arranging an assignation?"

He ought to know. However, he went on before I could say anything about it. "But we hadn't actually progressed to informality..."

I arched my brows. "You were on kissing terms with this woman, but she didn't call you by your first name? What on earth did she call you, then? Lord St George? My lord?"

"One of those," Crispin said, with a hint of a flush in his cheeks, "yes."

I sniggered. "My lord? Really? I'm sure you enjoyed that, St George—"

"Moderately," Crispin said.

"—but that's simply vile. Out of curiosity, did you return the favor?"

His brow curved up. "Of course not. I called her Miss de Vos. As was proper."

Of course. "It leaves the field a bit more open, though, doesn't it? *Dear Crispin* is one thing. Or *Dear St George*. Just plain *C* is another. There's Christopher and Constance, just to name two other options."

"She'd hardly arrange an illicit assignation with me," Christopher said.

"But she might have with Constance. Not an illicit assignation, of course, but if she was devastated enough by being rejected by St George, she might have wanted another woman to talk to. Lady Peckham was gone, and Lady Laetitia was out of the question, of course, and I'm sure she had figured out that I wasn't likely to be a sympathetic ear..."

Christopher and Crispin both snorted.

"—but she and Constance had lived in the same household for years. She might have been self-centered enough to think she could cry on Constance's shoulder."

No one said anything for a moment.

"The initial was curly enough to have been a G, as well," I added. "That means Gilbert and Geoffrey are in the running. They both wear cufflinks. If the onyx pair isn't yours, St George, they had to have come from somewhere."

"But the cufflink rather takes Laetitia out," Crispin said, "doesn't it? Isn't she your favored suspect, Darling?"

"You don't think she knows where her brother keeps his cufflinks?" I arched a brow at him. "If the cufflink was planted, it doesn't follow that whoever planted it is someone who wears cufflinks, you know. I can guarantee you that she's familiar with her brother's cufflinks, and I'm sure she knows yours—you might even have worn the onyx back in January when you took her to bed, mightn't you?—and who had a better reason for wanting to punish both of you? Johanna for taking you away from her, and you for letting her do it."

He had no answer to that, so I turned back to Christopher, who asked, "Do you think Johanna wrote the note to someone else, then, Pippa? Maybe even at a different time? And someone decided to make use of it?"

"It's possible," I said. "It wasn't dated. Maybe Constance found it slipped under our door this morning—I might have missed it in the dark; I was up early—and she decided to use it to incriminate St George."

"Why would Constance Peckham want to incriminate me?" Crispin sounded sincerely baffled.

"If she killed Johanna?" I said. "She'd want to incriminate anyone she thought she could make look guilty, I imagine. And there was certainly no love lost between them. If Lady Peckham's death was a murder, Constance had motive to want to get rid of them both."

"You think that mousey little thing could commit two murders?"

"It's often the quiet ones," I said, although my only real evidence for that was from murder mystery novels. And from Her Grace, Duchess Charlotte of Sutherland, I suppose, but it didn't seem polite to bring that up. "If they were both murdered, someone had reason to want them both dead. If we can think of someone like that—and I can think of Constance—it behooves us to consider them, no matter how mousey they are."

"I thought I heard you tell Pendennis that Constance couldn't have done it because you shared a room and she didn't leave last night."

"I don't think she left," I said. "But I couldn't swear to it. It's possible I might have slept through it, if she did. I don't think I would have—I woke up several times—but I couldn't swear. I don't want her to be guilty, but between the three of us, she had motive, and I can't say with a hundred percent certainty that she didn't have opportunity."

Crispin shrugged. "So now what?"

"I suppose I should go have a conversation with Constance," I said. "See what, if anything, she has to say about any of this. Christopher, perhaps you can go find Tom. See if he'll spare you a few moments. Make it seem as if you're worried about your cousin..."

"I *am* worried about my cousin," Christopher said.

"—and maybe he'll feel compelled to tell you something comforting that'll move us forward."

Christopher nodded.

"St George..." I eyed him. "How do you feel about Lady Laetitia?"

"Why, Darling—"

"No," I said. It had been a rhetorical question, nothing more. I didn't actually want to know. "She seems to want you, at least as long as someone else does. Spend time with her. If nothing else, she won't try to frame you anymore, if you pay her enough attention."

"I don't think she'd try to frame me in the first place," Crispin said.

"I wouldn't be too sure. A woman scorned and all that. Just don't propose to her. Unless you do want to marry her, of course. But just in case she's a murderess, don't go and get yourself engaged to her right now. Aunt Roz told me specifically to make sure you didn't get yourself compromised while you were here."

"Did she really?" Christopher asked with a fond smile.

I nodded. "She really did. And made me promise. So don't make me out to be a liar, St George."

"If I had wanted to get myself engaged to Laetitia," Crispin said, "I'd have done it in January. It's been months since I've seen her other than in passing."

"Why on earth would she care that you'd let yourself be vamped by Johanna, then?"

"Pure acquisitiveness," Crispin said. "She'd had her fun and moved on, but she didn't want me to. Especially not to someone who looked like Johanna."

So that was it. "You were a toy she had finished playing with, but woe to anyone else who picked you up and wanted to play with you?"

He shrugged, a bit pink about the cheekbones. "Something like that."

"You're the one who put it like that, St George." And a sad state of affairs it was, too. "If that's the case, we may be out of luck. With Johanna gone, perhaps you'll fall back into obscurity again."

"That's easily fixed, Pippa," Christopher said, smirking. "Just pretend you're a bit goofy about Crispin, and he'll be all the rage."

"Don't be ridiculous, Christopher," I said, "nobody would believe—"

Meanwhile, Crispin snapped, "Not on your life, Kit!"

"There's no reason to take that tone," I told him. "I realize nobody sane could possibly believe it, but—"

"For pity's sake, Darling, that isn't why—"

"Stop it," Christopher said, "both of you. Crispin—"

"If Laetitia killed Johanna," Crispin said, "what's to keep her from coming after Philippa next?"

"You, I suppose," I told him. "You'll simply have to keep her away from me, now that we know about the danger."

He gave me a look, which I ignored in favor of turning to Christopher with a more salient point. "That doesn't mitigate the fact that nobody would believe it. Everyone knows we despise each other."

"I don't despise you, Darling," Crispin said. "There's a degree of animosity there, certainly—"

"Oh, excuse me. Everyone knows there's a degree of animosity between us, then—"

"Stop it," Christopher said again. "Your degree of animosity looks a lot like something else sometimes, so I daresay plenty of people would believe it."

"Ridiculous," I grumbled, while Crispin nodded.

"I'll do my best, of course, Kit, but I can tell you right now that—"

"Don't do me any favors, St George," I told him. "Besides, *I'm* the one who's supposed to look like I've lost my mind over *you*, not the other way around."

"Actually..." Christopher said, and didn't get any further, because Crispin bared his teeth.

"I don't know that it matters how *you* feel about *me*, Darling. What matters is whether *I* pay *you* attention. And for that—"

"That's not what matters, you nitwit. Johanna—"

"Stop!" Christopher said. "Pippa, what are you wearing for supper?"

I blinked at the sudden change of topic. "I suppose I ought to wear black, really..."

"She wasn't *your* mother," Christopher said.

"My yellow dress with the silver spangles, then, if you think it'd be all right. I only brought two evening dresses, and I wore the green yesterday."

And had been called edible for my trouble. I leveled a displeased look at St George.

"Remember the yellow dress with the spangles, Crispin?" Christopher asked.

Crispin nodded.

"Between now and supper, you need to come up with something to say about it. Make it the sort of backhanded compliment you're so good at."

The corner of Crispin's mouth turned up.

"Cause a lovely little scene, just like you did yesterday. Finish it off with a smirk at some point during supper, but don't overdo it..."

"What do you mean, don't overdo it?"

Christopher arched a brow at him and he flushed. "Fine. I'll be careful."

Christopher nodded. "And Pippa, if you want to look like you're dreaming of murdering him, that's all right. It's usually quite effective."

"Wonderful," I said. "It comes naturally to me most of the time."

Neither of them said anything, and I continued. "So for now, you'll go find Tom, I'll go find Constance, and St George will spend the next few hours trying to come up with something clever to say. If you can spare the effort, St George, you may want to spend some time with Peckham and Marsden this afternoon, too, in between your mental gymnastics. If it wasn't Laetitia, it might have been her brother. He was certainly very persistent with me yesterday—"

Both their faces darkened at the reminder.

"—and if he managed to get Johanna to himself in Lady Peckham's room, and she rejected him, I wouldn't be surprised if the situation turned nasty. He's the type who wouldn't take kindly to being told no. Talk to him about women—Marsden leans toward gutter talk anyway, I've noticed—and see what, if anything, you can discover."

Crispin nodded, even as his lip curled up in a sneer. I

deduced he wasn't any fonder of Marsden's conversation than I was.

"Until dinner, then. I'll go in first. Good luck, both of you."

I headed for the front door. When I glanced back over my shoulder before turning the corner, Crispin had his cigarette case out and was offering it to Christopher, and they both looked completely comfortable and ready to settle in for a prolonged break.

I FOUND Constance in the reception room wringing her hands over a trunk and a toiletries bag I remembered from Wednesday afternoon, when they had arrived at Sutherland Hall.

"Your mother's things?" I asked sympathetically.

She nodded. "I don't know what to do with them. Her room is a crime scene, and even after the police are finished, there's no point in unpacking, when she isn't going to come back to wear or use any of it. But it doesn't feel right to simply throw away the trunk, either, especially without looking at what's inside."

I nodded sympathetically.

"And then there's everything else." She looked up at me with tears in her eyes. "What's going to happen to us, Pippa? This was Mother's house, which she got to live in because she was the widowed sister of one of the Marsdens. But Gilbert and I won't be allowed to stay here. Nor will he want to, I'm sure. He'll want to go out and find a wife and have a family of his own now, somewhere away from here. And then what will become of me? I'll be all alone."

I opened my mouth, and closed it again. I had no idea what to tell her. I'd come to live with the Astleys after my German father was drafted for the war effort and my English mother refused to leave him. I'd ended up with Aunt Roz and Uncle Herbert as substitute parents, and I also ended up gaining three —then—pseudo-brothers and a pseudo-cousin who didn't like me much, but who was still a part of my life and probably always would be. The idea of being alone in the world and having to make my way without any support at all was foreign.

"You're related to Lady Laetitia and her brother, aren't you? Maybe you and she...?"

"I hate Laetitia!" Constance burst out. "She's as bad as Johanna, or worse. Beautiful, and wealthy, and in with the popular set. The last thing I'd want is to become a companion to Laetitia!"

I hadn't really meant to suggest that she should take a job as a companion, but I could see where she might have got that idea. I could also see, quite clearly, why it didn't appeal. I felt my own nose wrinkle involuntarily. "It would be the last thing I would want to do, too." I could barely stand Laetitia now. The thought of having to spend months, perhaps years, with her, was abhorrent.

"So you see why I can't do that. And I'm not qualified to do anything else, Pippa. I was never clever, the way you are. I had a difficult time at Godolphin. All I ever wanted to do, was have a family of my own."

"So find someone to marry," I said.

"Do you suppose it's that easy?" She pinned me with a stare, and her eyes were furious behind the glistening tears. "I walk in anywhere behind someone like Johanna, or Laetitia—or you!—and no one even notices I'm there."

"I'm hardly in their category..." I protested, and then I realized I was focused on entirely the wrong thing. "I don't think that's true, Constance. There are plenty of men who would rather have you than Laetitia."

Francis, for one. Not that I was about to express that sentiment aloud. It was up to Francis himself to broach, if he so desired.

"She's not very nice," I added. "Even Crispin says so. And Johanna is dead."

And hadn't been very nice, either. Not that it's kind to say something like that about someone who's recently deceased. But she would never get the chance to outshine Constance again, so at least there was that silver lining.

"And that's another thing," Constance said and lowered her voice. "Someone killed her, Pippa. Someone here at the Dower House strangled Johanna. And he's still walking around! What's to stop him from strangling someone else?"

"I'm sure he must have had a reason," I said, choosing to continue with Constance's pronoun instead of mentioning that the killer might not be a man at all, "and it would have been a reason that doesn't apply to anyone else. None of the gentlemen here are serial murderers. If there had been a string of young women strangled lately, we would have heard about it."

Constance didn't seem at all reassured by that. "Perhaps she's the first!"

"I suppose she might be. But I think it's more likely that whoever did it had a reason beyond just liking to strangle women. Besides, you and I are all right. We're sharing a room. We'll keep the door locked, and we'll stick together and make sure we don't get caught anywhere alone."

Constance shot a fearful look over her shoulder and lowered her voice another degree. "What about Mr. Astley? I've been spending a lot of time with him."

"Francis?" I shook my head. "Francis wouldn't hurt a fly. He saw so much death and devastation in the war, he's scarred for life. It's not my place to tell you this, really..."

"It's all right, Pippa," Constance interrupted. "Mr. Astley...

Francis—" She flushed, "has already told me that he takes a sleeping draught sometimes because the memories of the war haunt him. On the day of the funerals he showed me the bottle and told me he'd taken a small dose that morning, to make it through the day—just enough to calm his nerves—and he said he'd likely have to take a bigger dose that night, because funerals are difficult for him..."

I could well imagine that they were. He had been through so many, starting with Robert's, and then a long line of friends' and fellow soldiers' on the battlefield. Not that funerals are necessarily any easier for the rest of us. "Did he also happen to mention—?"

"That he drinks too much sometimes?" Constance asked. "Or that he occasionally indulges in some other form of narcotic?" She nodded. "He told me everything. Or at least I think he told me everything. I can't imagine what else there might be."

That sounded promising, anyway. Francis wasn't keeping secrets.

"That's good," I said. "Although I was actually going to ask whether he had mentioned sharing his dope with St George that day. Crispin was practically comatose by the end of his mother's funeral..."

Constance patted my hand. "He didn't say, Pippa. I'm sorry. Gilbert came along at that point, and Francis dropped the bottle back into his pocket—"

"He had it with him? At the funerals?"

She nodded. "I imagine he wanted to have it handy in case he needed more, you know?"

Or in case someone else needed some, perhaps. I wondered whether Francis had foreseen his cousin's need and brought the bottle because he thought Crispin might need it. Kind of him, if so.

"He said he'd be able to stop," Constance said softly, but without looking at me. "I don't know if that's true."

I didn't know whether it was true, either. Although I hoped for both their sakes that it was. Constance seemed taken with Francis, and if he had shared all these personal details about himself—he'd never told *me* any of these things—it appeared he must return her feelings. For the sake of their potential future relationship, as well as for all of us who loved him and didn't want to lose him, I hoped Francis was right and he could stop.

SIXTEEN

WE ENDED up putting Lady Peckham's trunk and bag in the box room under the stairs, since neither of us wanted to drag it into our room, and since the Dowager's Chamber was still a crime scene. The local mortuary had removed Johanna's body, after Tom had taken photographs and Finchley fingerprints, and now she was down in the village being examined by Doctor Curtis from Scotland Yard along with the local coroner. I doubted an autopsy was necessary, since Johanna's cause of death was surely obvious, but an examination was undoubtedly in order. After all, we didn't know what, if anything, might have happened to her before she died, did we?

After that, we headed up to our shared room and started our preparations for supper. "Will this be all right?" I asked Constance, as I held up my yellow spangled dress. "I have a black dress, but it's an afternoon dress, not an evening dress, that I brought for the funerals."

"You can wear whatever you want, Pippa." She kept her back to me as she examined her own gowns in the wardrobe.

"Mother wasn't your mother, and Johanna wasn't your... whatever she was supposed to be to me."

Not sister, clearly. "I don't want to be insensitive, though. I can wear the black, but it isn't a dinner dress."

"Wear the yellow," Constance said, with a glance over her shoulder. "It's a lovely dress. I enjoyed wearing it earlier this week when you let me borrow it. I must wear black, and Lady Laetitia doesn't seem to wear much else—"

And looked marvelous in it, annoyingly.

"And of course all the men will be in black tie..."

Of course. Black and white all around.

"—so you'll be the only bright spot we're likely to get." She nodded decisively. "Wear the yellow."

I'd wear the yellow, then, with her permission. It was probably a good thing, since Crispin had spent all afternoon thinking of something witty to say about it. It would serve him right if I showed up in something else, and forced him to come up with another backhanded compliment—as Christopher had put it—on the spot, but if the yellow didn't bother Constance, then it certainly didn't bother me.

And St George rose to the occasion beautifully. "Why, Darling," he caroled when I entered the parlor for before-supper cocktails, "don't you look—"

"If you say, 'good enough to eat,' I shall pummel you, St George."

"I wouldn't dream of it," Crispin said, with the air of someone who would absolutely dream of it, and had, in fact, said exactly that just yesterday. "Although there is something quite—"

He looked me up and down, "—quite banana-like about it, isn't there? So very yellow. And also something—*je ne sais quoi*—something almost uncultured and practically savage about the color."

The phrase dropped from his lips in melodic, unaccented French. I stared at him blankly, wondering what on earth he was going on about. There's nothing uncultured or savage about yellow, is there? There was certainly nothing uncultured about my very pretty dress, which wasn't even French, but which had come from Norman Hartnell's studio on Bruton Street in Mayfair.

And then Crispin smirked evilly. "If the gramophone comes out after supper, will you favor us with your own *danse sauvage* tonight, Darling?"

And that was when the penny dropped, and my jaw did too, and my cheeks flooded with color.

For those of you who didn't catch the reference—both the mention of the *danse sauvage* and the emphasis on the yellow fruit—let me call to your mind the scandalous American *danseuse* Josephine Baker, with her famous banana skirt and bare breasts, who was causing a sensation on the other side of the channel practically as we spoke. She had taken Paris by storm last year, in La Revue Nègre at the Théâtre des Champs-Élysées, and now she had moved on to the Folies-Bergère, where she was dancing with a ring of bananas on a string around her hips, and precious little else. She was a spectacle, the costume was unutterably risqué, and the comparison between that and my yellow dress was... appalling, to say the least.

"Oh," I choked, "you *bastard*."

Constance gasped, and so did Laetitia. Francis practically strangled on a laugh. In the background, Marsden muttered something to Peckham, who sniggered.

"Now, now, Darling," Crispin drawled. "You know very well that I'm a Sutherland through and through."

Yes, he was. There was, unfortunately, no denying that. He had his mother's hair, and her gray eyes instead of the Astley blue, but in every other respect he was a perfect replica of Christopher. There was no denying his heritage. Nor had I been trying to.

"You know that wasn't what I meant, you deplorable cad. How dare you compare my perfectly modest dress to—"

"Darling." He snatched up my hand, and it was enough to stop my tirade mid-sentence. "I apologize."

He raised it... not to his lips, which was what I expected.

No, he pulled it to his chest, where he held it against his heart. I could feel the beat against my palm. My mouth dropped open, and it took me a second too long to pull my arm back. My voice might even have been a touch breathless, although if anyone asked—Christopher, for instance—I was fully prepared to chalk it up to my brilliant acting. "Whatever are you doing? Keep your hands to yourself, St George."

I took a step back, just in case he might be thinking of making another assault, and added, "Whatever's gotten into you?"

"Perhaps I feel bad for upsetting you," Crispin said, with a soulful expression that certainly made him look as if he felt terrible. He even went so far as to put his own hand over his heart this time.

I blinked—it looked real enough to give me pause for a second, and of course he knew it, because the smirk made another appearance. "Will you forgive me, Darling?"

"As long as you promise not to do it again," I told him. "I can't go through life thinking you care, St George. I'd never get a good night's sleep again."

He nodded solemnly. "Of course, Darling. Complete and utter disinterest from this point on, I promise."

"Thank you, St George," I told him, and waved a hand dismissively. "As you were, then."

He clicked his heels together and gave me a bow before he

turned his attention back to Lady Laetitia. She gave me a slightly longer look before withdrawing her attention. Searching my face for something, unless I misread her expression.

Christopher tucked his hand under my arm. "Come on, Pippa." His voice was uneven with laughter. "Let me get you a cocktail."

"Thank you, Christopher. After that display, I could use a stiff drink."

I let him tug me away from Crispin and Laetitia in the direction of the bar cart, and of Marsden and Peckham, who were standing there with glasses of something that didn't look like cocktails. Bourbon or brandy, most likely. They both looked me up and down as I came closer. Trying to mentally replace the yellow dress with the banana skirt Crispin's words had conjured, no doubt.

Damn him.

I planned to treat him to a piece of my mind about it later, but there was no denying that it had been effective. Both men eyed me speculatively, and Lady Laetitia's examination had been a clear case of sizing up what she thought might be competition. The piece of my mind I planned to offer needed to include a compliment on a job well done too, it seemed, much as I would hate to convey it.

"Miss Darling," Marsden said with a small bow and a barely concealed leer. "St George has it right. You do look ravishing in yellow."

"Thank you, Lord Geoffrey." I managed a semblance of a curtsey, even as my cheeks flushed—part embarrassment, part anger. Edible is one thing, ravishing quite another, especially in combination with Marsden's proclivities for pawing at women. "St George likes to have his fun."

I glanced over at the latter—he was smiling at Laetitia—and

let my eyes linger for a second. With murder in mind, naturally, but no one else needed to know that. With any luck, my smoldering glance would convey jealousy instead.

"What would you like to drink, Miss Darling?" Peckham wanted to know. "Perhaps a Hanky Panky or a French 75?"

When I turned my attention to him, his eyes, small and muddy brown, were twinkling with a combination of malice and glee.

"I'll have a Last Word," I told him sweetly, "if that isn't too difficult. Otherwise, a Gin Rickey will do."

He smirked, but turned to the bar cart. And allowed me to have the last word, at least for right then.

CHRISTOPHER TOOK me in to dinner, but since we were now an even eight and not nine, and only three women but five men, the seating arrangements were just as unorthodox as the night before.

Dawson had removed leaves to give the table a comfortable eight seats in total, and I ended up in the middle of one long side with Christopher on one side of me and Lord Geoffrey on the other. Laetitia had the opposite seat, with Crispin on one side and Francis on the other. Francis was properly partnering Constance on the hostess's end of the table, while Gilbert had seated himself at the other end, the only place where the proper man-woman-man seating arrangements didn't work out. He spent half the meal engaging Christopher in discussion, which forced me to talk to Marsden, and the other half talking to Crispin. Constance would much rather spend the time talking to Francis—for which no one could blame her, certainly not me—and so entertaining Marsden fell on my shoulders.

It was an uncomfortable meal. The murders, not to

mention the presence of Scotland Yard in the Dower House, had no doubt discombobulated the below-stairs, and the food was not up to the standard of yesterday's supper. The meat was overcooked and the potatoes hard. Whenever Crispin was talking to Gilbert, Laetitia eyed me across the table in a disconcerting, vaguely calculating manner. Marsden's conversation was one innuendo after another, and he kept chasing my foot with his under the table. Francis was showering attention on Constance, too busy to notice my plight, while Christopher was being monopolized by Gilbert, perhaps so Marsden could have this go at me. And Crispin, of course, was either talking to Gilbert or to Laetitia, and was too far away to notice the footsie going on at my end of the table.

By the time Constance placed her napkin beside her plate and stood, I was exhausted. And that was just the beginning of the evening.

"What are we supposed to do now?" Laetitia wanted to know as we drifted out of the dining room towards the parlor. "I don't suppose dancing would set the right tone."

Decidedly not. Although I was rather impressed that she realized it.

"Card games?" Constance ventured. "Whist? Bridge?"

Laetitia wrinkled her nose.

"Or maybe board games? Chess? Ludo?"

Laetitia waved the suggestions away the same way one would a gnat.

"Feel free to suggest something that would be more to your liking," I told her. "But you simply cannot use dancing as an excuse to drape yourself all over St George tonight. With a murder in the house and Scotland Yard still working in the library, it would not be appropriate in the least."

She looked at me, and for a moment there was something

very cold and calculated in her eyes, before she turned away, languidly. "Crispin, darling."

She accompanied the words with a stroke of her hand over his sleeve. I was reminded of Johanna doing the same to the Hispano-Suiza.

She had caught him in the process of lighting a cigarette, and he had to take it out of his mouth to be able to answer her. "Laetitia?"

"You'll dance with me, won't you?" Her eyes were limpid, huge and imploring, and she kept the hand on his arm. She made quite the pretty picture as she looked up at him, transparently earnest and stunningly lovely.

"Oh." Crispin looked from her to me and back. He cleared his throat diffidently. "I'm sorry, Laetitia, but I think Philippa's right, you know?"

Laetitia pouted prettily. "Are you sure, darling? We could play soft music and dance slow..."

She flicked a glance my way, so quickly it was almost unnoticeable. She wanted to see how I reacted to that suggestion, I assumed. A suggestion that would certainly bother me if I did nurse any variety of tender feelings for St George.

"Your boy's right, Letty," her brother cut in. "It wouldn't set the right tone to have a dance party tonight. This is a house in mourning, and we owe it to our cousins to be sensitive to their loss."

"But I'm bored," Laetitia whined. "Crispin..."

"For God's sake, St George," I told him. "Keep your girlfriend under control, can't you? We cannot dance tonight. I don't care how much the two of you want to. It's inappropriate. Find something else to do with your time."

"Perhaps a romantic walk through the grounds?" Laetitia suggested. She had moved her hand from the top of Crispin's arm to his elbow now, and the grip looked firm.

"The rest of us will just sit here in silence and wait for you to come back, then, I suppose? Make sure you bring a clean handkerchief, St George. Judging by yesterday's display, you'll need it."

I strode into the parlor without giving either of them a second look. I could feel eyes following my progress, though, and I could also sense Christopher's amusement. My performance, and Crispin's, seemed to meet with his approval. And it was obvious that Lady Laetitia had bought into it. She was staking her claim on St George just as hard as she could to keep him away from me.

However, Marsden detached his sister from Crispin's arm as soon as they entered the parlor, and took her aside for a stern talking-to about proper behavior, so the romantic stroll through the garden didn't come off. Laetitia pouted about it, but Crispin looked relieved, unless that was just in my imagination. And it was Laetitia who finally came up with the evening's entertainment.

"Maybe we should have a séance."

There was a beat of silence.

"A séance?" I repeated, incredulous. If music and dancing were improper, surely a séance was abominably so?

She tossed her neck. Her hair swung. "Just think about it. If Johanna's spirit is still around, we could ask her what happened. And then the crime would be solved and the police would go away..."

And we could dance again, I realized. "Surely you understand that it would be in atrociously poor taste?" Not to mention that the detectives from Scotland Yard wouldn't take the results of a séance as evidence of anything whatsoever.

But Gilbert, surprisingly, seemed in favor. "It can't hurt, certainly. I'm sure none of us are believers—" he gave Laetitia an apologetic look, "—but if we're wrong, maybe we'll learn something, and if not, maybe it will be fun."

"I don't know..." Constance demurred, with a glance at me. We had certainly sat around on the floor of our dormitory at Godolphin back in our school days on plenty of evenings, playing spiritual games in the dark with nothing but a lot of frissons down our spines to show for it. I thought it was a load of tosh, personally, and if it had been my mother who died last night, I wouldn't have wanted to turn her death into entertainment for Lady Laetitia. But I wasn't in charge here. The Dower House wasn't mine—nor was it Constance's, actually; it was really more Laetitia's, wasn't it?—and perhaps she felt like she couldn't say no in stronger terms than she already had.

So we ended up around a table in the darkest corner of the parlor, with all the electric lights out—the spirits are affected by too much light, Lady Laetitia claimed. I could see Christopher's lips compress at the sound of that, and had to agree that it was ridiculous. Spirits aren't physical, so why would anything in the physical world bother them?

It was, of course, much more likely that Lady Laetitia didn't want anyone to know that she was pushing the planchette—or more accurately, the glass.

We played the old-fashioned way, with circles drawn on pieces of paper with letters and numbers and 'yes' and 'no' scribbled on them, and with a cocktail glass with a stem—that was important, somehow—that Laetitia held over the flame of a candle before putting it down, bottom up, on the table.

"Everyone put their fingertips on the glass," she instructed.

There were eight of us, so sixteen fingertips, which of course took up rather a lot of room. But we managed, somehow, to each rest the tips of two fingers on the edge of the glass.

"Elbows off the table," Laetitia ordered. We all obeyed. And there we sat, while the candles flickered, and the darkness got darker, and the silence more oppressively silent. Marsden took a finger off the glass to rub his nose, and Laetitia scowled at him. "You're not taking this seriously, Geoffrey!"

"No," Geoffrey said. "This is silly, Letty. Let's just play Ludo."

"Hush!" someone hissed—I think it might have been Gilbert Peckham—and they both fell silent.

Constance tittered nervously. Marsden, directly across the table from me, pressed his foot down on top of my toes. I moved my foot out of the way and accidentally nudged Gilbert instead. He was next to Marsden, on the other side of Constance (and Francis, who was to my right). Gilbert smirked. I scooted my chair an inch closer to Christopher, on my other side, and tucked my feet underneath, out of the way. Crispin, on Christopher's other side, glanced my way and arched a brow. I shook my head, and saw that Laetitia had noticed the by-play.

"No talking," she said severely. "Everyone look at the glass."

We looked at the glass, with its smoky inside. There was something very hypnotic about the whole thing, and of course that was the point. When Laetitia finally intoned, "Is there a spirit present?" in her best sepulchral voice, both Constance and I jumped. Gilbert giggled.

Apparently no spirit was present, because nothing happened. We sat in silence for a while longer. My own nose itched, but I knew if I took my fingertips off the glass to rub it I would be yelled at, and the longer we sat here, the more annoyed I got. I leaned over and rubbed my face against Francis's shoulder instead. He grinned.

"Shhh!" Laetitia hissed. "Is there a spirit present?"

Apparently there was, because the glass jumped. Or perhaps—much more likely—it was just one of us.

Laetitia decided on the former. "Can you tell us who you are?"

The glass hesitated, and then moved, with increasing speed, toward the letter R. When it went from there to the letter O and then B, I felt Francis stiffen beside me.

"Robert?" Laetitia said. "Is that right?"

The glass zoomed, with all our fingers on it, to the circle with the word 'yes.'

"No," Francis said and took his fingers off the glass. "Absolutely not."

Laetitia hissed and Marsden grumbled, but I nodded. "I agree. Parlor games are all well and good, but some of us here have suffered losses, and dredging up our dead is not going to win any points."

Christopher nodded, and so, a little to my surprise, did Crispin. Laetitia pouted but relented. "Oh, very well. Sorry, Robert."

I narrowed my eyes, and she added, "Everyone be quiet."

We sat in silence again. The candles sputtered. Marsden's foot searched for mine under the table. He must have hit Francis instead, because the latter shot him an unkind glare, and Marsden subsided, at least for the time being.

"Is there a spirit present?" Laetitia intoned.

The glass wobbled toward 'yes.'

"Can you tell us your name?"

C, spelled the glass. H. A.

"No," I said, as it moved toward the far end of the alphabet and the R. The glass stumbled, or someone's fingers did. Crispin looked up at me. I met his eyes as I shook my head. "Absolutely not. I don't want to talk to my dead aunt, or my dead cousin, or my dead mother or father... No, wait. Actually, I would like to speak to my dead father. If someone can conjure up my dead father, I'd be happy to speak to him."

There was a pause.

"Very well," Laetitia said. "Can we have Miss Darling's father? Is he here?"

The glass stood stock still, of course. Nobody knew my father's name—or rather, Christopher or Francis, or perhaps Crispin, might have heard it at some point, but neither was likely to remember it now. And I didn't think either of them had been pushing the glass in the first place. Francis clearly hadn't been any happier to recognize Robert's name than I had, and Crispin had flinched when he'd realized the glass was spelling out his mother's name. And Christopher... well, Christopher just wouldn't, that's all.

So we spent a few minutes waiting for the spirits to settle down again. My father never appeared, of course. Eventually, Laetitia tried again. "Is there a spirit present?"

The glass twitched.

"Can you tell us your name?"

The glass moved backward towards the middle of the alphabet. Several people held their breaths when it approached the J, but instead of stopping there, it moved on to the I. Then the R, and back to the I.

"Mother?" Constance breathed.

The glass abandoned the letters in favor of the 'yes,' where it lingered, seemingly waiting for another question.

"Lady Peckham?" Laetitia tried. "Is that you?"

The glass stayed where it was. Obviously, as it was already firmly planted on the affirmative.

"Mother," Gilbert said. "Do you have something to tell us?"

The glass seemed to hesitate, then started moving. L-O-V-E, it spelled out. L-I-G-H-T.

I thought about rolling my eyes, but decided that under the circumstances it would be insensitive. Gilbert seemed invested in the actions of the glass, and Constance didn't seem opposed, so my skepticism might not be appreciated.

"You're happy?" Gilbert ventured, while Constance choked back a little sob.

The glass signaled an unhesitant 'yes.'

"Can you tell us what happened to you?" Laetitia asked, and the glass went into a frenzy of movement, all of it in the first half of the alphabet. A-C-C-I-D...

"An accident?" Gilbert asked, as it made its way unhesitatingly toward the E.

The glass zoomed toward the 'yes,' so quickly that Crispin, who was farthest away from the 'yes'—as well as from the first half of the alphabet—lost his connection with it. It didn't seem to matter. The glass arrived triumphantly at 'yes' and stayed there.

"Thank you, Mother," Gilbert said humbly, while Constance sobbed quietly beside him. She'd always been a bit gullible, even back in our Godolphin days, and under the circumstances... well, if it had been my mother who'd died today, I might have been overcome, too. She would surely realize, at some later point, that she hadn't really communicated with her dead mother, and Lady Peckham hadn't really sent her children love and light from the beyond.

Then again, did it really matter if Constance believed it? If it gave her some kind of peace, could it really hurt?

While I cogitated, we had lapsed into silence again. And— "Is there a spirit present?" Laetitia intoned.

The glass twitched, then headed for the J. Then the O. Then the H.

Someone drew in a ragged breath.

"Johanna?" Laetitia said, and to my surprise, her voice wobbled. In my mind, she had certainly been the one manipulating the glass earlier, but in this moment, at least, it sounded as if she truly believed.

Either that, or she was terrified. And if she had strangled Johanna, maybe that wasn't surprising.

The glass circled the 'yes,' before settling firmly on top of it.

"Johanna?" Laetitia said again. "If it's you, can you give us a sign?"

The next moment, a stentorian thud split the silence. Followed by two more.

SEVENTEEN

LAETITIA'S EYES rolled to the back of her head. She went limp in her chair and slid halfway under the table. The glass tipped sideways and rolled in a half circle, while Marsden let out a bellow of concern and Constance a shrill scream.

"Come in!" I called over the babble of voices. "Can someone turn on a light?"

Marsden and Crispin were both bent over Laetitia, hauling her back up onto her chair, slapping her hands and fanning her face, while Francis was trying to calm Constance's hysterics. She was sobbing, tears running down her cheeks. It was Christopher who pushed his chair back as the door to the reception room opened, silhouetting a tall, imposing form. "What's going on in here?"

"Séance gone wrong," I said, as calmly as I could considering all the hubbub swirling around me. "Can you open the door all the way, so we can see what we're doing?"

Tom grumbled something about stupidity, and the gullibility of people who believed in spiritualism, but he pushed the door all the way into the room and walked in. The electric light from the reception room made the scene around the table look all the more lurid. Constance was weeping in Francis's arms. Gilbert sat like a statue, as stiff and pale as marble. Laetitia was equally colorless, dead to the world (if you'll pardon the expression) and her brother was trying to dribble some of his brandy between her lips while Crispin helped by holding her head upright. I met his eyes across the empty place where Christopher had been. "Is she all right?"

A corner of his mouth turned up. "Overcome by the excitement. What about you?"

"I'm fine," I said steadily. "I don't believe in any of it."

He nodded. "Good thing."

Yes, it was. Over at the small side table, Christopher had got a lamp going, so we could see a bit better, and after a quick look and an equally quick inquiry as to whether Christopher was all right, Tom raised his voice. "I knocked on the door to let you know we're done for the evening and on our way to the pub in the village, where we've taken rooms for the night. We'll be back in the morning."

Gilbert pulled himself together enough to nod. "Thank you, Officer."

Tom was hardly an officer, and it showed in the rise of his eyebrows, but he didn't say anything. Perhaps he could see that Gilbert was pale and clammy and not fully in his right mind, so it wasn't worth the correction.

"Are you any further along?" I wanted to know, since I'm sure we were all wondering. Or if we all weren't, I knew I was.

"We're getting closer," Tom said. "We're not in a position to arrest anyone yet, but we have a better idea than we did."

"I don't suppose...?"

"No," Tom said. "Just go about your business as usual." He glanced at the circled letters and sooty glass on the table. "And no more séances. All it does it make things worse. Play a nice game of Snakes and Ladders instead."

He glanced around the table. Laetitia was coming to now, sitting up and sipping from the glass her brother was holding to her lips while she clutched Crispin's hand in a death grip. Constance had calmed herself down—or perhaps it was Francis who had done it—and was sniffling quietly into a handkerchief. His, judging by size. Peckham still looked shellshocked, while Christopher was standing by the side table beside the lamp he had just lit, watching Tom.

Tom had his hands in his pockets and was watching the rest of us. "No one is to leave the house tonight. Attempting to run will look like an admission of guilt, so don't do it. If you need fresh air, don't go beyond the patio."

"Have you... are you..."

I wasn't quite sure how to finish the sentence—'Did you post guards to stop us from leaving?' sounded a bit ominous—so I ran down without asking what I wanted to know. Tom met my eyes for a moment before he said, "Just go to sleep like it's any other day. It should all be over by tomorrow evening."

Scotland Yard must be quite a lot farther along in their deductions than I was in mine, then. To me, the field of suspects was wide open, and I was no closer to naming a single culprit than I had been when the day started.

But I nodded. "Sleep well, Tom. We'll see you tomorrow."

"Good night, Miss Darling. Miss Peckham. Lady Laetitia. Peckham, Astley, Marsden, St George." He turned to Christopher. "Kit—"

Christopher nodded and fell in behind Tom as he headed out.

"I could use a drink," I said and turned towards the bar cart.

"Allow me." Peckham got there first. Perhaps he needed one, as well. "Another Last Word?"

"I honestly don't care, as long as it's alcohol. I'd take straight gin at this point."

"I feel the same way," Peckham confided as he filled two glasses, one for himself and one for me. Not with straight gin, of course. He created some kind of concoction with a half dozen ingredients, of which gin was just one of many. I honestly didn't pay too much attention, since by now Lady Laetitia had moved from merely clutching Crispin's hand to holding it against her cheek, and I was watching him squirm uncomfortably. Gilbert finished my glass with two olives on a stick and handed it to me. "There you are."

"Thank you." I picked it up and sipped. It was sour and not really to my taste, but I didn't feel like I could say that, not to my host and the man of the house, so I just smiled. "Delicious. Thank you."

"Bottoms up," Gilbert said and raised his glass, but of course cocktails aren't meant to be tossed back, so I let him take a gulp of his own drink and limited myself to another exceedingly small sip of my own. "That was quite the show earlier."

I nodded. "Good to know your mother is happy and at peace."

I had meant it sarcastically, and Christopher would have caught on—so would Crispin and for that matter Francis—but Gilbert looked touched. Maybe this hadn't been his first—or even his second—glass of brandy this evening. "It was nice of the old girl to stop by."

This, too, sounded like a joke, but must have been meant sincerely. "I lost my mother when I was sixteen," I said. "I'm sorry for your loss."

"Thank you." He gulped another mouthful of brandy. "Do you suppose it was really her?"

Of course it hadn't been her. I wasn't sure who—or what—it had been, but I don't believe the spirits of the dead communicate with us through smudged cocktail glasses and circles drawn on paper. But it seemed like he wanted to believe that his mother had got in touch to tell him that everything was love and light, so I said, "I don't see who else it could have been, do you? I mean..." I grinned at him, "You didn't push the glass, did you?"

He looked some variety of deeply offended and horrified that I'd ask. "Of course not."

"Then I don't see who else would have. Do you?"

He shook his head, although he gave me another one of those looks. "I'm glad she told us it was an accident. I can't imagine who would have wanted to hurt my mother, so I thought it had to be. But it's good to know for certain."

"Of course," I nodded, while I wondered whether he really was gullible enough to believe that anything had been settled by that 'conversation.'

"Here, let me refresh that for you."

He took the glass out of my hand and turned back to the bar cart. I hadn't taken more than a couple of small sips—the drink really wasn't to my liking—but he'd tossed back rather a lot more than that, and if he was going to refresh his own glass, I guess courtesy dictated that he do mine at the same time, whether it needed it or not.

I let him get on with it while I scanned the room. Christopher was still gone, off somewhere with Tom. Francis was murmuring sweet nothings to Constance, and Marsden was now eyeing his sister and Crispin from over by the window. She had practically crawled into his lap and he looked uncomfortable. When he caught my eye across the room, I arched my brows at him and made him grimace in return.

"Something going on with you and St George?" Gilbert wanted to know as he handed me the refreshed glass. It had more gin in it now, but otherwise it tasted the same. Just stronger. I took a polite sip and shook my head.

"Nothing at all. Do you think I'd let him carry on like that, with both Lady Laetitia and Johanna, if there was something going on between us?"

Gilbert had no answer to that, so I added, "Just out of curiosity, how did your mother and Johanna get along?"

He blinked, and I added, "For the few days that I knew them, I thought your mother seemed very fond of Johanna. And Johanna seemed to return the sentiment."

Gilbert nodded.

"Johanna wouldn't have had any reason to want your mother dead, would she?"

He opened his mouth, and then closed it again, as if this was something that hadn't crossed his mind at all. It had just now crossed mine, to wonder whether it was possible that the same person hadn't killed both victims.

And yes, Lady Peckham's death might still—as the séance had tried to convince us—have been an accident. But if not, was it possible that Johanna had doctored her medicine, and then someone else had killed Johanna in retaliation?

It would almost have to be Gilbert, in that case. Constance had had her own reasons for wanting them both dead—or had at least had her own reasons for disliking them both—but if she had found out that Johanna had killed Lady Marsden, Constance's first instinct would have been to have Johanna arrested, I thought, not to kill her.

But Gilbert, if he had loved his mother and had come to find out—how?—that Johanna had taken steps to kill her, was it possible that he might have strangled Johanna for it?

Unlikely, I thought. He would have had to have come to that realization last night, before Lady Peckham died, and if he had learned of it then, he would have rung up Sutherland Hall, surely, and tried to prevent his mother from drinking any of the doctored medicine. If he'd cared enough about her demise to kill Johanna because of it, he would have cared enough to try to stop it, if he could have.

"No," Gilbert said finally. "My mother loved Johanna, and Johanna loved Mother. I can't think of any reason why Johanna would have wanted to kill her."

"If she refused to let Johanna marry St George?" I pushed. "Would Johanna have killed her over that?"

Gilbert looked pensive. "I didn't get the feeling that my mother opposed Johanna marrying your cousin," he said. "Although I suppose she might have learned something to incline her otherwise. Is there a reason St George would be an inappropriate match for my mother's ward?"

"Oh, lots of them." I smiled toothily. "Lady Laetitia you already know about, but there have been so many others. The Honorable Cecily Fletcher. Lady Violet Cummings. Millicent Tremayne..."

"The actress?"

I nodded. "I could give you the names of at least three or four more, that he's dallied with in the past year. And that's in addition to the girl with the baby at Sutherland House, of course. You heard me mention her earlier today, I think?"

"Good Lord," Peckham said, looking faint. "Yes, if Mother knew about all that, she might have had second thoughts."

He glanced at Crispin and Laetitia, and then at Marsden, who was scowling over by the window. "Does Geoffrey know about this?"

"If he doesn't, I think he ought to, don't you?"

Peckham nodded. "If you'll excuse me?"

"Of course." I waved him off with a wiggle of my fingers and watched, amused, as he crossed the room to where Marsden was standing. Crispin arched a questioning brow at me, and I smirked, which did nothing to reassure him. Then Laetitia tugged at his sleeve, and he turned back to her.

"What did you do now?" Christopher's voice asked next to me, and I glanced at him.

"Told Peckham all the reasons Crispin shouldn't be allowed to marry Lady Laetitia. He scurried off to share them with her brother."

"You're evil," Christopher said.

I scoffed. "It's not like he's in love with her. Besides, would you want Laetitia Marsden to be part of your family forever? Face her over plum pudding at Sutherland Hall every Christmas? No? Then let's not pretend I'm not doing you a favor."

Christopher shrugged. "Everything all right in here?"

"Just fine. Peckham gave me a horrible cocktail I'm pretending to like, but now that he's gone, I guess I can forget about being polite."

I looked around for somewhere to put the glass, and then stopped when Christopher took it out of my hand. He raised it to his mouth for a sip and shrugged. "I've had worse."

"Truly?" That was hard to believe, but we all have different tastes, I suppose. "Peckham's relieved his mother stopped by to notify us all that her death was accidental."

"Is he really?"

I nodded, speaking fast because I didn't think we'd get a whole lot of time to ourselves where no one could overhear. "He can't think of any reason why anyone would have wanted to kill Lady Peckham, but when I suggested that Johanna might have, if Lady P told her she couldn't have Crispin, he sounded like it might have been a possibility after all."

Christopher nodded.

"And Constance knew that Francis takes Veronal and that he had some in his room at Sutherland Hall, so she would have known where to find it and what it does. Even if Francis didn't tell her about Aunt Charlotte dipping into his stash, I'm sure she and Gilbert both know that Aunt Charlotte's death was due to an overdose of Veronal."

"The last thing Gilbert did before we left Sutherland Hall yesterday morning, was run back inside because he said he forgot something," Christopher said. "And Tom said they're getting close to making an arrest, but he wouldn't tell me who, probably because he was afraid I would give something away."

"The only person I can think of with a motive for killing both of them is Constance," I told him, "but she was in my room last night, and I'm almost positive she didn't leave. I'm not sure she'd have had the strength to strangle Johanna anyway, she's such a small girl, and besides, it seems like she would have used the Veronal on Johanna, too, if she had it, instead of making it so obviously a murder."

Christopher hummed agreement and took another sip of his—my—drink.

"Whoever did it had access to a note with Johanna's handwriting, so it would have been easy—or fairly easy—to make it look like a suicide. Copy the handwriting and put the blame for Lady Peckham's death on Johanna, too. Everything would have been tied up with a neat bow."

Christopher nodded.

"But whoever killed Johanna didn't do that. He—or she—used the note and cufflink to try to implicate St George, but he—or she—didn't use the Veronal. So were they two different people? Or was Lady Peckham's death an accident, and Johanna's murder unpremeditated, and whoever did it decided to frame St George afterwards?"

Christopher shook his head. "No idea. Although I hope for Francis's sake that it isn't Constance."

I nodded. "On the other hand, it would be quite convenient

if it were Lady Laetitia. Solve the murder and get her away from St George in one move."

Christopher arched his brows. "Are you sure you don't just want her away from Crispin, Pippa?"

"Positive," I said. "Honestly, Christopher, aren't you the one who told me to pretend so Lady Laetitia would think someone else was interested in him? Of everyone here, *you* should know better."

He shrugged, conceding the point. "Do you think he means that much to her, though? That she'd commit murder to keep him?"

"If he told the truth when he said that he hadn't seen her since January, perhaps not. Although as long as someone else looks like they're trying to take him away, she seems keen enough."

I eyed her. "She's quite as tall as Johanna was, so she would have had a much easier time strangling her than someone small like Constance. And she was alone in her room last night, so she could easily have gone across the hall to the Dowager's Chamber and no one would have known better. She was the last one down for breakfast this morning, too."

"What does that matter?" Christopher wanted to know.

I glanced at him. "That cufflink and note in St George's pocket wasn't put there while the three of you were in the bedroom, asleep. It had to have been done after you all came down for breakfast this morning. That's the only time your room was empty between the time Johanna was strangled and when Tom and Constable Collins searched everyone's room. At that point, only Constance and Laetitia were left upstairs."

Christopher looked enlightened. "So Constance could have done it, or Laetitia. Or, I suppose, Crispin, although that doesn't make any sense."

No, it didn't. He'd been the last of the three of them out of their shared room this morning, so in that sense he could have hid the evidence in his own pocket, but it made absolutely no sense that he would have done.

"Peckham left the dining room for a couple of minutes," Christopher added, "didn't he? To talk to Dawson about luncheon? He might have had time to run upstairs and plant the cufflink and note."

He might have. The note could have been written to him, where it had obviously not been written to Lady Laetitia. Although she might have appropriated it from her brother, who had also ducked out of the dining room for a minute or two this morning. Perhaps not enough time to run upstairs and plant evidence in Crispin's pocket. Then again, maybe it had been enough.

"Look," Christopher said, nudging me. "Her brother is taking her away from Crispin. And Peckham's waiting."

"Planning to enumerate all the reasons St George is bad news, I expect." I sniggered. "Go fetch him, Christopher. Let's see if he's learned anything new in all this time of her hanging on his arm."

"It'll be more effective if *you* go fetch him," Christopher said.

I cut my eyes to him. "Surely I've debased myself enough for one evening?"

He merely looked at me, and I sighed. "Fine. St George!"

Crispin turned at the sound of my voice, and I crooked my finger at him.

"That's one way to do it," Christopher muttered as his cousin obediently started across the floor toward us.

I smirked. "Surely it's even more effective if I simply call his name and he comes running?"

"Yes, Pippa." It was his turn to roll his eyes, although he

had got them under control again by the time Crispin reached us.

"Let me guess, Darling." He glanced over his shoulder at where Laetitia stood beside her brother, with Gilbert Peckham hovering two feet away. "Your doing?"

"I just happened to mention to Gilbert all the many, many reasons you're not an acceptable suitor for his cousin's hand. Funny enough, they all had female names." I smirked. "He thought her brother ought to know."

"Although by now," Christopher added, "I'm sure they all think you only did it so you could get Crispin away from Laetitia and over here."

I sighed. "What tangled webs we weave..."

"Yes, yes, Darling," Crispin interrupted. "What did you want?"

"To know whether Laetitia has said anything useful. Peckham actually seems to believe his mother came through from the other side to assure him that she died by accident, and he seemed quite gratified to know it, too..."

"No," Crispin said. "Mostly she spent the time asking me about you."

"So it worked?"

"She seems convinced you're after me," Crispin confirmed. "Be sure to lock your door tonight. If she did kill Johanna, she might try to kill you, too."

"Do you think she might have?"

He merely shrugged, and I added, "I'm sharing with Constance. We'll be all right."

"What if you're wrong about Constance, and she's the killer?"

"Then I suppose I'm just out of luck," I said. "There's nowhere else I can sleep. I can't share with Laetitia, for obvious reasons, and the Dowager's Chamber is off limits. And I hope you're not suggesting that I share with you?"

He glanced at Christopher, and then back at me. "You'd be safer with us than anywhere else. At least, with four of us in the same room, no one would get at you."

"But Laetitia would have a fit, her brother and Peckham would both be scandalized, and so, undoubtedly, would Constance. I'm better off where I am."

I hesitated a moment before I added, "I don't really think it's Constance, anyway. She has the motive, but I don't think she has the personality. And I'm not sure she'd actually be strong enough to strangle Johanna."

Crispin watched Constance, small and dainty beside Francis, for a moment before he nodded. "Still, be careful."

"You, too," I told him. "Better get back to Laetitia. She's put her brother and Peckham in their places and is staring at you. If she thinks you're not paying enough attention to her, she might decide to kill you and not me."

He rolled his eyes, but nodded. "See you later, Kit. Keep an eye on her."

He vanished, back across the floor to where Laetitia was waiting, ostrich feather fan tapping impatiently at her thigh.

"Her?" I inquired.

"You," Christopher said.

"I never thought I'd see the day when Crispin St George was concerned about my safety."

I was still watching as he crossed the floor, and when he reached her, Laetitia lifted the fan and tapped him on the cheek with it. I winced.

"Looks like it goes both ways," Christopher said blandly.

I glanced at him. "There was absolutely no need for her to hit him. That wasn't a love tap, in case you didn't notice. Not quite the same as the full palm and four fingers, but it got the point across."

"I guess she's making sure he knows what happens if he thinks about straying again before she's done with him."

So it seemed. "Make sure he gets in safely tonight, too, Christopher. I don't want you to keep all your attention on me while she murders him behind some door somewhere. Your mother told me to make sure he didn't get himself in trouble while we were here. I think she was mostly concerned that he'd end up in some sort of breach of promise suit or something like that, but I don't think she'd want him to be murdered, either."

"Likely not," Christopher agreed. "I'll make sure you both get to bed in one piece. And you're sure you'll be safe with Constance?"

"I'll borrow a bread knife from the kitchen and hide it under the mattress if you think it's necessary," I said, "but yes, I think I'll be safe with Constance. Even if she did kill her mother and Johanna, she has no reason to kill me. I didn't like them either, and she knows it."

Christopher looked unconvinced, and I added, "And if she says or does anything strange before we go to bed, I'll come find you and spend the night with you instead, even if it would scandalize everyone else in the house. At least it would make St George's day. Or night."

"That would do it," Christopher agreed, and let the subject rest.

EIGHTEEN

"WHAT DID you think of the séance?" Constance wanted to know as we were getting ready for bed.

I had already changed into the blue silk pyjamas Aunt Roz had given me for Christmas last year, and I was sitting on the bed, arms around my knees, watching Constance get ready. Unlike me, she dressed not in modern pyjamas, but in a soft, white, lawn nightgown with embroideries, very two decades ago.

It suited her, though. Even with her bobbed hair, there was something very ingenue and innocent about Constance. She wasn't a modern girl at all, really, nor did she seem to want to be. Under the modern hairstyle and red lipstick—which she only wore sparingly—was a traditional girl with old-fashioned sensibilities who dreamed about a husband and babies.

"I think Lady Laetitia is full of—"

I stopped myself before I could complete the sentence and tell her what I really thought, but Constance caught enough to giggle anyway. "She believes it enough to faint when that handsome policeman knocked on the door, anyway."

Yes, she had. Although it had been (somewhat) easy to believe at that point.

Not that I had. Believed, I mean. But after a long time of sitting in the dark, listening to everyone breathe, with the flickering candles and the darkness pressing in from all sides, and the eerie sensation of the glass moving on its own, even when you know it isn't possible for a glass to move across a surface independently and spell out words...

At any rate, it wasn't terribly surprising that someone like Lady Laetitia, who I judged as quite high strung to begin with, might have become a little overwrought by her (self-imposed) role as mistress of ceremonies for the séance. When the knock on the door had come, seemingly in response to her request for a sign, it had taken me a moment of elevated heartbeat and cold sweat to put two and two together, too.

Not that I had any intention of admitting that.

"I don't believe in the supernatural," I said firmly, and watched Constance's face drop. "I admit it was all very eerie. But I think that was partly the atmosphere, you know? The darkness and the sound of people's heartbeats and Marsden's foot chasing mine under the table..."

Constance tittered, but persisted. "But you don't think there's anything to it? That the dead can..." She hesitated, "—communicate from where they are?"

I hesitated, too. It was clear what she was talking about, after all, and I didn't want to cause her undue pain if she had gathered some comfort from believing that her mother still existed and was at peace somewhere. So much had happened today that it felt like an eternity had passed since this morning, but it was less than twelve hours since Constance had learned that she had lost not just her... almost-sister? almost-friend? friendly enemy?... but her mother, as well. Even if she clearly hadn't cared much for Johanna, they must have had a relationship of some sort. They'd spent years across the hall from one another, after all. Years of meals and shopping trips and passing each other going in and out of the lavatory door. I don't care much for St George, but we've spent years as part of the same family, and if he died, I certainly wouldn't be able to act as if nothing had happened less than twelve hours later.

And then her mother. While there'd undoubtedly been resentment there—I had seen it myself—Lady Peckham had been Constance's *mother*. She had dried her tears as a child, and had read her stories—unless there'd been a nanny for that—and they must have had a more normal mother-daughter relationship at some point, before Johanna came along and took Constance's place.

Or maybe they hadn't. Maybe the relationship had always been peculiarly unloving, with Lady P showering all her attention on Gilbert before Johanna came along, so Constance always got the short end of the stick. Maybe she truly had killed them both, and I was simply spinning stories about things that hadn't been true.

But if not, if Constance had lost a mother and a girl she had grown up with today, then I owed her some consolation and sympathy.

So I thought back to what she'd asked before I'd gone on my track of causes and counter-causes—could the dead communicate from where they were?—and said, carefully, "I'll admit I'm not terribly superstitious myself. And I certainly don't believe in Laetitia Marsden as a spiritualist."

She tittered, and I added, "But do I think there's something after death? Absolutely. We all lost so many people during the war and after, in the influenza epidemic. I lost my mother and father, and my cousin, and I'm just one person. I'm sure Francis's loss was magnitudes greater than mine. He lost his brother, and I'm sure untold numbers of friends and allies over the couple of years he spent fighting. I don't think they just vanished. I think, after what they went through and what they sacrificed, they went somewhere better."

"Yes," Constance whispered.

"And if they're somewhere, then I suppose it's possible that they're able to communicate from there. Perhaps even in spite of Lady Laetitia. Your mother seemed to me to be a strong-willed sort of woman when I met her..."

Constance nodded, sniffling. There were tears in her eyes that she fought to hold back.

"If she wanted to communicate to you and your brother that she's at peace and comfortable, I think she could maneuver around Laetitia Marsden's shenanigans, and any of our doubts and reservations, to do it."

Constance nodded. "Thank you, Pippa."

"Don't mention it," I said, completely sincerely, since I wasn't sure whether I believed what I had told her or not. That there was something after death, certainly. I don't think—I don't want to think—that people just die and are gone. I wanted to believe that my mother and father, and Cousin Robbie, and the late Duke of Sutherland, and Crispin's mother, and Grimsby, and Lady Peckham, and yes, even Johanna... that they were somewhere nice, somewhere they were at peace beyond all the cares and worries that had been their lives. At least some of them deserved that.

Whether they could come back and communicate that to us? That was a different story. And that Lady Peckham had come back and done just that? Very doubtful indeed.

But of course I didn't tell Constance that. I just reached out and took her hand and squeezed it. "I'm sure your mother is somewhere better than here. Somewhere peaceful and lovely, where there's no pain and no cares or worries. Johanna, too."

"I don't care about Johanna," Constance said, clutching my

hand. Tears were gathering in her eyes again. "That's a horrible thing to say, but I don't. I didn't like her."

"I didn't either, so I can hardly blame you for that."

She sniffed. "She took my mother and my brother away from me. To Mother, she was the daughter I'd never been. The pretty one, the one who cared about all the things Mother thought were important. Pretty dresses, and handsome men, and estates and titles and money."

I nodded. "I'm sure your mother was a great beauty in her day." Back in the Gay Nineties of the previous century. The era of wasp waists and padded bosoms and fluttery fans. The young Lady P had been the toast of London, no doubt, along with Aunt Charlotte, who had also been exactly that type. No wonder they'd been friends.

"And Gilbert," Constance said. "We always had a good relationship, you know. We're only a year and a little more apart in age. We played together a lot as children, and he never thought I fell short. I was his sister, and he loved me. He actually probably liked that he didn't have to fend off his friends' advances on my behalf, that I wasn't the kind of girl who made men flutter around. We were happy. Until *she* came."

The level of poison she managed to put into that single pronoun was quite astonishing.

"And she was everything I wasn't. Mother liked her better than me, and all of Gilbert's friends started coming around more, but not for Gilbert—or for me, of course. It was all for Johanna. Gilbert became exceedingly popular. And then he started spending all his time with her. Escorting her to luncheons and balls. Leaving me to fend for myself."

"That must have been difficult," I said, as I tried—and failed—to imagine Christopher abandoning me at home to escort some other cousin, prettier and more sought after, to balls and luncheons.

"I hated her," Constance said through tears. "She absorbed all the attention. Whenever she walked into a room, no one saw me. Not even my own family."

I couldn't even imagine, honestly. I had shown up on the doorstop of the Astley family at eleven, long-legged and skinny and awkward, at the beginning of a war in which my father fought on the other side. It might have been my father who killed Robert, and no one had ever said it, or made me feel any different because of it. I had been Aunt Roz's dear niece from the moment I arrived, and Francis's and Robbie's Pipsqueak, and Christopher's best friend and almost-sister. Even Crispin, for all his dislike of me—and of the way I had taken Christopher's time and attention from him—had never made me feel like I wasn't part of the family.

"I don't care where Johanna is," Constance said wetly. "I don't care whether she's at peace or not. I don't care about her. But I don't want my mother to suffer. I was angry with her, but I wouldn't want her to suffer. You don't think she suffered, do you, Pippa?"

"When she died, do you mean?" I shook my head. "I don't think so, Constance. I think she just took a swallow or two of her medicine, or what she thought was her medicine, and went to sleep, and just never woke up."

I hesitated for a moment before I added, "Aunt Charlotte died from an overdose of Veronal, you know, and she looked like she was asleep. Very peaceful, with her hands folded and everything. Not as if there had been any discomfort at all. Just as if she'd fallen asleep and died without ever realizing it."

Constance nodded. She passed her hands over her eyes and cheeks and then against the skirt of her nightgown to get rid of the wetness. "Thank you, Pippa."

"Don't mention it," I said. "I don't think your mother even realized what happened. She just slipped from sleep into death without noticing the difference. Now Johanna, on the other hand..."

"That's right. You saw her." Constance lowered her voice. "Was it awful?"

I conjured the picture of Johanna in my head—limbs twisted in the bedclothes, face discolored with her tongue sticking out—and shuddered. "Yes. It was terrible. I've seen violent death before—Grimsby, Christopher's grandfather's valet, was shot, so there was a lot of blood—but I've never seen anything like that."

"Tell me," Constance prompted.

"Well, she was strangled, so her face was purple. Her tongue was sticking out. Her eyes were bloodshot. Her clothes were twisted, as if she'd fought. Her necklace was broken, there were pearls everywhere..."

"Mother gave her that necklace," Constance said softly. "Last Christmas. She gave me one, too. And Gilbert gave us both lockets. Mine had my picture in it, and an empty place where he said I could put a picture of my husband..."

Her eyes filled with tears again.

"I'm sorry," I said. "I'm sure Francis would be happy to put his picture next to yours in your locket. If you two are serious about each other, of course. I think I'm a bit young to get married, myself, although of course Francis is almost thirty—"

"Francis won't want me," Constance hiccoughed, "after this weekend."

"After the murders, you mean? Don't be silly, Constance. It's hardly your fault that your mother and Johanna died. You didn't kill them, did you?"

I hadn't meant it seriously, of course. But then she looked at me for a second without answering—long enough for my blood to run cold—before she smiled. "Of course not, Pippa."

I blinked. "You're sure?"

She giggled. "Of course I'm sure. I was in this bedroom with you all last night, remember? I couldn't have killed Johanna even if I'd wanted to."

I nodded. "Of course."

"I'm just rather glad that she's dead, that's all. I'm sorry my mother had to die, but I'm not sorry Johanna is gone."

After a moment, she bit her lip and added, "Even if now I have to find somewhere else to live, and some way to make money. Unless I can snag a rich husband, of course. Francis isn't rich, is he, Pippa?"

"No more than the rest of us," I said. "He's comfortable, I suppose."

Or would be if he didn't spend all his money on dope. And considering that Aunt Roz had been forced to sell gossip to the tabloids to help pay for Francis's habit, I could only imagine how much it cost on a yearly basis.

Then again, if he could stop using it, just think of the savings.

But there was no need to tell Constance any of that. She might not be serious about Francis, or he might not be serious about her—all appearances to the contrary, on both of their parts—and anyway, it was for him to share with her, not me, if he chose to.

"I haven't noticed him take any of his medicine since we got here," Constance said, "even with everything that's been going on. Although I suppose he might need some tonight..."

He might. And she seemed very understanding of it, which was nice. She even called it medicine, which of course it was, technically, and not dope, which was how Francis used it.

At least she wasn't one of those people who were shocked and appalled that after surviving the war and the trenches, after watching friends and fellow soldiers die horrible deaths,

Francis wasn't able to go on as if nothing out of the ordinary had happened.

"Maybe you and Gilbert can do what Christopher and I did," I said, "and share a service flat in London. At least until one of you gets married and moves out. And then the other can get married and have the husband or wife move in. Christopher and I have room enough for the two of us plus a child or two, or we would have if we shared a room and our children shared another."

"But I thought..." Constance trailed off. "You and Christopher, you said?"

I nodded.

"But aren't you and Lord St George...?"

I shook my head. "Oh, no. No, no. I told you that back at Sutherland. There's nothing going on with me and Crispin."

She looked confused, and I added, "Earlier tonight, that was just for Lady Laetitia's benefit. We need her to keep talking to him—someone has to keep an eye on her; she might have killed Johanna—and she only seems to want him when someone else wants him, too. So I pretended at jealousy so she'd think she had competition for his affection. And it worked beautifully, as you saw. She'll hardly let him off her arm now. Did you see the way she swatted him with her fan when she called him to heel?"

Constance nodded. "So you're not...?"

"No," I said. And reinforced it. "Of course not. You heard me. He's insufferable. I'd kill him within the first week, and that's if he didn't kill me first."

"He's clever," Constance said.

Yes, he was, and that was partly what made him so difficult to deal with. "He'd be easier to manage if he were a little less clever. At least I could argue him into silence, then."

Constance's lips twitched. "You seem perfectly able to

argue him into silence now. And you have to admit he's handsome. They all are."

Of course they were. Not that I'd admit that out loud. "You think Francis is handsome, do you?"

She blushed. "Of course. Who wouldn't?" But then her voice changed from breathy to chiding. "But we weren't talking about me and Francis, Pippa. We were talking about you and—"

"Please," I cut her off. "Not in the same sentence, I beg you."

She blinked, and I added, "It was all for show, Constance, I promise. We worked it out after tea. Including that imbecilic banana skirt comment. Christopher asked what I'd be wearing to dinner, and I told him my yellow dress, and he tasked Crispin with coming up with something clever to say about it—one of his 'backhanded compliments'—and that's what he came up with, the bastard."

"Now, now, Pippa," Constance drawled, in a not-terrible imitation of Crispin, "you know he's a Sutherland through and through."

I rolled my eyes. "He is, at that. But with that kind of behavior, you can understand why I told you we wouldn't last a week if we had to live together. Crispin lives at Sutherland with his father. He comes up to Town occasionally, and goes to a party, and gets drunk, and crashes a car, and beds a girl, and then he goes home again until the next time. Meanwhile, Christopher and I are quite happy in our service flat. And you and Gilbert could be happy in one of your own."

Or she could marry Francis and live happily in one of the minor Sutherland properties.

Or in Beckwith Place, if she didn't mind sharing with Aunt Roz and Uncle Herbert.

Or she could do any number of other things. Go off to

Africa and become a missionary, or to Paris and give Josephine Baker a run for her money. Or to some miserable watering hole on the coast, or a sheep-infested village somewhere in Scotland, somewhere one can live cheaply for a long time and not talk to anyone.

It was Constance's life and Constance's problem, and I wasn't going to get in the middle of it. I had problems of my own.

"Ready for bed?" I jumped down and tugged the counter-pane away from my side of the mattress while Constance did the same on her side. "Did you lock the door?"

She nodded. "But you can check again."

I did check again. And then I checked that I'd checked, just one more time for good measure. And then, when I was in bed, I slipped my hand under the pillow to make sure that the hat pin I had tucked there—because who needs a bread knife when you travel with a three inch long stiletto in your reticule?—was still where I had put it, in case Constance turned evil and decided to attack me in the night.

All that done, I put my head on the pillow. "Good night, Constance."

"Good night, Pippa." She turned her head to look at me, her eyes like pale glimmers of light in the darkness of the room. "Thanks for being my friend."

"It's entirely my pleasure," I told her, which wasn't too far from the truth. The unassuming little girl I remembered from Godolphin had grown on me over the past few days. "I know it feels like a lot right now. Your mother and Johanna dead, a murderer on the loose. But the police will figure it out, and so will you. They'll figure out the murders, I mean, and you'll figure out your life. It'll be all right. I promise."

"Thank you, Pippa."

She closed her eyes, and after a few moments her breath

turned deep and even. If she had a guilty conscience, it clearly didn't keep her awake at night.

I didn't—have a guilty conscience, that is—but I stayed awake quite a lot longer while I went over the conversation in my head, and wondered whether I ought to leave Constance to her sleep, and scurry off across the landing to the room where the Astleys slept the sleep of the innocent, before she woke up again and tried to murder me.

IT WAS LATER, but I don't know how much later, when I was startled out of sleep. It might have been thirty minutes, or it might have been several hours. From the deep darkness of the room and the lack of any light coming in around the draperies, I guessed it was sometime in the later part of the night, the hour or two before dawn.

There was movement on the other side of the bed, soft mutters and the slide of fabric and skin before Constance's voice rang out, rusty with sleep. "What's happening?"

"I don't know," I said, since I was wrestling with my own bedclothes and hadn't got any farther than she had. "Someone's making a lot of noise."

It was by way of stating the obvious, since it sounded like the entire first floor was having a party outside our door. I could hear several different voices, steps, movement, and the shrill screams of Lady Laetitia Marsden rising above it all.

"Good Lord," I said, "what has St George done now?"

"I don't think it's your cousin this time, Pippa."

Constance was already on her way towards the door, bare feet pattering on the wood floors. I took the time to slip my own feet into a pair of quilted mules before I followed.

NINETEEN

I CONTEMPLATED SNATCHING my hat pin from below the pillow in case there should be need of it, but in the end I decided against it. I didn't want to accidentally stab anyone, and given the level of activity outside the door, that seemed a possibility.

By the time I caught up, Constance had got the door unlocked, and had flung herself through and into the crowd on the other side. "What's happened? Is someone hurt? What's all the screaming?"

I followed, doing my best to see. The landing was in the middle of the house, with only one window of its own at the top of the stairs, and no one, it seemed, had stumbled upon the idea of turning the light on in one of the surrounding rooms and letting it spill out through the door so we could see each other and get an idea of what was going on.

Then again, I hadn't thought of it either, so it wasn't as if I was any cleverer than anyone else present.

And before I could do anything about it—before I could do

anything at all, except start to ask, "What's going on?"—I ran into a male body, or it ran into me.

They were all male, except for Constance, whose nightdress I could make out as a faint, pale gleam in the dusk, and Lady Laetitia, who I could place, based on her now thankfully diminishing shrieks of terror, still inside her room.

I bounced back. A pair of hands grabbed my arms and held me steady, and I looked up into Crispin's... no, Christopher's... no, it really was Crispin's face.

"Pippa?" he said. "Are you all right?"

He looked like Crispin. He sounded like Christopher, or at least the name he called me did. Crispin would have called me Darling. Although in the dark, it was difficult to be entirely positive.

Nor did it matter a whole lot, I decided. "I'm fine," I said and took a step back, so his hands fell from my arms. "What's going on?"

"Something seems to have happened to Laetitia." He turned his head to look in the direction of her half-open door. From behind it, we could hear soft sobs and a male voice— Marsden's, I assumed, although if I really was talking to Christopher, it might be Crispin—murmuring reassurances in soothing tones to calm her down.

The longer our conversation went on, the more certain I became that I was, in fact, speaking to Crispin, though. And if so, it was likely to be her brother in with Laetitia. None of the other men would have dared to breach that barrier, I thought.

Although perhaps it was best to make certain.

I crossed my fingers. "St George?"

I had time to realize that if it turned out to be Christopher, I would likely never live it down, before he hummed a response. It sounded affirmative. So at least I knew for certain which Astley I was conversing with (and Christopher would never know that for a moment or two, in the dark, I hadn't been positive).

"When you were dancing with Johanna night before last, was she wearing a locket around her neck?"

He looked at me for a moment. "Yes?"

"And in the garden?"

He nodded. "Yes. Why do you ask?"

I wasn't sure myself. Just— "Gilbert gave it to her. He gave them each one. Constance told me."

Crispin's eyebrow shot up, but before he could comment, another wail from inside Lady Laetitia's room reached us, and we both flinched.

"You're not planning to go in there," I asked, "are you?"

"Good Lord, no." After a moment he added, "Not unless she asks for me. If she does, I guess I won't have a choice."

"You most certainly do. Just because a woman crooks her finger at you, doesn't mean you have to obey, you know."

"Oh, really?"

That was when I remembered that I had, in fact, done just that to him this evening. Crooked my finger and expected him to come.

"That was different," I said, while I was glad the darkness covered the blush that crept into my cheeks. "We'd planned that."

"Oh, had we?"

He let me stew for a moment, and then he added, "It wouldn't be the first time I've been in a woman's bedchamber, you know. It wouldn't even be the first time I've been in Laetitia's. Or she in mine, at least."

"I'm sure it wouldn't. Thanks so much for reminding me, St George, since I'm sure I would have forgotten otherwise."

He hadn't anything to say to that, so I added, "But going in there now, with her brother present, and both your cousins, not to mention the Peckhams, would be tantamount to a declaration. And unless you're willing to declare yourself, and you're willing to marry her, you're better off staying out."

There was a moment's pause. Then—

"I had no idea you were so old-fashioned, Darling. Declare myself, truly?"

"Call it whatever you want," I told him. "Aunt Roz tasked me with making sure you didn't get yourself in any trouble this weekend, and getting engaged to Lady Laetitia Marsden would definitely qualify as trouble. I'm not going back to her and telling her I allowed you to do that."

"How are you going to stop me, Darling?"

His voice had a disconcerting note of flirtation—it was the darkness, I assume; it's a lot easier to be brave in the dark, unless I was simply imagining it—and I told him, as prosaically as I could, "I'll knock you down and sit on you if I have to. Francis will help me. Won't you, Francis?"

I snagged the elder Astley's arm before he could push past. My eyes had mostly adjusted to the dark now. I could clearly see that I was talking to Crispin, and I had also spied Francis making his approach, probably on his way towards Constance, who was still behind me somewhere, trying to get her head around what was happening.

He glanced down at me. "Won't I what, Pipsqueak?"

"Help me keep St George from compromising himself by going into Lady Laetitia's bedroom."

He glanced from me to Crispin and back. "How do you plan to do that?"

"You hit him, I keep him down," I said.

Francis's teeth flashed in a grin. "I'd be delighted to help with that. You just tell me where you want him hit and I'll do it."

I gave Crispin an arch look for which he returned a roll of

his eyes. "Some cousin you are, Astley. You'd turn on your own blood because she asked you to?"

"I like her better than you," Francis told him, and glanced around. "Any idea what's going on?"

I shook my head. "I'd just got out here when I ran into St George. I assume we all heard the same thing...?"

Francis nodded. "Someone screaming bloody murder—Lady Laetitia, it seems, since it wasn't either you or Constance—and then a lot of footsteps and noise."

"Where's Christopher?"

"I don't know," Francis said and glanced at Crispin. "St George?"

Crispin shook his head. "I'm not sure he was there when we woke up."

My blood ran cold, and I turned to look at him. "Surely you're not suggesting...?"

"No, Darling." He turned his head, and a lock of fair hair he hadn't slicked back for the day yet flopped over his eye. "Of course not. Kit would never—"

"Then where is he?" I looked around. "You don't think anything's happened to him, do you?" I raised my voice. "Christopher?"

"Christopher!" Francis bellowed.

"Kit!" Crispin added his slightly higher tones to the call.

There was no response, or none from Christopher. He didn't come running, and didn't stick his head out through Lady Laetitia's door to tell us he was inside, offering whatever assistance he could.

"Go make sure he's not in your room," I told Crispin or Francis, whichever one was likely to obey me, while I turned to the stairs. "I'm going downstairs."

One of them headed for the other side of the landing. It must have been Francis, because when I clattered down around the bend in the stairs, Crispin was keeping pace with me. "Where to?" he asked when we reached the reception room floor.

I had no idea, of course. I was running blind, on instinct. If Christopher wasn't upstairs, he had to be down here, and—

There was a breeze coming from somewhere. I could feel it move the soft ends of my bob against my cheeks, and it also ran across the soft silk of my pyjamas and rustled the fabric.

I headed towards where I thought it came from—the open door to the parlor—but before I could take make it past the doorway, a wordless bellow came from upstairs.

"Francis!" Crispin spun on his heel, going back up the stairs again two at a time, abandoning me.

I barely hesitated at all—half a second, perhaps, with a glance toward the parlor door—before I ran back up the stairs towards Francis's voice. By now, it had resolved itself into words, some of which I recognized (and thought perhaps I'd rather I hadn't, because they were blisteringly profane) and some I'd never heard before. Interspersed with the curses was Christopher's name. "Come on, Kit. Wake up! Wake up!"

My legs being shorter, it took me longer than it took Crispin to make it back up to the first floor. He took the stairs two at a time while I had to settle for stepping on each one.

I got to the landing in time to see the edge of his pyjama legs flick around the corner into their shared room, across the landing from Lady Peckham's closed and locked door.

It was also where Francis's voice came from, and I scurried after them both. I had to push Constance out of the way to do it. There was very little left of Lady Laetitia's tantrum, just some soft sniffles and her brother's soothing tones from behind the half-open door to her room, so perhaps Constance felt she could now devote herself to the next cataclysm.

Or not cataclysm. Dear God, no more cataclysms. No more problems of any kind.

I wasn't even aware I was praying, sending mostly wordless requests and desperation ahead of me as I burst into the room the three Astleys had shared for the past two nights.

Christopher had to be all right. He had to be. Please, God, let him simply be asleep, not dead, and that was the reason Francis couldn't raise him.

Asleep. Not dead.

Not Christopher.

The room was larger than the one I had shared with Constance, and it had a double bed as well as a settee along one wall that was made up with what was now a rumpled pile of pillows and blankets, some of them dragging on the floor. One side of the bed was empty, with the counterpane thrown back. Whoever had been sleeping there must have tossed off the covers and run onto the landing with the rest of us when Lady Laetitia started screaming. So, clearly, had whoever had been sleeping on the settee.

Crispin on the settee and the two Astley brothers in the bed, I surmised, or perhaps Francis, the former soldier, had assured his little brother and his much more delicate cousin that he'd slept in worse places in his time, and he had made himself comfortable on the settee while they shared the bed.

It didn't matter, anyway. Just the useless calculations my mind made to keep itself busy so I didn't have to focus on what was going on on the other side of the bed.

Francis and Crispin were both standing there.

Or perhaps that gives a much too peaceful picture of what was going on. Francis had ripped the blankets off his brother, and was busy slapping him across the face and yelling at him. "Wake up, Christopher! Come on, brother. Shake it off and open your eyes. Talk to me. Kit!"

He was clearly frantic, his voice shaking, and I could see tears on his cheeks. The faint light from the window reflected in them.

Crispin, meanwhile, was doing his best to stop Francis from actually hurting Christopher. He was clutching at Francis, trying to drag him back from the bed. "Easy, Francis. Take it easy."

I choked back a sob. If Crispin was trying to stop Francis from hurting Christopher, that must mean that hurting Christopher was possible. Christopher must be alive. Although from where I stood, he didn't look as if he were. He was as unresponsive as a rag doll as Francis shook him. His head lolled, his arms flopped, his wrists hung limp. There wasn't a sound or a movement out of him.

But Crispin was closer to them both than I was, and perhaps he had seen something I hadn't.

Please let Christopher still be alive. Please let him be alive.

"Dear God," Constance whispered behind me, "what's happened?"

"Light," I told her hoarsely. "We need light!"

She ran for the nearest lamp and flicked it. Nothing resulted, of course. I could have told her that. The lights seemed to be out on the entire first floor. Perhaps in the entire house.

I dragged my mind into coherence, even if just for a single thought. It felt like it took untold effort. "Main fuse panel?"

Constance looked blank for a second, and then her eyes sharpened. "Box room under the stairs."

"Can you—?"

She sent one agonized look Francis's way, and then she whirled away to hurry out of the room, white gown fluttering. I turned back to the scene at the bed.

"Stop it, Francis!" Crispin was saying now. "You're hurting him. Stop it!"

He physically threw himself at Francis and pushed him back from the bed, forcing him to let Christopher go. Christopher flopped down on the mattress, lifelessly, and Francis bared his teeth in a snarl. For a moment or two, I was afraid he'd hit Crispin, and not in the way we'd joked about on the landing earlier.

No, his whole body went taut, his hands clenched, his muscles bunching with effort. He was bigger than Crispin—than Christopher, too. Stockier by nature, more muscular with age. Crispin and Christopher were both still boyish, slighter, without Francis's packed muscles.

If Francis wanted to, or if he lost control, he could do lasting damage to anyone who stood in his way. Which was exactly where Crispin had put himself: between Francis and Christopher.

I held my breath, waiting.

Crispin didn't. He wasn't worried, or didn't seem to be. Perhaps he just didn't understand how far he had pushed Francis. Francis had lost one brother; he clearly wasn't about to lose another. Not if there was anything he could do about it.

And that included waking Christopher from the dead himself, through sheer force of will.

But Crispin didn't even seem to realize it. He knocked Francis back a step and turned his back on him, as if he weren't worried at all.

"Kit." His voice was soft, and his hand gentle when he put it on Christopher's chest. "Can you hear me, Kit?"

There was no answer from Christopher, and Crispin moved his hand from Christopher's chest to his throat, and from there to his cheek. Behind him, Francis shifted from one foot to the other, fists still clenching and unclenching as he undoubtedly had to talk himself out of going for Crispin's throat when it was obvious that Crispin wasn't doing anything to harm Christopher.

When he pushed one of Christopher's eyelids up and bent over him, it ended in an irritated huff. "Can't anyone light a candle or find a torch? I can't see!"

"I sent—" My voice was froggy, and I cleared it. "Constance went downstairs to look at the fuse panel. Hopefully—"

And yes, just like clockwork, like an answer to prayer, the landing lit up. Or at least it felt as if it did. The light was actually pretty faint, spilling up the stairs from the reception room downstairs, but it was electric light, and after so much darkness, it felt like a flood of brightness.

Francis lunged for the lamp at the bedside and flicked it on. Light streamed from that, too, and we all squinted against it as it lit up Christopher's face and Crispin's finger, holding Christopher's eyelid back.

Francis let out a *whoosh* of breath—relief, I thought—and Crispin nodded, with a relieved—if less explosive—exhale of his own. But before he could say anything, there was the clatter and patter of footsteps on the stairs. Two pairs: Constance's almost silent bare feet, and a pair of heavier shoes that thumped on each step. I expected Constance to be accompanied by her brother, but instead it was Tom who burst through the door just ahead of her.

He took in the scene in a single glance, and his jaw dropped. Constance, meanwhile, threw herself at Francis, whose arms came up just in time to catch her.

"Kit!" Crispin was forced to take a step back as Tom lunged for the bedside and began going through the same cycle of tests that Crispin had employed. Chest, throat, cheek, eye.

"He's doped to the gills," Crispin commented calmly, as if, just a few seconds prior to this, we hadn't all been frantic with worry. "His pupils contracted when the light came on, so he's responding to stimuli. He's breathing and his heart's beating, but it's slow."

Tom shot him a look. "Had some experience with dope, have you?"

Crispin just shrugged, since the answer was obvious. "Better find him a doctor, don't you think?"

I looked from one to the other of them. "What do you mean, he's doped? Christopher doesn't take dope!"

"He did tonight," Crispin said, and I rounded on him.

"What do you mean, you utter twit? We spent the evening together! I would know if Christopher had taken dope, and so would you! We were together most of the time."

"I spent the latter part of the evening with Laetitia," Crispin corrected, without so much as a glance out the door and across the landing at the room where Lady Laetitia was still sniffling.

"Well, I spent it with Christopher, and I would have seen him do something that stupid. We live together, and I'm telling you, Christopher doesn't take dope!"

"Then someone else gave it to him," Tom said, from where he was still bent over Christopher's prone body. Now that the light was on, I could see that Christopher was, indeed, alive. He was breathing, slowly but steadily, even if his chest didn't rise or fall far inside the striped pyjama top. And of course he wasn't responsive at all, to Francis's shaking or shouts, Crispin's firm administrations, and—now—to Tom's clinical examination.

Francis made an inarticulate sound, and abandoned Constance to run to one of the weekender bags. He fell to his knees next to it. Seconds later, things started flying from inside to land on the floor all around. Shaving tackle, suspenders, cuff-links, unmentionables...

Then he rose to his feet with a cry, small twists of paper

clutched in both hands, cheeks flushed in what looked like anger.

We were all staring at him by then, and now Constance let out a moan. She wasn't looking at his face, however, but at the papers in his hands. Crispin's lips were compressed in a tight line that was quite different from his usually expressive pout, while Tom looked serious.

"How much is missing?" he asked.

I didn't understand what he meant—my brain seemed to be dragging, not capable of keeping up with everything that had happened—but Francis did. "Looks like a hundred grains, at least. Maybe more."

"Enough to kill someone twice over," Tom said, and Constance let out a cry. Turning on her heel, she ran, still padding on bare feet, out of the room.

For a second or two—a crazy slice of time that lasted a lot longer in my mind that it did in reality—I was certain it was an admission of guilt. Hadn't I suspected her, after all? Hadn't I reasoned that she knew about Francis's Veronal and where to find it, and hadn't I thought that she might have used it to kill her mother?

And now Francis had discovered a lot of his Veronal missing—enough to kill two people, according to Tom, who ought to know—and Constance was running away.

Francis tore after her with a bellowed, "Constance!"

"Stay with him!" Tom ordered. Crispin nodded, and Tom pushed past me with a murmured apology. I turned to stare after him, blankly, while Crispin dropped down on the edge of the bed next to Christopher and let out his breath.

TWENTY

"GILBERT!" Constance howled from out on the landing, and I heard what I assumed was a door opening and then slamming against the wall before bouncing back. "Gilbert!"

I realized, for the first time since I'd been woken from dead sleep by Lady Laetitia's screams, that at no point had I heard Gilbert Peckham's voice, not from inside Laetitia's chamber, nor from anywhere on the landing. Nor had I at any point seen his face or any other part of him.

"What's happening?" I asked Crispin.

It was more a request for understanding what my brain couldn't seem to grasp on its own, than the actual belief that he knew something I didn't. Because of course he didn't. He couldn't possibly.

And he didn't seem to, because he merely shook his head before looking back down at Christopher. "Putting two and two together, I'd say someone has stolen more than a hundred grains of Cousin Francis's Veronal. Enough to kill someone twice, according to Detective Sergeant Gardiner."

I nodded. I had caught at least that much. "It's not possible to kill someone twice."

"Of course not," Crispin said. "But it's possible to kill two people."

Yes, it was. But— "Christopher isn't dead."

"No." Crispin laid a hand against Christopher's cheek, perhaps to check his temperature, or perhaps just to reassure himself that Christopher was still there, and still warm. "He isn't."

"He—" I cleared my throat. My voice was rusty, as if I hadn't used it for a long time. "He got lucky."

Crispin nodded. "I'd say so. Unless whoever gave it to him didn't want him dead, of course, just out of the way for a while."

"Who would want Christopher out of the way? Why Christopher?" If it had been Crispin, that would have been a different story. I could imagine that lots of people might want him out of the way, permanently or just for a while. But— "He wasn't a threat to anyone, and he's much less objectionable than you are."

"Same to you, Darling," Crispin said, which was fair.

"Besides, what good would it do to get either of you out of the way when the three of you shared a room, and you and Francis were wide awake as soon as the ruckus started? That makes no sense."

He shook his head. "Maybe there's another reason he isn't dead. Maybe whoever gave him the drug miscalculated the dose. Or just wanted to give us something else to think about for a while so we wouldn't worry about whatever else might be happening in or around the Dower House."

Maybe so.

Up until now I had concentrated on Christopher, but now my ears and my brain started serving up a few impressions from outside the room as well. Laetitia and her brother must have been alerted by Constance's mad rush across the landing, or perhaps the door slamming against the wall. Or perhaps they simply realized they couldn't ignore the rest of us any longer.

At any rate, they had appeared on the landing at long last. Marsden was dressed in stripes, and his hair stuck straight up on one side. It made him look a bit more human, less glossily perfect, and as such, I thought it was an improvement.

Lady Laetitia, meanwhile, cut a stunning figure in a slinky nightgown and matching negligee, and the slight dishevelment of her usually sleek bob only served to enhance her amazing good looks. Her eyes were puffy from crying, she was pale and devoid of makeup, and she still managed to look like something that belonged on a silver screen above us all. The gown and negligee, like everything else she had worn this weekend, was black: sheer in places, with strategic applications of lace everywhere that mattered.

Tom did a double-take when he came out from Gilbert's room and saw her, and even Francis's eyes widened for a second before he turned away, deliberately, to put his hand under Constance's elbow as she exited the room as the last of them.

"Well?" I managed, certain they'd tell me that Gilbert was inside, dead to the world, or more likely simply dead, from an overdose of Veronal.

But Tom removed his gaze from Lady Laetitia to look at me, and shook his head. "Empty."

I blinked. "Where is he?"

"That's what I'd like to know," Tom said grimly, and Constance, now clinging to Francis's arm, whimpered.

"Perhaps he went below-stairs to talk to Dawson?" I suggested, since I was honestly a bit surprised that the staff—or at least Dawson and Nigel the hallboy—weren't milling around with the rest of us, trying to determine what was going on.

"There's a lot of padding between downstairs and up," Constance said apologetically, her voice soft. "Mother—"

She had to stop to clear her throat. "Mother didn't like to hear the sound of the servants moving about."

Of course not. God forbid that the other people who lived in her house, the people who made her life comfortable, made too much noise. She had probably been the kind of mother who believed that children should be seen and not heard, too. That would explain rather a lot about Constance, actually.

"Never mind Dawson," I told Tom, "or for that matter Gilbert Peckham." If he wasn't dead in bed, who cared about him? "What are *you* doing here? Didn't you tell us earlier that you were going to the village for the rest of the night? You couldn't have heard the screaming all the way from there. I know Lady Laetitia was loud, but surely she wasn't that loud?"

Laetitia sniffed, deeply insulted, but she didn't say anything. Couldn't deny it, I suppose.

"Where's St George?" she asked instead, with a flick of her eyelashes at me. And then, when she realized he wasn't present, "Dear Lord, has something happened to St George?"

I opened my mouth to reassure her—or more honestly, I suppose, I opened my mouth to say something scathing—but before I could, Tom told her, "St George is sitting with Christopher Astley. They're both fine. Or will be. Can anyone tell me what happened tonight?"

"I woke up," Lady Laetitia declared, "with the overwhelming feeling that there was a presence in my room."

I refrained from rolling my eyes, but only barely. "Left over from the séance earlier, I suppose? Did you get the impression that it was Lady Peckham, or Johanna? Or perhaps someone else? My cousin Robbie, perhaps? My father?"

"I don't know who it was," Laetitia said, and under the circumstances, I had to—much as I hated to do it—commend her for the dignity she managed to show in not snapping back at me. "It was dark, and I had been asleep, and when I woke up, someone was leaning over me. I couldn't make out his—or her—features. It was very dark. But I could hear someone breathe. And feel it. Hot on my face."

She shuddered, and if it was feigned, she could have given the divine Josephine a run for her money.

"What happened then?" Tom wanted to know. He sounded, thankfully, not at all influenced by her lurid tale.

"I screamed," Laetitia said simply. "And I continued to scream. When I opened my eyes again—"

I got a mental picture of her, eyes squeezed shut and mouth wide open, that was not at all flattering.

"—the figure was gone. I was alone in my room."

Francis leaned down and murmured something to Constance. She nodded. I didn't have to be next to them to guess that Francis had chalked the whole thing up to an over-wrought imagination after the séance, and Constance had agreed.

Laetitia didn't pay them any attention. "But it was dark," she continued with a shiver, "and my lamp didn't work. I heard noises outside my room. Feet running. And then Geoffrey came in and held me, and I felt better."

The look she gave her brother was one of adoration. And much as I disliked Lord Geoffrey and his wandering hands, I was glad that at least he treated his sister right when she needed him.

"Did he say anything?" Tom asked. And clarified, "This shadow you said you saw. The figure in your room. Did he say anything?"

"He said..." Laetitia gulped. "He said, 'you know what you did. You should confess.'"

There was a pause as we all digested this statement.

"And what did you do," Tom asked finally, dryly, "that you need to come clean about?"

Francis whispered something else to Constance, who nodded. Again, I could guess what it was, and agreed with it. There hadn't been anyone in Laetitia's room. Between the excitement of the séance and whatever it was she had done, her own guilty conscience had caused her to imagine the figure and the words.

She glanced at me, almost as if she could feel my disbelief, and then looked away again. Her mouth opened, but if something came out, it was too faint for me to hear.

"What was that?" Tom leaned closer.

"I gave Gilbert," Laetitia whispered, "a few grains of a sleeping powder and told him to put them in Miss Darling's drink when he mixed it."

"*What?*"

It wasn't Francis's voice, as I might have expected it to be. And of course it wasn't Christopher's. He was unconscious in the other room.

It wasn't even Tom's.

No, it was Crispin who had somehow made it over to the door of the bedchamber without me noticing, and who was staring at Laetitia with shock and horror in his eyes.

"You—" He could barely get the words out, his voice was shaking so much. "You spiked Philippa's drink and almost killed Kit? *Why?*"

"It was hardly enough to kill anyone," Laetitia said petulantly. She tossed her head so the glossy, black hair swung and settled back into its usual sleek bob. "Just a few grains. Not even a full dose. She's smaller than I am, so I didn't want to give her too much. I just wanted her out of the way for the night."

My jaw dropped. After a moment I realized I was gaping, and I lifted it back up again.

Nobody bothered to ask *why* she had wanted me out of the way. I guess it was obvious. That little performance we had put on must have worked better than any of us had dared to hope. Laetitia must have thought I was actually going to give her competition for Crispin's affections, and she had decided to get me out of the way for the rest of the evening.

When she'd started screaming, she'd been alone in her—in Johanna's—room, though, and he had been in his own bedroom along with Francis and Christopher, so something must have gone wrong with the plan somewhere along the way.

Unless the plan had simply been to prevent *me* from spending time with Crispin, and not so she could spend the time with him herself.

And all that aside, Christopher had clearly ingested a lot more than an extra-small dose of sleeping draught. If she had given me—or given Peckham to give to me—less than she normally took herself, it should have had even less of an effect on Christopher.

"You tried to drug me?" fell out of my mouth. "You tried to drug me to keep me away from St George, and instead you drugged Christopher and *he almost died?*"

"I didn't drug anyone!" Laetitia protested. "I gave Gilbert a few grains of sleeping powder to mix into your drink. Just a few, I swear. It was supposed to make you drowsy, nothing more. I just wanted to make sure you'd go to bed and stay there. That's all!"

"Oh, that's all?" Crispin asked, somewhat bitterly, from the doorway where he was still leaning. He had his mouth open to say something else, but Tom looked at him, and he closed it again.

"Kit doing all right?"

Tom's voice was bland, but just the question was enough to make Crispin pull a face and disappear back into the room. I wasn't worried, though, nor, I expected, was Tom. If Christopher hadn't been all right, Crispin wouldn't have left him, not even to stand in the doorway and talk to Lady Laetitia. Whatever other faults he had—and they were plentiful—he clearly cared about Christopher's wellbeing.

"So you gave Gilbert Peckham a few grains of a sleeping powder to put into Miss Darling's drink," Tom said. "This was in the parlor last night?"

Laetitia nodded. "He mixed her a drink before dinner, after that exchange—" She cast a glowering look at the door where Crispin had disappeared, "—about the yellow dress."

"There was nothing whatsoever wrong with that drink," I said. "It was a Last Word, and it was delicious."

"You always do enjoy having the last word, don't you, Darling?" Crispin's disembodied voice said from Christopher's bedside.

I glowered at the door, too. "I do, thank you very much. Now pipe down, St George. Nobody asked you."

I think this might have been greeted by a snigger from inside the room, but I can't be sure. At any rate, Tom continued the conversation—or questioning—without paying attention to it. "So there was nothing wrong with your Last Word?"

"Nothing at all," I confirmed. "I finished it, and I felt fine."

Laetitia nodded. "After dinner, while we were setting up for the séance, I asked Gilbert, if he had a chance to mix another drink for you, whether he'd be willing to add a couple of grains of something to it. He said he would, and I watched him put the powder paper in his pocket."

"And he didn't question it at all?" Tom wanted to know. "Not what it was or what you wanted him to do with it?"

Laetitia shook her head. "I told him it was a sleeping draught, and that I wanted her out of the way for the rest of the night. That it wouldn't harm her at all, it would just make her go to sleep and wake up tomorrow morning like nothing had happened."

And instead Christopher was in the next room looking like the next best thing to a corpse.

"Then," she said, "in the parlor after the séance, he mixed another drink, and he tipped me the wink that he had added the powder."

"So that was why he scurried over to Marsden to get him to talk to you," I said, enlightened. "It wasn't about St George and his peccadillos at all."

"I know all about Crispin's peccadillos," Laetitia said, with a haughty tilt of her chin. "Better than you do, I imagine."

Maybe, maybe not. Grimsby's dossier had been fairly comprehensive in that regard. However—

"What happened to the drink?" Tom wanted to know.

I turned my attention back to him. "It tasted awful. Bitter and sort of sour. Once Peckham ran off to tell Marsden all about St George's women, I thought I'd throw it into a handy aspidistra. But Christopher tasted it and didn't think it was as awful as I did, so he ended up drinking it."

No one said anything for a moment. Tom directed a grim look at the room in which Christopher lay.

"But it was just a few grains," Laetitia protested again. "I swear. I'm quite used to..."

She trailed off, blushing slightly.

"Doping other women to keep them away from the men you want?" I suggested. She gave me a crushing look, but no answer.

"I don't understand," Marsden said after a few moments. It would be Marsden, of course. "What happened to Astley? Where's Peckham? And what are you doing here, Gardiner? I thought you were going to the pub for the night."

Tom nodded. "That's what I said I'd do, Lord Geoffrey. But

two residents of this household have died under suspicious circumstances in the past two days, and there's still a murderer on the loose. We don't actually leave the premises and go off to the village pub to sleep under those circumstances."

He waited a second while that information sank in, and then he added, "Constables Collins and Burke were on guard outside the house, while I set up in a quiet corner of the dining room. I didn't think it likely that I would be spotted there at that time of night."

"So you've been sitting in the dining room in the dark for..." I glanced around for a clock. When there was none to be found, I estimated, "—four hours? Waiting for what, exactly?"

"Waiting for someone to make a move," Tom said coolly. "Waiting for something to happen. Or more precisely, for someone to try to make a bunk, so I could arrest him."

Lord Geoffrey's lips curved in a way I didn't like. "And did you?" he inquired.

Tom leveled a look at him that ought to have had him quailing in his... well, bare feet. It's hard to be angry with a man who is standing in bare feet on the upper landing in the middle of the night, although Tom gave cold professionalism a try. "I did not. When the something I was waiting for happened, it wasn't what I expected."

He turned back to Lady Laetitia. "You said you thought someone was in your room when you woke. Someone who told you to confess."

She nodded.

"And when you opened your eyes again, the figure was gone. But you heard footsteps."

"I did," Laetitia confirmed. "It was either the man—the figure, the person—running away, or it was Geoffrey running towards me."

"Geoffrey's in bare feet," I pointed out. "He wouldn't have made any noise."

Tom nodded. "When you heard your sister scream, Lord Geoffrey, and you left your bed, can you remember whether Gilbert Peckham was in the room with you?"

Marsden threw his mind back. It looked painful. "No," he said eventually, and while I wanted to blame him for not being more observant, I realized that neither Crispin nor Francis had noticed that Christopher was there with them, and unwell, when they had scrambled out of bed—or off the settee—at the beginning of the ruckus, either.

Constance looked like she was swaying, and Francis must have thought so too, because he put an arm around her. She drew in a breath. "Detective Sergeant Gardiner?"

Tom turned to her. "Miss Peckham?"

Constance had to take in another breath before she could speak again. "Where is my brother?"

"That's what I was trying to convey, Miss Peckham," Tom said with a grimace. "Constable Burke was stationed in the back garden, to keep an eye on the double doors with the exit from the parlor. When the screaming started upstairs, Burke ran towards the house to help. Upon arrival in the parlor, he encountered a person coming in the opposite direction. This person fell upon Constable Burke, and knocked him down for long enough to allow this person to make his escape through the door, over the wall at the end of the garden, and away."

Constance stared at him, her eyes enormous in her pale face.

"Given present company," Tom said, eyeing the circle of us, and the door to the room where Christopher lay with Crispin watching over him, "we assume the person who fled to have been your brother, Gilbert Peckham."

TWENTY-ONE

IT WAS STILL VERY EARLY, the sun hadn't risen yet, but after an announcement like that, I guess nobody wanted to go back to bed. I sat with Christopher for long enough to let Crispin change out of his pyjamas and brush his teeth, as well as slick that wayward lock of hair back against his scalp again, before he walked back into the bedroom. "Your turn."

I got to my feet with a last look at Christopher's peaceful face. "You'll let me know if anything changes?"

"Of course." Crispin sat down in the spot I'd vacated and ran a hand absently over the counterpane that covered Christopher's chest. "But I think he's going to be all right. This amount of Veronal would likely have killed you, had you finished the drink with the powder in it—"

The look he directed up at my face was turbulent, "—but Kit's bigger than you are, and with more muscle mass. If he were going to die, he'd be dead by now. I think he'll just sleep it off in time."

I folded my arms across my chest. It's a defensive mechanism, and I recognized it as such, although I can't tell you what

I was defending myself against. He wasn't even baiting me at this point. "How much time are we talking about?"

"Hard to say," Crispin said. "A regular dose wears off after eight or ten hours. This came close to killing him, so I think it could take several days. But I'm hardly an authority on Veronal. Francis is the one you should ask."

Or perhaps Lady Laetitia.

I had my mouth open to say as much when Crispin glanced up at me again. "I guess I did my job a little too well last night. I'm sorry I almost got you killed."

"You didn't almost get me killed," I said, dropping my arms so I could curl my hands into fists. "*Christopher's* the one who almost died. I was *fine*."

"But if you'd finished the drink the way you were supposed to, you would have been the one who was dead. It's not as if Laetitia planned for Peckham to mix a disgusting cocktail you couldn't stomach. Veronal is tasteless, you know. If the drink had tasted good, you would have finished it. And we'd be sending you off to the mortuary right now."

His hands were fisted too, I noticed, clenched on top of his thighs.

"But it didn't happen," I said. "And you said it yourself: Christopher's going to be fine."

"I *think* Christopher's going to be fine. I don't actually know that he is. We should have a doctor look at him, at the very least."

"We will," I told him soothingly, "as soon as the sun's up. To be honest, I don't think you and I have to worry about it. I think Tom will make sure the doctor's here at first light. He does seem to care about Christopher's wellbeing, you know."

Crispin shrugged, and glanced down at Christopher's face. "I'd like to kill her," he said, so seriously that it took me a moment to come up with anything to say.

"I don't like it any better than you do, you know, but wasn't her fault. You heard her. She only gave Gilbert a few grains, so I would be sleepy and wouldn't get in the way of her seducing you."

"That's what she says," Crispin said bitterly.

I squinted at him. "What does that mean? Didn't you believe her?"

He shot me a look. "I don't know why *you're* so quick to believe her, Darling. You seem perfectly willing to accept that she'd give Gilbert dope to put in your drink. Why do you quibble at the amount? If she wanted you out of the way for the evening, what makes you think she wouldn't want you out of the way permanently?"

Well, because that would be crazy, wouldn't it?

I opened my mouth, and then I closed it again because I had to admit that he had a point. "I suppose I thought she sounded sincere?" I said, uncertainly. "There's a significant difference between getting someone out of the way for a few hours, and killing them. Do you really think she's a murderess?"

"I thought you thought so?" Crispin retorted. "Wasn't that why we created the big deception in the first place, because you thought she might have killed Johanna?"

Well, yes. It had been.

"If you think she'd kill Johanna because of me," Crispin said, "what makes you think she wouldn't kill *you* because of me?"

"Well, because no one in their right mind would actually believe—"

Except someone in her right mind, if that was an accurate description of Laetitia, had in fact believed that something was going on between me and Crispin. Enough of it that, if she hadn't actually wanted to silence me permanently, she'd at least taken steps to keep me away from him in the short term.

"Gilbert's the one who ran away," I said, a bit desperately. "Not Laetitia. Surely that means he's the killer. Doesn't it?"

He lifted a shoulder. "Why ask me, Darling? I'm just not quite as ready to forgive her as you seem to be. She *doped* you. I don't understand why you seem ready to put it behind you, just like that."

"I suppose it's because I don't think she intended—" I glanced at Christopher, so still and pale, "—this."

"But even if she didn't intend this, she intended something. You were in her way, and she wanted you gone. It's no better than hitting you over the head and leaving you in a corner, is it?"

Perhaps it wasn't. Even if it felt quite a bit better without the headache.

"I would have thought you'd take it as a compliment, St George," I said, in an effort to get back on comfortable ground. The sort of ground where we poked at each other for fun and he wasn't looking at me like he cared that someone had tried to harm me.

He grimaced. "You would, would you?"

"Well, she wants you badly enough that she'll literally take out the competition to keep you. Surely that must be a boost to your self-esteem?"

"You'd think," Crispin said, "but somehow I find the prospect of someone committing murder over me less of an aphrodisiac than you might expect."

Well, yes. When he put it like that.

And since he didn't seem inclined to want to play along with me to get our relationship back on its usual footing, I decided I might as well leave him there with Christopher and give us both time to get our respective equilibriums back.

"I'm going to go check on Constance," I told him.

"Isn't she with Francis?"

"I'm sure she is. But they won't mind if I cut in for a few moments. It won't be as if they're doing anything I can't interrupt."

With Peckham missing, presumably the murderer we'd all been looking for, and the police in hot pursuit—or so I assumed—not to mention the two deaths yesterday, that she was still undoubtedly processing, Constance was most likely a blubbering mess on some sofa somewhere, crying on Francis's shoulder. He wouldn't mind if I interrupted that, and Constance might want something else to focus on for a while.

"Be careful," Crispin said.

"Of course. Although with Peckham gone..."

"You didn't suspect Peckham. You suspected Laetitia and Constance."

"But Peckham was the one who ran away."

"We don't know why Peckham ran away," Crispin pointed out. "If he even did. He could be lying in wait in the box room, for all we know. He could be *dead* in the box room, too. The police haven't finished searching the house yet. But even if he did run away, Laetitia was the one who tried to harm you."

"Laetitia was the one who tried to put me to sleep," I corrected. "Gilbert was the one who mixed the drink."

"One or the other of them," Crispin said with emphasis, "added enough sleeping powder to that drink to put Kit into a coma and to kill you. Peckham might be gone—or he seems to be, at least until we learn differently—but Laetitia is still here. So just do me a favor and *be careful!*"

He practically yelled the last two words, and I took a step back, not just because of the volume of his voice, but because of the level of anger in it.

And he noticed—of course he did—because he closed his eyes and took a breath in—deliberately, through his nose—before he opened his eyes again, clear gray now, and added, more calmly, "You know how you don't want to go back to Aunt Roslyn and tell her I've got myself entangled with some woman who's only after the Sutherland title and money?"

I nodded.

"Well, I don't want to go back to Aunt Roslyn and tell her that not only is her youngest son unconscious, but her sister's daughter is dead, and I did nothing to stop it. So for *my* sake, Darling, and for your Aunt Roz's sake, please be careful."

"I'll be careful," I said.

He nodded, and I turned on my heel and left the room, since that was all the emotion I could handle for the time being. More emotion than I'd wanted to handle, if I'm honest. A sincere St George was rather difficult to stomach.

UPSTAIRS, the door to Lady Laetitia's—formerly Johanna's—room was shut, and I heard a murmur of voices from within. She was still talking to her brother, presumably, unless it was a more formal interview with Tom or Inspector Pendennis, where everything she said was taken down and could be used in evidence. I wondered whether anything would come of her confession of having drugged me against my will, even for such an ignominious purpose as to get me away from Crispin for a few hours. It couldn't be legal, surely, even if the ultimate goal hadn't been to harm me permanently.

And that was if she was telling the truth, and the amount of Veronal she had given Gilbert for my drink was only intended to make me drowsy. If she was lying, then she had given him enough to kill me, and almost kill Christopher.

But even if she hadn't done that, and Gilbert Peckham had added the deadly dose of Veronal of his own volition, one could claim that she was partially responsible for what had happened to Christopher, couldn't one? It was negligence, if nothing worse. Deliberate disregard for life and safety, or something like that. If she hadn't given Gilbert the small dose of dope in the first place, who knew whether he'd have thought of doing this on his own?

I tried to imagine Lady Laetitia Marsden going to trial and being sentenced to a nice, long imprisonment at Holloway, and then I shook my head. The press would have a field day over two well-bred women going to such lengths over a notorious playboy—never mind the fact that I didn't actually want him.

I could just imagine the headlines. *Catfight over Crispin!* and *Irresistible: Crispin St George and the women who love him.* My face contorted.

Someone at The Daily Yell seemed to have it out for Crispin anyway—he was featured on the front page every other weekend, it seemed, and rarely in flattering terms. That, combined with the prospect of having my own name dragged through the mud next to his, was enough for me to decide that under no circumstances would I allow it to come to that, even if that meant that Lady Laetitia wouldn't be held responsible for anything she had done.

The police—Scotland Yard with support from the local constabulary in Marsden-on-Crane—were still searching every nook and cranny of the house and grounds, including the garage and cars, as I made my way downstairs. I ran into a couple of constables I didn't know in the foyer, putting trunks and bags back into the box room after making sure that Gilbert —or perhaps as Crispin had suggested, his body—wasn't hidden inside any of them.

I gave them a pleasant nod and carried on. There was a light on in the dining room despite the early hour—the police search of the below-stairs must have knocked up the staff—and Dawson was setting up for breakfast. He gave me a nod of good morning when I walked in. "Tea, Miss Darling? Coffee?"

"Later," I said with a grimace. My insides were still a bit queasy from the realization that it could have been me lying unconscious—or worse, dead—in a bed upstairs. It would be a while before I let anyone mix me a drink again.

Granted, the tea was probably all right. If it were poisoned, it would poison everyone in the household. But still, better safe than sorry. I'd wait until everyone else was partaking, too, to minimize my chances of being exposed to anything unsavory.

"I'm looking for Constance," I added. "Miss Peckham. And Mr. Francis Astley."

"Outside on the terrasse," Dawson told me. "Miss Constance mentioned a desire for fresh air."

Yes, with her mother dead, Johanna dead, and her brother on the run, presumably for having killed them both, not to mention the police crawling all over the Dower House, I'd be looking for a spot of fresh air, too. Or an excuse for getting out of the house, on a day when the terrasse was as far as she could reasonably move without setting off suspicions that she was making a bunk, as well.

I thanked Dawson and headed for the parlor, where I found Finchley on his knees in front of the bar cart. He was in the process of dusting fingerprint powder all over the bottles. Not that I think any of us were in any doubt that it was Gilbert Peckham who had mixed the almost-fatal drink. Laetitia had handed him the powder, and he had handed me the drink, so there wasn't much of a question about it. But I'm sure Scotland Yard, being Scotland Yard, had to eliminate even the unlikely possibilities.

Finchley nodded to me, and I nodded back, and then I vanished through the doors on the other side of the room onto the terrasse, and drew in a deep breath of fresh air.

It was the start of a lovely day, in spite of everything. The sun was just peeping over the horizon, painting the sky in shades of peach and gold against pale blue, and Constance and Francis were sitting side by side on the balustrade with no room between them. Like me, they had changed out of their nightwear into morning clothes. Constance was wearing a pleated skirt with a fluffy blouse, while Francis was in plus fours and argyle and a knitted jumper that matched the socks. His hair was slicked straight back from his face, and his eyes were the clear blue of the sky, awake and alert with no signs of dissipation or overindulgence in anything.

Constance had her eyes fastened on the flagstones and her mouth was moving, but when they heard my footsteps, they both lifted their faces to look at me.

"Pippa," Constance said. It wasn't a greeting, nor a question or an exclamation of surprise. More than anything, it was simply an acknowledgement that I was there. We were all a little goofy after the night we'd had.

I nodded. "Constance. Francis."

"Kit all right?"

"I left him with St George," I said. "If he hadn't been, Crispin would have let me know. He thinks—Crispin does—that it might take some time—maybe even days—but that Christopher will wake on his own when the sleeping draught wears off, and he won't be any the worse for it."

Neither of them said anything, and I added, "I hope he's right."

"There have been times," Francis said reluctantly, without looking at me or for that matter at Constance, "when I've taken enough Veronal to sleep around the clock. And I had a friend who once took enough to sleep for several days. He woke up again eventually, although I'm not entirely certain that it was intentional."

I had my mouth open to ask whether it was the overdose that had been unintentional, or if the friend simply hadn't planned to wake up after taking it, but in the end I decided against asking, and closed my mouth again. I might not like the answer, I realized. The past tense verb hadn't escaped me—he'd had a friend—and I didn't want to dredge up bad memories.

"I'm sure Tom will have the doctor look at him as soon as it's late enough," I said instead. "And he doesn't seem to be suffering. He's breathing, and his heart is beating, and St George doesn't seem as worried anymore as he was in the beginning."

Francis nodded. "I imagine Cousin Crispin's had some experience of his own with dope. I'm sure he's seen worse than this."

No doubt. Crispin's set of Bright Young People dabble in quite a lot of things they shouldn't be dabbling in, and he had probably come up against much worse than Veronal in his time.

"He's quite angry," I said. "Well, you heard how he talked to Lady Laetitia earlier. That ship has sailed, I'm afraid."

I made no particular effort to sound like I felt bad about it, and they both looked at me. I added, "Well?"

"You don't have to sound so pleased about it," Francis said. "Or do you?"

"I'm sure I don't know what you're talking about."

He snorted, and I added, "Fine. She tried to drug me. I don't want her in the family."

"There was never any danger of that," Francis said.

"You don't think so?"

He shook his head. "He's not stupid, contrary to what you might think. Contrary to his own usual behavior, too. He may act like an idiot a lot of the time, but he knows what he wants. Or who. He just can't have her. But he's not going to settle for Laetitia Marsden in the meantime. Not for anything more permanent than a roll between the sheets, at any rate."

"Do you know who—?" I began, because to be perfectly

honest, until quite recently I had never considered the possibility that Crispin was capable of falling in love. I would have put money against it, as a matter of fact. But no one else seemed to doubt that he fancied someone, and I'll admit that I was curious. She had to be quite something, if she had managed to impress him where Lady Laetitia Marsden and Johanna de Vos and all the others from Grimsby's dossier hadn't.

"It was Gilbert," Constance said.

I blinked. "Pardon me?"

This was clearly not the answer to the question I hadn't got around to asking, but at the same time, I wanted to know what she was talking about, especially since it sounded as if she was accusing her brother of...

"It had to be," Constance said with a nod. "I'm almost certain of it."

"That it was your brother who...?"

"Killed Mother and Johanna," Constance said.

"But..." I said, "why?"

She shot me a look, one that veered off, back to her lap, before it connected. "I think it was Johanna's fault. Or because of Johanna."

She had her hands in her lap, and was twisting them together, over and over again. Until Francis reached over and gently untwisted them, and then took one between both of his own and kept it there.

"I don't understand," I said, although of course I did. Or was beginning to, anyway. "Did Gilbert... was he in love with her?"

"I think he must have been," Constance said, and her eyes were shiny with unshed tears. "She was so beautiful, you know? I think every man who ever saw her fell in love with her."

Francis cleared his throat, and I smiled.

"Oh, you," Constance said, and swatted him, but her cheeks were pink and pleased. "You know what I mean. Even your cousin Christopher lost his breath for a second or two."

He had. And Crispin, who was certainly used to pretty women, had lost his mind for longer than that. "And your brother fell in love with her?"

"I think so," Constance said. "And I think she might even have considered marrying him. Except Mother wouldn't have stood for it. She expected all her children to make advantageous marriages. Me and Gilbert and especially Johanna. She was so pretty that she could be expected to turn the head of a duke or an earl, at least."

"Just out of curiosity," I said, "was there a reason Johanna didn't want to marry Lord Geoffrey? He comes with a title and an estate, or he will come into both at some point, I assume. Surely your mother must have thought of it. Her own nephew...?"

"Geoffrey's a cad," Constance said. "You think your cousin is bad? Geoffrey is all hands, and he'll bed anything that moves. The Manor has a problem keeping female staff for longer than a month, because of the way Geoffrey moves through them."

I made a face. That sort of behavior is just unsavory, and at least Crispin, for all his faults, doesn't seduce the staff at either the Hall or Sutherland House in London.

"So Johanna wasn't interested in Geoffrey, in spite of his title and money. But your brother wanted to marry her—"

"No title," Constance nodded, "but a small fortune, and she knew he'd never cheat on her. She'd have had to share Lord Geoffrey with any woman who took his fancy, and most of them do."

"And yet she seemed perfectly willing to marry St George, whose reputation isn't exactly lily-white, either."

Nobody answered, and I added, "I told her, you know,

what he's like, that first afternoon at Sutherland Hal. She called it—" I made quotation marks in the air with my fingers, "boyish exuberance."

Francis snorted.

"Well, before your cousin came along," Constance said primly, "Gilbert showered her with attention and gifts, and she knew he would never, ever stray. So yes, I think she thought about marrying him."

"You said he gave you both lockets for Christmas last year?"

She nodded, with a shy look at Francis. Thinking about his picture opposite hers, I assumed.

"What did you give him?"

"I gave him cufflinks," Constance said, "and Johanna gave him the matching shirt studs."

"Onyx, by any chance?"

She nodded. "Why?"

"Just curious," I said. "So Gilbert wanted to marry her, and she might have wanted to marry him back, but your mother wouldn't hear of it?"

Constance shook her head. "When Lady Charlotte died, she took us all to Sutherland Hall. Gilbert didn't want to go, and Mother told him he could stay home, but she was insistent that Johanna and I come. She probably thought she'd make a play for the duke herself, although she would have given him up to Johanna if he'd shown the slightest interest."

"But he didn't."

"He'd been widowed for all of two weeks," Constance said. "I don't know what she was thinking."

No, I didn't either. Uncle Harold and Aunt Charlotte had never seemed to have a warm relationship—not like Uncle Herbert and Aunt Roz—but they'd been married for more than twenty-five years. You don't just pick a new wife before your old one is even in the ground.

"But by then she had already hooked St George anyway."

Constance nodded. "And Gilbert noticed. But I think she convinced him that it was just because she had to make things look good for Mother. Make them look realistic. Because Mother really did push Johanna to go after your cousin, you know. It wasn't just her own idea."

"I'm sure it wasn't," I said.

"And I think," Constance continued, "that Gilbert thought, when we arrived back here, and Mother stayed behind at Sutherland Hall, that Johanna would stop making eyes at Lord St George."

"But then Lady Laetitia was here, and it turned into a competition for St George's attention."

Constance nodded. "But before that, while we were still at Sutherland Hall, I think Gilbert made his way into Francis's room, and took some of Francis's Veronal, and put it in Mother's medicine bottle. I think he hoped it would look like an accident, and I think he wanted her to die after we'd left for home, so we wouldn't be blamed for anything. And then he'd be able to marry Johanna, and everyone would be happy."

"And I suppose," I said, "once we got here to the Dower House, he probably told Johanna what he'd done—for love of her, no less—and she decided she was better off with St George, who at least hadn't killed anyone."

"Or he didn't tell her," Francis added, "because if he told her, she might call Sutherland Hall and tell Lady Peckham, and then it would have been for nothing. Or worse than nothing: he would be arrested, and would lose his position, and his money, *and* the girl. So he might not have dared to tell her."

No, he might not. He might just have watched Johanna pursue Crispin that whole afternoon and evening, all the way up to the screaming match in the parlor between her and Lady

Laetitia. And then he might have watched the girl he loved run into the garden after St George.

He might even have followed her, and heard her declare her love, and beg for marriage.

"He intercepted her when she came inside, and strangled her," I said, and Constance nodded.

"I'm almost certain he did. He took her into Mother's room because Lord Geoffrey was sharing his own room, and Lady Laetitia was in Johanna's, and all the Astleys were in the spare room, and Dawson was downstairs. But Mother was gone and her room was empty, and he'd know that there was extra padding, just like between the upstairs and the downstairs. Mother didn't like noise."

"And then he strangled her," I said, "and ripped her locket off, the one that he had given her for Christmas," the one that might have contained a photograph of him, "and he left her there, and went to his own room and to sleep as if nothing had happened. And Marsden was already sleeping and didn't notice..."

And the next morning Gilbert had taken his remaining cufflink, the one Johanna hadn't ripped out in her fight for her life, and had put it, along with a note Johanna had once written to him, in the pocket of Crispin's dinner jacket, during the time he left the dining room to, ostensibly, consult Dawson about the menu for luncheon.

"Lord Geoffrey was probably drugged, too," Constance said. "Don't you remember? He said he'd fallen asleep right away. That he took an aspirin for the hangover and went right to sleep."

I nodded. Now that she mentioned it, I did remember that.

"Gilbert was mixing all the drinks again that night. Perhaps he used a few grains of the sleeping powder to put Lord Geoffrey out. He probably noticed what Geoffrey did to you, Pippa, and how your cousin looked like he'd like to murder him for it..."

"So he made sure Marsden wouldn't get up to any more trouble," Francis nodded. "Lady Peckham wasn't a large woman, and Pippa isn't, either. And Lady Laetitia gave him a little extra powder, anyway. Between the dose that killed your mother, and the one that didn't kill Pippa but knocked Kit unconscious, there'd be a few grains left over to put Marsden out for the night."

"I'd like to put Marsden out permanently," I grumbled.

"You and every other woman he's ever touched against her will," Francis said. "And one of these days someone will."

He looked past me into the dining room. "Looks like breakfast is on. Is anyone hungry?"

"I could eat," I said. Supper last night hadn't been anything to write home about, and we'd had rather a lot of excitement since then. And I should also go and relieve Crispin so that he could get something to eat, while I sat with Christopher.

"Let's go." Francis put out a hand and helped Constance to her feet. She looked less enthused about the idea of food than either of us, but when Francis put a hand against her back and nudged her forward towards the parlor doors, she went willingly.

He did the same to me; put a hand against my back and gave me a push. "Come along, Pipsqueak."

"Coming," I told him, and let him guide us both into the Dower House.

TWENTY-TWO

"CRISPIN," Lady Laetitia's voice said from inside the room where Christopher lay, and I slowed to a stop a few feet away from the door, hopefully before either of them noticed me being here. "Darling..."

It was thirty minutes or so later. I had sat in the dining room with Constance and Francis during that entire time, poking at a kipper and a boiled egg while we waited for someone else to appear. When no one did, I'd left the two of them alone and gone upstairs to relieve Crispin of duty so he could get something to eat.

And as I approached the door, I heard Laetitia's voice. I had no idea how long she'd been in there, but her tone was exasperated, so I surmised I wasn't listening to the beginning of a conversation.

Or perhaps it wasn't a conversation at all. Perhaps she'd been trying to get him to talk for a while, and he wouldn't, and that was why her voice had that note of wanting to slap him that was so often present in my own.

Her next words reinforced this impression.

"Crispin St George, if you don't start talking to me right now—!"

"You'll do what?" Crispin wanted to know, his own voice as disagreeable as ever. "Good God, Laetitia, does it really surprise you that I don't want to talk to you after—"

"I told you!" Her voice was shrill, loud enough and whiny enough that I felt it going into the back of my head like a sharp spike. "I wasn't trying to hurt her! I just wanted her out of the way for a few hours—"

"It doesn't matter!" Crispin yelled. "It isn't about her. My cousin could have died! Kit could have died because you couldn't stand to have me pay a compliment to another woman!"

"That's not—" Laetitia tried, and he went on as if she hadn't said anything.

"She doesn't even like me, you know! No—"

She must have tried to interrupt, and he had waved her to silence. Or maybe not: once he started speaking again, it seemed as if it might have been himself he had stopped and not Laetitia at all.

"That's not true, actually. It's not that she doesn't like me, although she doesn't. She doesn't like me *so much* that she wouldn't throw me a rope if I were going down for the third time. *That's* how much she doesn't like me. And for you to almost kill my favorite cousin over her—"

"I said I was sorry!" Laetitia yelled, and in her favor I will say that I almost believed she meant it.

"I'm sure you are." The words were understanding, but Crispin's voice was not. "If Gilbert had succeeded in murdering her, you would have been an accessory, you know. And all because you couldn't handle the idea of a little competition."

Laetitia sniffed. "It was simply that after Johanna..."

"Oh, come off it," Crispin said rudely. "I wasn't in love with Johanna, and we both know it. As for Philippa, that was all play-acting. She's not interested in me. She just got it in her head that you might have killed Johanna—"

Laetitia squeaked, and Crispin smirked. I had seen that smirk enough to recognize the voice that went with it. "Oh, yes. Hadn't you figured that out? She thought you might have strangled Johanna—you were the only one of us with your own bedroom, you know, and you can't deny you had a motive—and she wanted me to keep close to you in case you let something slip."

There was a beat of silence in the wake of this statement.

"She thought *I* killed Johanna," Laetitia said incredulously, "over *you*, so she pretended to be enamored with you so that she could figure out whether I'd killed Johanna? Didn't it occur to her that if I killed Johanna over you, I might kill her over you, too?"

"I imagine it must have," Crispin answered, "although I didn't get the impression that it was very important."

"That seems stupid."

"She's not," Crispin said. "She just acts without thinking sometimes. Even if—" his voice turned sour, "—in this case it almost did end up getting her killed."

"Not by me," Laetitia pointed out. "You believe that, don't you?"

"I suppose I'll have to, won't I?" He didn't wait for her answer. "I wonder what she said to Peckham that made him decide he had to get rid of her."

Now that he'd mentioned it, I wondered myself, something I hadn't actually done so far. I'd been appalled that Laetitia had tried to drug me, and upset that Christopher had almost died, but I hadn't thought to go back over the conversations I'd had with Gilbert last night to try to pinpoint what I might have said to make him feel like killing me was a good idea.

What was it we had talked about just before he had handed me the drink and the conversation had turned to Crispin and his misbehavior? The séance, wasn't it?

Yes, that was right. We had talked about the séance, and I had asked him about Johanna and whether he thought she might have murdered Lady Peckham. He had seemed reluctant to entertain the thought at first, but then he had seemed to come around to it.

As well he would if he were looking for someone else to put the blame on, I reminded myself. He had every incentive to be happy about another possible suspect. And he had seemed delighted about his dead mother appearing to affirm her death as an accident—as of course he would be, if he had poisoned her.

And I had said something like, "You didn't push the glass, did you?" and he had denied it, of course, and then I'd said something else, something along the lines of, "Well, I can't think of anyone else who would have, can you?"

Which of course hadn't meant that I suspected him, because I hadn't. But if he had pushed the glass during the séance, which seemed obvious now, and he had killed his mother and Johanna, my innocent question might have been enough to put his back up.

And yes... it was after that, wasn't it, that he had taken the glass out of my hand and said, "Let me refresh that for you," even though it hadn't needed it.

And I had turned my back on him to watch Crispin and Laetitia, while he'd dumped a fatal dose of Veronal into my glass and topped it off with more gin.

I came back to myself and to the present in time to hear Lady Laetitia say, "I wish you'd get over this idea that you have to marry for love, Crispin. We could have so much fun, you and I."

Something in her tone made my nose wrinkle involuntarily, and while I couldn't see into the room, I was absolutely certain that she was touching him. It was the sort of tone that went along with touching. The sort of tone—and touch—someone might use when they were trying to convince someone else to go along with what they wanted.

Coaxing, or cajoling. Cooing. Caressing.

"I'm sure your father would approve," Laetitia added, invitingly. "He won't let you marry *her*—" and there was a wealth of disdain in that one word, from which I gathered that she knew exactly who Crispin's penniless, foreign, common-as-mud beloved was, and she didn't like the idea any better than Uncle Harold did, "—but he'd let you marry *me*. And I'm certain I could make you happy..."

She trailed off, enticingly.

There was a moment's silence, during which I wondered whether Crispin had given in to whatever it was she was doing. I thought about turning around and tiptoeing back down the stairs to give them the privacy I assumed they needed to continue what they were doing. But then—

"My father won't live forever," Crispin said coolly.

I arched my brows. Uncle Harold was only in his late fifties, so he could certainly live for quite a long time yet. His father, the late Duke Henry, had been almost ninety when he died, and that had been murder, not natural causes. The Sutherlands tended to be long-lived when left to their own devices.

Laetitia's voice changed from wheedling to annoyed, so she must agree with me. "Are you really going to sit around and wait thirty years for him to die before you can marry the woman you want? What's to stop her from marrying someone else in the meantime?"

"Nothing at all," Crispin said, "and I'm sure she'll do just that one of these days. There's nothing I can do about it. Without Father's permission, I have nothing to offer her. And I'll be damned if I do what he suggested and ask her to be my mistress while I marry someone else."

"I doubt she'd agree anyway," Laetitia said.

"She absolutely wouldn't. Nor would I want her to. But I'm not marrying you just because I can't have her. I know you think we'd get on well, and you're probably right, but you deserve better than a husband who's in love with someone else."

She didn't protest that, at any rate. "I just worry that you're going to end up sad and alone, darling."

Crispin snorted. "I'm hardly alone, Laetitia. I have plenty of company. You should know that better than anyone."

I imagined him shaking his head, dislodging the whole conversation, before he told her, his voice lighter, "Go on down to breakfast. I can smell the bacon from up here. And if you see Philippa, tell her to get herself upstairs, because I'm starving."

"I'll absolutely tell her that," Laetitia promised, and there was a smirk in her voice too now.

"Not like that, for God's sake. I told you that was all play-acting. I need her to come sit with Christopher so I can go eat something. Let her know if you see her."

Laetitia promised she would, and I heard her footsteps come towards the door.

I glanced around the landing, looking for a way out, but as there was nowhere to go, I put the best face I could on it, and—when she appeared in the doorway looking like her usual vision, this time in an elegant black and white day-dress with white cuffs and a white collar—I smiled sweetly. "Good morning, Lady Laetitia."

She looked me up and down. "Miss Darling."

"I was just coming up to relieve Crispin," I said. "If you'll give me a moment, you can take him down to breakfast."

She didn't say anything, just nodded. I walked past her and into the room. "St George."

"Darling." He was still sitting on Christopher's bedside, and still looked the same as he'd done when I left. Whatever the conversation with Lady Laetitia had been, it hadn't had any visible effect on him.

"Dawson's started serving breakfast," I said. "I thought you might be hungry."

He got to his feet. "Starving."

"I'll stay with Christopher for a while. Anything I should know?"

He shook his head. "He's still asleep. Still breathing. Everything looks normal. I think it'll just take time."

"Then go get yourself some food before you waste away." I turned toward the bed.

"Thanks, Darling. I'll be up later."

"Take your time," I said. "I don't imagine we'll be able to leave before they track down Gilbert Peckham, anyway. It's going to be a long day of doing nothing, if I have my guess."

I perched on the edge of the bed and flapped a hand at him. "Shoo, St George. Lady Laetitia is waiting."

"Yes, Darling." But he hesitated, looking at Christopher. "You'll let me know if anything changes?"

"You'll be the first," I said. "St George...?"

He turned around in the doorway and arched a brow questioningly.

"That first day at Sutherland Hall, when Constance and I caught you and Johanna in the garden maze..."

He winced, but nodded.

"Did you spend the rest of the evening with her?"

"With the things you'd said about me?" He shook his head. "Good Lord, no, Darling. I dumped her on Peckham at the first opportunity and hid in my room until I was forced to come out by the supper gong. I don't think I've ever been so embarrassed."

"So if I told you that I saw Johanna going into her room around seven-thirty, with her hair a mess and her lipstick gone..."

"It wasn't me," Crispin said promptly.

I nodded. "If it wasn't you, and it wasn't Christopher, and it isn't likely to have been Francis, and I hope to God it wasn't Uncle Herbert or your father..."

"It was Gilbert," Crispin said.

"That's what I was thinking, too. Constance bought him onyx cufflinks for Christmas."

He didn't say anything, and I added, "Thank you."

"My pleasure." He ducked out the door, to where—I assumed—Lady Laetitia was still waiting. I turned to Christopher and settled in to wait for something to change.

NOTHING HAPPENED for the rest of that day, though.

Or rather, quite a lot happened, of course. Scotland Yard spent the day investigating the physical aspects of the Dower House—photographs, fingerprints, searches; still looking for Gilbert and any clues as to where he might be headed. They interviewed us all again about last night and what, if anything, Gilbert had ever said about either his mother's death, or Johanna's, to any of us. Constance told them about him and Johanna, and I told them about the séance and the conversation I'd had with Gilbert afterward, during and after he mixed my almost-fatal drink.

Of Gilbert himself, there was no sign. He wasn't anywhere in the house, and it looked like he might have taken a small knapsack with him when he left, so it had clearly been planned, down to the smallest detail. He must have figured out, when Tom so ostentatiously announced his intention to sleep at the pub but that they were planning to make an arrest tomorrow—today, now—that there would be guards posted outside in case anyone tried to make a bunk. He had deliberately caused the scene in Lady Laetitia's room in the hope that it would draw the constables from outside into the house so he would have a chance to make his escape.

And so he had. On foot, since all three motorcars—the Bentley, the Hispano-Suiza, and Tom's police car—were still in the garage and not even a bicycle was missing.

We were, on average, twenty-five miles from both Salisbury and Bournemouth, and Tom had phoned the railway office in Salisbury and the docks in Bournemouth to tell them to be on the lookout for a man fitting Gilbert's description. With the railway workers and dockworkers both on strike, there was a question of what, if anything, anyone would do if they did see Gilbert, of course, so Tom had also rung up several of the local constabularies between the two with the same message.

Southampton, to the east, was a bit farther away, but also a possibility for someone who might want to leave the country by boat, so they got a call as well. And since Portsmouth was only a few miles further, so did they. People all over southern England were looking for a tramp with Gilbert's features, wearing plus fours and sturdy brogues and a brown newsboy cap, with a knapsack over his shoulder.

But by evening the first day, there had been no sign of him.

By evening the first day, Christopher hadn't awoken, either.

The local doctor from Marsden-on-Crane, a small man with a very large mustache, had turned up at the Dower House in the late morning. He had examined Christopher—listened to his heart, measured his breaths, peeled his eyelids back and shined a light into his eyes—before confirming Crispin's diagnosis.

"If he isn't dead by now, he'll likely pull through. He'll wake once the medicine has run its course, hopefully none the worse for wear. Just give it time."

The news hadn't been terribly encouraging, if you asked me—too many likelies and hopefullies in that statement—but since the doctor hadn't seemed actively concerned about any of it, I managed to refrain from physically grabbing him by his thin shoulders and shaking something more definite out of him.

Crispin's hand on my shoulder—he must have noticed the light in my eyes—had helped keep me from committing physical assault, as well. Not a statement I'd ever expected to make about St George.

But the next morning we were sitting down to breakfast in the dining room when Tom burst through the door, eyes shining and high color in his cheeks. "They got him!"

Constance turned pale, of course, and Francis put a hand over hers.

By now, it was just the four of us at table, with Gilbert gone and Christopher still abed upstairs. Lady Laetitia and Lord Geoffrey had been allowed to withdraw to Marsden Manor yesterday afternoon, after their statements had been taken and it was obvious that they'd had little to do with anything that had happened.

(Laetitia was to escape prosecution for having tried to drug me, it seemed, while Geoffrey would surely get in trouble for putting his hands on some unwilling woman at some point, but it wasn't going to be this weekend. And yes, Scotland Yard had searched Marsden Manor from top to bottom for Gilbert before they allowed the Marsden siblings to return there.)

And now someone had found him, it seemed.

"Where?" Francis wanted to know.

Tom snickered. "He walked into the railway station in Salisbury this morning, looking for the train to London. Of course, there wasn't one—"

"Wasn't one?"

"*Et tu,* Francis?" I asked. "Weren't you present when I lectured Peckham and Marsden on the general strike two days ago?"

"It was hardly a lecture, Darling," Crispin said. "A single sentence about the railroad workers, as I recall."

"But I mentioned that Christopher and I might find it hard to get back to London as a result. He should have put two and two together."

I stabbed my spoon into my egg.

"At any rate," Tom said, "we've got him. Salisbury City Police dressed Constable Elsie Mouland in mufti and sent her to the station—"

"Pardon me?" This was Crispin holding his own spoon up to stop Tom's recitation. "Did you say Elsie Mouland? Her? A woman constable?"

"Salisbury has had women constables since 1918," Tom said. "Pippa—"

I nodded.

"You and Miss Peckham met at the Godolphin School in Salisbury, isn't that correct? You may remember a teacher there, by the name of Miss Florence White."

I looked at Constance. She looked at me. We both shook our heads.

"Well, she taught there until 1914," Tom said, "when she left to join a women's street patrol in Somerset. After the war, she joined the City of Salisbury police and was attested as a constable. When she transferred to the Birmingham police last year, Elsie Mouland took over her position."

"Women police constables?" Crispin had a faraway look in his eyes. "Are there any of those in London?"

Tom opened his mouth, but I got there first.

"Planning where you might misbehave next, St George? If you have a fancy for handcuffs, I'm sure Lady Laetitia would oblige."

He flushed, and so did Constance. Tom didn't react beyond a twitch of his brow. "Constable Mouland arrested Mr. Peckham," he said, "on suspicion of murder, and escorted him to the police station on Endless Street in Salisbury. I'm going there now, to fetch him back."

"Have something to eat first," I told him. "He's not going anywhere, and you can spare five minutes."

He eyed the door, and then eyed the food, and then eyed me. It looked like he might have considered protesting, but in the end he just said, "I suppose that's true."

"Bossy," Crispin muttered beside me while Tom headed for the sideboard.

I shot him a look. "Really, St George? Weren't you the one who just fantasized about being arrested by a woman constable? She'd be bossy, too, I assure you."

On the other side of the table, Francis chuckled, and bent to whisper something in Constance's ear. She smiled.

Crispin scowled. "You're awful, Darling. Have you no concept of proper breakfast conversation?"

"You're the one who brought it up," I told him. "If you'd just keep your prurient fantasies to yourself, this wouldn't be an issue."

"All I asked was whether there were woman constables in London!"

I fixed him with a glare. "I know what you were imagining, St George. We all do. And I'm sure it's quite a far cry from reality. If Miss White taught at Godolphin before Constance and I started there, and it is now 1926, she must be as old as your mother, at least. Maybe as old as Aunt Roz. Maybe older! Not at all the nubile young woman in uniform I'm sure you pictured."

"I pictured no such thing!" Crispin snarled. "You're vile, Darling."

He tossed his napkin on the table next to his half-eaten breakfast and pushed his chair back.

"I'm going up to sit with Kit."

He stalked out of the dining room practically radiating anger. Francis sniggered. "Well done, Pipsqueak. It's quite a gift you have, the way you manage to send him to the brink of madness in every conversation."

"He has a quick temper," I said. "It isn't hard to do."

"You seem to manage it with more ease than anyone else, however." He tilted his head to contemplate me. "Have you ever considered—"

"No," I said, because I hadn't, and furthermore, I didn't want to. When someone asks me to consider something about St George, it's invariably something I wish I hadn't considered.

And in this case I didn't have to, because Dawson whisked away Crispin's plate, and then Tom dropped down on the empty chair beside me and put his own plate on the table where Crispin's had been.

"Any news on Kit?" he wanted to know as he shook his napkin open and spread it over his lap.

"No change this morning. Or at least that's what Francis and Crispin told me when I came down to breakfast. I haven't seen him yet myself."

"You're free to go home," Tom said. "Or back to Sutherland

Hall, I suppose. Or Beckwith Place. Wherever Lord and Lady Herbert are right now, and wherever you can get to, without the railway."

I winced. "I haven't informed them what happened. Have you, Francis?"

Francis shook his head. "No need to worry the old folks unduly, I figured. If Mum knew what was going on here, and that both of you came close to dying, she'd only fret, and there is nothing she can do about any of it. Although by now I daresay she might want the chance to fuss over Kit."

"We could load him into the backseat of one of the motorcars," I suggested. "I could sit back there with him and make sure he didn't rattle around too much."

Francis nodded. "If we start packing now, we can be back at Sutherland by this afternoon. Mum and Dad will still be there. I took their car, after all."

So he had. They were stuck until he fetched them, or unless they talked Uncle Harold into lending them Wilkins and the late duke's Crossley.

"Shall we do it?" I looked at Francis. Francis looked at Constance.

"Oh," she said faintly.

"You don't want to stay here, surely? Not by yourself?"

She shook her head.

"Then come to Sutherland Hall and meet my parents," Francis said. "And we'll figure the next step out from there."

Constance nodded, with two perfect tears running down her cheeks. I glanced at Tom, who tipped me a wink before he devoted himself to his steak and eggs.

EPILOGUE

WHERE WE HAD LEFT Sutherland Hall with seven people and two vehicles, there were now only five of us. We could have fit into a single motorcar, but of course there was no question of leaving Aunt Roz's and Uncle Herbert's Bentley behind at the Dower House, nor was there any chance at all that Crispin would agree to not drive his beloved Hispano-Suiza back home. The only question was how to divide the passengers and luggage between the two vehicles.

"You're an absolute menace on the road," I told Crispin. "I drove down here with you, don't forget, and besides, I know what you did to your Ballot last year."

"What did you do to the Ballot?" Francis wanted to know. "That was a beautiful motorcar. What happened to it?"

I had my mouth open to tell him that Crispin, under the influence of rather a lot of alcohol, had managed to wrap it around a light pole somewhere in the West End, and destroy it. But before I could, Crispin scowled.

"I was drunk then. I am not drunk now. And if I'm carrying

Kit, I'll go as carefully as if I had a load of explosives in the back."

A moment later he added, pensively, "With you back there, it comes to the same thing, really, doesn't it? You'll scream loud enough to make my ears bleed if anything happens to him."

"What did he do to the Ballot?" Francis asked again, of me this time.

"He crashed it into a light pole. Damaged it beyond repair. Walked away laughing. Somehow managed to stay out of jail, as well as out of the hospital."

I turned back to Crispin. "You know, you're not the only one of us who can drive a motorcar. Perhaps *you* should sit in the back with Christopher, and *I* should be behind the wheel."

He stared at me, bug-eyed, for what felt like a full minute, opening and closing his mouth. "You—" he finally managed. "You can't be serious!"

"Oh, can't I? You don't think women can drive motorcars?"

He opened his mouth and closed it again, since clearly there was a correct answer here, and he hadn't been about to give it.

"It's not that..." he tried. "It's just... you..." He flapped his hands. "You can't!"

I snorted. "It's not as if I'm suggesting I wear your trousers, St George. It's a motorcar. Anyone can drive it."

"Not you! Not *my* motorcar!"

I wouldn't have been surprised to see him throw himself in front of it, arms extended, to physically keep me away.

"Then promise me you'll drive carefully," I said.

"I will!" He caught himself just before folding his hands in supplication. "I promise, Darling. I will be so careful you could balance an egg on a spoon the whole way home. I won't go above thirty the whole way. I promise!"

Behind him, Francis handed Constance into the Bentley

with exquisite care, and a broad grin on his face. When he noticed me looking at him, he winked.

"Very well," I said and opened the back door of the Hispano-Suiza. Crispin let out a breath of air that I'm sure he would have preferred for me not to hear, but which was such a sigh of relief that he just hadn't been able to keep it in.

I gave him a look down the length of my nose—not an easy task when he's several inches taller than I am. "Help me with Christopher, please."

He nodded eagerly. Anything to keep me in a good humor so I wouldn't threaten his precious motorcar further, I assumed.

Between him and Francis, they had carried Christopher down from the first floor and made him comfortable in the back seat of the Hispano-Suiza. We had taken the liberty of borrowing a pillow from the Dower House, on which Christopher's head was resting. I wiggled myself underneath it while Crispin held Christopher's head up, and then we eased him back down into a comfortable position with his head in my lap. Through it all, Christopher continued to sleep the sleep of the innocent—or the deeply drugged—with his face peaceful and his breath even.

"Very well," I told Crispin, as he latched the door behind me and made sure it was secure. "Home to Sutherland, if you please, St George. Carefully."

"Yes, Darling," Crispin said, and headed around the motorcar to the driver's side to start the slow drive back to Wiltshire.

Dear Reader,

First, the standard warning about the language. I've written almost fifty books in American English. This book is written in a mixture of that and British English, since it takes place in England with British characters, and I couldn't see my way clear to having them use American expressions when I knew the difference. So there are flats (apartments) and lifts (elevators) and biscuits (cookies) and ground floors (first floors) and first floors (second floors) and lots of little things like that. At one point, before I caught the mistake, Gilbert Peckham was wearing knickers—which of course are women's underpants in the UK—and not plus fours, those extra-long, four-inches-below-the-knee knickerbockers, which is what he was really wearing.

But while I caught that one, I'm sure there are others I didn't, so I apologize for the errors. I didn't have the book Brit-picked and I'm only human, so there are bound to be mistakes. I've done my best, and that's all anyone can do, really. This is intended as light entertainment, nothing more, and while I've endeavored to get the details right, sometimes I haven't.

And speaking of details... this book takes place a week or so into May 1926, just about two weeks after the events of the previous book, *Secrets at Sutherland Hall*. Pippa mentions the General Strike, which really did take place during that time. The miners were striking, for the usual reasons—more money, better working conditions—and the railway workers and dock-workers and quite a few others were also striking in solidarity. Public transportation did shut down for a while, so railway travel through England would definitely have been affected. I cheated a little by getting Christopher and Pippa *to* Sutherland Hall in the first place, though, when that would have probably been as difficult as getting them back at the end of the weekend.

The strike started at one minute to midnight, 23:59 or 11:59 pm if you're American, on the 3rd of June, a Monday, so for all intents and purposes, it ran from Tuesday, May 4th to Wednesday, May 12th, 1926. If you're interested in reading a mystery set in the days just before the strike, Laurie R. King has one, called *Touchstone*, which lays out all the issues and counter-issues during the week or so before the strike itself.

The expression 'screaming meemies' harken back to the Great War, when there existed a German artillery weapon that made a sound like *meem* or *meemee* when it was fired. Later on, the expression came to mean an attack of nerves, not coinciden-tally because the men who came home from the war with shell-shock had been affected by the Germans' screaming meemies. Pippa is using it in the sense that she's threatening to be both very loud and very shrill.

One of Crispin's little byplays in this book centers on Pippa's banana-yellow flapper dress. Josephine Baker was, of course, a real person and the toast of Paris in the mid-1920s.

She was picked out of the chorus in a nightclub in Harlem in 1925, and brought to Paris for La Revue Nègre at nineteen years old. A year later, she was dancing at the Folies-Bergère, and at one point during 1926 or 1927—the records are vague—she did do her famed *danse sauvage* in a ring of bananas and not much more. The pictures and videos I've been able to find are dated 1927, but some sources say 1926, so I'm stretching the performance forward a little bit, to give Crispin his 'back-handed compliment.' The film and photographs would have been taken after the dance premiered on the stage anyway, so I'm somewhere in the ballpark.

Josephine Baker's life is an amazing story, from her leaving America to find success on the Continent, to her undercover work for her adopted homeland during WWII, to her family. I grew up hearing about Josephine Baker's Rainbow Tribe, and I remember being enthralled with the idea of a family of adopted children living together in a castle in France with a famous mother and a cheetah. It sounded like the setup for a series of children's books of the kind I would have enjoyed reading at that age.

Now, too, maybe.

Norman Hartnell, another real person, was born in London in 1901, and he designed Pippa's yellow dress. He opened his first design business on Bruton Street in Mayfair in 1923, but didn't really rise to prominence for a few years after that. He dressed the British royals until his death in 1979, but at the time of this book, he was best known for designing wedding and evening gowns for the debutantes of the upper classes and the Bright Young Set in London.

Constables Elsie Mouland and Florence Mildred White were likewise real people. White did teach at the Godolphin School in Salisbury, which Pippa and Constance attended, but she left roughly two years before the girls started, to join a women's street patrol in Somerset. In 1918, she became an official constable in Salisbury, and when she left in 1925 to join the Birmingham police, Chief Constable of Salisbury, Ernest Frank Richardson, replaced her with Elsie Mouland.

The London Constabulary also had WPCs, but was a bit slower to accord them the same respect that Chief Constable Richardson accorded White and Mouland. With that said, it's certainly not impossible that Crispin may come across a WPC during his adventures at some point.

Thank you for taking a chance on this story. If you feel compelled to leave a review, I'll love you forever. I'll love you even more if you buy the next book.

Till next time!

ABOUT THE AUTHOR

New York Times and *USA Today* bestselling author Jenna Bennett (Jennie Bentley) is the author of almost fifty books, most of them in the genres of mystery and suspense. The Pippa Darling mysteries is her most recent project.

For more information, please visit Jenna's website, www.jennabennett.com